MW01537727

SECRETS OF THE CRIMSON VEIL

LOIS E. LANE

This book is dedicated to the best friends in this life...the ones you can laugh with until you cry, those you can cry with when times are difficult, and those that you can share everything with, no matter what it is. If you have even one friend like this, you are truly blessed. I have two of these...you know who you are.

"My best friend is the one who brings out the best in me."

HENRY FORD

CONTENTS

PROLOGUE

Franklin Kennedy stood in front of a massive wall of windows on the top floor of his Denver home, staring out onto the snowcapped mountains of the Rockies, but not seeing them. His mind was on Oliver Anderson. It had been many years since the two of them had spoken, even more where they had not seen eye to eye on certain decisions that had been made. He stood there, balancing himself with a walking stick, an ivory skull for the handle where the eye sockets gleamed ominously with dark crimson jewels. He rested his hand there, knowing that he would have to see this through. There was too much at stake. And now, some girl may be living in the only place that hadn't been searched. A sharp knock on the door brought him out of his reverie.

"Come in," he said, his voice strong, belying the condition of his aging body. A young man walked in.

"Mr. Kennedy, you rang for me?" he asked formally.

"Yes, yes, Ethan, please, be seated," said Franklin Kennedy, moving toward a comfortable wingback chair and sitting down slowly.

Ethan took a seat opposite his employer and waited. He knew that Franklin Kennedy would get to the point quickly.

"There are some things of which you are not aware, Ethan, but in the weeks ahead, I will be briefing you," he began. "I don't want to reveal too much too soon, as much of the information is highly confidential and protected and if the wrong person were to gain knowledge of it, it would be devastating, even criminal."

Ethan, thinking Mr. Kennedy was being a bit melodramatic, spoke clearly, "We no longer live in a cloak and dagger society, Mr. Kennedy. I think we are safe to speak of anything here without fear of discovery."

"That is where you are wrong!" Franklin Kennedy practically shouted. Seeing the look on Ethan's face, he schooled his own. "I know of things that only one other person knew, and he is now deceased. He was very well hidden in this country, in plain sight you could say. He selected a family to act as his own and adopted a young girl as his granddaughter. He was very intelligent and cunning. He was privy to much information that could derail the lives of several high-level persons in this country. Knowing him, he would have recorded information that, if found, could wreck lives, possibly cause deaths. Do you understand?"

Ethan, still a bit skeptical, spoke, "Yes, I

understand. So, what do you want me to do for you?"

Franklin Kennedy sat quietly for a moment before speaking again. "I have located his residence, and I must acquire it. However, the woman who owns it now has not responded to my offers. I don't think she is holding out for more money because from what I understand, she is quite wealthy, thanks to Oliver."

"What did you offer?" asked Ethan, curious if it was a sum he would have accepted from someone he didn't know.

"Ten million dollars," Franklin said calmly.

After digesting that information, Ethan looked directly at Franklin, "That, Mr. Kennedy, would be a sum of money that would not be believed. However, if they were to research you and your assets, they would see that you are quite capable of paying that amount of money. Now, however, she may now be considering why it would be so valuable, and if there was anything hidden there. You may have just tipped your hand a bit."

"Yes, I admit I had that thought as well. But I am desperate to have the property, examine it with a thorough search that only I could do, because I am the only one left who would know what was real and what was fake," he said, slightly agitated.

Looking directly at Franklin Kennedy, Ethan spoke, "I can see that this is a very delicate matter and utmost secrecy is required. What do you want me to do?" Ethan repeated his earlier question.

"I want you to go there as my liaison, to broker the deal for her property. It is located in Germantown, Tennessee. I'll send all of the information to you via the VPN. How soon can you go?" Franklin Kennedy asked, leaning forward to emphasize that speed was of the essence.

"I can go as soon as tomorrow. If the owner doesn't want to speak with me, do you have any direction in mind that you would want me to go?" asked Ethan, mentally preparing himself for this assignment.

Having thought about it, Franklin spoke, "If you have trouble convincing her, let her know that even though I am old and frail, I will travel to meet with her in person. In the meantime, we need to find someone that would not mind getting their hands dirty, if you know what I mean."

Ethan sat thoughtfully for a full moment. Quietly, he spoke, "I had an acquaintance at one time that would do odd jobs with no questions asked. But then, he sort of went silent. I didn't think of him for years but saw his name in relation to a prisoner who committed suicide. He lives here in Colorado, outside of Denver as a matter of fact. I can put some feelers out to get some more information."

"Hmm, sounds promising. Who is this person, if I may ask?" Franklin was very interested.

"He had contacts with ex-military and others who could obtain whatever he needed. His name is Lenny Crocker," said Ethan. "I'll see what I can do."

"Good. Do not engage him until I have an opportunity to check all of his credentials," said Franklin.

"Are you sure you want to be involved? I think the less you know, the less culpable you will be," advised Ethan.

"Believe me when I tell you, I am already culpable. I will be informed of every aspect of this situation and any person involved. When you return, I will brief you on as much as you need to know," Franklin said.

"Very well, Mr. Kennedy," said Ethan, rising to leave. "I will prepare to leave tomorrow and if I have any questions for you, I will reach out to you before I leave. You have my number if you need anything else."

"Thank you, Ethan," said Franklin, already thinking of Oliver Anderson and his heir, Marly Anderson.

CHAPTER 1

Marly was sitting in her cozy living room, in the small wingback chair that sat near her grandfather's chair, his glasses still sitting on the side table by a book he had been reading. She got up and picked it up, looking at the cover. Smiling, she placed it back on the table, thinking he was always reading books on espionage, secret identities, and anything dark and mysterious but this was The Screwtape Letters by C. S. Lewis. Maybe he realized his time was getting short. He was the kindest man she had ever known. He truly loved her in a way that her own family didn't. Why did her thoughts always come back to them? She never felt that they wanted her around and most of the time, her mother sent her to live with her grandfather. Now that she thought about it, she did live with him more than with her own family. Funny how much like strangers they felt and the fact that Poppa left her everything in his will, didn't help the situation. They contested it, of course, but after a short period of time, they dropped it. When they had asked for financial help, she had given it without question but when it got to be too frequent, she stopped. The entire family stopped speaking to her, even snubbing her in public when their paths crossed and never inviting her to any family functions. It didn't bother her that much now. She considered Lucy, Kate, and Seth her family and now there was Rafe. They were the people in her life that she could depend on for love and support. Shaking her head, as if to get rid of the depressing thoughts, Marly was startled by her telephone ringing.

"Saved by the bell," she said aloud. Picking up her phone, she answered, "Hello?"

"Hello," said a male voice. "Am I speaking to Marly Anderson?"

Not recognizing the voice, Marly asked, "Who is calling?"

"My name is Ethan Longmire, from Denver, Colorado," he said confidently.

She responded, "Yes, this is Marly Anderson. What can I do for you, Mr. Longmire?"

"I was hoping that we could meet regarding the recent offer made to you by Mr. Franklin Kennedy, my employer."

Silence.

"Are you there, Miss Anderson?" Ethan asked.

"Yes, I'm here. I was hopeful that if I didn't respond, Mr. Kennedy would drop his offer and leave me alone," said Marly emphatically.

"On the contrary, Miss Anderson, he is most anxious to acquire your property, for personal reasons," said Ethan, not willing to give any more information unless it was needed.

"I'm sorry, Mr. Longmire, I am not interested in selling my home," said Marly.

"Could we at least meet for dinner and discuss it? I flew all of this way and would at least like to talk about it further with you," said Ethan, hoping that she would take pity on him since he was already in town.

"Mr. Longmire, you should have called before you flew here, putting me in an awkward situation. Mr. Kennedy should have known that, even if he is a reclusive and eccentric billionaire," said Marly, all warmth gone from her earlier tone.

"I do apologize, Miss Anderson. I am just doing my job, and I agree, he is very eccentric and insisted that I fly here today and meet with you. I totally understand how it makes you feel. I tried to tell him, but he is elderly and quite set in his ways. I did not mean to offend you," Ethan tried to schmooze Marly, pretending that he didn't want to intrude on her like this.

"Thank you, Mr. Longmire, I appreciate your candor," said Marly, relenting somewhat. "I have several appointments today, but we could get together this evening. I can meet you somewhere for dinner, if that will work for you."

Elated, he calmed himself and said evenly, "Are you sure? I feel that I am putting you out."

Marly didn't want his trip to be a total loss, and

she said, "I'm fine with meeting you. I'm just not interested, and I didn't want to waste your time or his, for that matter."

"Thank you. Do you have a suggestion, since I am not familiar with your city," said Ethan.

"I like the Moondance Grill for casual dining," said Marly. "I'll meet you there around 7:00 p.m. if that will work for you."

"Yes, I'll meet you there. Would you like for me to pick you up?" he asked, knowing that she would decline, which she did.

"I'll meet you there, Mr. Longmire," said Marly and she disconnected the call.

Ethan was relieved that she agreed to meet with him. He had warned Mr. Kennedy that a surprise visit might not work but she was very gracious. He returned to his hotel, the DoubleTree outside of Germantown, and called Mr. Kennedy.

"Hello Ethan," said Franklin Kennedy, "how did it go?"

"As I suspected. She was not pleased with being caught off guard and refused to see me at first," began Ethan.

"Ahhh, but that means you persuaded her, yes?" Franklin said, excited.

"Yes, after I told her I had advised you against a surprise visit. I did what I had to do to have her take pity on me," said Ethan, hoping that his employer would understand.

"Of course, of course," said Franklin. "So, what did she say?"

"About the deal? We didn't even approach it. She had some appointments this afternoon, so we are meeting for dinner this evening. I won't be able to fly back until tomorrow," said Ethan.

"I don't care how long you are there, Ethan. I want this deal done. If you think staying longer will help, then do it. You have a black card so use it," he said, making his wishes known. He wanted Ethan to stay until he convinced Marly to sell her building.

"I'll see how this evening goes, Mr. Kennedy. I should be able to get a feel for the situation. I do know that she was very firm on the telephone when she said she was not interested in your offer," revealed Ethan.

"Did she say why?" he asked.

"No, she didn't and maybe I can uncover her reasons this evening. It may be late so do you want me to call you, no matter the time?" asked Ethan, knowing he would.

"Of course! I will be waiting to hear from you as soon as possible," said Franklin.

"Yessir," said Ethan as he heard the click of the call ending. *So much for pleasantries*, he thought.

Ethan sat down in a chair and turned on the television. He had quite a few hours to kill before dinner, and he was fully armed with his information. A little relaxation was in order because he was sure that he would have to be on his toes for dinner.

Marly was feeling many things at the moment. Anger, frustration, curiosity, and some feelings that she couldn't explain. It was very presumptuous of Mr. Franklin Kennedy to send a lackey to her for the sale of her home. No advanced warning or a courtesy call. Of course, she thought that was exactly what he was hoping he could do to put her off balance. She had let her kindness make her feel sorry for the man that worked for him. She was determined to get some information from Mr. Longmire and also, a free dinner. She was definitely going to let him pay for it. That was the least he could do. But, now, she had to get in touch with Lucy and Kate. Marly called Kate, who was staying with the Cavanaughs at the winery in Blanco. She was recovering from a head injury that occurred a few months ago.

"Hello," said Kate.

Hi Kate," said Marly. "How are you doing?"

"Hi Marly, I'm doing very well. Therapy will be completed next week and then I have to decide if I am going to return to San Antonio or just stay here. Seth would want the latter," Kate laughed, thinking of her fiancé.

"I know that's true," said Marly. "How's Lucy and Rafe?" Marly was chatting before she delved into the real reason for her call.

"They are great," said Kate. "They are both at

the winery today, but Lucy said she would be home early. So, what is going on with you? I know you don't call in the middle of the day unless something has happened."

"You are very astute, Kate. I think maybe you are fully recovered!" laughed Marly. "I had a telephone call a few moments ago from a guy that works for Franklin Kennedy. He is here in town and wanted to meet with me about selling my home."

"Wow, Marly. He must be serious. What did you tell the guy?" asked Kate.

"I told him the same thing I tell you guys. I'm not interested in selling my home. I felt bad for the guy because he said he knew a surprise visit wasn't going to work. I took pity on him and agreed to meet for dinner," said Marly.

"You didn't!" said Kate. "If he works for a man as rich and influential as Franklin Kennedy, he will know exactly what to say to get you to feel that way. I bet he was playing you, Marly."

"Damn it, I didn't think of that!" Marly was furious at herself and at him too. "What should I do, Kate?"

Kate thought a moment. "You could cancel but I bet he already has your address, and he would probably just show up. It can't hurt to meet him in a public place, and a free dinner is always nice. But no wine!"

They both laughed, knowing they all enjoyed a bit of the vino.

"I've got an appointment with my financial advisor about the empty bookstore, but I will FaceTime you and Lucy when I get home. Maybe I will have more information to share. Now, instead of being nervous, I'm a little bit angry, which is probably helpful," said Marly.

"Yes, it probably is. He isn't going to pick you up, is he?" asked Kate.

"No, I will get an Uber, even though I know you don't approve," said Marly. She didn't like driving around town alone and usually took a ride share service if it was local.

"Just be careful, Marly. I'll fill Lucy in, and we'll look for your call later," said Kate.

"I will. Thanks for the advice Kate. I may need more before all of this is over," said Marly, ending their call.

CHAPTER 2

The meeting with her financial advisor, Jerry Fielding, went smoothly. They discussed some options for the empty space, which included renting it out as office space or another retail venture. Marly trusted Jerry as he had been her grandfather's choice.

"Can I think about it, Jerry?" she asked, looking at the numbers.

"Sure, there isn't a rush. I just don't want the taxes on an empty space to kick in. You have a little bit of time, a couple of weeks maybe," said Jerry.

"Is that all?" asked Marly, clearly agitated.

"What's wrong, Marly? You don't seem like yourself," observed Jerry, knowing Marly as calm and levelheaded.

"I'm sorry, Jerry, but I have been approached about selling the building where I live," said Marly. "And for an exorbitant amount of money."

"What was offered, if you don't mind me asking," said Jerry. "I can always advise you if it's not a fair market value."

"Oh, it's more than fair. It's almost too much.

I was offered ten million dollars," said Marly, watching Jerry's face. As she suspected, it was a shocked one.

"Are you kidding me?" asked Jerry. "There isn't a building in this whole town that's worth that much. Do you know who the buyer is?"

"A man named Franklin Kennedy. He lives in Denver, Colorado. He's a recluse, from what I can find online about him, very wealthy, usually gets what he wants, but I don't want to sell the only home I have known. It makes me wonder if there is something there that I don't know about," said Marly.

"I've heard about that guy. Pretty eccentric from what I have read too. Just tell him no," advised Jerry, knowing that Oliver Anderson would not want that building sold to anyone.

"I've said that, but he sent someone to town today to meet with me, unannounced I might add," said Marly, clearly frustrated.

"A ploy to get you to make decisions you aren't ready to make," said Jerry, wondering himself about the old building.

"I know that now, Jerry, but at the time, I did feel sorry for the guy. I agreed to meet him for dinner and now I am regretting that ten times from Sunday!" Marly was clearly upset.

"How are you getting there?" knowing that Marly used Uber drivers most of the time.

"Uber. I definitely wasn't going to ride with a person I didn't know," admitted Marly.

"Do you want me to go with you? I can be there as your financial advisor, if you want," volunteered Jerry.

Smiling at her friend, she said, "What about Belinda and the girls? They probably want you home for dinner."

"I hardly think so. Belinda took the girls to their grandparent's house for a few days, and she decided to stay too. They will be back this weekend," confessed Jerry.

Thinking it over for a few minutes, Marly said, "If you are willing, I am glad to have you. Maybe I should have some surprises for Mr. Kennedy!"

"I can pick you up, Marly, unless you have a crush on your latest Uber driver," laughed Jerry.

"You can pick me up, Jerry. We are meeting at the Moondance Grill at 7:00 p.m. How does that sound?" asked Marly.

"I haven't been there in a while. It sounds great," said Jerry, already salivating.

"I am picking up dinner, unless he opts to pay for all of us," said Marly. "I will not take no for an answer."

"Hey, I'm willing to be fed for free," said Jerry, "but technically I will be working."

"This makes me feel so much better about tonight, Jerry. Thank you for being a good friend. I'm lucky to have you," said Marly sincerely,

"I think we are both lucky, Marly. Oliver was a smart man, and he knew exactly what he was doing. I think you are right to consider there may be something in that building that this person wants. Do your own sleuthing," said Jerry.

"That is my intention. Is there anything else we need to discuss? I think my initial investment in the Vine to Vino Winery is paying off," said Marly.

"It is. We received a wire transfer for half of the initial investment, which is phenomenal. It has been deposited to your broker who will invest it when you notify him," Jerry informed her.

"If you ever get the chance to go to Texas, Jerry, take Belinda there. It is the most beautiful place and so luxurious. And, I know I can ensure you will get the VIP treatment," grinned Marly.

"Sounds good. Maybe for our anniversary this year. It will be our tenth," he said.

"That would be perfect, Jerry. Let me know and I will help you with all of the arrangements," said Marly.

"I'll let you know a date when I get it figured out," said Jerry, closing the folder on his desk. "Otherwise, I think we have covered everything. Think about what you want to do, and we'll make it happen. If you want to open a bakery, by all means, we can make it work or lease it out. Make some money without the work!"

Standing up from the chair, Marly said, "I'll let you know in a few days, Jerry. I want to review all of the options that we discussed. I'll see you tonight, about 6:30 p.m.?

"Yep, I'll pick you up then. Bye, Marly," said Jerry, waving at her as his phone rang.

Marly walked out of Jerry's office feeling a bit better about tonight. She wasn't comfortable about the meeting, but Jerry would be a great buffer. She was still upset at herself for not seeing through the guy's pity party, but it just made her more determined to be on her guard around him. She walked a few blocks back to her house and went up the stairs. She still had some books that didn't sell, and she wanted to box those and get them ready for donation. She was going to donate them to another small bookstore and giving them some new inventory might help.

The afternoon flew by, and Marly heard the grandfather clock chime 5:00 p.m. She was startled that it was so late, and she stopped what she was doing to get ready for her dinner meeting. She showered and washed her hair, letting it hang loose, the auburn tresses framing her face. She dressed in a green blouse with tiny yellow flowers on it and put on a darker green jumper. Slipping her feet into some brown leather ankle booties, she was ready. She had put on minimal make-up because she didn't want Mr. Longmire to get any ideas, not that he would. At promptly 6:30 p.m. she heard a knock at the front door. Heading down the stairs, she opened the door to see Jerry in his business suit and briefcase in his hand.

"I thought I would dress for the part," he said, grinning.

"Perfect! But I hate you aren't comfortable," said Marly, smiling.

"Hey, I'm used to suits and I wore one of my best ones, to impress the guy," laughed Jerry and Marly joined in.

"I'm ready," said Marly and they both walked toward Jerry's Lexus. He held open the door for her and then got in the driver's seat.

They had a casual conversation on the way to the restaurant and after parking, made their way inside. The hostess met them, and Marly informed her they were meeting someone.

"Mr. Ethan Longmire," Marly gave his name, and she looked at them.

"Oh, I'm sorry, I understood it was a party of two," she said, a bit flustered.

"Is that a problem?" asked Jerry.

"No, not at all. I will relocate him to a four top which will be more comfortable for the three of you," she said, hurrying over to Mr. Longmire and ushering him to the larger table. She then returned to escort the two of them to the table.

Ethan Longmire was confused when Marly was brought to the new table with a gentleman in tow. This was an unexpected twist.

Ethan stood as Jerry pulled out a chair for Marly. She made the introductions.

"Jerry, this is Mr. Ethan Longmire, from

Denver, Mr. Kennedy's representative," said Marly. "Mr. Longmire, this is Jerry Fielding, my financial advisor."

Not letting the surprise show on his face, Ethan spoke, "Nice to meet you, Mr. Fielding."

For the next few moments, the server came over and took their drink orders. Ethan got a vodka tonic, Jerry ordered a sweet tea, and Marly chose water with lemon. When the server left the table, they all perused the menus he had left, deciding on their dinner.

Marly could tell that Ethan Longmire was taken aback when they had arrived. She was glad that Jerry had volunteered to escort her, and it never hurt to have two sets of eyes and ears when you didn't know what the situation was going to be. When the server returned to their table, they placed their orders.

Marly said, "I'll have the Lemon Caper Chicken with the bed of wild rice."

"Excellent choice," said Clint, their server.

"I've been drooling thinking of the Maple Bourbon Glazed Salmon and I'll have that with steamed broccoli," said Jerry, closing his menu.

"Very good, sir," said Clint, then looked over at Ethan.

Ethan, closing his menu, said, "Everything looks delicious, but I have decided on the Lobster Ragu."

"It is very good, sir, you won't be disappointed," said Clint as he left the table to put in their orders.

Ethan was a bit off balance with the addition of Jerry Fielding, but maybe it was an indication that she would be willing to sell. One thing that he wasn't expecting and that was that Marly Anderson was very beautiful. This was going to be an interesting evening.

CHAPTER 3

"Ethan, I hope you don't mind that I asked Jerry to come tonight. When it comes to financial matters and decisions, I depend on his advice," said Marly, apologetically.

"No, not at all. It shows you are a smart businesswoman," said Ethan, smiling at her.

Marly was not expecting this suave man sitting before her. He had jet black hair, styled to look casual and he was wearing black slacks, and a black shirt with a white tie. Very modern and somehow, he looked dangerous.

Ethan didn't wait long before leading the conversation to the subject at hand.

"Miss Anderson," he began.

"Please, that is so formal. You may call me Marly," she said.

"Okay, thank you, Marly, have you thought any more about Mr. Kennedy's offer of your property?" asked Ethan.

Jerry interjected, "Do you know why he is so set on acquiring this property? It has been the only home Marly has known most of her life and it has great sentimental value. Surely Mr.

Kennedy can understand that."

Ethan wasn't prepared for an additional person, but he had been in difficult situations before.

"Mr. Kennedy has some personal reasons for wanting the property, of which I am not privy to at this time. I do know that he had a personal relationship with your grandfather, Marly, and I think that is part of the reason," said Ethan, giving her the crumb that he thought she would want more of.

"He knew my grandfather? From when?" asked Marly, not expecting this information.

"Apparently they worked together many years ago. The elderly like to relive their pasts as they age, I'm sure you know that from living with Mr. Anderson," said Ethan, very smoothly.

Marly thought his explanation sounded rehearsed, but it had a ring of truth to it. But how much of it was true? To Ethan she said, "Yes, we discussed many things from his past before he died. So, I do understand how Mr. Kennedy is feeling. But is that a reason to buy a building in a city he doesn't even know for such a large sum of money? It doesn't make a lot of sense, even for someone waxing sentimental."

Ethan realized that this wasn't going to be as easy as he thought. She apparently has brains as well as beauty.

"I can't answer that question. Mr. Kennedy has more money than he can spend. He has no heirs and will be leaving his wealth to many charities which he has named in his will. He seems to be laser focused on your building," explained Ethan.

"I understand that Mr. Kennedy has offered ten million dollars for the building," began Jerry. "There isn't a building in this town worth that amount of money."

"Maybe not, but to Mr. Kennedy, it is. He offered to come here in person, Marly, even though he is elderly and frail," said Ethan.

At that moment the server came to their table with their entrees, and they began eating in silence.

Marly spoke first, between bites. "I am not trying to be difficult. Losing my grandfather was an emotional blow to me, and we shared this home together for many years. The memories we have there are not something that I am ready to part with, if ever. I would not want Mr. Kennedy to travel such a long distance only to be disappointed at the outcome. At this time, I am not leaning toward selling."

Nodding, Ethan spoke, "I can certainly understand your position and I respect it. I am just doing the bidding of my employer and, might I add, having the pleasure of dinner with a beautiful woman."

Blushing slightly, Marly put another piece of chicken into her mouth, taking away her necessity to speak.

Jerry decided to weigh in and test the waters. "If Mr. Kennedy would be more forthcoming with his reasons for wanting the building, maybe Marly would be willing to accommodate him if there was a memento he is remembering and would like to find. That would surely be a cheaper solution than buying the building."

"I agree with you, Jerry," said Ethan with a smile that didn't reach his eyes. "But, he is a very stubborn man. If Marly is willing to make that concession, I can certainly present it to him." Looking at Marly, he raised one of his dark brows in question.

"I would consider it, or I could even find it for him. I'm sure he would be the only one that could recognize it, if it is something that he and my grandfather knew about," said Marly.

This was definitely not going the way Ethan had intended. Marly was quite intelligent, and it would not be easy to change her mind, if it were even possible. He could tell when he had hit a brick wall, and he would back off...for now.

As they finished their meal, Ethan spoke, "I will take your suggestions back to Mr. Kennedy. Although I know he will be disappointed, he certainly will be able to understand your reluctance to sell your home."

"Thank you, Mr. Longmire," said Marly, never addressing him by his first name. "Let me know what he says about the alternative plan."

Reaching into his pocket, Ethan pulled out a

business card and handed it to Marly. "This is my personal cell phone number. You can contact me at any time."

"And, I know that you already have my number," said Marly.

The server brought over the check and Ethan held out his hand for it. "This is on Mr. Kennedy," he said, putting a black card with the ticket. Clint's eyes widened and he looked at Ethan with much respect.

"I'll be right back, sir," he said as he disappeared into the restaurant.

"I'm sorry that this isn't the outcome you were hoping for, Mr. Longmire. Please impress on Mr. Kennedy that I cannot leave my home. It is my touchstone," said Marly, smiling slightly.

"Of course, I expected as much after our conversation today, but I have to do my due diligence for Mr. Kennedy. I'll be in touch with you regarding your offer," said Ethan.

Jerry looked at Marly and asked, "Are you ready to go?"

"Yes, I am Jerry. Thank you again, Mr. Longmire, for a lovely dinner. I look forward to hearing from you," said Marly as she stood and walked away with Jerry.

Well played, Marly Anderson, well played.

Jerry and Marly walked to his car, and he helped her in. Sliding into the driver's seat, he grinned at Marly.

"I don't think it was a very successful night for Mr. Longmire," he said as he started the engine.

"I think you are right, Jerry. You were not what he expected. I think he thought I would be a pushover, just like I was when I agreed to dinner," admitted Marly.

"He was floundering, but he covered it well," said Jerry. "I've seen people in that situation before. And believe me, Marly, when I tell you that he knows more about the situation than he is letting on. He is good but you don't work for someone like Franklin Kennedy unless you have been thoroughly vetted and trained to do his bidding. I hope you don't mind that I threw out an alternative."

"No, not at all. It was actually brilliant. I could tell he wasn't expecting that, and he quickly regrouped. I am so grateful to you for coming tonight, Jerry," said Marly.

"I'm glad I came too because that salmon was spectacular!" he said, laughing and she joined in. "And, there is something else, I can feel it. There was tension in him, like a clock wound too tight. Be careful with him, Marly. He could be a dangerous threat."

"I think so too, Jerry. I've had my fill of dangerous people and situations," said Marly, knowing that Jerry would know what she meant. She had shared with him about Raven Silvers from college who turned out to be a serial killer, who had Marly kidnapped and then about the crazy woman who set the vineyard on fire while Marly was catering the grand opening of her friend's winery, not to mention that her friend Kate was recovering after being kidnapped and almost killed.

Nodding his head, he agreed, "Yes, you have had an eventful few years. Let's hope this doesn't turn out to be a repeat performance!"

Stopping in front of her building, Jerry got out and walked her to the door, keeping alert for anything out of the ordinary. Marly was grateful for his vigilance.

"Thanks Jerry. I'd have you for my wingman any time," said Marly, hugging her friend.

"Glad to do it, Marly. Let me know if you hear from them, and I'm betting that you will," said Jerry as he returned to his car after she closed her door.

Marly went inside, setting the alarm and set up her tablet to FaceTime Kate and Lucy. After their initial greetings, Marly got right into the situation, dinner, telling them that Jerry, her financial advisor, went with her and that it put the guy, Ethan Longmire, off balance. Kate agreed that it was a great idea and was glad that Marly didn't have to navigate the meeting alone. Lucy was irate that the man couldn't take no for an answer but was glad that Marly stuck to her original decision. She wasn't happy that Marly offered the old man to search for whatever it was he was looking for, if it was anything. Marly was calmer after talking to her best friends. It was the best relationship in her life. They were her family and would do anything for her.

"Marly, how about me and Lucy coming for a few days to help you look around your house?" asked Kate.

"Oooh, yes, a mini girl trip!" agreed Lucy.

Marly laughed and said, "That would be perfect...as long as it isn't like the last girl trip we took!"

They all laughed at that reference and agreed.

CHAPTER 4

Ethan drove back to his hotel and prepared himself to call Mr. Kennedy. It wasn't the outcome he had hoped but the addition of Marly's financial advisor to the meeting changed the way he would have handled it. Knowing that Mr. Kennedy would not be pleased, Ethan postponed the call for a little bit. He thought about everything that had transpired. He definitely knew that Marly Anderson was not interested in selling her home just from the way she spoke about it. The alternative of letting Franklin Kennedy look for the "memorabilia" would not be acceptable to him. He wanted the entire building to search and destroy the remnants of the past. Although Ethan was not yet fully read in on the information, he knew enough. Whatever the organization was that Franklin Kennedy and Oliver Anderson were a part of was not one to be tampered with. He could tell that by the desperation in Franklin's quest for this property. And he knew that Oliver Anderson's granddaughter would just be collateral damage. Sighing, he thought he should get the call over with and picked up his phone. Franklin Kennedy answered on the first ring.

"Hello Ethan, how did it go?" he asked anxiously.

"Hello Mr. Kennedy, I'm sorry to say that it didn't go as I expected," confessed Ethan.

"Why, what happened?" barked Franklin.

"First, I was blindsided by the fact that she brought her financial advisor with her," said Ethan, still stinging a bit from that fact.

"Oh, she did, did she? Hmmm, she may be smarter than I anticipated. So, what happened?" Franklin asked again.

"She is not interested in selling the home," said Ethan bluntly. "The guy, a Jerry Fielding, threw out an option of letting you look for whatever sentimental memento you were looking for, because I had to explain that you knew Marly Anderson's grandfather."

"How did she react to that tidbit?" Franklin asked, interested.

"She was actually surprised, and I believe intrigued. He had apparently not shared your name with her, although she said he had talked about his past with her before he died. From how she spoke, I don't think he shared anything about the period of time he worked with you," explained Ethan.

"I don't imagine that he did. Neither of us talked about it because in our line of work, it was a matter of life and death. Even now," said Franklin Kennedy gravely.

Silence followed until Ethan spoke, "What do you want me to do now, sir?"

"You can come back, Ethan, and I will be devising another plan. I may want to reach out to her personally, but I must be careful about it. I know that Oliver, if he retained information instead of destroying it, would have hidden it very carefully. I could be wrong about it, but I highly doubt it. Did you get a look at the building?" asked Franklin.

"Yes, I drove past it. It appears to be a three-story building. The first floor looks to be a retail space, and I saw that there was a sign announcing the bookstore was closed. I think that was Miss Anderson's business. I am assuming that the second and third floors are the living spaces," said Ethan.

"Could there be a basement?" asked Franklin, very interested.

"Yes, there could be, but I didn't see any outside entrance to one.," said Ethan.

"Hmmm, it could be a basement with no exit, which wouldn't be legal but, knowing Oliver, it would be a perfect setup for hiding something. He may have even had it modified so that there wasn't an entrance or exit," mused Franklin, more to himself than to Ethan.

Ethan waited a few moments before speaking, "So, I will get a flight back tomorrow and then we can regroup."

"Yes, yes, that sounds good. Do you think she might be curious enough to start looking for something?" Franklin was a little worried about that possibility.

"I don't think so. She thinks if it is anything, it is a memento from the past. She offered to look for something if you wanted to let her know what it was and I told her I would present that to you," said Ethan.

"Good, good," said Franklin. "We'll talk more when you return. Do you have anything for me on Mr. Crocker?"

"Davis is working on it and should have it ready for me when I return," said Ethan, referring to his associate Davis Berg.

"Excellent, I look forward to getting it," said Franklin, preparing to end the call.

"I'll see you tomorrow sir," said Ethan as he heard the call disconnect.

That went better than I thought it would, thought Ethan, as he reached out to the airline and scheduled his return flight for tomorrow morning.

Marly always felt better after talking to the girls. There was something about their relationship that was calming, and they always found something to laugh about. When Kate suggested they come and have a 'search party', it was exciting. But, looking around the living room with the large bookcases filled with books, she didn't know what they might be looking for. She had already gone through her grandfather's desk after he died, and she didn't find anything out of the ordinary. But, she wasn't really looking for anything specific. Maybe Lucy and Kate would have some ideas too. One thing was for sure, she was already looking forward to the prospect of them visiting. Marly went upstairs to the third floor where the bedrooms were located. She opened the door to her grandfather's room. It was just as it had been the day he died. She didn't really look around much in here because it was his personal space. But, now that someone was wanting something of his, she should probably do a more thorough search. She didn't want to think that her grandfather was involved in something nefarious, but the whole situation was feeling more and more like a dark mystery. Maybe she had read too many books on espionage and secret identities herself! Closing the door to his room, she made her way across the hall and went into her room. She loved this place, and she could never part with it. There were so many good memories here. She got ready for bed and picked up the book she was reading, laughing at herself when she realized it was a murder mystery. She sat down on the chaise lounge in her room and began reading, although she kept reading the same page over and over. Her mind was on the evening with

Ethan Longmire.

He seemed nice and even handsome on the outside but there was something about him that wasn't true. She didn't know what it was but felt that he was holding back something, some information that she needed to know. She was pretty confident that Mr. Kennedy was not going to accept the offer to let him look for whatever it was that he wanted. In her heart, she knew that it was something very important for him to find, based in part on the amount of money he was willing to spend to obtain it. She didn't remember until this very moment that there was a clause in Poppa's will that addressed the sale of the property. She would have to get it out of the safe and reread it. Funny that she just thought about it. But when Poppa's lawyer read the will to her and the other family members, she was still grieving for him. She still grieved for him.

Kate and Lucy were sitting at the kitchen table where they had spoken to Marly earlier on FaceTime.

"Wow, Marly has a situation going on," said Lucy.

"I agree and I don't think it is as simple as she is trying to make it. No one is going to offer that much money for a building just because of some memento," said Kate. "I think there is a lot more to the story than she even knows."

"I agree and I think the sooner we go to help

her, the better it will be. I think we should try to figure out when we can go. Let's talk to Seth and Rafe," said Lucy.

"Talk to Seth and Rafe about what?" asked Seth, as they both walked in the door. They had been working at the winery late tonight.

Lucy got up to embrace Rafe while Seth leaned down and kissed Kate.

"What are you two planning?" asked Rafe, smiling into Lucy's violet eyes.

Kate proceeded to fill in both of them about Marly's situation.

"We thought we would go see her and together we would search her home," said Kate, looking directly at Seth. "I think I am able to travel. My therapy will be done this week."

"Sounds like you have already made up your mind about this," said Seth, smiling at Kate.

Lucy interjected, "I'll take care of her, Seth. We won't be doing anything too strenuous, just poking through dusty old boxes and such. I'll make sure she doesn't get too tired!"

Rafe stood there, smiling at the woman he loved. "So, am I to assume, this is the plan? May I ask when you are thinking about going?"

Lucy looked at Kate who spoke up, "I think we could leave Thursday, after I get released from the therapist. Would that be okay?" Even though she wasn't asking for permission, she didn't want to worry Seth too much. They had both been through a lot lately.

Seth agreed with some stipulation, "I think it will be okay, but you need to keep us updated. The man who is making this offer has a lot of power and money, obviously, and he is determined to find whatever it is that he thinks is hidden there. It could be dangerous."

"I agree," said Rafe, somewhat worried. "You know how the three of you seem to attract trouble and danger like a magnet."

"I promise we will call every night," said Lucy, with Kate nodding behind her.

"Rafe and I will cover the winery, and Cory will fill in when he is needed. I think we will be able to manage things. Do we have any upcoming events?" asked Seth.

"There's a wedding at the end of the month, but I'll be back to handle that," said Lucy, feeling excited that she and Kate would be at Marly's within the week.

"We'll call Marly tomorrow and work out the details and give you guys the itinerary," said Kate, smiling at Lucy, as she too was excited about this trip.

"Okay, so do you have some dinner for us two working guys?" asked Seth, and Lucy and Kate got up to put their dinner on the table.

CHAPTER 5

Marly had a fitful night, waking up frequently, feeling anxious. She checked the security alarm several times, but each time it was still armed, the way it had been all night. She didn't realize how much all of this was affecting her. She definitely didn't want any more dangerous drama in her life. She was ready to have a quiet life and enjoy everything it had to offer. She went downstairs and made herself a cup of coffee and toasted a bagel. Doing something mundane seemed to calm her a bit. As she was sitting there, her phone rang. Seeing it was Kate, she answered it quickly.

"Hello Kate," said Marly, smiling.

"Hi yourself, Marly," said Kate. "What are you doing on Thursday afternoon?"

"Whatever it is, it can be cancelled!" laughed Marly, suddenly feeling lighter. "Am I to assume that I will be having visitors?"

"Yes, Lucy and I spoke to Seth and Rafe last night. Seth was a bit hesitant I think, but he knew that I had made up my mind. Both he and Rafe approved us to travel. I have my last therapy session on Wednesday, so we are going to book our flight for Thursday. Will that work for you?"

"Oh yes, definitely!" said Marly, the excitement evident in her voice. "You two don't know how much this means to me. I didn't realize how much all of this was making me anxious. I think I'll feel much better with you and Lucy here."

"Good. I'll make the travel arrangements and will send you our itinerary. Will you be able to pick us up?" asked Kate.

"Yes, I will. I normally Uber around town and sometimes to the airport, but I will be able to pick you up. Are you flying into the Memphis airport?" asked Marly.

"That was the plan. I'll message you when it is all finalized. So, am I to assume you are feeling upset about this situation?" asked Kate, being very aware of Marly's emotions.

"I have to admit, I didn't sleep well last night. I kept getting up and making sure that the security system alarm was on. Of course it was, but this whole thing is making me feel jittery. It's not what has happened but the anticipation of what might happen," confessed Marly.

Knowing how Marly was feeling, Kate said, "Never fear, my friend, the cavalry is on its way! We will get there and before you know it, we'll find what Mr. Kennedy is looking for, whether he likes it or not!"

Laughing at the picture in her mind of Lucy and Kate, riding up on white horses to save the day, Marly said, "I hope you are right, Kate. I just want to put this behind me and move on to the next phase of my life."

"I know that's true, Marly. I am trying to put the past few months behind me too. Seth has been wonderful and so attentive," said Kate.

"Of course he has! He loves you, Kate and has, for a very long time. And just when he thought you two were going to have a happily ever after, you got kidnapped and almost killed! He probably doesn't want to let you out of his sight!" said Marly.

"You know, he said we had to check in every day, so you are correct. But I don't mind. And, if we need reinforcements, I know that he and Rafe would be there as quick as possible," admitted Kate.

"All I can say is that I can't wait for you girls to get here!" Marly was ecstatic. "I am already planning menus in my mind!"

"We can't wait either, Marly. I'll keep you updated on our plans and we'll see you soon," said Kate, ending the call.

Somehow, Kate's phone call had changed Marly's entire outlook. She knew that Lucy and Kate would help her and maybe together, they would uncover the secrets that Franklin Kennedy thinks are here. Because, the more she thought about it, the more she figured out that it was something he and her grandfather had shared when they worked together. Her mission was to find out what type of work they did and maybe they would find a clue that would guide them in the right direction.

Ethan sat in the Memphis airport, waiting for his flight to be announced and thinking back over the prior evening. He had concluded that there was nothing he could have done differently to change the outcome of the meeting with Marly Anderson. The fact that her financial guy had tagged along made him realize that she wanted a buffer there, to ensure that nothing would be misconstrued. It was one of the few times that he had not been prepared for all scenarios. Of course, he would never admit that to Franklin Kennedy. In his defense, however, no one could have anticipated that move. The one thing he didn't know was that she was quite beautiful. That was an unexpected pleasure of their meeting. But, knowing some of the plans for the Anderson household, it would not do any good to get involved, at any level. That seemed to be his lot in life. Bringing him out of his thoughts was the ringing of his phone.

"Hello," he answered.

"Hello Ethan, it's Davis. You busy?" he asked.

"Just sitting in an airport, waiting to fly back to Denver. What's up?" asked Ethan, knowing that Davis probably had something to report.

"I was looking into that Lenny Crocker and

found something very interesting," said Davis.

"Oh? Please share," said Ethan.

"It seems that Mr. Crocker knows Marly Anderson. He was involved with kidnapping her in partnership with some crazy bitch in North Carolina," said Davis.

"You're kidding!" exclaimed Ethan. "What happened?"

"Apparently the Anderson woman was an old college roommate of Raven Silvers who was using a fake identity. Anderson recognized her and identified her by her real name and Silvers put out a contract on the Anderson woman and Crocker kidnapped her. I can't get all of the details yet, but I am working on them," Davis explained.

"Interesting. It would seem that he might be perfect for the job, since he already knows her," said Ethan, wondering how it all had ended.

"I'll reach out to you when I get more information. The FBI was involved, and you know how hard it is to get all of the information, unless you have a contact there. Do you?" asked Davis.

"No, but Mr. Kennedy might. I'll check in with him when I land and will ask him," assured Ethan. "Good work though, buddy."

"Don't thank me yet. Let me make sure of the outcome," said Davis.

Smiling, Ethan said, "Okay, okay. But, I know he has had questionable activities before that and maybe we can convince him it would be worth his while."

"I'll let you know," Davis reiterated. "We don't want to make any mistakes."

"Definitely," said Ethan. "Talk soon."

Davis disconnected and Ethan sat there pondering this new information. If Marly Anderson knew Lenny Crocker as her kidnapper, she would be afraid of him. That would be a clear advantage. Hopefully, Davis would uncover what they needed to know.

The announcement that Ethan's flight was boarding brought him back to the present and, gathering his things, he made his way to the gate. It was an uneventful flight back to Denver and he loved seeing the snow-capped mountains as they landed. He didn't have any checked baggage, so he was able to quickly exit the plane and make his way to his car, which was parked in long term parking. At the time of his trip, he didn't have any idea how long he would be gone, but it was much shorter than he had anticipated. Getting into his Mercedes, he pulled out of the space, paid his fee at the kiosk and drove toward the Kennedy estate. After he got out of the city, the trip was much faster and with a lot less traffic. He drove down the long circular driveway and parked in front of the imposing structure. Franklin Kennedy had not spared any expense when having his retreat built. It was a

Greek Revival home with large ornate columns on the front, framing the massive double mahogany doors. Walking up to the door, he rang the bell, and it was opened quickly by Mr. Kennedy's manservant.

"Hello Victor," said Ethan.

"Hello Mr. Ethan, Mr. Kennedy is waiting for you in the third-floor library," announced Victor, as Ethan made his way to the elevator. He could have taken the long, spiral staircase but he knew that Franklin Kennedy would not have wanted to wait. Selecting the third floor, the elevator silently rose quickly and opened across the hall from the designated place. Ethan walked into the library to see Franklin Kennedy seated in a leather club chair, sipping what he assumed was a brandy.

"Ah, hello Ethan, welcome back. How was the flight?" asked Franklin, very uncharacteristically. He must have already had a couple of brandies.

"Typical, Mr. Kennedy. But, no turbulence and it wasn't a full flight," Ethan gave a few details but knew that wasn't what he wanted to hear.

"Anything new to report?" Franklin asked, sipping his drink.

"Actually, while I was waiting for my flight, Davis Berg called. He had some interesting information regarding Lenny Crocker," revealed Ethan.

"Really? What pray tell was it?" asked

Franklin.

Ethan wanted to be sure he relayed the message correctly and began telling Franklin what Davis had uncovered.

"He is still trying to find out the final outcome but the mere fact that he kidnapped the Anderson woman certainly indicates that he is not out of the game," said Ethan confidently.

"Hmmm, could be," said Franklin. "But we must make sure that all is what it seems. When did Davis say he would get back with you?"

"As soon as he can get some confirmation on some facts with the FBI," said Ethan.

"I may can help with that," said Franklin, a slow smile curling his lips.

CHAPTER 6

Kate and Lucy made their plans. They would drive to San Antonio on Wednesday for Kate's therapy and then stay overnight, driving to the airport to catch their flight to Memphis. Both of them were getting very excited with the fact that they would all be together again, even for a short while. Their plan was to fly back to San Antonio on the following Wednesday, giving them five whole days to see if they could find out anything. Seth had been taking Kate to her therapy sessions, so he wasn't happy that Lucy was doing it, but he knew it made more sense than two round trips to San Antonio. He didn't know if Kate would be up to all of that traveling. Knowing he was concerned, Kate made sure that she had time with Seth to discuss everything.

"I know you usually go with me, but this makes more sense. Don't you agree?" she asked.

"Of course it does, Katie. But, just because it makes sense, doesn't mean that I like it," he said, smiling at her, trying to convey he wasn't upset.

"I know that, Seth. And you have so much more to do, with Lucy gone for a week. Is everything going to be okay?" asked Kate, thinking about the hardship they were putting on the men.

"Hey, Rafe and I can handle anything. Besides, we'll do some man things, like cooking out and drinking beer," laughed Seth, trying to lighten the moment.

"Sure you will. I can see you both working hard all day, barely eating dinner, and falling asleep in front of the television," laughed Kate. "Seriously, I am going to be fine. I will call you as soon as my appointment is done and give you all of the updates."

"You better. When you get back, we need to have another discussion...like, what is going to be your decision about your job in San Antonio. Have you spoken to Steven lately?" asked Seth, wondering what her boss was thinking.

"I spoke with him last week. Everything is going fine. They brought in another attorney while I was out so if I do decide to stay here, he won't be shorthanded. Of course, I'm sure they aren't as good as I am," joked Kate to which Seth said he agreed.

Kate moved into Seth's arms, nuzzling his neck and pulling him to her for a deep kiss.

"Oh Katie, I'm going to miss you here," said Seth, returning her kiss.

"I'll miss you too, but you know, Marly needs us. We can't have some shyster threatening her," said Kate, seriously.

"I know that," said Seth, "but at the first sign of something dangerous, call the police."

"We will definitely do that," said Kate. "We've been down this road before."

"I know, that's what worries me," said Seth, grimacing.

Kate laughed at the face he made and said again, "We will be careful, and it might not be anything except an old man wanting to recapture something from his past. Hopefully, that is all it amounts to. Don't worry!"

"Okay, Katie, I won't worry, and I won't breathe either," said Seth wryly.

Hugging him tightly, Kate knew there was nothing else to be said.

Wednesday morning came quickly, and Seth and Rafe saw the girls off before they left for work. They had loaded the luggage in the SUV and said their goodbyes. As they left, Kate sighed a little.

"Are you okay, Kate?" asked Lucy, looking at her friend.

"Yes, I'm just going to miss your brother, Lucy. He has been so good to me since everything happened," said Kate.

"That's because you love each other and it will be okay, Kate. Sometimes a little absence does make the heart grow fonder, as they say," said Lucy, the forever optimist.

"True. So, are we ready to hit the road?" asked

Kate.

"Yep, let's do this," said Lucy, making sure they didn't leave anything and headed down the long driveway towards San Antonio.

The trip didn't feel very long as they had their favorite songs playing on the radio and they were laughing and talking. Both of them were stoked about the opportunity to be with Marly for a few days.

"This will almost be like a girl trip," said Lucy. "I'd like for one of our trips to have no issues, just fun. Maybe this one will be it!"

"I hope you are right, Lucy. And, I brought plenty of pajamas!" said Kate and they both laughed.

Pulling into the Medical Center parking lot, they both made their way to the Neurology Therapy Center. After checking in, Lucy and Kate sat there, waiting and talking quietly.

"Ms. Butler?" said Angela, Dr. Boren's nurse.

Kate got up and looked at Lucy, "Wish me luck," she said.

"No luck needed," said Lucy grinning at her friend.

Kate disappeared through the door with Angela and Lucy sat there, waiting to see what the verdict would be. She was in there quite some time, but Seth had warned her the wait was usually about an hour. Lucy leafed through a magazine, not really reading it but looking at the pictures.

After about an hour and a half, Kate emerged from the back, smiling brightly.

"Well?" asked Lucy.

"Good to go," said Kate. "I need to come back in six months, but I can resume all activities, even returning to work, if I choose to."

"You better call Seth then," said Lucy, "because you know he is a worrier."

They got in the car to head to the hotel and Kate called Seth. He answered on the first ring.

"Hey Katie, what did the doctor say?" asked Seth before she could say anything.

"Everything is great Seth," Kate said and proceeded to give him the good news.

"Awesome Katie! I'm so happy for you. Now, you and Lucy enjoy your time with Marly and keep us updated. Have a safe trip and remember, I love you."

"I love you too, Seth, and we will, on all counts," said Kate as they disconnected the call.

Franklin Kennedy had reached out to an old associate who had been his FBI liaison. He still had friends he could call on to get information. Derrick Porter took the name of Lenny Crocker and said he would see what he could do. Franklin was hopeful they could get this inquiry done quickly. True to his word, Derrick Porter called back within a couple of days.

"Hello," said Franklin as he answered his phone.

"Franklin, Derrick here," Porter said. "I have that information for you." It was just like Derrick to get right to business.

"What can you tell me, Derrick?" asked Franklin, getting anxious.

"The file on Lenny Crocker was sealed at the FBI but I have a guy there that did a bit of snooping. It appears that Mr. Crocker made a deal with the FBI by agreeing to testify against the woman, Raven Silvers," said Derrick.

"What about the kidnapping charge? Did it just go away?" asked Franklin, thinking that was highly unusual for a federal crime. Maybe Crocker had a lot more information they could use.

"Apparently, there were some extenuating circumstances and after the deal was done, the woman committed suicide in jail. So he got off scot-free," Derrick filled in.

"Interesting," said Franklin. "It sounds like Mr. Crocker is willing to make a deal with the devil, when it suits his purposes."

"Yeah, he had some pretty dark things in his file, so he's no goody two shoes," said Derrick.

"Nice work, Derrick. I have already sent a deposit to your account," said Franklin, knowing that Derrick would come through for him.

"I appreciate that, Franklin. Let me know if I can do anything else for you," said Derrick, signing off.

Scrolling through his contacts, Franklin

selected Ethan Longmire and listened as the phone rang.

"Hello sir," said Ethan, "how can I help you?"

"It is I who is helping you, Ethan," said Franklin Kennedy, a smug smile on his face.

"What is it, sir?" asked Ethan, knowing he must have heard from his contact.

Franklin hesitated a moment before he revealed his information. "I did hear from my FBI contact and apparently Lenny Crocker got off on the kidnapping charge in exchange for testifying against his partner. But, when she committed suicide, he got off without any time served. I think you are free to approach Mr. Crocker and see if he would like to be gainfully employed by me. Let me know what he says," said Franklin, ending the call before Ethan could reply.

Ethan called Davis Berg, and he answered quickly.

"Yes?" Davis said.

"Ethan here," he said. "Mr. Kennedy heard from his FBI contact and gave the go ahead on Lenny Crocker. No need to keep looking into him as Mr. Kennedy feels he is the right man for the job."

"Are you sure?" asked Davis. "I'd hate to overlook something."

"Yes, I'm sure. If something is overlooked, it is not your responsibility," Ethan assured him.

"Okay, brother, let me know if you change

your mind," said Davis, and he disconnected the call.

Ethan felt a little uneasy with stopping Davis, but Mr. Kennedy had some very connected people at his disposal, and he was sure that everything had been examined. At least he hoped so.

CHAPTER 7

Lucy and Kate checked into the hotel by the airport and had a very leisurely evening. They had room service for dinner and lounged around in pajamas watching sitcoms until about 10:00 p.m. Lucy noticed that Kate was yawning.

"Are you ready to go to bed, Kate?" asked Lucy, feeling a bit tired herself.

"I think I am Lucy. We have a busy day tomorrow and you know there will be no rest once we get to Marly's place," said Kate.

"I know that's right!" agreed Lucy.

As the girls got into bed, they both were thinking about Marly.

"What do you think he wants?" asked Lucy, knowing Kate was listening.

Kate was thinking the same thing. "I don't know Lucy, but I hope, that whatever it is, we find it first!"

"Amen," agreed Lucy. "Goodnight Kate."

"Goodnight Lucy," she said, and it was lights out.

Marly was up early, scurrying around, getting the bedroom ready for her guests, although they weren't really guests. They were her family, her best friends. She was really looking forward to being together and reconnecting. Of course, they had another mission as well, but she was sure they would have some down time to play. The large bedroom Marly had designated for guests had two queen beds, separated by an antique table. A tiffany lamp in pastel colors sat in the center of it on top of a scarf that Kate had given her several years before. Over each bed was a framed print of pastel flowers that Lucy had gifted her one Christmas. A large oak wardrobe sat against one wall with enough space for hanging clothes with two drawers in the bottom. The room was large enough for a sitting area and Marly had put a small cream-colored sofa there as well as a dark pink chaise lounge chair. A low coffee table completed the area and Marly was satisfied, knowing the girls would be comfortable. Heading down the stairs to the living area and kitchen, she surveyed the cozy space to make sure everything was ready. Now all she had to do was wait until time to pick them up at the airport.

Ethan was up early and was reviewing the file he had on Lenny Crocker. He didn't know him personally but had used his services years before. There hadn't been any issues at that time, and he hoped everything would go as smoothly this time. But first, Mr. Kennedy would give the final word on how to proceed. Ethan was to meet with him this morning and they would discuss reaching out to Crocker. For some reason, Ethan was nervous about this one.

Franklin Kennedy sat in the library, sipping his morning cup of black coffee. He had not slept well again, with visions of his old life interrupting his slumber. Oliver leading the last meeting he attended, Oliver saying something is not right, Oliver disappearing with highly confidential information, Oliver dead. They are some of the same images that haunt him when he is awake as well. If he could just be sure that there is nothing in the Anderson home that would compromise hidden clients and government assets, then he could rest easy. It would be so simple if Oliver's granddaughter would sell the property to him and then he could just destroy it. He could then be at peace when his time came.

Victor appeared at the door of the library, "Mr. Kennedy, Ethan Longmire has arrived."

Surprised that so much time had passed with his reminiscing, Franklin said, "Send him in, Victor."

Victor disappeared and in a few moments, Ethan walked in, carrying the file on Lenny Crocker. He strode over to the chair opposite Mr. Kennedy.

"Good morning, sir," greeted Ethan. "I hope

you rested well last evening."

"Truthfully, no, but at this point, it doesn't really matter," he said. "Let's discuss Crocker. You have dealt with him in the past and my contact feels certain there isn't anything that would compromise him. What are your instincts, Ethan?"

Ethan had decided long ago that being honest was the best way to respond. Clearing his throat, he said, "I am a bit uneasy that we discontinued the deep dive into Lenny Crocker. Davis also felt he should continue in case your contact may have missed something."

"I do not think that is the case, Ethan. Do you not trust my judgement?" asked Franklin pointedly.

"That isn't it at all, sir. You have always impressed upon me to not leave any stone unturned, and this felt as if we were not being as diligent as in other situations," Ethan explained, hoping that Mr. Kennedy would understand his reasoning.

Franklin sat there in thoughtful silence. This was the way he had taught Ethan, but again, Derrick was a trusted friend and contact. He had never gotten bad intel from him once and that swayed him to stand by his earlier decision. "I appreciate your thought processes, Ethan, and yes, I have always kept digging, even when we found out it wasn't necessary. However, Derrick Porter is a long-trusted colleague and friend, and

I have never been disappointed with him or with what I have requested of him. I believe you can trust me when I say we have enough information to move forward with Mr. Crocker."

"Yes sir," said Ethan, letting the subject drop. "What next then, sir?"

"I would like to contact Miss Anderson again, before we move forward. Call her and find out if she has had a change of heart. Maybe see if she is really willing to allow me to search her home," Franklin stated.

Ethan, fairly certain that she would not want that, did not state that but simply said, "Yes, I'll contact her today. If she asks about when, what would you want to do then?"

"Arrange it for as soon as possible, this weekend even," Franklin didn't want any more time to lapse, if possible.

"I'll call her this morning," Ethan said, not mentioning Lenny Crocker again.

Franklin was silent and Ethan thought he was done, but he suddenly spoke, "Ethan, Oliver and I were part of a secret organization that did work for high level individuals. Work that involved making them disappear."

"Disappear? What do you mean?" asked Ethan, shocked and intrigued at the same time.

"As technology was invented, we incorporated much of it into our work. Oliver was a genius and could do anything. We specialized in digital erasure, concealment of information, and protected high-profile individuals who needed their pasts to disappear," Franklin explained.

"Who were these people?" asked Ethan.

"They were whistleblowers, defectors, and people entangled in dangerous political or corporate wars. It was our mission to make sure that whatever it was, it had to disappear without a trace. In some cases, the person themselves disappeared, to live forever in anonymity," Franklin explained.

"So, they are out there but no one knows who they are? And they have secrets, if they are found out, could..." Ethan said.

"Destroy our world as we know it," Franklin admitted.

"Do you think Mr. Anderson kept the intel he was to erase?" asked Ethan, mesmerized with the story.

"Something happened or went wrong. I don't know what because during Oliver's last assignment, he abruptly left the organization and withdrew into obscurity. I have spent the better part of two decades searching for him and only recently tracked his whereabouts to Tennessee. He was a master of deception and misdirection," said Franklin. "If he did keep something that should have been destroyed, he probably hid it somewhere. And knowing Oliver, it would be something that he wanted to keep close."

Ethan looked at Mr. Kennedy and asked, "Does

this organization still exist?"

"In some sense, yes, but the work of the Crimson Veil is over. It is the protection of the people whose identities we obliterated that is our priority," said Franklin. "There are members still associated with the Veil and only members can communicate with one another. That is all you need to know."

Realizing that he was being dismissed, Ethan stood. "I'll let you know what Ms. Anderson says."

"Good, and if we are unsuccessful, we will move forward with Lenny Crocker," said Franklin, dismissing Ethan.

Ethan walked slowly down the spiral staircase, mulling over what he had just been told. He didn't even think about using the elevator, so absorbed as he was in his thoughts. He could understand the urgency of Mr. Kennedy's request more now but was positive that Marly wasn't going to be agreeable to a search of her home. Her concession had been to find a memento or to find it for him. In fact, it wouldn't surprise Ethan if she wasn't suspicious. Who demands access to your home without a good reason, especially a stranger? Maybe Mr. Kennedy was getting a little senile with unreasonable expectations. He reached the bottom floor and Victor walked to the door, opening it for him. He went down the front steps to his car and drove back to his apartment. Even though it wasn't yet noon, he needed a drink before he called Marly Anderson. That was going to be a difficult story to sell.

CHAPTER 8

Marly had her SUV serviced and it was parked out front. She was going to leave for the airport in about thirty minutes. She was sitting in the living room, trying to read a book but she was so excited she couldn't concentrate. She finally gave up and placed the book on the side table when her phone rang.

"Hello," she said.

"Hello Marly. This is Ethan Longmire," he said, dreading this conversation.

Taken off guard, Marly wasn't sure how to respond but said, "What can I do for you?"

Ethan took the plunge, "I spoke with Mr. Kennedy about your alternative solution, and he wanted me to ask when he could come and look for the item he was remembering. I could give you an idea, but he wouldn't tell me."

Frustration was in her voice when she answered him, "I believe that I said I would look for the item first and then, if I couldn't locate it, maybe I would allow him to look. I think it is a great invasion of my privacy. I do not know this man and yet, he wants to come into my home and look for some unnamed object and I am just supposed to allow him to waltz in and take whatever he wants? I don't think I am comfortable with that, on any level."

Ethan cringed inwardly, but pushed on, "I certainly understand that, Marly. I actually told him something along those lines as well, but he was insistent. He said he would even come this weekend."

"Absolutely not!" Marly said emphatically. "I have houseguests for the next week, and it would not be possible at all, even if I had been willing and I'm not. Am I going to have to get a restraining order against Mr. Kennedy to get him to leave me alone?"

"No, no, not at all. I was just relaying his request, but he would never come without your permission," Ethan scrambled to calm things down. "Don't worry about it. Maybe we can come to some other solution, after your guests leave. I'm sorry to have upset you."

"There are limits, Mr. Longmire, to my patience and Mr. Kennedy has exceeded those limits. Now, if you will excuse me, I have to go," said Marly, disconnecting the call without anything further.

Ethan sat there with the silent telephone to his ear. Slowly he put it away and thought, '*well that was a total disaster*'. He knew that he needed to call Mr. Kennedy but he needed to finish his drink first and then frame his report in a less hostile manner. She definitely was upset. Sighing, he drained his vodka tonic and leaned his head back to think.

Now she was late! She was so angry as she grabbed her purse and keys, leaving the house and getting in her car. She drove toward the Memphis airport, seething. '*The audacity of Mr. Franklin Kennedy and his lackey, Ethan Longmire. I don't care how much money he has, he doesn't have a right to come into my life and turn it upside down*'. By the time she pulled into the short-term parking lot, she had calmed down. Getting out, she headed to the baggage claim area to wait for Kate and Lucy. She didn't have to wait long.

"Marly!" screamed Lucy, as she and Kate hurried to their friend. A group hug was inevitable.

"Kate, how was the trip for you?" asked Marly, concerned because of her recent injury.

"She did great," said Lucy and Kate smiled.

"Yes, it was fine. I called Seth as soon as we landed and let him know as well," said Kate.

"Good, I was worried because of the altitude and cabin pressures," said Marly, always thinking like a caregiver.

They walked toward the carousel and waited for the baggage to appear.

"How has your day been, Marly?" asked Lucy, teasingly. "Have you found anything mysterious in the house?"

"No and I haven't been looking. But, I have something to tell you when we get in the car," said Marly, obviously miffed.

"Oh my, sounds like another encounter with Franklin Kennedy," guessed Kate.

"Yes and I have had it with him," said Marly.

"Oooh, I can't wait to hear this story," said Lucy. Suddenly, the luggage started falling onto the carousel and they stood there until their bags appeared. Lucy picked up hers and pointed to Kate's and Marly scooped them up.

"I can do that, Marly," said Kate. "I'm not an invalid, remember."

"But, I can do it easier. Come on, let's get out of here," said Marly, leading the way to her car.

After loading their things in the back of her Tahoe, they all got in. Kate called dibs on the front and Lucy didn't fuss. She still worried about Kate too.

"So, what happened today, Marly?" asked Lucy.

Marly proceeded to tell them about the call from Franklin Kennedy's associate, Ethan Longmire, and the request to search the house. He even suggested this weekend! Marly told them how she had refused and that she had never offered to let him search her house carte blanc. She had even threatened to get a restraining order against him.

"Oh my," said Kate.

Lucy piped up, "Kate, could she get one of

those?"

"Yes, and I can help you do that, if you want to go that route. But, be very careful, because he is a very rich and powerful man. I'm sure there are a lot of people who would do his bidding without any consideration of a restraining order," she said.

"I know, I know, it was sort of an empty threat, but I was just so angry. He is so pushy. I don't know what it is that he wants to look for, but if it's there, it can wait a bit longer. I told Ethan Longmire that I had houseguests for the next week, and it wouldn't even be possible. Hopefully, he will relay that to the mighty Mr. Kennedy," said Marly, as she drove toward Germantown.

"Woohoo, our Marly is fired up! I love it!" said Lucy, laughing.

Marly gave a chuckle herself. "It really bothers me that he is so presumptuous. I'm not on his schedule, whatever that is. But, for now, let's not talk about it. We will have plenty of time for that in the next few days. For tonight, it's going to be about us,"

"Agreed," said Kate and Lucy echoed the sentiment.

Marly parked in front of the building, and they took the luggage inside and up the stairs. Marly went outside to move her car to the garage in the back. She went up the stairs in the garage and opened the door to the second floor, making her way into the living room.

"Okay girls, let's get you upstairs to the guest room. I'm sorry about all of the steps, Kate," said Marly.

"Actually, I have been doing exercises to help with my strength and balance so this will be good for me," confessed Kate.

Marly ushered them into the guest room, and they loved it. The décor was perfect and the atmosphere so calming.

"Maybe you should come sit in here, Marly, after a conversation with Mr. Longmire," laughed Lucy.

"Very funny, Lucy," Marly laughed with her. "Maybe next time, I will."

After they were settled in, they all trooped downstairs and to the kitchen. Lucy found the wine glasses and a chilled bottle of Cavanaugh Vineyards wine.

"Oooh, this wine is excellent!" she said, winking at her friends.

"Actually, it is," said Marly. "I know the wine maker."

Lucy poured and then they toasted, "To the best friends ever!" said Marly.

"I'll drink to that!" said Lucy.

"Here, here," said Kate, and their glasses clinked together.

"Mmmm, this is good wine," said Kate, as they all made their way into the living room.

"So, what is on the menu tonight, Marly?"

asked Lucy.

Marly said, "I kept it simple. I made a rice pilaf and I'm going to sear some salmon steaks and steam some broccoli. I made homemade yeast rolls this morning."

"Oh my god, I can hardly wait!" said Lucy.

Kate agreed, "It sounds marvelous.!"

They spent the next hour catching up.

Ethan took a deep breath and called Franklin Kennedy. As always, he answered immediately.

"Hello Ethan, what did Miss Anderson say?" he asked without preamble.

"She was put out with the request and said that she had offered to search for the item you were looking for, although you had not identified it. I couldn't tell her anything, so I pressed for this weekend. She has guests for the week and said it would not be possible. She got a bit irate, threatening a restraining order," Ethan gave him all of the information.

"A restraining order, eh? She's spunky, I'll give her that much. Let her have guests and when they leave, I may approach her again or by that time, we may have a plan in place with Mr. Crocker. I'm getting impatient with Miss Anderson. Time is of the essence, and I will not be held off indefinitely," Franklin Kennedy was adamant.

"I understand sir," said Ethan. "Let me know what you want me to do."

"We will wait. I'll have one of my contacts keep an eye on Miss Anderson and her guests. When they leave, I'll make the decision as to what will be our next move," Franklin stated and ended the call.

This was not going to end well.

CHAPTER 9

Dinner was a delicious affair as well as entertaining. Marly, Kate, and Lucy never had any trouble picking up where they left off, and stories always were spun when they were together.

"What do you say we get in our pajamas and retire to the sitting area in your room," suggested Marly.

"I thought you would never say it!" laughed Lucy.

"Yes, I've been ready to slip into my pj's too," said Kate, laughing.

"Well, you girls should have said something. I mean, I practically live in mine when I'm at home," said Marly. "Go on up and I'll join you in a few minutes. I just want to check the doors and set the alarm."

"Are you that uneasy, Marly?" asked Kate concernedly.

"I have to admit, it has made me a bit nervous. But, it doesn't hurt to take precautions, right?" Marly added.

"You're absolutely right, Marly," said Lucy.

"And I dare anyone to try to get to you while we're here. We are a formidable force to be reckoned with!"

"Definitely," agreed Marly as she checked on the house while the other two went upstairs. *'Oh Poppa, what could possibly be here? Please give me a sign.'*

After Marly got into her pajamas as well, she joined her friends in their room. They began to think about the task at hand.

"Have you gone through your grandfather's desk and library, Marly?" asked Kate.

"Actually, I did a cursory search, but I didn't really think it was necessary. All of his legal papers were filed with his attorney, so I didn't have to look for anything when he passed away. The attorney contacted me and informed me that I was the sole heir to the estate," Marly said.

"Wow, I bet that made Lucinda angry," said Lucy, referring to Marly's mom.

"Yes, she and my dad were furious. Of course, my brother and sister joined right in with them in trying to get me to let go of some of the assets. But I couldn't. Grandfather had explicitly stated in his will that everything had to remain in my ownership or be sold and donated to charity," explained Marly, curious about that stipulation. "Is that ever done, Kate?"

"It's quite telling, actually, that he didn't trust them to be good stewards of the holdings. He trusted you to do what he would have done,

Marly. With that stipulation, they definitely could not contest it," Kate stated.

"It certainly put an end to my family relationship, as if there ever was one. I still don't know what I ever did to be treated the way I was, even before Poppa died. I always felt like I didn't belong there, and they were more than happy to ship me to Poppa's house. I think I lived with him more than I did my own parents," said Marly.

"Marly!" said Lucy, "you were just a child. You didn't do anything. If anyone is at fault, it's Lucinda and Thomas. The fact that your siblings didn't come to your side just tells me that they are selfish and greedy people. I just want to say, they are adults supposedly, so grow up!"

Marly smiled at her friends. They were all the family she needed, and she told them so. After another hour, the travelers were starting to yawn and Marly insisted they all get some rest.

"We will be busy in the morning," said Marly. "We'll start in the living room and go through his desk and library, although I'm sure we won't find anything."

"Don't be so sure, Marly," said Kate. "Sometimes things are kept hidden in plain sight."

"Well, I for one can't wait!" said Lucy. "I always wanted to be a detective, before I got into the wine business, that is!"

They all laughed, hugged each other goodnight, and went to bed.

Franklin's phone rang about 2:00 a.m.

"Hello," he said, knowing who was on the other end of the call.

"Have you found anything yet?" the voice asked.

"Not yet but I'm working on getting access to the last place where he lived," Franklin said.

"So what's the hold up?" the voice continued.

Franklin, irritated at the caller's attitude, said, "It's not so easy to do when someone else lives there."

"Buy the place," the caller suggested.

Franklin snapped back sarcastically, "Oh, why didn't I think of that? I did, of course, but the owner is not interested in selling. I am working on getting inside to search for myself, but we have to be careful and not arouse suspicion. Unless, of course, you are okay with that?"

The caller backed off somewhat, "No, of course not. I'm just anxious and want some assurance that I will continue to be safe."

"That is the goal, and we are proceeding as quickly as possible with the obstacles we have to overcome," said Franklin, speaking firmly.

"Do you have any idea when your 'obstacles' will be overcome?" the voice hissed.

"I think I will be able to have answers for you in a couple of weeks," promised Franklin, hoping that he was right. "Next time we speak, I will call you."

The caller realized that Franklin Kennedy wasn't someone you should bully, and said, "I'm sorry if I pushed too hard. But, it is my life at stake."

Relenting somewhat, Franklin said, "I understand and believe me when I tell you that I am doing everything I can to expedite this mission."

"Thank you," the voice said quietly, and the line went dead.

Long after the conversation ended, Franklin lay in the darkness of his room, mulling over everything. *'Why did you have to die first, Oliver? Now I have to deal with all of this shit. I hope for her sake that your granddaughter relents and lets me search your house. Lives depend on it, maybe even hers.'*

Early the next morning, Franklin contacted Derrick Porter.

"Hey, Frank, what's going on?" asked Derrick, surprised to hear from him again.

"Unfortunately, I need a favor," said Franklin. "I will make it worth your while."

Derrick always liked doing favors for Frank. He was very generous when he wanted a favor.

"If I can help you, I will. What do you need?" asked Derrick.

"I need someone in the Memphis area to surveil someone, off the books. I'm not interested in doing anything, just recording the people and their activity at an address in Germantown," explained Franklin.

"Hmmm, tricky. I'll have to involve someone not on my payroll," said Derrick. "For how long?"

"A week, starting immediately. I will pay extra so that you have enough to incentivize your person. Do you know anyone in that area?" asked Franklin.

"Do they have to be with the Bureau?" asked Derrick.

"No just someone you trust to do the job," Franklin was getting worried.

"Hang on just a second," said Derrick. Silence filled the gap while he was waiting, and Franklin wasn't sure Derrick could help.

After a few minutes, Derrick was back. "I have someone that can do it today through the weekend. Can you arrange someone else after that?"

Franklin immediately thought of Lenny Crocker and made a quick decision, "Yes, I can have someone there by Monday. You can send me the report from your guy. What did you offer him?"

"A thousand a day," said Derrick. "He wasn't cheap, I know."

"No problem. I'll wire ten thousand to you and you can pay him out of that, keeping the rest," said Franklin.

"Thanks Frank, I'll get him right on it," said Derrick, ending the call.

Feeling some relief, Franklin picked up the file on Lenny Crocker. It contained his address and telephone number. He thought about calling him, but he felt that he would have a better outcome if he just showed up at his cabin. He didn't even loop Ethan in on this decision, because the less people knew, the better and more secret it would remain. Looking at the map, he found Snake Hill Road outside of Denver about twenty minutes from his estate. But, the road itself looked quite curvy and dangerous. Picking up the phone, he called Samson Travers, his chauffeur.

"Hello sir," said Samson. "Do you require a ride somewhere?"

"Yes, I do, Samson. Please get the car ready and I will meet you out front in twenty minutes," said Franklin.

"Yes sir," was the reply and Samson went to prepare the Porsche Cayenne ready. At the appointed time, he was waiting out front for Mr. Kennedy.

Victor wasn't happy with Mr. Kennedy's decision. "Sir, you really shouldn't be outside in this weather," indicating the drizzle of rain that had begun.

"Victor, I will be fine. If anyone calls, I am under the weather and in bed," he instructed.

"After this, you possibly will be sir," said Victor, opening the door for his employer.

Franklin Kennedy slowly made his way down

the rounded stairs and Samson met him halfway, helping him into the back seat of the black SUV.

"Where to, sir?" asked Samson.

Franklin handed a card to Samson and on it was the address on Snake Hill Road. Putting it into the GPS, the Cayenne slowly went down the circular driveway and into the road.

CHAPTER 10

Marly got up early and started making waffles, cooking bacon, and heating maple syrup. The smells made their way upstairs and it wasn't long before Lucy and Kate were headed downstairs toward the delicious aroma.

"What are you doing?" asked Lucy. "It smells heavenly down here!"

"It certainly does," agreed Kate, sneaking a piece of bacon. "And delicious too!"

"Hey, no fair," said Lucy, snatching the half-eaten piece of bacon from Kate.

Laughing, Marly said, "There is plenty to go around. There's also some fresh orange juice in the fridge and if you want a mimosa, some champagne too."

"Marly, you think of everything," said Lucy, opening the fridge and taking out the juice and bubbly. "I had to rush Kate off of the phone with Seth so we could get down here."

Blushing a little, Kate said, "I promised him I would keep him updated!"

"And you should, Kate," said Marly, "or he would worry."

"I know, I know," said Lucy, "I'm just kidding, sort of."

Breakfast was a fun affair and soon, everyone was so full they were miserable.

"We cannot eat like this every day, Marly," said Kate, picking up the dishes and putting them in the dishwasher.

"For real!" echoed Lucy, who was putting leftovers in baggies.

"I just wanted your first day here to be memorable and now, it's cold cereal for you guys," laughed Marly as she put things away in the pantry.

When they finished in the kitchen, they went into the living room and surveyed the area.

"I'll start at the desk if you two want to go through the bookcases," said Marly, indicating the three large ones against the wall.

"I think we got the hardest job, Kate," said Lucy, grinning.

"I'll help when I'm done here," said Marly, sitting down at her grandfather's desk. She was a little nervous, not because she was afraid of what she would find but just invading his privacy. But, it was necessary, because of Franklin Kennedy.

The three of them worked in silence, a comment about a book or a movie reference being interjected occasionally.

Kate slid a book out of the bookcase, but it was just the hardcover of a book. Inside was a journal.

"Look Marly," said Kate, excitedly.

Marly came over and took it from Kate. "What is this?" she asked.

"It appears that your grandfather was hiding something, and maybe not just this either," said Kate.

"I knew Kate would find something first," said Lucy, pouting.

Marly turned the journal over in her hands and then opened the leather cover. It seemed like gibberish, nothing made sense to her. She turned it so that Kate and Lucy could see.

After a few moments, Kate said, "It could be encoded information. Maybe the key to it is hidden in a different book?"

"We would definitely need something to decipher this because it means nothing to me," said Marly, baffled.

"Let's just keep looking. We've already found something, and we've only been at it for an hour. No telling what we are going to come across," said Lucy, energized.

Marly went back to the desk, and she had only found old newspaper clippings of people she didn't know, some empty folders, and some pages with symbols on them. Nothing looked important but Marly wasn't going to dismiss them...yet. The bottom drawer was locked, and Marly had found some keys. However, none of them fit the lock on the drawer.

"Kate, Lucy, I found a locked drawer but none

of these keys fit. Do you think we should break it open?" asked Marly.

"It's your desk, Marly," said Kate. "You can break it open."

"I'm not sure I know how," said Marly, looking confused.

Lucy said, "Look, I have jimmied a few locks in my time. Let me take a crack at it."

Marly got up and Lucy sat down. She picked up a letter opener and a paper clip.

"Oh so those are the tools of a drawer jimmy?" asked Kate, teasingly.

"Very funny, Kate," said Lucy, smiling. She worked on the lock for a few minutes and suddenly, it was unlocked. Lucy laid down the tools she was using and got up, indicating to Marly she should be the one to open it.

Marly didn't realize she was holding her breath until she sat down. She let it out and slowly slid the drawer open. In the bottom was a single manila envelope. It had Marly's name written on it in her grandfather's handwriting. She sat there, looking at it, reluctant to open it.

Kate spoke up, "You don't have to open it now, Marly."

"I want to, but I'm afraid. What will I find?" she asked.

"You won't know until you do," said Lucy. "But remember, we are here for you, no matter what is in that envelope. It changes nothing between us."

Smiling at them both, she opened the envelope and pulled out two documents. Marly read them in silence and then reread one of them. She slowly looked up at her friends and they could tell she was shocked at what she had found.

"My grandfather was hiding something," she said, as tears formed in her eyes.

The road was winding and steep and Samson was using all of his skill to navigate Snake Hill Road.

"Who would want to live up here, Mr. Kennedy?" he asked, taking another sharp curve slowly.

"Someone who doesn't want to be found, I would imagine, Samson," said Franklin.

They finally turned the last curve in the road and there was a small but sturdy-looking cabin with a porch across the front. The trees towered around it, and it was so quiet you could hear a pine needle hit the ground. There wasn't a sound and Samson asked his boss.

"Do you want me to go to the door sir?"

"No, Samson, I will, if you will just help me up the steps," said Franklin. Getting out of the car, he walked to the steps and Samson helped him make it to the porch.

Franklin Kennedy wasn't afraid of anything, but he realized he was in a vulnerable position right now. He knocked on the door, listening for any signs of life inside.

Lenny heard the sound of a vehicle coming up the road. He was curious because he never had any visitors. The last ones he had, took him into custody after he had kidnapped Marly Anderson. These people must be lost. He heard the knock on his door and walked to it, opening it widely to see a frail old man standing there.

"Are you lost?" asked Lenny.

"I am, if you are not Lenny Crocker," said the man, balancing with his ornate walking stick.

"Who wants to know?" he asked, never willing to give out information to someone he didn't know.

"I'm Franklin Kennedy and I have a proposition for you," he said firmly, belying his age.

The name Franklin Kennedy was well known, and Lenny was no exception. He knew he was a very rich and powerful man, but he was curious about his reason for coming.

"Come in, Mr. Kennedy," said Lenny, stepping aside so that he could enter the cabin.

Franklin noted that even though it seemed simple on the outside, the inside was well furnished, with high-end furniture, electronics and appliances, and everything a person would need to exist. Lenny noted his perusal.

"You have a very nice place, Mr. Crocker," said Franklin.

"Thank you, I have updated it to meet my

needs," said Lenny, without further explanation.

"Let me get to the point, Mr. Crocker," said Franklin. "I have a delicate situation at the moment. I need to search a property, but the current owner has not given me permission to do so. It is possible that I will be allowed to conduct my search in a couple of weeks but in the meantime, I need the person surveilled. Would this be something you would be interested in?"

Lenny wasn't one to bite quickly. Once he got out from under Raven's influence, he had not been involved in anything illegal.

"That is not the type of thing that I do," said Lenny.

"I know that, with kidnapping being more your style, eh?" said Franklin, showing Lenny that he knew about his past.

Showing no emotion to his dig, Lenny said, "You can hire a private detective to do surveillance for you."

"True, but I might need you for something else after the surveillance is done. Money is no object, if that is your concern," Franklin said.

"Look around, Mr. Kennedy, I do not need money," said Lenny.

"I see that, but I think you are acquainted with the person I want you to surveil, and I can ensure that you can finish the job you started a couple of years ago," he said smugly.

"Oh, and who might that be?" Lenny asked, curious.

"Marly Anderson," said Franklin Kennedy, dropping the bombshell and seeing the reaction on Lenny's face.

CHAPTER 11

"So, you remember her?" asked Franklin, knowing that he did.

Lenny was silent, contemplating where this was going.

"I wouldn't say I didn't finish the job. I was supposed to kidnap her, and I did," replied Lenny in an even voice.

"Well, I don't have all of the pertinent facts, but I assure you I don't want her kidnapped. I just want you to watch her place for a week. She has something that belongs to me, and I intend to get it, one way or another," said Franklin, stretching the truth a bit.

Lenny quickly did some thinking. If he turned down this offer, Marly might be in greater danger. If he took it, he could protect her from whatever this guy was planning, provided he found out the end game.

"So do you want me to get whatever it is of yours that she has?" asked Lenny, leading Franklin to believe he would take the offer.

"No, no, it is something that only I would recognize, as it is personal. As I mentioned, I have approached her, but permission is pending," lied Franklin, feeling certain she would never give him access.

Lenny didn't speak for a good full minute. "Where does she live? When I grabbed her, it was in North Carolina," said Lenny, trying to get as much information from Franklin as possible without raising suspicions.

Franklin forged ahead, "She lives in Germantown, Tennessee, in a three-story structure. Part of it is an empty retail space and then the living spaces. I'm not sure of the layout but I'm expecting blueprints from the city. She stated to my associate that she had guests for the week, and I just want to keep an eye on her and make sure she does have guests. She might be lying, for all I know."

If he knew one thing about Marly, Lenny knew she wasn't a liar. But, he didn't want to let on that he knew her better than this guy thought he did.

"That's a long way from my cabin. I'd have to get a hotel or an Airbnb," mused Lenny, as if he was thinking out loud.

"I will finance the entire trip and lodging as well as your fee. Money is no object," said Franklin, trying to convince Lenny.

"I'd like to think about it before I decide," said Lenny, trying to stall.

"I'm sorry, but I don't have the time. I have someone watching the house this weekend, but

I must have someone else there by Monday. If you can't decide now, I'll have to reach out to someone else," Franklin said, hoping that the urgency would help him decide.

"What are you offering for the job?" asked Lenny, buying some time.

"All expenses paid, travel and lodging as well as $20,000.00 for the week," said Franklin, making it more than lucrative for him.

Lenny knew he had to do it. He couldn't risk Marly getting hurt or worse. After a few minutes, Lenny spoke.

"I'll do it. I'll drive my vehicle, because I am comfortable taking my own ride. I'll find a place to stay and keep my receipts. You can advance the fee," said Lenny, seeing if he was serious.

"I'm delighted, Mr. Crocker. I actually came prepared to pay you today," Franklin said, getting up and waving to Samson who was waiting outside. Samson came to the door with a briefcase in his hand. Franklin opened the door and took it from him, closing it again.

Franklin handed the briefcase to Lenny, saying, "You will find $30,000.00 in cash in the case and if your expenses exceed the excess of your fee, just let me know."

Lenny took the case and popped it open. Lying in neat, banded stacks were $100 bills. He closed the case and held out his hand and Franklin shook it.

"You just hired me," said Lenny. "I'll be there

on Sunday. Do you have the address?"

Franklin pulled a card from his pocket and handed it to Lenny. "You will find all of her information on this."

"Do you want daily reports?" asked Lenny, trying to cover all of the details.

"Only if something out of the ordinary arises. I don't want to alarm her...yet," said Franklin.

Lenny kept his features expressionless as he opened the door for Franklin Kennedy and watched as Samson escorted him to the SUV and started making his way back down the mountain.

"What is it, Marly?" asked Kate.

Silently she handed the first document to Kate and she and Lucy read it. It was from an adoption agency and showed that Marly was adopted by Oliver Anderson. She was from an orphanage in Arkansas and was three years old at the time of the adoption. There was no family information in the records, and it was a private adoption.

"But what about Lucinda and Thomas?" asked Lucy. "When did they adopt you?"

"They didn't," said Marly, handing over the second document. This one was a contract between Oliver Anderson and Thomas and Lucinda Weston.

Reading this document, they learned that the Westons agreed to act as Oliver's family, taking the name of Anderson. All legal documents were forged and signed by the Westons and Oliver Anderson. They were paid a sum of $100,000 at the onset of the agreement and were paid $25,000 each quarter every year.

"So, they pretended to be your family for money? That's outrageous!" said Lucy, her temper flaring.

Kate was concerned about Marly and asked, "Are you okay, Marly?"

"I don't know what I am. Everything I thought about my life was a lie. My family, no I have no family, have lied to me all of my life. No wonder I never felt I was a part of them. It's because I'm not. I'm part of a big, fat lie!" Marly shouted out and then broke down in tears.

Lucy and Kate surrounded Marly, hugging her and letting her cry. This was certainly not the way they thought this day was going to go. This elaborate cover up makes what is happening a lot more dangerous.

Lucy spoke quietly, "Marly, you do have a family. Me, Kate, Seth, Rafe, and our families are yours. You will never be alone, and you are loved more than you know." Tears were slipping down Lucy's cheeks as well.

"I know, I know, and that's the way I feel. To think I have given those imposters money since Poppa died...I don't even know if I should call him that," cried Marly.

"Yes, he has been your Poppa for a very long

time, Marly, and it is obvious that he loved you dearly. This whole scheme makes me think that Franklin Kennedy knows your grandfather has something that he desperately wants and I'm afraid that he will do anything to get it. It makes this whole situation much more dangerous," said Kate.

At that moment, Marly's phone rang. She looked at it and saw unknown caller. She let it go to voicemail.

"I just don't feel like talking to anyone," said Marly. A few minutes later, he called again.

"Just see who it is," said Kate. "Put them on speaker."

"Hello?" said Marly, sniffling.

"Marly, are you okay?" he heard the tremor in her voice.

"Lenny? Did you get a new number? I'm okay and I have you on speaker and Kate and Lucy are here with me," said Marly.

"Good, because I need to tell you something. Can you all hear me?" asked Lenny.

Looking at each other, the girls nodded, and Marly said, "Yes, we can hear you."

"I'm calling from a burner phone. Listen, a Franklin Kennedy came to see me today," he began.

"What? Are you kidding? What did he want?" asked Marly.

"To hire me to watch your house," Lenny began but was interrupted.

"What the hell?" said Lucy. "Did you kick his ass out?"

"No, I didn't and please, listen," said Lenny.

Kate motioned for everyone to be quiet, and she spoke, "What do we need to know, Lenny."

Lenny explained what Franklin Kennedy proposed and that he hired Lenny for a week with a possible job after that one. Lenny let them know that someone was watching the house now, to see when they left and returned.

"I don't know what's going on, but I thought if I took the job, I could somehow protect you girls. I don't know what else he is planning but he wants to get into your house Marly and find something he said you have of his," Lenny finished.

"That's a lie! He wants something that my grandfather had, and I have no idea what it is, and he won't say. I'm thinking it must be something they worked on together years ago, but I don't know for sure. I'm tired of Franklin Kennedy thinking he can bulldoze his way into my home. I won't have it!" said Marly emphatically."

"He offered me the job because I had kidnapped you. He thinks I'm still that type of person. I used his misinformation to get the job. I plan to be in town on Sunday but whoever is watching you now will be there until Monday. I won't be contacting you unless I hear about any other plans. Also, keep this number because

I bought this phone so that my communication with you couldn't be traced," said Lenny.

"Thank you, Lenny, for wanting to protect Marly, and us by proxy. But, you are putting yourself in a dangerous position, from what I can gather," said Kate.

"I'm pretty sure you're right, but I have a lot to pay for from my past and I want to do the right thing, Kate. I want to do this for you, Marly, and your friends. I will do whatever you want me to," said Lenny.

"Thank you Lenny for letting me know. I'm glad you will be the one watching," said Marly.

After the call, the three of them looked at each other, wondering what else could happen.

CHAPTER 12

Ethan arrived at the Kennedy estate and walked to the front, ringing the bell. He wasn't scheduled to come by, but he felt he should discuss things with Mr. Kennedy. Victor opened the door and greeted him.

"Good morning, Ethan. Did you have an appointment today?" asked Victor.

Surprised, Ethan said, "No, but I needed to see Mr. Kennedy in person."

Knowing that his employer wanted secrecy about his mission today, Victor said, "I'm sorry, Ethan, but Mr. Franklin is ill. The doctor has confined him to his bed. He is not even taking calls today."

Ethan guessed that anything could happen to him at his age, so he told Victor he would call later and left.

As the door closed and Ethan walked back to his car, he thought it odd that Mr. Kennedy hadn't said anything about feeling sick. Of course, he always wanted to appear perfectly fine at all times and hated weakness. He drove back to his apartment and decided to research Marly

Anderson some more. It never hurt to have as much information as possible.

Marly looked at Kate and Lucy and said, "What should we do now? I don't feel like looking for anything else today."

Kate agreed and suggested they go to a couple of shops and then get a light lunch somewhere.

"Especially after that huge breakfast you made Marly! Which was fabulous. But I don't think I can eat a big lunch," said Lucy.

"That's because you had two waffles!" laughed Marly. "But, I agree. If someone is watching the house and reporting back to Franklin Kennedy, we should give him something to report. If we never leave the house, he may think we are searching it."

"That's a good idea Marly," said Kate. "So, any cute shops around here that you like to go to?"

"Yes, there's a cute dress boutique a few blocks over and then down the street from it is a cute little bakery that has light lunch options," said Marly, thinking of the area.

"That sounds good," said Lucy. "I would like a new dress to wear the next time we go to Fort Worth to see Rafe's family."

"How's his mom doing, by the way?" asked Marly.

"Much better," replied Lucy. "They put her on some medication for her blood pressure, and she hasn't had any other episodes. Gosh, though, it was scary, especially for Rafe."

"I know it must be hard for him, living so far from them," said Marly.

"True, but the other boys live on the property, so he knows they are in good hands," explained Lucy. "Besides, we will go anytime we need to, and they know that."

"Do we walk or drive? Kate, do you feel up to walking?" asked Marly.

"Actually, I need the exercise. If I get too tired, I'll let you know," said Kate.

"Let's get ready and give the guy something to watch," said Lucy and they all laughed.

Dan Ricter was thinking he had a piece of cake job. He hadn't seen anybody come out of the building and it was getting close to noon. But he wasn't complaining because he was making 1K a day to sit and watch. He was sipping a cup of coffee that was getting cold when he saw the door open and three young women come outside. They were laughing together, walking down the street. He watched as they turned the corner and then got out of his car, walking in their direction but hanging back to keep from being noticed.

It had been a while since the three of them had been shopping so they were really enjoying the day. The weather was cooperating too.

"I loved that last shop we went in, Marly. The dresses were too cute" said Lucy.

"I guess so," said Kate, "since you bought two of them!"

Marly laughed, "But they did look so good on you. I think Rafe will really like the red one."

"Me too," said Lucy, "but now, I think I need some shoes!"

Laughing, the three of them kept walking down the street until they got to a small shop that carried designer shoes.

"I think you will like this one too, Lucy," said Marly and they walked in.

Dan Ricter casually walked into the smoke shop across the street and pretended to look at a row of vapes. The owner came over and was telling him all about them. He listened halfheartedly and watched across the street. He almost missed them coming out and heading out.

"Sorry, I can't decide," Dan said. "I'll think about it." Hurriedly, he walked out, keeping the trio in his line of vision. *'Damn,'* he thought. *'If I had known I would be walking today, I would have worn sneakers.'* His feet were burning in his leather boots. He almost lost them but turned a corner in time to see them go into a small bakery. Hurrying down the street, he saw them sitting at a table, obviously going to eat there. He was hungry and needed something to eat, so he walked into the shop, the small bell announcing his arrival. He went up to the counter and ordered a coffee and a ham sandwich, sitting several tables away from the women.

"Whew, I think I am done for today," said Lucy.

Looking at the bags hanging on the empty chair, Marly laughed at her friend, "I would think so. You didn't have to buy something at every store!"

Kate laughed too and Lucy joined in.

"I didn't know everything was going to be so cute and on sale!" said Lucy, trying to justify her purchases. "I just hope it all fits in my suitcase."

"I can always ship it to you," said Marly. "Yours too, Kate, eyeing the several bags she had sitting on the floor.

"Good because I don't want my new shoes to get crushed," said Kate, smiling at her friend. "They were just the right heel and who knows, I may be a working girl again soon."

"Are you leaning that way, Kate?" asked Lucy. "I know Seth has other ideas."

"I know but I have to be productive. Maybe I can work remotely for a while. Steven did suggest that the last time we spoke. I just don't know," said Kate.

At that moment, their number was called and Lucy got up to get their lunch. She brought back three chicken salad sandwiches and three raspberry teas.

Kate had seen the man a few tables over and had an eerie feeling. She just knew this was the guy following them. She leaned in and whispered to Marly and Lucy and told them to laugh, covering up her message to them.

The man thought he had been made but when they laughed, he felt he was safe. *'Just silly women spending some man's money. What a waste of time this assignment was'*, he thought, as his number was called.

He didn't unwrap the sandwich, picked up his coffee and headed out the door. Walking another block, he could still see the shop and sit on a park bench to eat his lunch.

"I think we fooled him," said Marly.

"I do too," said Kate. "He thinks he is being so smart by leaving. I wonder if there is a back door in this place."

Lucy got up and talked to the young girl at the counter. In a few minutes, she was back.

"Yep, there is one. I told her some guy was following us, and could we use it when we left. She said sure," said Lucy, taking another bite of her chicken salad sandwich.

"Great," said Marly. "Won't he be disappointed?"

"After this, I think I am ready to go back to the house," said Kate.

"I agree," said Marly. "Let's relax this afternoon and get back to the search tomorrow. After the desk and the books, we can head to his room upstairs."

"Are you ready to tackle another search, Marly?" asked Lucy.

"No, but it must be done," said Marly. "And, the

sooner we uncover whatever it is, the sooner all of this will be over, and I can get back to my life, whatever that may be!"

Kate said thoughtfully, "Your life is going to change, Marly. You now have information about yourself that you didn't have before. How you approach that will be your choice."

"I know," said Marly. "I want to confront the fake Andersons but not now. I want to be ready when the time comes. But for now, I just want to finish this search, especially since the two of you are here to help me. I don't know what I would have done if I had been alone when I discovered my adoption papers."

"I'm just glad that we were here with you," said Lucy. "And, we will be here with you through all of it."

"Indeed," said Kate, "are we ready to lose our tail?"

Giggling, they got up and asked the girl about the back door. She showed them the exit, and they found themselves one street over and headed back to Marly's.

Dan finished his lunch and kept watching the bakery. *'They are making an afternoon of it,'* he thought. Getting up, he walked by the bakery and saw there was no one there. *'Damn, I must have missed them.'*

Hurriedly retracing his steps, Dan rounded the corner at Marly's street and saw the women going inside the front door. *'Whew, that was close. I don't know how I missed them but nothing to report except a shopping trip.'*

Dan got back in his car down the street and watched the front of the building, vowing to be on his toes. He definitely didn't want to botch this job.

CHAPTER 13

Samson made it down the mountain more quickly than the trip up and by noon, he was pulling the car to the front of the Kennedy estate.

"Thank you, Samson, you did great on that treacherous road. I'm glad you were in the driver's seat," said Franklin.

"I had a few moments, Mr. Kennedy, but you're back now, safe and sound," said Samson, glad to be back. "Will you need the car any more today, sir?"

"No, I'm a bit tired and need to rest. Oh, and by the way, we never left today," said Franklin.

"I've been here all day," said Samson, winking at his boss.

Victor opened the front door and came down the stairs to help Mr. Kennedy, if needed.

"Any calls today, Victor?" he asked, making his way up the steps and into the house.

"No but Ethan stopped by to see you. I told him you were ill and were resting," said Victor.

"Hmmm, he never comes by unannounced. I wonder what that was all about," mused Franklin.

"I am not sure sir, he just said he needed to see you," answered Victor. "I'm sure he will call you, but it may be tomorrow."

"Good, because right now, I want to rest," said Franklin.

"I'll bring up your lunch, sir," said Victor as Franklin got into the elevator.

Ethan was sitting at his desk, poring over online articles and information about Marly Anderson. She went to college in Texas, lived in Germantown since childhood, was very wealthy, invested in a winery in Texas owned by friends, owns a cabin near Gatlinburg, TN, had a bookstore which is now closed, went to culinary school, and is estranged from her family. Mr. Kennedy said that Oliver Anderson had selected a family to pretend to be his own and apparently, Marly Anderson is not aware of that fact. Maybe they would be willing to share any information about Oliver Anderson and if he had a place where he kept personal belongings. He *would* ask Mr. Kennedy about it but since he is sick, he didn't want to bother him. It didn't take long to get the names, address, and telephone numbers of the Anderson "family".

Ethan was preparing to call Lucinda Anderson when his phone rang. He didn't recognize the number, so he cautiously answered.

"Hello?" he said.

"Hello yourself, Dahling, it's been ages," said

the woman on the call.

"Hello Brittany, how have you been?" asked Ethan, surprised to hear from his old flame.

"You would know if you called me sometimes," she said, somehow working a pout into her words.

"I was under the impression that you were involved with someone else," said Ethan drily. "Besides, you must have a new number."

Brittany giggled and said, "Yes, I do. Oh, that was nothing, Ethan. Not like what you and I have."

"Had, Brittany. We are no longer together," said Ethan, wondering about her motive. She was the last thing he needed now.

"Ethan, how can you say that? What we have is so special, that not even time nor distance can stop it," Brittany said with a purring cadence to her voice.

"Brittany, I don't know what you want but I am very busy. I don't have time to play games so what is it?" Ethan was a bit abrupt.

Silence and then a small, hurt voice, "Never mind, Ethan. I can see that you don't have time for me anymore."

"Brittany, you left me, remember?" said Ethan. "What was I supposed to do?"

"Follow me, chase me, find me," she said, "just like I hoped you would. But you didn't and I was trapped in a terrible relationship."

A sudden feeling of anger came over him,

"What happened?"

"I left him, Ethan," she said, almost in a whisper. "But, I know he will come looking for me and he is cruel. Please help me."

"Where are you?" he asked, hearing a lot of noise in the background.

Brittany spoke again, "At a bus station in New York. I don't have anywhere to go, and I hoped you could tell me what to do."

Getting involved with Brittany again would be suicide but a part of him still cared for her. He had to get her to Colorado.

"Are you safe right now?" he asked.

"Yes, but I don't know for how long," she admitted.

"Is your ID still in Brittany Solara?" he asked, punching numbers in his American Airlines account.

"Yes, but Ethan, I don't have any money. I just ran and left everything," she said.

"Call an Uber using my credit card number. I'll text it to you. Go to JFK and there is a ticket in your name at the American Airlines counter for a 7:45 p.m. flight to Denver. You should arrive here at midnight, and I'll be there to pick you up," said Ethan, giving her direction quickly.

"Oh Ethan, thank you, thank you," she said, finally breaking down with a sob.

"Stop Brittany. You don't have time to get emotional. We'll figure everything out when you get here, okay?" said Ethan. "I'll see you tonight."

"Okay, I will. Goodbye Ethan, I'll see you soon," said Brittany, feeling some relief flood over her.

Hanging up the phone, Ethan felt that old web wrapping around him. He had a soft spot where Brittany was concerned. He had loved her, maybe he still did but he didn't want to get involved with her again. He had to help her out of whatever mess she was in now. He turned off his search and decided to take a nap. He was going to have a late night.

After shopping and walking today, they were all tired. Marly suggested they order a pizza and everyone agreed. They got into their lounging pajamas and waited for the delivery, talking about the man following them today.

"I wouldn't have noticed him if you hadn't pointed him out, Kate," said Marly.

"I guess my senses are heightened after what I went through in San Antonio. Or maybe I'm just suspicious of everyone!" she laughed.

"I hope we lost him," said Lucy. "But, even if we did, he'll be back out there, reporting our activities to Mr. Kennedy."

"I doubt he cares about our shopping trip but if we were to start throwing stuff out of the house, he'd probably be notified," said Marly, with a wicked smile.

"I don't think that is a good idea, Marly. We don't want to draw attention to what we are actually doing," said Lucy.

"I know, but it would make me feel better," Marly said, hearing the doorbell. "Dinner is here!"

She went to the door and picked up the pizza, bringing it in the house. She noticed a car down the street and figured it was their stalker.

Putting the pizza on the island, they ate directly out of the box.

"No need to make a mess with dishes," said Marly, handing out napkins to everyone. Kate had poured everyone a glass of red wine from the Cavanaugh Vineyards. It was quiet for a few minutes while everyone was eating.

"Oh, I think I saw our stalker's car down the street. I guess he will be pretty bored tonight," said Marly.

"Good, and I noticed the guy today was wearing leather boots. I bet his feet ache too, with all of the walking we did today!" said Kate, laughing.

They finished their dinner and did the minimal cleanup and headed upstairs after Marly set the house alarm. They discussed everything they found today and decided to tackle the rest of the books in the morning.

Kate asked, "Were you done with the desk, Marly?"

"I think so. I didn't find anything else in the drawers," she said.

"What about a secret drawer or panel?" asked Lucy. "You know, like in the movies."

"Do you think that is possible?" asked Marly, never thinking about that possibility.

Kate thought a minute and said, "It wouldn't hurt to check. You never know. It is apparent that your grandfather had secrets and people with secrets tend to hide things."

"Okay then," said Marly. "I'm pretty beat, girls. I think I'll head to bed."

"I'm there with you," said Lucy. "No big breakfast in the morning, though. Let's have cereal."

"Sounds like a plan, Lucy. I love you two, I hope you know that. And right now, I need your love and support," said Marly sincerely.

"Right back at you, Marly," said Kate, as all three of them hugged. "Goodnight."

The lights in the building went out and Dan figured they were calling it a night. He was glad because his feet were on fire. He called Derrick Porter, the FBI agent that hired him.

"Hello," said Derrick.

"Hey, just checking in. The woman has friends staying with her. Today, they shopped all day, ordered pizza tonight and just turned out the lights," Dan reported.

"Nothing out of the ordinary?" asked Derrick.

"No, it was a very boring day," Dan said, aching to get to the motel.

"Thanks for the report. I'll talk to you tomorrow night," said Porter, ending the call.

'*Now to get these damn boots off and sleep*', he thought as he drove into the night.

CHAPTER 14

Ethan was at the airport at 11:30 p.m., waiting for Brittany's flight. The flight schedule shows that it will be on time. He sat down and waited, watching the people milling around. It was a busy place, even though it was almost midnight. Then he saw her.

Brittany was walking through the terminal, looking around, as if she was being followed. He observed her for a few minutes before she saw him. She seemed afraid and it was then that he noticed the bruising on her eye and cheekbone.

"Brittany!" he called out, getting her attention.

She rushed to him, grabbing him tightly.

"Thank you, Ethan," she said, with a tremble in her voice.

Holding her back from him, he looked at her critically.

"What happened?" he asked.

"It's nothing, don't worry about it," she said. "I'm safe now."

Sensing that she didn't want to discuss it now, and they were in a busy airport, he tabled the talk until they were at his apartment. She didn't have any luggage, just a backpack, so they headed out of the airport and to the parking lot. He helped her into his car and got in, driving through the Denver streets until he reached his apartment.

Helping her out of the car, he said, "Here we are."

Taking the elevator to the fifth floor, they exited and walked across the hall to his apartment. He opened the door and ushered her in.

Brittany had been quiet on the ride to his place, but she turned to him, "Thank you, Ethan, you don't know how much this means to me."

"What the hell happened to you?" asked Ethan, indicating her bruised face.

"I told you he was cruel, and he was. He didn't use to be but some relative of his died who was going to leave him a lot of money, according to him, but that didn't work out. After that, he was in a bad mood all the time and I was the closest thing he could take it out on," she explained.

"What's this bastard's name?" asked Ethan, vowing to do something about him.

"Tom Weston, but it's not important now," said Brittany. "He can't hurt me now."

Wanting to get more information, Ethan stopped asking questions. Tomorrow they will discuss it in more detail but right now, she looked dead tired.

"You can sleep in the guest room," he said. "I put one of my t-shirts on the bed for you. I didn't know if you would have a suitcase or not, so I'm glad I did. I also put some toothpaste and a toothbrush in the bathroom."

"Thanks Ethan. I don't deserve your kindness but I'm so grateful for it," said Brittany quietly.

"No matter what happened between us, Brittany, we are still friends, and I care about you. We'll talk more tomorrow. Get some rest, you look wiped out," said Ethan.

"I am. Goodnight, Ethan," said Brittany and she disappeared behind the bedroom door.

It took Ethan a long time to fall asleep, imagining all of the things he would do to this Tom person if he ever encountered him.

Lucy and Kate came downstairs, dressed and ready for the day. They found Marly sitting at her grandfather's desk, looking at the journal they had found yesterday.

"Good morning, Marly. You are up early," said Kate.

"I had trouble sleeping and thought I could use my time better by checking out this journal," said Marly.

"Any revelations?" asked Lucy.

"Actually, yes. I believe that the journal we found is the encryption of whatever my grandfather was involved in and that there is another journal that is the key to the encryption. If we find that, we can possibly figure out what was going on," explained Marly.

"That makes a lot of sense, but I think it is highly unlikely that he would hide the key in the same location as the journal," surmised Kate.

"You're probably right, Kate, but I still think we need to keep searching the bookcases, just in case there is something else there," said Marly.

They all agreed and, so after a quick breakfast of cinnamon rolls Marly had baked this morning, they got to work. It was quiet as they worked, with the occasional, 'oh I haven't read this book in ages' to 'I would never want to read this book', they methodically pulled out each book, flipping through the pages.

Suddenly, Lucy exclaimed, "Hey, I think I found something!"

They all stopped and looked at her and the small manila envelope she held in her hands. She gave it to Marly who slowly opened it. Inside were black and white photographs of people Marly didn't know. She turned them over, finding the same type of coded information on the backs.

"Look at this," said Marly. "These codes match the codes that are in the journal. I wonder if the information in the book concerns these people?"

Kate looked at the photos and concluded that Marly had pointed out something important, saying, "I think you are right, Marly."

Even though they didn't know what any of it meant, it seemed as if their searching was not in vain.

"Do you recognize any of these people?" asked Kate.

"No, but maybe we can use the internet to search and find out who they were," said Marly. "I'm sure there is a face recognition program we can use."

"That's a great idea, Marly," said Lucy.

Energized by finding the photos, they continued going through the remaining books. At the end, they had found four more small manila envelopes with similar pictures of people.

"By their clothes, some of these were at least forty years ago," said Lucy, examining the photos on the counter where Marly had laid them out.

"Yes but then some of them seem more recent than that so it could represent a period of time in his life that he was involved," said Kate.

"Did you find any secret compartments in the desk?" asked Lucy?

"I didn't even look because I was going through the journal and baking cinnamon rolls," Marly said.

"Which we are so thankful for!" said Lucy. "They were the bomb dot com!"

Lucy walked over to the desk, saying, "Mama had a hidden desk drawer that she didn't think I knew about, but I figured it out." She sat down and pulled out the drawers and felt underneath them with no luck. She pulled the long middle drawer completely out of the desk, looking at the back. There was a slight indention which Lucy pushed, and it opened, revealing a small cavity.

"Oh my goodness," said Marly, as the three of them looked into the small opening. Inside was a very small manila envelope which Lucy handed to Marly. Inside of it were three keys but to what?

Kate spoke, "This tells us that there are at least three places that are locked and hidden somewhere. Are they here in this house? I don't know but we have our work cut out for us!"

"Do you think there are any places in here where we need to look, Marly?" asked Lucy.

"These were the only things I had never looked through because they were his spaces," said Marly. "I guess the next place to look would be his room."

"Don't forget that we are being watched and if we don't leave the house, they may suspect we are searching it," said Kate.

"Yes, he is back. I saw his car in a different spot this morning in the other direction, but it's the same car," said Marly.

"I can't afford to do any more shopping!" said Lucy, laughing with her friends.

"How about a museum or a bookstore?" asked Marly.

"Let's do a museum and see if they have a back door too!" said Kate. "Is there one within walking distance or will we need to drive to it?"

"The Tennessee State Museum is pretty far so I think we should drive. Let's grab a bite somewhere and then go spend a few hours at the museum," said Marly. "I'll go grab my keys and bag."

Lucy and Kate followed her up the stairs to get their bags as well and then they were walking through the lower hallway to the garage.

"This is a pretty hidden garage," said Kate.

"Yes, our stalker may not see us leave but we want him to. I'll make the block so that he sees us," said Marly.

She drove around the building and into the street. They had the windows rolled down and they all laughed when they drove by the car.

Almost on cue, the car started up and slowly began down the street behind them.

"Mission accomplished, girls," said Marly and she drove to find a place for lunch.

Dan was startled by the laughing as the silver Tahoe drove past, and he looked up in time to see the women driving down the street. He started his car and slowly followed behind them, keeping them in his sight. He definitely didn't want to lose them today. They pulled into a Red Robin, a local burger chain and went inside, apparently for lunch. He waited about ten minutes before going in and sat at the bar, where he could have a vantage point for observing. He could see their table in the main dining room, and they were being served their lunch. He ate a sandwich too and when they were finishing, he paid for his meal and went outside to wait until they left. It wasn't long before they were getting in the SUV and backing out of the parking lot. Dan pulled out behind them, thanking his lucky stars that he had put on sneakers today, just in case they were shopping!

CHAPTER 15

Ethan's phone rang while he was sitting at his desk. Seeing it was Mr. Kennedy, he answered immediately.

"Hello," he said.

"Good morning, Ethan. I'm sorry I missed you yesterday," said Franklin.

"I'm sorry you were ill, sir," said Ethan. "I hope that you are better today."

"Yes, I am much better. It must have been a bug of some kind," he replied. "What did you want to talk with me about."

Ethan began, "I wanted to know if you were ready for me to approach Lenny Crocker. I know we want to have a plan in place at least by next week when Marly Anderson's guests have left. That is, if she really does have guests."

"Yes, she has guests Ethan," replied Franklin. "I had that confirmed yesterday from my FBI contact. Apparently it is a type of girl reunion. But, on the subject of Crocker, no need to contact him as I have already done so."

Ethan was a bit surprised that Mr. Kennedy had not mentioned it, but sometimes he was very secretive.

"Oh, I wasn't aware, sir," said Ethan. "Anything I need to know?"

"Nothing in place yet," said Franklin. "He will be watching the house in Germantown beginning Monday and after that, we may have another job for him."

"I understand," said Ethan. "I had thought about contacting the Anderson family that Oliver Anderson recruited to pretend to be his family. Since his death and the obvious fact that he didn't leave them anything monetarily, they may be willing to talk and possibly reveal something about him or other properties we don't know about."

"Hmmm, not something I had yet considered, but I don't see why not. They may stonewall you, but we may hit the jackpot as well," said Franklin. "Good job, thinking outside of the box, Ethan. Anything else going on?"

Always open and honest with his employer, Ethan said, "Brittany Solara contacted me yesterday."

"Oh? And why? I mean, she left you without any word. Was she in trouble?" asked Franklin, always being very astute.

"Yes, she was with some guy in New York, and she was scared. I arranged a flight for her last night, and she is here with me," said Ethan.

"What was she afraid of?" asked Franklin.

"When I picked her up, she had a black eye

and a bruised face. He was using her as a punching bag when he was in a bad mood, which apparently was all the time," explained Ethan.

"I'm sorry to hear that," said Franklin. "Do what you can for her."

"I will, sir," said Ethan. "I'll report back to you when I speak to the fake Andersons."

"Excellent, Ethan," Franklin said before disconnecting the call.

At that moment, Brittany walked out of the bedroom, dressed in her clothes from the night before.

"Good morning," she said softly.

"Good morning, Brit," he said, falling back into his habit of shortening her name.

She smiled, "I like that. I always did. Are you working today?"

"Not really, just some project I was discussing with Mr. Kennedy. I'll probably make a call or two, but I think we need to go shopping and get you some clothes," said Ethan, letting her know that he was aware she didn't have much with her.

"You don't have to do that, Ethan. I'm sure I can call my dad and get him to send me something," she said, although she certainly dreaded making that call. Her dad was the type that always said, 'I told you so'.

"Wouldn't you rather not call him?" he asked rhetorically. "There's bagels in the kitchen. Go eat something and then we'll go shopping."

She walked up to him and gave him a hug and

walked into the kitchen. In the meantime, he sat back down and looked at the screen with the information he had been researching. Picking up his phone, he dialed the number he had found.

"Hello?" a woman's voice came over the line.

"Hello, is this Lucinda Anderson?" he asked.

"Maybe, who's calling?" she asked warily.

"I'm sorry to be calling on a Saturday, but I was trying to get some information on Oliver Anderson," said Ethan politely.

"What kind of information?" she asked.

"Have I reached Lucinda Anderson? I wouldn't want to waste your time if I had the wrong number," he said, trying to get confirmation. He was recording the call but didn't inform her.

"Yes, I'm Lucinda. Mr. Anderson is dead," she said bluntly.

"I am aware of that, Mrs. Anderson, but I work for a finders group," said Ethan, making things up as he went along, "and we are trying to confirm if he had any properties other than the home in Germantown and the cabin in Gatlinburg."

"What for? Is there any money involved, like a fee for finding it? I could use some extra money," said Lucinda.

Ethan thought he would bait her a little bit, saying, "But Mr. Anderson had quite a large estate. Weren't you an heir?"

She laughed without mirth. "You'd think so, after all we did for him."

"Oh, were you his caregiver?" Ethan asked, knowing that she wasn't.

"Uh, no, but we were his only family, other than the granddaughter he adopted. Thomas and I had two children too and he left them out of the will altogether."

Now that she had an audience, she was very willing to talk about Oliver Anderson, and not in a very flattering light.

"That didn't seem fair. Did you have a falling out of any kind?" Ethan plunged ahead.

Clearing her throat, she said, "Not really. He was failing in his health, and the subject of his will came up once. I didn't want him to die without one, but now I wish he had because he left everything to that granddaughter!"

"So she wasn't your daughter?" he asked.

"Hell no, he saddled us with her when she was small, and he was flitting around the globe. But I sent her to him every chance I got. Then, when I had my own kids, I didn't have time for her at all. She lived with him mostly, so I guess she got under his skin and told him to leave us out," Lucinda was manufacturing lies as she spoke.

"Really? That is terrible. Surely you could contest the will," said Ethan, poking the bear.

"We did that, of course, but, there were extenuating circumstances that prohibited us from moving forward. So now, we don't even get our monthly stipend to help make ends meet," she moaned self-servingly.

"That is very unfortunate. If we uncover any other properties, however, they possibly will not be linked to the current will. Maybe there would be some money in it for you, in that case," said Ethan, making up anything he thought would keep her talking.

"No, I don't think anything will help us out. It was iron clad and very intentional. I guess we got all we were going to get while he was alive," she said, clearly not going to reveal any other information.

"Do you still live in Tennessee?" asked Ethan, making sure of their location.

"Yes, my husband Thomas and I do. Our children have gone off on their own. My daughter moved to Nashville and works for a veterinary clinic and our son moved to New York. He thought he would find fame and fortune there, since he wasn't finding it here. He was devastated when Oliver didn't leave him anything in the will."

A warning bell went off in Ethan's head. New York. Relative that didn't leave him any money. "What is your son's name?"

"Tom. He is trying to break into theater. He's very talented," she said, her voice proud.

"Tom Anderson, I'll have to keep an eye out for a new rising star on Broadway," said Ethan.

"No, no, he goes by another name. He is Tom Weston, not Anderson," she said. Suddenly, he heard a male voice talking to her and she immediately said, "I have to go. Please don't call again." The call was done.

What a coincidence! Who would have guessed that Brit's abuser was the son of the fake Andersons. This would be interesting to Mr. Kennedy, and it was for him too. He might have to take a trip to New York.

Marly had a season pass for the museum and got them all in free. They walked around leisurely, learning about the history of the state Marly lived in.

Lucy was reading a display and said, "I didn't know Mountain Dew started here. I'll have to tell Rafe. He loves that drink!"

"Hey," said Kate, "cotton candy and Moon Pies were born here too!"

"We've got all the good stuff," said Marly, laughing.

"You sure do, I mean, Elvis Presley lived in Memphis and Nashville is the home of country music, for crying out loud," said Lucy, suitably impressed.

Dan was following them around in the museum and he was getting bored. This was not his cup of tea. He figured they would be here all day. He stepped outside for some fresh air.

"Our tail is outside right now. Let's see if we can find a back exit," said Kate.

They walked toward the back of the museum and found an employee exit. No one was around so they slipped outside and walked to the side where they parked. Quietly getting in the car, Marly drove out of the back gate and headed to the house.

CHAPTER 16

Dan went back in the museum, showing his wristband so he wouldn't have to pay again. *It sure was expensive to read crap in this place*, he thought. He walked back to the area where he last saw them but didn't find them. *Probably in the ladies' room*, he thought, and he loitered around one until he started to get looks from the security guard. He wandered around for about thirty more minutes and wondered if they went outside. He walked out and looked for their car in the parking lot. It was gone! Damn, he had lost them again. *This didn't look good on my record. At least no one else knew about it...yet.* Hurrying to his car, he got in and drove back to the building and didn't see any sign of the car. He was just going to have to wait until they came back home. He hit the steering wheel with his fist to deal with his frustration. What was he going to tell Porter?

Thomas Anderson, a.k.a. Weston, Sr. was furious with his wife. "Are you crazy? Talking to a stranger about Oliver? Do you even know who it was?" he shouted.

"Don't yell at me!" she shouted back.

"Lucinda, you know that what we did was illegal, don't you? If we get caught, what if we have to pay all of that money back to Marly? We don't have that kind of money!" he said, in a more normal voice, but still angry.

"Surely she wouldn't make us pay it back," said Lucinda. "We are family."

"That's just it, Lucinda. We aren't family and with the relationship we have now, she wouldn't be willing to help us, you know that," Thomas said, more calmly now.

"Maybe I should try to reach out to her," said Lucinda. Although she would hate to do it, she definitely didn't want to pay any money. She had enough with all of Oliver's money.

"My question is, why is someone just now reaching out," said Thomas. "It feels off. What did he say, exactly?"

Lucinda thought for a minute, then said, "He was with some finders group, looking for other properties Oliver had. He already knew about the Germantown building and the cabin in Gatlinburg."

"Why did he ask about Tom Jr.?" asked her husband.

"I don't know...oh yes, he was going to look for a Tom Anderson on Broadway, but I told him he was using the name Weston. That's all it was, Thomas," said Lucinda.

"Still sounds fishy to me. Don't speak to

anyone about Oliver, Lucinda. It will just be best if we forget about that part of our lives," said Thomas.

"Can we go back to being Westons?" asked Lucinda. "And maybe move back to Michigan?"

"I'm working on it, Lucinda. Just be patient," Thomas said, walking out .

Ethan didn't get much information regarding Oliver Anderson, but he did get an unexpected bonus. Tom Weston was Tom Anderson. Now what was he going to do with that information? He would have to think about it very carefully.

Brittany came out of the kitchen and asked, "Are you still working?"

"Nope, I'm done for the day. Are you ready to go shopping?" he asked, smiling. He hurt inside when he saw her bruises.

"Yes, I'm ready," she said, walking to the door and they both headed to the elevator and down to the parking garage. Getting in his Mercedes, he drove to Cherry Creek shopping center.

When they arrived, Brittany spoke, "I don't need to get much, Ethan. Just a few things to get me through a week or so."

"Sure," he said, although that wasn't his intent. Mr. Kennedy said to take care of her, and that was exactly what he planned to do. They walked in through Nordstrom, and she didn't even stop.

"Hey, I like this dress," said Ethan. "Why don't

you try it on?"

"Ethan, this is an expensive store," she said, looking at the price tag. "Very expensive."

"Please, just let me see you in it," he said.

"It has short sleeves," she said.

"So, what does that matter?" he asked and then realization struck. She must have more bruises on her body. "Ok, no short sleeves. Here's one with a jacket."

Reluctantly, Brittany tried it on. It fit very well, and Ethan said they would get it. And that's how the day went. By the end of the day, they had bags from Urban Outfitters, lululemon, Levi's, LUSH, Bath & Body Works, Neiman Marcus, J.Crew, North Face, Anthropologie and Macy's.

Even though she didn't want him to buy these things, she had such a good time and told him so. "Thank you, Ethan. I'll pay you back, I promise."

"No you won't because I won't let you. I can afford it, and I wanted to do it. So just enjoy your new things. I know I will, especially that lingerie you got," winked Ethan.

She blushed and took his hand, and they walked outside to his car, putting her bags in the trunk.

"You hungry? I know that I have worked up an appetite," said Ethan, starting the car.

"Yes, I'm starved," she said.

"Let's go to 801 Chophouse. I feel like a steak," said Ethan and he headed to the restaurant.

Brittany settled back and thought *I'll never*

leave Ethan again.

Marly and her friends peered out of the upstairs window to see if the stalker was back. He was but Marly wasn't sure he knew they were back. Giggling, they walked to Oliver Anderson's bedroom.

"This is probably going to be emotional for you, Marly, so just say when you need to stop," said Kate.

"Okay, but I think I'll be alright, especially with the two of you here," Marly said, and they all entered the room.

It was dim with shadows falling across the bed. Marly switched on the overhead light, brightening up the room.

"Much better," said Lucy. "Where should we start?"

"Kate and I will search the nightstands and Lucy, you check out the wardrobe," said Marly and for next 45 minutes, they searched, but nothing was found.

Lucy spoke up, "This coffee table has a drawer, but it's locked."

"What?" said Marly. "I never noticed that before."

"It doesn't have a handle, but I see the keyhole," said Lucy, pointing to the small lock.

"Where are those keys we found?" asked Kate.

"I have them right here," said Marly, pouring them into the palm of her hand. A small silver key looked like it might fit. She tried it and it opened the drawer. A sealed envelope with Marly's name on top, lay in the bottom of it. Taking it out with shaking hands, Marly slid her finger under the flap and pulled out a handwritten letter.

'My dearest Marly,

If you are reading this letter, my death and the secrets surrounding my life are being discovered. Let me say first that you were the most wonderful addition to my life. When I saw you in that orphanage in Arkansas, my heart leapt within my chest. Your red curls with your expressive dark brown eyes captivated me. I knew I wanted to give you a life that would be better. Typically, a single man would not be allowed but I had connections and soon you were part of my family.

I know this next revelation will be a shock to you, but I must protect you, if I can, from the grave. My life before you was a dangerous one. I was a member of an organization known at the time as the Crimson Veil. Sounds mysterious, right? We specialized in digital erasure, information concealment, and the protection of the individuals whose pasts we erased. These people were corporate and government whistleblowers, defectors, and others who needed to protect their lives. My last assignment was to make sure that a government whistleblower with classified information disappeared, without a trace. But something went wrong, and he was killed. I felt we had been compromised, and I left the organization and withdrew into obscurity. If you are being contacted, my whereabouts have been found out.

I tell you this now because you need to know that the family you thought was your own, is not. I hired them to be my family, in case I had to suddenly leave. That didn't happen and I'm sorry for the time you spent with them. I knew you were not happy there, but I had to keep up appearances. I left everything I had to you because I loved you more than anything, and it may have caused you more harm than good. Unfortunately, I later found out the Westons were greedy people.

I believe the organization still operates on a smaller scale and someone in particular may come knocking at your door. Beware. He does not hesitate to get what he wants by any means. If you are approached by Ramondo Breviat, know that he means you harm. He may use an alias, the last I knew was Franklin Kennedy. Take every precaution.

Your loving grandfather,
Poppa

"Oh my god," said Marly, handing the letter to Kate and Lucy to read. The need to find the items her grandfather had hidden was now imperative. Not knowing how many things needed to be found, Marly was hoping they accomplished it quickly. She looked at her friends.

"Are y'all up for this?" she asked, seriously. "It is apparently dangerous."

"All for one, and one for all," said Lucy, and they did a group hug, ready to tackle whatever they might discover.

CHAPTER 17

Lucy, Marly, and Kate continued searching Oliver's bedroom, but nothing else was found.

"How about a break?" suggested Marly. "Then we can tackle the basement. I've never been down there so I'm not sure what we will find."

"Sounds good," said Kate, "I could use one."

Lucy checked the car parked down the street and confirmed he was still there. "I imagine this is the most boring job he ever took on!"

"Serves him right," said Kate, not feeling sorry for him at all.

"Is anyone hungry? I have deli meats and cheese and some croissants. We can have a sandwich unless you want to go out," offered Marly.

"A sandwich is perfect for me," said Lucy. "I'm going to call Rafe and check on things at the winery. Be right back."

While Marly was getting out the sandwich fixings, Kate called Seth.

"Hey Katie, how are you?" asked Seth, happy to hear from her.

"Hi Seth, I'm good," she answered. "How's

everything going there?"

"Other than I miss you like crazy? Nothing, just making some wine," Seth said, laughing. "How's it going there? Finding anything?"

"Actually, yes," said Kate. She paused to check with Marly about telling Seth and got the thumbs up from Marly. "Marly found out she was adopted, and her family was hired by her grandfather to pose as her family."

"For what purpose?" he asked, curious.

"It's a lot to go into on the phone but the house is being watched, and we are finding some hidden items. We are tackling the basement next," said Kate.

Seth was somewhat alarmed, "Kate, if the house is being watched, there is something very sinister going on. Do you need me and Rafe to come? We can have Cory cover for us at the winery for a few days."

"I don't think that is necessary, Seth, but you can discuss it with Rafe. Lucy is upstairs calling him now," said Kate.

"I don't like this, Katie, I can tell you that," confessed Seth. "I'll let you know what we decide to do."

"I love you, Seth," said Kate, feeling very cared for and loved.

"And I love you too, Katie," he said. "I'll call you later."

Marly looked at her friend, "He's worried, I can tell. I can't blame him either. I feel like I have put you and Lucy in a dangerous situation."

"You didn't put us here, Marly. We volunteered. Besides, neither of us wanted you to go through this alone," Kate assured her.

"Alone? Who's alone?" asked Lucy as she re-entered the kitchen.

"Seth is worried, and Marly is feeling guilty for putting us in this situation," explained Kate.

"We chose to come, Marly. We wouldn't have it any other way. You are our best friend, and we won't let anyone hurt you, no matter what!" said Lucy, passionately.

"I love you guys," said Marly, her eyes glistening with unshed tears. "You will never know how much you mean to me."

"I think we do because we feel the same way," said Lucy. "And, Rafe is worried too. He is going to talk to Seth, and we may be seeing a little more muscle around here."

"We'll take all we can get!" said Marly. She set a tray of sandwiches on the island with some assorted chips and said, "Dig in. We have to keep our strength up!"

As they ate in the kitchen, they talked and laughed and tried to keep the subject away from what was happening to Marly. They would think about that later.

Ethan and Brittany arrived back at his apartment after a great meal. He noticed that Brittany didn't eat much but she did bring it home with her. He didn't make comment about it because she was adjusting to a lot right now. As he opened the door to his place, his phone rang. He looked and saw that it was Mr. Kennedy.

"I gotta take this call, Brit," he said, going over to his desk.

She carried her bags into the bedroom and started taking off the tags and putting them away.

"Hello Mr. Kennedy," said Ethan. "How are you today?"

Remembering that he had supposedly been sick, he responded, "I feel great today. I don't even feel like I was sick."

"That's good to hear sir. What can I do for you?" asked Ethan.

"I was curious as to whether you spoke to Lucinda Weston?" asked Franklin.

"As a matter of fact, I did," said Ethan, relaying to him the conversation they had.

"Interesting that her husband didn't want her to talk to you," mused Franklin. "But the fear of having to pay back whatever money Oliver paid them was definitely driving him. Must have been quite a tidy sum."

"I thought the same thing," said Ethan, turning around to make sure the door to the bedroom was closed. "Also, I found out that their son is in New York, going by his real name, Tom Weston. And that is the son of a bitch that Brit was with and the one responsible for all of her bruises."

"That is a twist," said Franklin. "I don't want you to do anything about it, Ethan. There is too much going on here and I will send someone to take care of Mr. Weston."

"But Mr. Kennedy," began Ethan but Franklin cut him off.

"I'm serious, Ethan. I do not need you distracted by this situation with Brittany and Mr. Weston. I said I will take care of it, and I will. Do you have his address?" asked Franklin.

"No sir, but I'm sure that I can get it," he said, reluctant to have Mr. Kennedy take care of it but relieved at the same time.

"Do so and email it to me. I don't know if you can do this or not but try to document her bruises. Having proof of something is better than not," said Mr. Kennedy.

"I'll see what I can do, sir. Thank you," Ethan said. "Was there anything else you wanted?"

"No, enjoy the rest of your weekend. My reports are that the Anderson woman and her friends are doing touristy activities, so I'm sure all is well there," he said. "See you Monday morning."

If he only knew.

After they ate, Marly suggested they take a walk around the block, to get some fresh air and let their tail know they were still around. As they walked by the parked car, Marly slowed down. She knocked on the window, startling the man inside. He rolled down the window.

"Hey, are you looking for someone? I noticed you have been here a couple of days," said Marly innocently.

Stammering, the man said, "Uh, no, I'm watching this house for the people that live there. They are out of town and their alarm system is on the fritz."

"Oh, I didn't know that. I thought they had moved!" Marly gave a silly laugh. "Do you need anything? I'm sure it gets hot out here all day."

"No ma'am, I'm fine. Thanks for asking," he said and immediately rolled up the window.

The girls continued on their walk and when they turned the corner, they all burst out laughing.

"Marly, you are terrible!" said Kate.

"I loved it," said Lucy. "At least he knows that we see him."

"And that's exactly what I wanted," said Marly. "That house has been vacant for about a month, but I have to say, he was quick on his feet with an explanation."

"Slick is how I would describe him," said Kate. "He reminds me of this guy named Peter that I worked with in San Antonio. He was a jerk."

"This guy is probably a jerk too, Kate. The world is full of them," said Lucy, thinking of Roger Preston.

Marly spoke up as they turned the next corner, "That, ladies, was your entertainment for the

SECRETS OF THE CRIMSON VEIL

day. Are we ready to get back to the task at hand?"

They all agreed as they made the last block to the front of the house. Marly unlocked the door, reset the alarm and they all headed downstairs, toward the basement.

Ethan picked up his phone and knocked on the extra bedroom door.

"Brit, are you decent?" he asked.

"Yes, come in," she said.

He entered and she was sitting on the bed, looking at a magazine that had probably been there since she had left the first time.

"I want to ask you something and you can refuse if you want," Ethan began.

"Ethan, it would be hard to refuse you after you treated me like royalty today," said Brittany.

"You might refuse this request. Mr. Kennedy wants Tom Weston's address, and he wanted me to document your bruises. If anything comes up, it would be good to have them," he tried to explain in a way she would understand the reason.

"I get it," said Brittany. Slowly rising from the bed, she slipped off her blouse, revealing black and blue bruises along her upper arm, chest, and side. She turned around and there were whelps along with some healing bruises, still green and yellow. She pulled her pants down to her knees, revealing more contusions along her thighs and hips. Ethan, his eyes tearing up, took photographs with his phone. Neither one of them spoke and when he was done, she re-dressed.

"Thank you, Brit," said Ethan, anger building inside of him toward Tom Weston.

CHAPTER 18

Franklin Kennedy heard the ping on his computer and opened his email, seeing one from Ethan. He opened it and found the address he had requested and there were multiple attachments. He viewed them and saw what he needed to see. Picking up the phone, he made a call.

"Hey Frank, what's happening?" asked Derrick.

"First, thanks for the update on the Anderson woman. Sounds like a tourist visit from her friends. But, I still want the house surveilled. Secondly, I have located a person that has abused a woman, who is a friend. I would like him taught a lesson. Can you handle something like that for me?"

"I'll have to use an informant or something," said Derrick. "Where is the guy?"

"In New York City. I have the address, and I can send it to you, along with photos of the woman he was abusing," said Franklin.

"So we're dealing with a sick bastard," said Derrick. "Roughed up or taken out?"

"Roughed up, for now," said Franklin. "I'll send the information to you in a minute through the VPN. Thanks for doing this, Derrick."

"No problem, Frank," said Derrick, wondering about the fee. He hadn't done anything like this for Frank before.

"I'll wire you $50K, Derrick. Will that be sufficient?" asked Frank.

"That's a bit much, Frank," said Derrick although he got excited. He didn't want to appear greedy.

"I think it's worth it," said Franklin. "Thank you," and as it was customary with conversations with Franklin Kennedy, the line went dead.

After he sent the information to Derrick Porter through the VPN, he thought nothing else about it. After all, it was a problem he had taken care of many times, and now it was someone else's responsibility. All he had to do was foot the bill.

Derrick received the email quickly and he reviewed the photos. It made him angry to see the abuse this woman had been through. He had a couple of low-life informants in the New York area and reached out via text to burner phones with the message 'CALL PORTER'. Now, all he had to do was wait. He didn't have to wait long and picked up the call on the first ring.

"Porter here," he said.

"Yo man, Wolfman calling, what's shaking?" the voice said.

"Got a job in your area. You up for it or know someone?" Porter said.

"What's the dime?" Wolfman asked.

"10K. Need a rough up," said Porter.

"I be your man," he said. "Where and when?"

"You have email on your phone?" Porter asked.

"Yo, I'm hip," he said.

"Message me and I'll send the info via your addy," said Porter, ending the call.

Seconds later his phone pinged, and he then sent the info to the address provided with instructions. *1230 125th St. NYC – Tom Weston – Send $$ to? Report needed.*

Derrick Porter was feeling good. $40K to make a phone call? Today was a very good day.

The door to the basement was locked and Marly hoped that one of the other two keys opened it. She tried one, but it didn't work.

"Fingers crossed girls," she said and tried the other one. It was hard to insert in the keyhole, but a hard jiggle made it work. The door creaked open.

"Geez, it already sounds spooky," said Lucy.

There were no windows in this basement and Marly searched around for a light switch. She finally found it and flipped it up. A dim light filled the room, creating shadows but revealed a few old furniture pieces, a couple of lamps, and several boxes. There wasn't much.

"Doesn't look very promising," said Kate.

"That's just what I was thinking," said Marly, "but I guess we won't be down here long."

"I have no problem with that!" said Lucy, and they all laughed quietly.

"Have you noticed how dampened the sound is in here?" asked Marly. "Hey!" she shouted to test it out. The sound fell flat.

"Soundproofed somehow," said Kate. "There has to be a reason for it, right?"

"I don't want to know," said Lucy, "this is creepy."

Marly looked at her friends, "Do you want to stop?"

"No!" they both said in unison. "Together, remember?"

They started with the boxes and found more books that didn't have anything in them, some old tools, and some baby clothes.

"I bet those were yours, Marly," said Kate.

"I remember this one in a picture he had in his desk," said Marly, a strange feeling to be holding these things.

After an hour of digging through boxes and under furniture, they concluded there was nothing there.

"I was almost sure we would find something else," said Kate.

"Me too, but I guess it is somewhere else," said Marly.

"Hey," said Lucy, "have you noticed that this room seems smaller than it should be? I mean, shouldn't it be the same length as the retail space?"

They looked around and Marly said, "You're right, Lucy. It should be bigger. What does that mean?"

"Maybe there is a secret room in here," said Lucy.

Getting excited, the girls started looking more closely and decided that the back wall would be the most likely place. Lucy went over to the tools and pulled out a hammer.

"Are you okay with me whacking this wall, Marly?" she asked.

"Whack away, my friend," she said, grinning in the dimly lit room.

Lucy hit the wall and broke a small hole in the sheetrock. Hitting it again, she pulled off enough to peer into it.

"Oh my god, Marly, Kate, there is another room!" said Lucy excitedly.

Lucy kept breaking the sheetrock as Kate and Marly pulled the pieces off. Soon there was a hole big enough for them to squeeze through.

"It's dark in here. I wonder if there is another light," said Kate.

They felt around the walls and Kate said, "I found one." Flipping it on, fluorescent light filled the room.

Marly looked around and saw a large desk with

file cabinets on either side. There was an old computer with a tower on a table and a couple of boxes.

"This, I think, is what we have been looking for," said Kate.

Relief flooded through Marly but also fear. What would they find, and would it put them in more danger? She looked over at her two best friends.

"What?" asked Lucy.

"It's getting late. Do you want to resume the search tomorrow?" Marly asked.

"Are you kidding me?" asked Lucy. "Just when we found a secret room! I want to check it out now!"

Laughing, Kate agreed, "I mean, we should, don't you think Marly? What are you afraid of?

"Of putting us in more danger than we already are," said Marly, a worried look on her face.

"The damage is already done, and we just need to see this through," said Lucy, eager to get started.

"Okay, let's do it," said Marly, buoyed by her friends' enthusiasm but still concerned.

Ethan and Brittany were seated in the living room when he suggested a movie.

"That sounds good," said Brittany, and Ethan started scrolling through the options on Netflix and Max.

"Do you want some popcorn?" asked Ethan,

trying to find something light and entertaining.

"That would be great. I'll go pop some. You do have some, don't you?" she asked.

"Isn't that a staple?" laughed Ethan. "What about this one, The Adam Project? I've heard it's pretty funny."

Brittany called out from the kitchen over the sounds of corn popping, "Sounds good. Popcorn is almost ready." She looked around and found a big bowl, filling it with the hot corn, putting some buttered salt on top. She carried it into the living room where Ethan had dimmed the lights.

"Oooh, just like a movie theater. I like it," she said, as she settled next to Ethan so they could share the popcorn. She was trying to act casually but her heart was pounding so loud she thought he could probably hear it.

Knowing Brit had been through a lot these last few months, Ethan was trying to keep things light and friendly. If something else were to come of their relationship, he was open to it but right now, she needed a friend, and he wasn't going to take advantage of her. So he settled back, and they watched the movie, laughing, eating popcorn, sometimes throwing it at each other, and sitting together comfortably.

It was a good night.

CHAPTER 19

Lenny was on Interstate 40 and just crossed over the Tennessee state line. He will be in Memphis tonight. He made good time, and it would be a day early, but he didn't mind. He was thinking about Marly and her situation. He had put out some feelers on Franklin Kennedy and one of his contacts came up with another name, Ramondo Breviat. He was still waiting for more intel on that name, but he was worried. This was sounding more complicated than just getting back something Franklin Kennedy said belonged to him. He hoped to hear something soon, so he would know how to plan. All of a sudden, his windshield wipers came on and it wasn't long before the light sprinkle became a downpour.

Great, that's all I need to slow me down, thought Lenny but he eased off of the accelerator and adjusted his speed for the weather. So much for getting there early.

Marly started pulling out the drawers of the desk while Lucy and Kate were going through the file cabinets. Marly found another journal and when she opened it, there were codes with meanings beside them. This had to be the key to the other journal.

"Look, I think this is the key!" cried Marly excitedly. Both Lucy and Kate came over to look at it.

"It definitely looks like the other one, except now, we have more information," said Kate.

"Look, here are some more photographs," said Lucy. "These have codes on the back. Do any of them match the ones in the journal?"

They all looked through it to see if one paired with the photo and suddenly, Marly found it. The code on the photograph matched a code in the journal which stated *David Holt, December 1967, African Prime Minister– EPR*

"What does EPR mean?" asked Lucy.

"I don't know," said Marly, flipping through the journal. Near the back, she found a list of codes like it. "Oh, here it is, Erased Personal Request.

"So he wanted to disappear and that's what your grandfather did or someone in the organization," said Kate, realizing this could have far reaching ramifications.

"Let's see if you can find another one. I mean, the African guy is probably dead by now, it was so long ago," said Lucy.

Matching another code on a photograph to one in the journal which said *Jeff Greason, April 2005. Racine WI, District Attorney – ESGR*

"Okay, what is ESGR?" asked Lucy.

Marly found it quickly and told them, "Erased State Government Request."

"Wow," said Kate, "this is scary, right?"

"Yes, what if someone who was erased wants it to stay that way?" asked Lucy. "That would be a reason to make sure none of it ever sees the light of day."

Lucy found a photo of a young woman. "What's her story?" She showed the code to Marly who found it more quickly, as she was learning how the journal was laid out.

"Okay, the notation says *Rachel Hollingsworth, March 2019, Republican Gubernatorial Candidate – EDNC* and before you ask, Erased Democratic National Committee."

"That's enough," said Kate. "We have to safeguard this information and get it to the proper authorities."

"But who would that be, Kate?" asked Marly.

"I don't know but I can research it. What about those FBI agents we met in North Carolina? Maybe I can contact them," suggested Kate.

"Edward Finch would know them," said Lucy, "you know, Marc's friend."

"Yes, I can reach out to Marc to get his number," said Marly, feeling some relief. "I don't want to keep this stuff here."

"We should gather all of this up and put it together. I found some floppy discs in this file cabinet, so they probably have information on them too," said Kate.

Lucy went through the hole that she had made in the wall and found a plastic bin. She sat it on the floor in the basement and Kate and Marly handed the items through the opening. She packed it all in the bin, closed it up and they turned out the light in the false room. Marly turned out the light in the basement and they carried the bin upstairs.

"Put it in my room," said Marly and they carried it in there.

"Whew, I'm glad that's done," said Lucy and the others agreed. "I'm hungry, what about you guys?"

They laughed and realized they had only a sandwich for lunch. They decided to have Italian and Marly ordered through Door Dash. That would alert the stalker that they were staying in and watching a movie because that is exactly what they planned to do. And drink some well-deserved wine!

Wolfman called Porter after he visited Tom Weston.

"Hello," said Derrick Porter.

"Yo, the deed is done," said Wolfman.

"What's the damage?" asked Porter.

"Broken arm, cuts and bruises, knocked out a tooth. Waited and got him in a nearby alley so it looked like a regular mugging," Wolfman said. "I took his wallet too, you know, for real, you know?"

"Thanks, I got your Western Union account and money moving now," Porter said.

"Good doing business with ya, Porter," said Wolfman, ending the call.

That's the way I like doing business, quick and tidy and my hands are clean, thought Porter.

The phone rang in the Anderson home and Thomas answered it.

"Hello," he said brusquely.

"Dad," said Tom, Jr. "I need help."

"What's wrong with you? I can barely understand you," Thomas said.

"I got mugged," he struggled to speak clearly. "They took my wallet."

"Where are you?" his father demanded.

"ER, need the insurance information," said Tom.

"I'll text it to you. How bad were you hurt?" asked his father.

"Not sure yet but I think my arm is broken. I'm bleeding and a tooth was knocked out," said Tom, wincing in pain.

"My god, Tom, come home. We worry about you in New York, and this will put your mother over the edge," Thomas said.

"Just send the insurance stuff, Dad," Tom said. "I'll call later when I get back to my apartment."

"Where's your girlfriend in all of this?" his father asked.

"She left me last week. Good riddance," said

Tom for his father's benefit but he was angry with her for leaving.

"Figures," said Thomas. "Call us back, and I'm sending the information to you now."

Ending the call, Lucinda had come in and heard some of Thomas' conversation.

"Was that Tom? Is he coming home?" asked Lucinda.

"No, he just needed the insurance information," said Thomas without explanation.

"What for? I sent him a card," said Lucinda.

Dreading what was to come, Thomas said, "He got mugged, Lucinda, and beat up. He's in the ER."

"Oh my god, Thomas. Do we need to go?" she asked.

"He's grown, Lucinda, and he can make his own decisions. I did tell him to come home but he really isn't in a position to talk right now. He said he would call us later," explained Thomas.

"I hate I'm not there with him. Do you know how badly he was hurt? Is his girlfriend there with him?" Lucinda peppered Thomas with questions and for some of them, he had no answers.

"We'll find out more later, Hon, just try to stay calm. The girlfriend left him last week so I'm sure he feels bad inside, and now out," Thomas said, hoping Tom would call back.

Lucinda started crying and murmured, "Everything is falling apart, I just know it."

Thomas was afraid she may be right.

Franklin Kennedy answered his phone quickly.

"Hello Derrick, good to hear from you so soon," he said.

"Hey Frank, so, the guy was taken care of and probably in the ER," chuckled Derrick. "I think he was suitably paid back, plus my contact also stole his wallet, to make it look like a mugging."

"Excellent, excellent," said Franklin. "At least that has been taken care of and not by anyone we know, so no culpability."

"Correct, and I've already rewarded the contact, so thank you," Porter said.

"You are welcome," Franklin said, knowing that Derrick probably kept the lion's share, but he knew who to call and to get it taken care of and that's all that mattered to him.

"Was that everything, sir?" asked Derrick.

"Yes, for the moment," said Franklin, feeling a bit tired. "I'll reach out if I need anything else."

"Yes sir," said Porter, ending the call.

CHAPTER 20

After a delicious meal of Italian food and some good wine, the girls watched a movie and then decided to make it an early night. They had been working hard, and they weren't sure what they were going to do tomorrow. At least, they had uncovered what Franklin Kennedy was after, they felt certain.

Kate called Seth and filled him in on everything they had found, and Lucy let Rafe know as well.

"Katie, this is very dark, and I think very dangerous," said Seth, extremely worried, especially after all that Kate had been through.

"I know, Seth, but we aren't doing anything but finding it. We plan to reach out to Marc's detective friend tomorrow and see if we can get some contacts at the FBI," Kate said.

"I don't mean to be negative, but how will you know that the FBI is not connected to this organization in some way. I would assume that they would have to have members or associates working in all of the government offices," said Seth.

"I didn't think of that," said Kate, a reminder that she wasn't back at 100% since her attack in San Antonio.

"Just wait before doing that," said Seth. "We need to find a safe place for all of that information. I'll be working on it."

"Thank you, Seth," said Kate, glad to have him on the case.

"You're welcome, Katie, I love you. We'll talk tomorrow. Get some rest," Seth said.

"I will and I love you too," said Kate as the line went dead.

Lucy was done with her call with Rafe, and she looked at Kate, "Rafe is worried and doesn't want us to do anything yet."

"Same thing with Seth, and he did bring up a valid point. What if someone in the FBI is associated with this Crimson Veil group? We could be walking right into the lion's den with exactly what they want," said Kate.

"Yep, you're right. I don't want to bother Marly with this tonight, but we will discuss it in the morning. I think we have to devise an alternate plan, that doesn't involve the FBI," said Lucy.

"Agreed," said Kate, yawning. "I'll be able to think better after a good night's sleep."

"Me too," said Lucy, as she turned out the light.

Marly got ready for bed, her eyes glancing over at the bin containing all of the documents and discs they had uncovered today. She couldn't believe everything they had found and to think that her grandfather was part of an organization that erased people. It was mindboggling and very scary. At least he got out of it when he realized they may have been compromised. She was thankful that he had been with her in her formative years, through high school and college and even as a young adult. But he still was accountable and no amount of money he left her could erase that fact. Her mind then went to Lucinda and Thomas Anderson. Why would someone give up their own identity to pretend to be someone else? Obviously for the money but didn't they think about what they were giving up, what their children were missing out on? It was a sad situation for them but, according to the contract she had found, they had been paid handsomely for their part in the charade. Looking out the window, she saw the man's car leaving and she could breathe easier. It has been so stressful, knowing that she is being watched. At least Lenny will arrive tomorrow. Maybe he could offer some advice. He knows about a lot of things, and maybe something that could help them. She wasn't sure that she would get any sleep tonight, but she drifted off, dreaming of being followed by masked men in red capes and running as fast as she could.

Lenny arrived at his hotel around midnight. Checking in, he went up to his room and crashed.

It had been a long road trip and one that he hadn't made in a long time. He knew he wasn't on watch duty until Monday, but he would call Marly tomorrow to let her know he was in town. He was worried about her and her friends, and he still hadn't heard back from his contact about Ramondo Breviat. This situation was getting more and more mysterious and dangerous. He knew one thing, and that was that he was not going to let anything happen to Marly. With that thought, Lenny fell into a deep sleep of exhaustion.

It was nearly midnight when Tom called his dad.

"Tom, is that you?" answered his father.

"Yeah, Dad, it's me," said Tom.

"Put it on speaker, Thomas," said Lucinda, sitting up straight in bed.

Thomas pressed the button for speaker but signaled to his wife to be quiet.

"What's happening?" his dad asked.

"I do have a broken arm, and they are going to do surgery in the morning to set it and put in some pins or something. It's pretty mangled. Bruised kidneys and multiple cuts and bruises," said Tom. "It could have been worse, I could be dead."

"Tom, don't say that!" admonished his father.

"Well Dad, I could. The guy came out of nowhere and started beating the shit out of me, like I had done something to him. I screamed for him to stop and of course, he didn't. When I was on the ground, unable to move, he took my wallet and ran off," said Tom.

"We can come to New York tomorrow, son," said Thomas.

"No Dad, I'm coming home after I get discharged. I'll get a flight and send you the details. I won't be able to travel tomorrow because of some anesthesia rules but probably Monday," said Thomas.

"Did you call your sister?" asked Thomas, wondering if Cindy knew.

"Nah, I'll do that when I get home," said Tom.

"Okay son, we love you. Call when you know your plans," said Thomas.

"I will, Dad. Love you guys too," said Tom, ending the call.

Lucinda was crying quietly and Thomas reached out and patted her arm.

"He sounded good, Lucinda, and he's going to be fine," said Thomas. "Try to get some sleep and I'm sure we'll hear from him sometime tomorrow." He turned out the light and rolled over, putting his back to her.

Lucinda slid down into the covers and closed her eyes, but she knew that she wouldn't be able to sleep. She kept thinking about how Oliver Anderson had ruined their lives, taking their legacy and making it his. Oh how she hated him and his granddaughter!

After the movie, Ethan and Brittany got up off of the sofa. Brittany cleaned up the popcorn remains and threw it in the trash. Ethan was turning out lights and making sure the door was locked.

"You ready to call it a day?" asked Ethan.

"Yes, I am. I forgot how tiring shopping can be!" she laughed, and he joined in.

Smiling, he said, "Goodnight Brit, I'll see you in the morning."

"Goodnight, Ethan, and thank you, for everything," she said, as she went into the guest bedroom.

He went into his room and started getting ready for bed when he heard his phone ping. Picking it up, he saw that it was a text from Mr. Kennedy.

ALL TAKEN CARE OF IN NY. That was all it said.

Good, thought Ethan, I hope that whatever he got was payment enough for what he did to Brit. Now, he would be able to forget about that scum and go to sleep. And that is exactly what he did.

The call came at 2:00 a.m., as usual. Franklin answered it quickly.

"Yes?" he said.

"What is happening? I'm getting impatient," said the caller.

"I am too, my friend, but we have to wait. The Anderson woman has guests and the less

SECRETS OF THE CRIMSON VEIL

interaction we have with other people, the better. They will be gone soon and then we will proceed," assured Franklin. "I'm having her watched and all the reports are very boring. Shopping, museums, movies, you know. Everything is fine."

"How do you know everything is fine? What if they are looking for the item you said Oliver had? What if they have already found more incriminating information?" the caller questioned.

"I know they haven't," said Franklin confidently. "They don't even know what they are looking for and I doubt that Oliver had anything in plain sight."

"You are probably right but I am very anxious to have this done and over with," the caller said, agitatedly. "Once we know everything is safe, I will rest easier."

"I think we all will," admitted Franklin. "But, it will be just a few more days and then we will resume our quest."

"Very good, Ramondo, we will speak soon," the voice said, and then ended the call.

Ramondo Breviat, aka Franklin Kennedy, smiled, pleased to hear his given name. It had been a while. Soon, he would be known by that name and no other. He closed his eyes and fell into a dreamless sleep.

Dan Ricter drove back to the front of Marly's

building and got ready for another boring day. He had sent his report to Porter which wasn't much of anything. They stayed in, took a walk, ordered take out and probably watched movies. They were definitely doing girl things. Even though the money was good, he was glad that today was his last day. It was Sunday so they probably weren't going anywhere today either. Oh well, he would sit here and take his 1K for doing nothing. He definitely didn't mention they talked to him yesterday. He figured out that they wanted him to know they knew he was out there. But, after today, some other schmuck would be doing it.

CHAPTER 21

Sunday morning dawned with light shining into all of the windows. Marly got up and dressed, going downstairs to figure out breakfast. She was surprised to find Kate and Lucy already in the kitchen.

"Hey, what's going on?" asked Marly.

"It was our turn to make breakfast," said Kate.

"Bacon, eggs, fruit and toast," said Lucy, finishing up at the stove.

"Wow, you guys, this smells wonderful. I can't believe I'm hungry after that dinner we had last night, but I am!" said Marly, laughing.

"I'm always hungry in the mornings," said Lucy. "I cook for Seth every day and now Kate, although she has been helping me lately."

"Yes, I have, but I thank you for all the times you did it all," said Kate.

"No problem," said Lucy, fixing each plate and placing it on the bar.

They all sat down and started eating and sipping the mimosas that Kate had prepared.

"A perfect way to start the day," said Marly, lifting her glass.

"I'll drink to that," said Lucy and Kate agreed.

"Marly, I spoke with Seth last night and he wants us to hold off reaching out to the FBI," said Kate.

"Why? I'm ready to get rid of this stuff," said Marly.

"I know, but he said, and I agree, that the organization probably has contacts in the FBI or even members. We don't know if we would be giving them exactly what they want," explained Kate.

"Wow, who can we trust?" wondered Marly. "I did think that Lenny might have some contacts. You know, he has a sketchy past and that might come in handy in this situation."

Lucy thought a moment, "That's not a bad idea, Marly. When is he getting to town?"

"Today, but he probably won't reach out until our stalker out there is gone. I wouldn't want him to get caught, because we aren't supposed to be on friendly terms," said Marly.

"Yeah, most people aren't friends with their kidnappers," said Lucy wryly. That made them all laugh.

"So, we just sit on what we found until we can figure out what to do," said Marly.

"Unfortunately, yes. We don't want to do the wrong thing, do we?" asked Kate.

Lucy spoke up, "Definitely not!"

"Okay, so what's on the agenda today?" asked Marly, when suddenly there was a knock on the door.

"Who knows? This may be something to do today!" said Lucy, laughing.

Marly opened the door, and you could hear the surprise in her voice. "What are you two doing here?"

Rafe and Seth walked in, and no one was more surprised than Lucy and Kate. Lucy was at a total loss for words which, as we all know, never happens!

After hugs all around, Seth spoke up, "After talking to Kate last night, Rafe and I discussed it and decided we needed to be here with you girls."

"Rafe, who's taking care of the winery?" asked Lucy, concerned but so happy to see him.

"Cory has it covered, and I called in a favor from my friend, Tommy, from Washington. He's just there to support Cory and has the knowledge needed to field any questions. We felt being with you three was more important right now, especially with what you have uncovered," said Rafe.

"I'm so glad to see you guys," said Marly. "Come in and we'll fill you in."

After everyone told their version of what was going on, Seth looked at Marly and asked her, "Are you okay Marly? This is a lot for you to deal with, especially finding out that you are adopted and that the family you thought was yours is no relationship at all."

"I'm still processing it all, Seth, and I know

that I will have to deal with it sooner or later, but right now, we have all of this confidential information, and we aren't sure who we can trust!" said Marly.

"Maybe we can help with that too," said Rafe. "If we all work together, we can come up with a good solution."

Marly spoke up, "Lenny will be here today because he has been hired to "watch" me and my house this week. I was hoping that we could get some insight from him, because we all know he has some nefarious people in his past."

"That could work," said Seth but he wasn't putting too much confidence in that plan.

"In the meantime, we took a redeye, so we are both starving," said Seth. "What's for breakfast?"

"You missed it brother but because you came all this way, I'll cook again for you two," said Lucy, grinning.

"Great," said Rafe and they all trooped back into the kitchen, talking, laughing, and feeling better. Seth and Rafe, because they were seeing Kate and Lucy, and the girls because they missed them and if they needed muscle, they had it.

Dan saw the two men arrive and thought maybe his day would be more interesting. He saw them go into the house and stay inside. Obviously, they must have known them. He would wait a bit longer to see if they put in another appearance. He reached into the box of doughnuts beside him and took one out, taking a bite and sipping his lukewarm coffee. Just one more day, he thought, just one more day.

After the second breakfast of the day, they cleaned up and everyone went into the living area.

"We can do a bit of shifting around, but of course, you both will stay here. Lucy, you and Rafe can take my room and Seth, you can be in the guest room with Kate. I'll sleep in Poppa's room," said Marly, laying it out for them. "No objections, okay?"

"Yes ma'am," said Seth and Rafe agreed.

"I'm actually relieved that we will be here with you," said Rafe. "We plan to fly home on Wednesday with you girls,"

"That's perfect, Rafe," said Lucy, smiling at him. She loved him so much and was glad that he and Seth took it upon themselves to come here.

"Okay, then, it's settled. So, what do we want to do today? We need to give our stalker something to do," laughed Marly. "I imagine we have been very boring."

"If he only knew, Marly," said Lucy. "We have uncovered a lot since he's been napping in his car!"

"Anything special you girls want to do? I was thinking we could go into Memphis and maybe tour Graceland, you know, Elvis' home," said

Seth.

"Yes, we know that's where Elvis lived," said Lucy, rolling her eyes at her brother.

Kate smiled at the interaction between the siblings and said, "I actually have always wanted to go there. I don't think we have anything else we can do here, do we Marly?"

"I think it will be a great distraction, for us as well as the guy out front," grinned Marly. "Guys, why don't you get your luggage, provided you brought some, and we'll head upstairs and switch things around to accommodate everyone."

Seth and Rafe went outside to their rental car to get their bags which consisted of two duffels and laptop cases.

Lucy, Kate, and Marly headed upstairs, with Lucy gathering her things to move to Marly's room and Marly was moving a few clothes and toiletries to her grandfather's old room.

"What about this bin, Marly?" asked Lucy, indicating the documents and photographs they had found.

"I think I will put it in the wardrobe in Poppa's room. Maybe he will guard it in some way," said Marly, hoping that would be the case.

Seth and Rafe came back in, heading up the stairs to find where they should put their things.

"Geez, is that all you have?" asked Lucy, seeing one duffel bag each and their laptops.

"Luce, guys don't need as much as gals," said

Seth, winking.

Rafe was a bit more gracious, saying, "I think what Seth means is that we appreciate everything you do to look as beautiful as you are."

"Oh, puh-leeze, Rafe," laughed Lucy. "But thanks."

After everyone was situated in their rooms, they headed downstairs.

"Anything else we need to do before we leave?" asked Rafe.

"No, I'll just set the alarm when we leave, and we can go. Do we want to take my SUV?' asked Marly.

"It would probably be roomier for everyone," said Seth. "I'll drive, Marly."

Handing him her keys, Kate said, "I'll take him to the garage, and we will meet you guys out front."

"Perfect," said Marly, as she, Lucy and Rafe walked out the front door, with Marly setting the alarm with her phone app.

In a few minutes, Marly's Tahoe came around the corner and Rafe got in the front with Seth and the girls sitting in the back seats.

"Everyone ready?" asked Seth, as he put Graceland in the GPS.

A chorus of voices said 'Yes', and Seth started down the street.

Lucy said, "It's Now or Never," quoting an Elvis song title, causing groans from the guys up front.

Laughter came from the back seat as Lucy said, "Hey, Don't Be Cruel."

It was going to be a fun day.

CHAPTER 22

Dan Ricter started following the SUV, hoping that they weren't going to another museum. He called Derrick Porter to report that two men had arrived at the Anderson house and that now they were all in the Anderson woman's SUV, heading toward Memphis.

"Did they look like law enforcement or detectives?" asked Derrick.

"Nah, they looked like boyfriends, and they plan on staying because they had bags," said Dan.

"Interesting," said Derrick. "Keep them in your sights and report back to me this evening. I will need to inform Mr. Kennedy about this development."

"Will do," said Dan as he disconnected the call and watched the back of the Tahoe in front of him.

Tom Weston got a flight to Memphis as soon as he could. He would arrive at the airport at approximately 8:30 p.m. Sunday night. He called his father to let him know so that they could pick him up at the airport. It was awkward getting himself to the terminal after checking his bag and when the desk agent saw his condition, she took pity on him.

"Mr. Weston, I can pre-board you since you are injured," said the agent named Danielle, according to her name tag.

"That would be great," he said, smiling at her. He was grateful for her consideration, knowing he must look pretty bad.

"If you don't mind me asking, were you in an accident?" she asked, processing his boarding pass to pre-board status.

"Unfortunately, I got mugged in an alley," he said. Seeing the horrified look on her face, he joked, "You should see the other guy."

"That's terrible, Mr. Weston, I'm so sorry," the agent said compassionately.

"I appreciate it but I'm feeling better today," he said, although he didn't look it.

"Just take a seat and when the plane arrives, I'll let you board," she said.

"Thanks," he replied, taking the short walk to the row of seats at the gate.

His phone pinged and Tom saw a text from his father, saying they would pick him up and meet him in baggage claim. He was glad of that because his dad could carry his luggage. Sending a reply simply stating he would see them soon, Tom closed his eyes and waited patiently until the plane arrived at the gate.

Victor brought a breakfast tray to the third-floor library where Franklin Kennedy was sitting. The elevator doors slid open silently and he walked in, setting the tray on the table beside Franklin.

"Ah, thank you Victor, I was starting to feel a bit hungry," said Franklin.

"Did you rest well, sir?" asked Victor politely.

"As well as I usually do, Victor. I don't have any appointments today so I will probably rest. I have some correspondence to take care of as well," Franklin said.

"Very good, sir. Do you want to remain undisturbed?" he asked.

"Yes, unless it is something that is emergent," said Franklin, dismissing Victor for the day.

Ethan was up early, and Brittany was still asleep, he assumed, since she had not come out of the guest room. He was thinking about the very enjoyable day they had together and how fun it was to watch a movie and pop popcorn. Just a normal evening between two people. His phone pinged and he picked it up, seeing a message from Victor. 'MR KENNEDY IS RESTING UNLESS YOU NEED TO SPEAK TO HIM'. That's perfect because he was hoping for another good day with Brit. Sending a short message of 'OK', Ethan put down his phone. He thought about the message he had received from Mr. Kennedy about the NY issue he had taken care of and wondered if there was any mention of it on the internet newspapers in NYC. He went to his desk and pulled up the Wall Street Journal and found a small story in the middle of the paper. It stated that another mugging had taken place near Broadway in NYC, and a young man was severely beaten sustaining multiple contusions, lacerations and a broken arm. Of note, a tooth had been knocked out as well. The man was being treated at a local hospital, and no description was obtained of his attacker. The identity of the victim was not released.

Ethan was sure this was Tom Weston, and he was grateful to Mr. Kennedy for taking care of him. Maybe he would think twice before striking another woman. He heard the door of the guest room open. Turning around, he saw Brittany enter the living room.

"Hey you," said Ethan, getting up from his computer.

"You don't have to stop working, just because I'm here," she said.

"I wasn't working, it's Sunday. I was reading the Wall Street Journal," he admitted, wanting to be as truthful with her as possible.

"So you don't work on Sundays? I seem to recall you used to," said Brittany, smiling.

"Not today. I received word that Mr. Kennedy is resting today," said Ethan. "So, I get a free day. What would you like to do?"

"I'm a little hungry," admitted Brittany.

"Me too, actually," said Ethan. "There's a diner

nearby called Pete's Kitchen. It's a 24-hour place and they have good reviews. How about that?"

"Sounds perfect," said Brittany, heading back to her room. "Let me get a sweater."

While he waited, he wondered if Mr. Kennedy was feeling well. He has been ill several days lately. Brittany returned quickly and the two of them rode the elevator down to the parking garage. They got into Ethan's car and headed to Pete's.

"Mr. Weston, Mr. Weston," said a voice but Tom was dozing. The agent touched his arm lightly, and he flinched.

"I'm sorry, Mr. Weston, but I called your name several times. I wanted to be sure you were alright," said Danielle.

"It's okay, you just startled me, that's all. Guess I'm a bit jumpy," he admitted.

"I would imagine you are," she said. "You can board now."

"Thank you, Danielle, I really appreciate this," said Tom, struggling to stand, and she helped him.

She led him over to the entrance and he showed his ticket to the agent and one of the flight attendants escorted him to the plane. When they entered the cabin, the attendant spoke.

"Mr. Weston, we were not full in First Class, so we have upgraded you so that you can be more comfortable," she said.

Pleased with this turn of events, Tom thanked the attendant and settled into the large seat with plenty of leg room and a place to prop his cast. He buckled himself in and was asleep again before the plane was ready for takeoff.

The next Graceland tour was about to start, and Marly led the group, with Rafe, Lucy, Kate, and Seth following her. They were going into the mansion and saw various rooms as well as the famous Jungle Room. It was unique with an indoor waterfall and animal statues. The guide also told them that this room was used for his recording studio.

"Wow, this is over the top," said Lucy, gazing all around.

"Don't decorate the Honeymoon Cabin like this, Luce, I don't think we could afford that!" said Seth and they all laughed.

Their tour went into the exhibits of some of his stage outfits and the car museum. This is where the guys geeked out, looking at what is now vintage automobiles.

"I heard he gave away Cadillacs," said Kate, wondering how the people felt that got one.

"He was a very generous man," said the guide, hearing some of their conversation.

Marly kept looking for their stalker and saw him several times, trying to look inconspicuous.

They ended their tour in the Meditation

Garden where Elvis and his family members are buried. Heading back to the car, they got in and Lucy piped up, "I'm hungry!"

They all agreed it was time to find something to eat, and they drove the short distance to Vernon's Smokehouse on the complex. They were seated and the smells were making them hungrier. Their server was very knowledgeable and gave a few suggestions. They decided on a sampler platter for everyone to try that included ribs, brisket and pulled pork. They ordered several sides, including turnip greens, sweet potatoes, and mac and cheese with cornbread on the side. When it came to the table, it was an enormous amount of food.

"I sure hope you guys are hungry enough," said Kate, looking at the mound of meat.

"I think we can do it justice, Kate, what do you think, Seth?" said Rafe, already putting some brisket on his plate and getting some of the sides. They all got what they wanted, and it was quiet for a few minutes while everyone was feeding their hunger.

"Mmmm, this brisket is so delicious," said Marly.

"You can't come to Memphis without trying their BBQ," said Rafe.

"It's not Texas BBQ," said Lucy, staying true to her heritage.

"No, but it's dang good, Sis," said Seth, eating his greens and cornbread.

"I guess, but I make better mac and cheese," she

said proudly.

"That you do, Lucy," said Seth. "Maybe you want to give them your recipe?"

Lucy glared at her brother and said, "Very funny, Mr. Cavanaugh."

It was a fun day and Dan the stalker spent the day trying to keep up!

CHAPTER 23

Thomas and Lucinda arrived at the airport around 8:00 p.m. and sat down in the baggage claim area. They hadn't talked much in the car and they both sat silently with their thoughts while they waited for Tom Jr. to arrive. His flight landed right on time and in about ten minutes, he came down the escalator.

"Tom!" shouted his mother, running to him, fresh tears filling her eyes when she saw his injuries.

"Careful, Mom, don't hug me too tight. I'm still pretty sore," he said, giving her a gentle hug.

"I'm sorry, I'm sorry," she said, moving to his side.

"Give him some room, Lucinda," said Thomas, and looking at his son, he grimaced.

"My god, Tom, how are you even walking?" he asked. "You look horrible."

"I feel pretty bad, but I needed to come home," said Tom. "I've got to see Dr. Laramore to fix my tooth they knocked out."

"Was there more than one of them?" asked Thomas.

"No, but it was almost like the guy was lying in wait for me," said Tom. "Just happened so fast."

"Did you fill out a police report?" asked Lucinda.

"Yes, Mom, but I don't think they will do much about it. I mean, I didn't get a good look at the guy, because it was so dark. I got in a few punches, but he was big and strong. I didn't have a chance, so I pretended to be knocked out and after a few kicks to my stomach, he left me alone," explained Tom.

"I'm sorry, son," said Thomas. "Come with me and point out your bags. I'll get them." The carousel had just started moving.

After a few minutes, his two bags dropped down and Thomas picked them up and they left the area, going out of the doors into the evening.

"We're over here in the short-term parking," said Lucinda, leading the way as she found the car. "I'll sit in the back, and you can sit up front with your Dad."

Tom didn't argue but he would rather have sat in the back. He wanted to take another pain pill but would do that when they got home.

"I called your sister and let her know what was going on," said Lucinda, trying to make small talk.

"I wish you hadn't, Mom," said Tom. "We don't get along that well, you know."

"Of course she would want to know about your condition, Tom. She loves you, as we all do," said Lucinda.

"Where is she now?" he asked.

"Nashville. She is a veterinarian at an animal clinic there," Lucinda said, with pride in her voice.

"Can we not talk anymore, Mom? I hurt all over and just want to get home and take something for pain," said Tom, closing his eyes.

The rest of the trip to the Anderson house was silent.

It was almost 9:00 p.m. when Marly and the gang got back to her house after their day in Memphis. It was a good outing, and Marly had to admit that it had taken her mind off of the problem at hand. But now that everyone was in bed and she was lying in her grandfather's room, she had time to think about everything. She was reviewing in her mind everything that they had found in the last few days and the truth about her family. That was the hardest secret to comprehend. Why did someone as intelligent as her grandfather think that hiring a family was the right thing to do? That was the reason she always felt disconnected from them, Her "brother and sister" never were close to her, even though she was the oldest. But that was probably because of the way Lucinda and Thomas treated her. She had been holding on to this house because of her love for Poppa but is that a reason to stay in a place where she didn't have any ties? No living family, no friends, really, so what was keeping her here? She was going to do some serious thinking about her life. Forcing herself to stop thinking, she closed her eyes and willed herself to fall asleep.

Lucinda was up early, drinking coffee and staring into space. She was thinking about Tom and his injuries. She heard him moaning during the night but when she checked on him, he was sleeping. Realizing it was probably the pain he was in, she crept back to bed and silently cried. Today, her eyes were dry, but she still hurt for her son. Her quiet reverie was interrupted by Thomas, coming into the kitchen.

"Morning," he said, headed to the coffeepot.

"Good morning," she said, but didn't say anything else. They had drifted apart over the years so, small talk in the morning wasn't expected.

"What are you going to do today, Lucinda?" asked Thomas.

Surprised, she said, "I am going to call Dr. Laramore's office as soon as they open and see if Tom can get in today as an emergency."

"Good. He looks pretty bad, don't you think?" Tom said, sipping his coffee and sitting down at the table with her.

"Yes, he does," she said, her eyes glistening again.

"Look, Lucinda, give him some space. He's

been through a lot, and I don't think he wants to talk about it," said Thomas, looking directly at his wife. "I know this is hurting you too because I want to find the son of a bitch that did this to our son and make them pay."

Shocked by the vehemence in his voice, Lucinda nodded, "I wish you could find him too. And all for a wallet. I hope he doesn't go back to New York."

"If he decides to, we have to let him. He is a grown man and needs to make his own decisions, but I agree with you. I wish he would just find a job here," Thomas said, finishing up his coffee. "I better get to work, don't want to be late." He got up and kissed Lucinda on the top of her head and left.

She sat there, thinking about their conversation this morning. It was unusual but Lucinda had to admit she liked it. It was almost like old times, before their lives were turned upside down.

Ethan got up and dressed for work. He will be going to Mr. Kennedy's estate today. He and Brittany had a good day. After eating brunch, they went to a park and walked on the trails, ending up near a fountain and sat on a park bench for a while, having casual conversation. Afterwards, they had dinner and drinks at a local eatery and then went home. Ethan didn't know what Brittany was going to do in the long term but right now, things were going okay with her staying at his place. So far it hadn't been stiff or awkward. He was drinking coffee when Brittany came out of the guest room, all dressed in jeans and a long-sleeved button-up blouse in blue and yellow stripes.

Whistling, he said, "You look wonderful in that color."

"Thanks," she said demurely. "I thought I'd go with you today to Mr. Kennedy's, if that's okay with you."

Surprised, he said, "Sure, that will be fine. While we are working you can hang out with Victor or read in the library. I'm sure he would love to see you."

"I want to thank him for letting you take care of me," said Brittany.

"Brit, that's not necessary," said Ethan.

"Maybe not for you, but it is for me. For the first time in months, I feel safe. I can sleep at night without fear of Tom getting angry for whatever reason and taking it out on me. It's a freedom that you cannot imagine," she said, revealing her inner feelings.

"I cannot imagine living with someone and being constantly afraid," said Ethan. "I'm glad you're here...with me," Ethan added that last part spontaneously, but he realized he meant it. He was hurt when she left him, but he eventually got over her, he thought. And now, it seems as if all of his feelings were surging back.

She smiled at him and walked over, putting her arms around him in a hug and he gently hugged her back. She smelled so good. Pulling away from him a bit, she kissed him tenderly on his lips. He answered her kiss with one of his own, making it more sensual, promising more.

"Okay, young lady, no more of that, at least not now," said Ethan, winking at her. "Let's get out of here and we'll stop and pick you up a coffee on the way."

"Sounds great," said Brittany, thinking that everything was going to work out. She was back where she belonged, and she was going to let Ethan know how grateful she was to him.

Everyone was talking and laughing about their trip to Memphis yesterday. Marly made French toast and Kate and Lucy cut up fruit to go with it. There was whipped cream freshly made by Marly, syrup, confectioner's sugar, and butter. The smells were delicious.

"I can't wait to dig in," said Seth, already buttering his toast.

"I'm ahead of you, Seth," said Rafe, taking a big bite of his and rolling his eyes. "This is fantastic, Marly."

"Thanks, Rafe. I did have two assistants this morning too," said Marly, grinning.

"I know I speak for Seth as well when I say, we are so lucky to have you three in our lives," Rafe said honestly.

Seth raised his glass of orange juice and said, "Here, here, I second that!"

Amidst the chatter and laughter, the doorbell sounded. Wiping her hands on a towel, Marly made her way to the front door and opened it.

There stood Lenny Crocker.

CHAPTER 24

"Oh, good morning Lenny," stammered Marly, as she had forgotten he would be here today.

"Good morning, Marly. Your house sure does smell good," he said.

"Oh, we were just having breakfast," said Marly, motioning him to follow her into the kitchen.

Lenny heard her say 'we' and he immediately thought about Marc Rivers. *This might be awkward*, he thought.

He followed her into the kitchen and saw Lucy and Kate and two people he didn't know.

"Everyone, this is Lenny Crocker, Of course you know Lucy and Kate and this is Rafe Sexton, Lucy's fiancé and Seth Cavanaugh, Lucy's brother and Kate's fiancé." Marly made the introductions.

Lenny shook hands with Rafe and Seth and nodded to the two women.

"Would you like something to eat?" asked Marly.

"As good as it smells, I have to pass. I ate the hotel breakfast, which wasn't great but filling," said Lenny. "Besides, I'm here to watch your house and keep tabs on you." Everyone laughed a bit nervously at that remark.

"I thought I would stop by and see if there was anything I needed to know about before I take up my post," he said.

"You guys finish up in here and I'll update Lenny," said Marly, leading him into the living area. The whole group could hear her, so they continued their meal.

Marly told Lenny everything that had been found when they searched the house and asked him if he knew what they should do with the information.

"I mean, it's very confidential and apparently highly classified, but how do I know if we are turning it over to a legitimate FBI agent or Homeland Security person. What if they are affiliated with this secret organization that erases people! I just don't know what to do," she said, her eyes pleading with him to have an answer.

Lenny was shocked by her revelations, and from what she revealed, he knew that it had to be handled discreetly. His military background and affiliation with different groups of people did give him some options.

"This is unreal," said Lenny. "I will reach out to some contacts and without mentioning anything specific, I'll see what chatter is out there."

"That would be great, Lenny. I have the

documents here in the house, and I think that is what Franklin Kennedy is wanting to find. But, we beat him to it and found the secret room but now, what do we do with everything?" asked Marly.

By this time, the others had joined them in the living room and were seated, offering suggestions and opinions.

"Where did you find the bulk of the information?" asked Lenny.

Lucy spoke up, "In a secret room in the basement."

"Was the wall damaged?" asked Lenny.

"Well, yeah, we had to bust a hole in the drywall," Lucy said, rolling her eyes.

Remembering she was a spitfire, Lenny said, "I ask because if we can repair the wall, it might deter them when they search this place…and one way or another, I believe they will search it."

Kate spoke up, "From what we have learned about Franklin Kennedy, he wants to personally look for the "item" he believes is here. So, I agree with you that he is determined to be involved in searching for it because, in reality, he is the only person who knows what needs to be found."

Seth looked at Kate, nodding, "I agree with you. But how do we protect Marly?"

"That's the million-dollar question," said Rafe, looking at Marly.

Suddenly, she felt very vulnerable, "I don't want any of you to put yourself in danger to help me. I can leave if necessary."

"It might come to that, Marly," said Lenny. "Since you didn't find any traps when you were searching, it appears that your grandfather didn't think anyone would come looking. In my experience, if you hide something and you want to protect it, you booby trap it."

"Are you suggesting we do that in the basement?" asked Marly.

"I think it would be a good idea. There isn't anything in there for them to find, but they don't know that. What if we repair the damage down there, and I can take care of setting some explosive charges that wouldn't kill anyone but would scare the shit out of them," Lenny said. "Excuse the language, ladies."

"It's okay, Lenny," said Lucy. "I've said much worse."

"Yes, we know," said Rafe, and everyone laughed, relieving some of the tension in the room.

Seth spoke up, "I think Lenny has a good idea. I can fix the wall downstairs, and we can even decorate it as a hangout space, making it more difficult to notice the room is a different size from the retail space. Isn't that how you noticed it, Kate?"

"Actually, Lucy noticed it first, and I didn't notice it, so that might work in our favor," said Kate.

Lucy spoke up, "If we paint, it will leave a smell

for a while which could tip them off. What about putting up some wallpaper?"

"That's a great idea, Luce," said Seth. "I knew that your decorator mind would come up with something else for me to do!"

"Hey, Rafe can help you," said Lucy, grinning, knowing that he was referring to all of the finishing touches she was having him do on the Honeymoon Cabin at the vineyard.

Marly spoke up, "Lenny, you would need to set the charges before the wall is repaired because everything we found was down there except for some items in his desk and books up here."

"I don't think anything in the living spaces would have been booby trapped if Mr. Anderson had taken those steps," said Lenny. "After I report to my employer, I'll locate some materials to set the traps. Can you guys go find a couple of pieces of drywall to make the repairs?"

"Yep, that will be our task today," said Rafe. "Lenny, you can report that the two men went out with golf clubs, but the women stayed home. We don't want anyone coming over prematurely."

"Sounds good," said Lenny, "I'll check back in later when I have everything I need."

Marly walked him to the door, "Thank you, Lenny. I appreciate what you are doing and putting yourself at risk."

"I owe you that much at least, Marly. I'm surprised that Marc Rivers isn't here with you," said Lenny.

"He doesn't know, and we aren't seeing each other anymore," she admitted.

"I'm sorry, if that was what you wanted," said Lenny. "He's a damn fool."

Marly blushed as Lenny walked out to his car and drove off.

Lenny pulled over a couple of streets away from the house. He picked up his phone and called Mr. Kennedy.

"Hello," said Franklin, not familiar with the number.

"Hello Mr. Kennedy, this is Lenny Crocker. I wanted to report that I was in place for the surveillance job."

"Good, good, Mr. Crocker. Anything happening?" asked Franklin.

"A couple of guys came out, looked like they were going to a golf course. The women didn't join them, so they are still there," Lenny reported his false narrative.

"Hmmm, I see," said Franklin, musing to himself.

"You want me to follow the men or the women?" he asked.

"Stay on the house. That's the most important thing. I don't believe that the men are a threat, as it appears they are on vacation," said Franklin.

"I'll let you know if the situation changes," said Lenny, ending the call.

Franklin Kennedy liked this Lenny fellow. He seemed to be very thorough in his observations. The man before him didn't have much to report and he wasn't very pleased with him. But, Derrick got him from a different source so he couldn't blame him. He was glad that he himself had moved quickly and hired Lenny Crocker and his previous association with Marly Anderson made him a bit more trustworthy in his eyes. Hearing the elevator doors, he looked up to see Ethan and Brittany walking across the hall.

"Ahh, lovely Brittany, it is so good to see you," said Franklin, as she came over to hug him.

"It is good to see you too Mr. Kennedy," said Brittany. "I insisted on coming here with Ethan today because I wanted to thank you for allowing him to take care of things for me."

He noted the bruising she tried to hide with makeup and the long sleeves that covered her arms and as he looked into her eyes, he gave her a sad smile.

"It was my pleasure to allow it, Brittany. You are a friend to us both and there should not be any question that we would stand up for you when someone was hurting you. I'm sorry that you had to endure pain at the hands of someone you cared for but now that is over. You are here and do not need to worry about what you left in New York," said Franklin.

Blushing at his reference of New York, she

knew that he was aware of the details and why wouldn't Ethan tell him? He had to be honest with him, and she was glad. Now she was in a good safe place and in a few weeks, she would get a job and make a new life for herself, right here in Denver.

CHAPTER 25

Lucinda called Dr. Laramore's office and requested an emergency appointment. The receptionist said they didn't have any openings.

"Please you don't understand," pleaded Lucinda. "My son was mugged in New York, and he flew home last night. His tooth was knocked out by the assailant, and it is imperative that someone look at it. We have been clients of Dr. Laramore for years, so if you will, please ask him to work us in."

"Hold for a moment," said the girl and in a few moments she was back.

"Yes, Mrs. Anderson, Dr. Laramore will see your son during lunch. Can you have him here at noon?"

"Yes, of course, we will be there," she said, ending the call.

Lucinda peered into Tom's darkened bedroom. She called out softly.

"Tom, are you awake?" she asked.

"Yeah, Mom, I'm awake," he acknowledged.

"Dr. Laramore will see you at noon today. It's 10:00 a.m. now and we should leave about 11:45

a.m." Lucinda told him.

"Thanks, Mom," said Tom, thankful for his mom taking care of things. "I'll get ready in a little bit."

"Do you need any help?" she asked, knowing he would refuse.

"If I do, I'll call out to you," he said, not knowing if he would need any help or not.

"Okay, love you," she said and walked away.

Tom set an alarm on his watch for thirty more minutes and drifted back off to sleep. At first, he didn't know what that buzzing sound was but realized the time had already passed and it was 10:30 a.m. Getting up gingerly, he made his way into his bathroom and took a quick shower. He got dressed slowly and it took him almost an hour. He walked into the kitchen to find his mother, preparing for dinner.

"What you making, Mom?" he asked.

"Oh, Tom, sit down. Do you need anything?" she asked, not answering his question immediately.

"Do you have some juice?" he asked, knowing that she would. She always had the fridge well stocked.

"Yes, of course," she said as she got a glass and poured it for him. "Here you go. I am making potato soup for dinner, so that it will be easier for you to eat. We don't know what Dr. Laramore will be doing today."

"That's true, but it sounds good, Mom," said

Tom, glad to be home and to be taken care of.

"I'm glad it sounds good to you," said Lucinda. "I need to get changed and then we'll go, okay?"

"I'll wait here for you," said Tom, sipping his juice.

True to her word, Lucinda quickly changed, and she and Tom left in her Cadillac, arriving at the dentist's office exactly at 11:45 a.m. They walked in and the waiting room was empty, and Lucinda was glad there were no stares or questions to evade.

Seth and Rafe found a Home Depot and got some drywall, tape, mud, hammers, and nails. They walked over to the wallpaper area and thumbed through the books.

"Do you know what you're doing, Seth?" asked Rafe, grinning.

"Not really, but I thought I'd take pictures of several and send to the girls," said Seth. "I like to play it safe!" They both laughed at that and when they found three they agreed would do, Seth texted the photos to Lucy and Kate.

The text he received said THE STRIPED ONE and Seth showed Rafe. "See, this is the one we thought they would pick!"

Paying for their purchases, including the wallpaper, which was an adhesive type, they got back in Marly's SUV and headed back to the house.

Lenny had contacts all over the country as

well as internationally, but he really needed someone close by to expedite things. He reached out to an ex-military friend who lived near Nashville.

"Hello?" said a voice answering the call.

"Hey, Jim, this is Lenny, Lenny Crocker from Denver," he said, identifying himself.

"Hey, Lenny, how are you doing? Staying out of trouble?" asked Jim.

"For the most part, I would say. I just have a little job I need to do in your neck of the woods and needed to procure some supplies. You have any resources I could get in contact with?" Lenny asked hopefully.

Jim thought a moment, "What type of supplies? I would say it depended on the size of the job."

"Not big, just some booby traps on some sensitive areas," said Lenny, wanting to get the right materials but not giving anything away. "Don't want to kill anyone, just hurt them a little if they come messing around."

"I totally understand. How close are you to Nashville?" he asked.

"I'm in Memphis but I don't think too far," said Lenny, not really knowing.

"It's about three hours or so," filled in Jim. "I can get you what you need if you want to come here. We could go grab a bite and catch up."

Lenny, relieved that he would get what he needed, agreed, "Yeah, that would be great. I'll head that way in about thirty minutes and see you about 1:00 p.m. Where you want to meet?"

"I'll meet you at Puckett's on Church Street. They got a great menu, and we can get a drink," said Jim.

"Sounds good," said Lenny, "see you then."

Ending the call, Lenny placed another call, this one to Marly.

"Hello," she said, in a sweet southern voice.

"Hey, it's me," said Lenny, "I got a lead on what I need but I have to go to Nashville to pick it up. I'll be back around 5:00 p.m."

"Okay Lenny, thanks for letting me know. The guys called and are on their way back to the house. We will have to get it done tonight because the guys need to finish in the basement tomorrow. Will that put too much pressure on you?" Marly asked.

Smiling as he remembered how she always worried about others, Lenny assured her, "It shouldn't take me long. Don't worry, everything will be fine."

As Marly ended the call, she turned around to see Kate and Lucy there, listening.

"Well, what did he say?" asked Lucy.

"He's getting what he needs but it's in Nashville. He'll be back here about 5:00 p.m.," said Marly.

Kate spoke, "Fortunately, Lenny knows what he is doing, which is good for us. One wall won't be too hard to do, and we'll help. We should also look around and see what furniture we can place in there too."

"True, and there's a television in Poppa's room that no one uses. We can put that down there, to make it seem as if it is a hangout type room," suggested Marly.

"That's good," said Lucy. "Also, I saw a couple of empty canisters in your pantry, we could fill with snacks. Make it look like your theatre room."

Laughing, Marly asked, "Should we move the wine fridge down there too?"

"That's not a bad idea," replied Lucy, laughing with her.

Marly suddenly got serious, "I can't tell you how much you two mean to me. I don't know what I would do without you."

"Thankfully," said Kate, "you don't have to. We are here for you, just like you would be there for us and have been in the past. So, let's just say, we're here for the party!"

Laughing together and lightening the mood was just what they needed. They got busy looking around and choosing items to put in the new room. It was just another girl adventure.

Dr. Laramore himself called Tom and Lucinda back to the examination room. Lucinda helped Tom walk through the doors and into the exam room.

"Good god, Tom, someone worked you over

pretty damn good," said Dr. Laramore.

"Yes sir, he did," admitted Tom. "He was a big guy, and he was waiting for me in an alley."

"Man, I'm sorry that happened to you. Did you report it to the police?" asked the dentist as he was examining the damage.

"Oh yeah, they came to the hospital where I was taken. I'm assuming the paramedics reported it. Of course, they aren't very hopeful that they can find the guy. I didn't get a good look at him because it was so dark and I was busy trying to fend off his punches," said Tom, sometimes garbled with Dr. Laramore's hands in his mouth.

After a few minutes, Dr. Laramore spoke, "I didn't find any other teeth damaged, but I need to remove the root of the broken one. We can do it now if you feel up to it."

"How will you replace the tooth, Dr. Laramore?" asked Lucinda, worried about her boy.

"I'll take an impression and make a cast. I'll send it to the lab and put a rush job on it. I can call when it's ready. It shouldn't take more than a day or two," he said.

"Lucinda, I'm going to ask you to assist me as my staff is at lunch. Are you okay with that?" he asked.

"Of course," said Lucinda. She would do anything necessary to help Tom.

For the next hour, Dr. Laramore extracted the

root, placed the rod where the false tooth would go and then he made an upper impression to send to the lab. It took about an hour and a half and Tom was exhausted.

"I'll call when I have your replacement, Tom. Lucinda, if I ever need an assistant, I know who to call. You did great," said Dr. Laramore and Lucinda smiled at him in thanks.

CHAPTER 26

Seth and Rafe got back to the house and unloaded everything in the garage. They didn't want any prying eyes to see what was going on, just in case they were looking. After bringing everything into the basement, the girls joined them to look at everything.

"Seems like you got enough stuff," said Lucy. "We're only doing one wall."

Seth looked at his sister, "Who is the carpenter in this group?"

Grudgingly, Lucy said, "You are, my brother, but we only..."

Interrupting her, Seth said, "I didn't want us to have to go back IF a mistake was made. I mean, we know how you measure things!"

While the others laughed, Lucy said, "That was one time, Seth. Geez, you never forget anything!" She laughed too and agreed it was a good idea.

"Heard from Lenny?" asked Rafe, when the noise settled down.

"Yes, he called earlier. He contacted someone in Nashville to get what he needs and will be back here around 5:00 p.m.," said Marly.

"That's going to cut it close, but I think we can do a wall in a day, even with mistakes," said Rafe, winking at Lucy.

"Oh, you guys are just so freaking funny!" said Lucy, punching Rafe on the arm.

Changing the subject, Seth said, "Something smells great, Marly. What's cooking?"

"I'm slow cooking some ribs in the oven and making some baked beans for dinner. Lucy made some coleslaw, and Kate was in charge of dessert," said Marly.

"A simple strawberry shortcake," said Kate, "after all of that rich food."

Seth looked at her and smiled, "It sounds wonderful, Katie. I guess we will wait until Lenny gets here to eat. So, who is interested in finding a burger joint because I'm hungry."

"When are you not hungry, bro," said Lucy, grinning at her brother.

"We spent a lot of energy getting manly things to fix the wall," said Rafe. "We deserve a burger."

"Oh, so now you are on his side, eh?" said Lucy. "I see how it is."

Marly joined in, "I have to say, I'm a bit hungry too."

"Okay, okay, I give in. I could eat something," admitted Lucy and they all went into the garage and got into the SUV.

"Wimpy's Burgers is good," said Marly, giving directions to Seth as he drove them to lunch.

Franklin Kennedy and Ethan were sitting in the designated work area in the library while Brittany went to find Victor and hang out in the kitchen.

"I've been thinking, Ethan, about sending you to Germantown again. I know that we have not been successful in getting Ms. Anderson's cooperation but maybe, after spending time with her friends and relaxing, she may be more amenable to my request," said Franklin, looking directly at Ethan.

"Of course, I will go Mr. Kennedy," said Ethan. "Is there anything new I can put on the table?"

"It's obvious she doesn't need the money. Maybe, instead of offering to buy the building, I pay her a finder's fee, something she would decide. I don't care what the price, of course, because I just need to get into the house and look. If I know Oliver, and I used to know him pretty well, he would have hidden things. Who knows, he may have another location where he may have hidden things or a lockbox at a bank, I just don't know. All I know is that the security of our high-profile clients is at risk if anything is uncovered by the wrong people," Franklin said, thinking of his late-night caller.

Ethan asked, "Is there a possibility that someone else will be looking for the same thing?"

"Unfortunately, there is. One of our clients is

desperate to ensure that all of their information is secured and since Oliver's death, it is in question," revealed Franklin.

"I am not trying to be impertinent, sir, but if this organization was so secret, how will anyone know where to look?" asked Ethan, seriously.

"If I can find out where Oliver Anderson, aka, Randolph Vinson disappeared to, then so can someone else, especially with a great motivation," said Franklin, wanting to make Ethan understand without revealing too much information.

Realizing that he wasn't going to get any more insight, Ethan simply said, "When do you want me to go?"

"I think this weekend would be good. I had my FBI contact look into who was visiting Ms. Anderson, and it is several old friends. They live in Texas and are scheduled to leave on Wednesday. So, I think fly in Thursday and have the weekend to meet with her," said Franklin, not leaving anything to chance.

"What about Brit, sir? Could I include her in the travel plans?" asked Ethan, not wanting to leave her alone.

"Excellent idea. It would give her a new place to see and possibly having her with you will make Ms. Anderson a bit more congenial. Make plans for both of you then. Find a nice hotel in Memphis and see the sights. As I recall from years past, there are some great nightclubs and restaurants in the area," agreed Franklin.

"I'll get on it right away, sir," said Ethan. "I'll find Brittany and we'll head back to my place. I'll make the arrangements there. Is there anything else sir?"

"No, I think that will do for now," he said. "Ethan, I appreciate your loyalty, and I will reward it."

"I'm not worried about that, sir. You are already very generous, and I'm honored to work with you," said Ethan, although lately he was afraid there was more behind the scenes than he ever imagined.

"Have Victor bring my tea, and I'll talk to you soon," dismissed Franklin, turning to his computer screen.

Ethan took that as his cue to leave, and he soon found Brittany in the kitchen with Victor. He relayed Mr. Kennedy's request and said goodbye to Victor. He led Brittany outside and down the steps to his car.

"All done for today?" asked Brittany.

"Just some work I need to do from home. So, how would you like to go to Memphis with me?" he asked casually.

"Oh yes!" she said excitedly, and Ethan smiled as he left the Kennedy estate.

Lenny walked into Puckett's and saw Jim, seated at the bar. Walking up to him, he tapped his shoulder and Jim spun around.

"Lenny! Long time no see!" said Jim, getting

down off of the stool and giving him a bear hug.

"Good to see you, Jim. It has been a long time," agreed Lenny.

Jim signaled the hostess, and she seated them at a corner table. She took their drink orders and walked away.

"So, man, what's been happening with you? See any of the old gang?" asked Jim, sipping the beer he brought over with him from the bar.

"Not really," said Lenny. "I've actually semi-retired and been staying on the mountain in my cabin. You know, hunting, fishing, enjoying the good life."

"Sounds great," said Jim. "I haven't seen many myself. Stan and I keep in touch, but that's about it. What about that chick you worked with a lot?"

"Sad story. She got involved in a murder and tried to blow up a bunch of people at the funeral of the guy she killed. Before her arraignment, she committed suicide in the jail," said Lenny, trying to keep passive.

"Whoa, man, that's wild!" said Jim. "You always did hang with the craziest people. I worried about you sometimes, man."

Chuckling a little, Lenny admitted, "I worried about myself a bit too. What's good here?" Lenny wanted to change the subject. Talking about Raven was still painful for him, because he just knew he should have seen her one last time. But, she was in control then.

"Everything is good here," said Jim. "You can't

go wrong."

"I've never had the Nashville Hot Chicken so I'm going to try that," said Lenny.

"Good choice," said Jim. "I'll have that too."

The server came over to their table with their drinks, took their order, and left quickly.

"So, Lenny, I've got what you need with me," said Jim, casually drinking his beer.

"Here? That's risky, don't you think?" said Lenny, a bit surprised. He thought he would have to go to a different meeting place.

"Nah, I had it at my place and thought, why don't I make the money. You were planning to pay for it, right?" asked Jim, eyeing Lenny.

Always prepared to pay for whatever he needed, Lenny said, "Of course, and I'd rather pay a friend than someone I don't know. What's the damage?"

"I'm thinking about $3,500, unless you think that's too steep," said Jim, knowing it was but he was in a financial crunch at the moment.

"A bit high but I did need it quickly. I'm okay with that," said Lenny, not blinking an eye.

Surprisingly, Jim said, "I could knock it down a bit, if you need me to."

Lenny, not wanting any questions about why he needed it, said, "Nah, what's $500 between old friends." Lifting up his beer, he held it up in a toast and drank it down. Now he needed to eat and get back to Memphis.

After lunch, they walked out to Jim's truck,

and he opened both doors to shield the transaction. Lenny handed him the money and Jim gave him a duffel bag with the supplies.

"I put a little block of C-4 in there, just in case you needed it later," said Jim, smiling.

Smiling at Jim, Lenny said, "Thanks, you never know in our line of work."

"True that," said Jim, getting in his truck and driving off, with Lenny getting in his SUV.

CHAPTER 27

Before leaving the parking lot of the restaurant, Lenny called Mr. Kennedy. This time, Franklin recognized the number.

"Hello, Lenny," he said. "How's it going?"

"Fine, the men returned a little bit ago and then they all left together. I followed them to a local restaurant, presumably for lunch. I'll keep close tabs on them until they return to the house," reported Lenny.

"Thank you, Lenny, you are very thorough. I wish I could say that for everyone on my payroll. I have a few loyal ones, but you can never be too careful," said Franklin.

If he only knew, thought Lenny, but aloud said, "I understand that, sir. I've had some untrustworthy people in my life, and it has been eye-opening, let's just say."

"Ah, I imagine you have," thinking back to the dossier he had on Lenny Crocker, and said, "I am sending one of my colleagues to Memphis at the end of the week. My intel is that the guests of Ms. Anderson will be leaving on Wednesday."

Surprised by the amount and accuracy of

his information, Lenny just said, "Will my role change at that time, sir?"

"Not yet," Franklin said. "but, it could, depending on the response he gets from Ms. Anderson. I'm changing my tactics a bit so we will see how it goes."

Not wanting to appear too curious, Lenny said, "I understand. Just let me know if you need any additional tasks performed."

"I certainly will, Lenny, and thank you for your cooperation," said Franklin, ending the call. He liked Lenny Crocker.

Lenny was going to send a text to Marly on his burner phone but thought better of it. Someone with Kennedy's power and money could get access to anything. He called her instead.

"Hello Lenny," said Marly. "Now I have two numbers for you!"

"Yeah, you do, but I won't be keeping this one when I'm done with the job," said Lenny. "I got the supplies, and I should be there around 5:00 p.m."

"Did everything go okay? Are you worried about anything?" asked Marly, always concerned.

Loving that about Marly, Lenny said, "Everything's okay. I'll see you guys later," ending the call.

Marly filled everyone in on Lenny's call, and they got ready to leave the restaurant. No one left hungry, that's for sure.

"On the way home, could we go by my financial advisor's office?" asked Marly. "You can drop me off and I know he will bring me home."

"We can wait for you Marly," said Seth, not sure about leaving her alone.

"Really, Jerry is a great friend, and I need to speak to him about some business transactions. We won't be too long, and I would rather not leave the house empty, if you know what I mean," explained Marly.

Reluctantly agreeing, Seth followed Marly's directions to Jerry Fielding's office.

"What if he's not here, Marly?" asked Kate.

"He is. I sent a text to him from the restaurant," said Marly.

"Pulling a fast one over on us, eh Marly?" said Lucy, grinning at her friend.

"I'm just efficient, that's all. I'll see you guys soon, I promise," said Marly, getting out of the SUV and walking into the office building.

Seth drove off, leaving Marly behind, and no one felt very comfortable about it.

Knocking on his office door, Marly waited for him to respond. In a few seconds the door swung open, and there was Jerry, smiling at his friend.

"Marly, you look good," said Jerry. "Has it just been a few weeks since you were in here?"

"Yes Jerry, did Belinda and the girls get back home from their trip?" she asked, remembering they were at their grandparents.

"Yep, they sure did and now they are spoiled rotten!" Jerry laughed. "I guess that is what grandparents are for, but Belinda was there too. She could have stopped it, but I think she was enjoying being pampered too."

Smiling, Marly thought back on her Poppa. He spoiled her too, but he also taught her good values. Aloud she said, "Yes, that's what they do but you are there to teach them the right way to do things. Let them enjoy the spoiling."

"You're right, Marly. So, what brings you here today? I don't have anything new to report yet on your holdings," said Jerry.

"I have been thinking about a lot of things, Jerry. Especially since I have uncovered some information that I was unaware of previously," said Marly.

Sensing this was a serious discussion, Jerry got up and closed his door. "So, what is it Marly?"

She began haltingly to tell Jerry what she had found about her birth and that the people who she thought were her family, were no relation at all. She revealed that her grandfather hired them to pose as her family.

"Wow, Marly, that had to be devastating to you! Why would your grandfather do that?" asked Jerry, puzzled.

Not wanting to divulge any of his past, she simply said, "I guess so there would be someone to care for me when he went on business trips. He didn't have any other family to depend on."

"I guess, but that is pretty bizarre. No wonder they dropped the lawsuit to contest the will. They absolutely had no legal legs to stand on," said Jerry.

"I know, but they extorted money from me after Poppa died, knowing they weren't entitled to it," said Marly.

"Do you want to take them to court? I don't know if you want to reopen all of that and make them repay it, but you could," explained Jerry, knowing it would be a very nasty court case. He had never liked the 'Andersons' and now he liked them even less.

"No, I don't want to do that, but in light of everything I found, I don't know that I want to stay in the house. Maybe selling it would be a good idea. Can you put out some feelers and see if anyone, besides Franklin Kennedy, is interested in the property?" she asked.

"Are you thinking about leaving the area or do you want a smaller place?" asked Jerry, afraid that she was going to leave.

"I don't know yet, Jerry. I just want to know what my options are and then I'll make some decisions. Somehow, I don't feel the same way about the place, knowing that I was there based on a lie," said Marly, tearing up a little.

"Marly, I knew your Poppa, and he loved you more than anything in this world. He may not have told you about your adoption, but he gave you everything he had," said Jerry, sad for his friend.

"I know, Jerry, and all of this is so new right now. I'm trying to wrap my head around it all, but I do know that I don't want to live there anymore. Just see what you can find out, okay?" asked Marly.

"Sure, Marly, you know I will. And, the girls will be sad if Miss Marly leaves, as well as Belinda and me," Jerry said sincerely.

"I appreciate that, Jerry. But, one thing I want you to know, that wherever this next chapter in my life takes me, there will always be room for the Fielding family," said Marly.

"Good, now, let's get you home and I'm taking the rest of the afternoon off," said Jerry, gathering his briefcase and leading her out back to his car.

When Marly returned home, she heard Kate and Lucy downstairs in the basement. She followed their voices and saw them moving the old pieces of furniture around to form a conversational grouping. Seth and Rafe had taken the television out of her Poppa's room and had it ready to install once the wall was done. They were all teasing and laughing together and Marly stood there for a moment, taking it in. Life with these people was the best!

"What's going on here?" she asked, looking around.

"We thought we'd get a head start on

arranging things down here. What do you think?" asked Kate.

"It looks great, like it's always been here," said Marly approvingly.

"If you have a tablecloth, we can put it over this beat-up sideboard and put a small refrigerator on it for soft drinks or something," said Lucy. "And we bought a refrigerator after we dropped you off!"

They all laughed, and Marly was overwhelmed with everything they had done.

"Y'all are the best friends ever!" exclaimed Marly, hugging her two best friends.

"I talked to Seth about making some personal sized wine bottles, you know, to fit in a small fridge. We may be able to market them really well," added Lucy, grinning.

Rafe came up behind Lucy, putting his arms around her, "That's my girl, always thinking business."

"Other companies do it," said Kate. "It would be great for single people."

"Can we write off this trip as an expense then?" asked Lucy. "We were working!"

Everyone laughed and they headed upstairs. It was almost 5:00 p.m. and Lenny would be arriving soon. Marly went to check on dinner and the others sat down in the living room, discussing the game plan for tomorrow. At that moment, the doorbell sounded, and Seth got up and answered it. There stood Lenny, with a duffel bag in his hand, looking at the group. His eyes landed on Marly, who was walking into the living room.

Holding up the bag, he said, "I got what I need. I can get to work now."

"After dinner, Lenny. Let's have a meal together," said Marly, not wanting to think about what he was going to do next. It was all getting very real.

CHAPTER 28

Ethan and Brittany returned to his apartment, and they had discussed the trip to Tennessee. Ethan asked Brittany to look at some hotels online with him in the Memphis area and he would book it with the airline tickets. Ethan wanted Brittany to feel as if she was a part of the process. They sat at the computer, looking at five-star hotels when Brittany spoke.

"I don't have to stay in a fancy place, Ethan. Something smaller is fine," she said.

"I know that, Brit, but Mr. Kennedy always wants me to stay in luxury hotels and enjoy the amenities they offer when I'm traveling for him. Believe me, he would be upset if we stayed at a motel," explained Ethan.

"Okay, then, look at this one," she said, pointing to the River Inn of Harbor Town.

"That looks swanky, and it's close to downtown and Beale Street. We'll want to take in those sights and eat BBQ, for which they are famous," said Ethan. He was looking forward to this trip more than he realized because Brit was going to be with him. Would this be the beginning of a relationship for them again?

"I must say, I don't think I've ever stayed in anything this posh," said Brittany, smiling at Ethan.

"Then that's the one we are going to stay in," he said, smiling at her. Going to his computer he quickly booked their flight and hotel reservations. "Done and done."

"That was quick," said Brittany. "I can go to my room while you do the rest of your work."

"I have a few things to do but it shouldn't take long. Then, we can talk about going to dinner," said Ethan.

"I do know how to cook, Ethan, remember? We don't have to go out all of the time," said Brittany.

"I know but we really haven't done any grocery shopping since you've been here. Let's plan on doing that when we get back, okay?" he asked.

"Sounds like a plan," she said, going into the guest room.

Ethan sat down at his computer and started searching the deed database for any properties owned by Oliver Anderson or Randolph Vinson, the name Mr. Kennedy had mentioned in passing. Nothing other than the Germantown property came up when he searched Oliver Anderson, but a sealed file came up with the name Randolph Vinson. Ethan tried to hack into the file but wasn't having any luck. Not wanting to get Mr. Kennedy's hopes up, he placed a call to his friend, Davis Berg. Davis was a much better hacker than Ethan and he wasn't afraid to admit it.

"Hello," answered Davis, the clacking of keyboard keys in the background.

"Hi Davis, Ethan here," he said.

"What's going on?" asked Davis, stopping his work to give Ethan his full attention.

"I was doing some research on a property, but I can't hack the file. Why it's sealed, I have no idea," said Ethan.

"Probably because the owner doesn't want you to know where it is," laughed Davis. "You want me to give it a go?"

"Yes, if you would," said Ethan, giving him the name of the property owner.

"Hold on a second," said Davis.

"You think you can get it that fast? I probably should call you back or better yet, you call me when you access it," said Ethan.

Davis chuckled a little and said, "I can call you back or give it to you now."

"What? You got it already?" asked Ethan, incredulously. "You are going to have to give me some more training, my friend."

"Anytime, Ethan. That person has a mountain cabin outside of Gatlinburg, Tennessee. There are two names on the deed, Anderson and Vinson. I'll send you the address. Anything else I can do for you?"

"No, but thanks for making me feel very inadequate," said Ethan, sheepishly.

"Anytime, that's what friends are for," Davis said, ending the call.

Ethan sat there, mulling over the information. Oliver Anderson, Randolph Vinson or whoever he really is was quite good at covering up his tracks. Probably in their day, hackers didn't even exist so they didn't know that anything could be found in today's society. He thought about holding on to the information but knew that Mr. Kennedy would not be pleased. He picked up his phone and called.

"Hello Ethan," said Franklin. "Did you need something?"

"Yes, Mr. Kennedy. When you mentioned the other name when speaking about Oliver Anderson, I remembered it and searched for any other properties he may own. I found one," said Ethan.

"Really? Where is it?" asked Franklin, excitement in his voice.

"It's a cabin located near Gatlinburg, Tennessee. Davis actually helped me with opening the file and he is sending the address to me," said Ethan.

"Excellent, Ethan! Send the address to me when you receive it and I will handle it from here. I'll arrange for someone to search the cabin. Do you know if anyone lives in it?" Franklin asked.

"No," said Ethan, "wait, just a moment. I'm getting an email from Davis."

After a few minutes, Ethan spoke, "It is on the Airbnb site and is rented most of the time except for a few weeks a year. It currently is rented until the end of the month and then there is a week in between the next rental agreement. That could be our window."

"Yes, perfect. Send that information to me, Ethan, and again, a job well done. I'm very proud of your initiative. And thank Davis as well," said Franklin, ending the call.

Well, well, well, Oliver. You can run, but you can't hide. I'll find what I'm looking for and do what I have to do to get it, Franklin thought.

The group had a great dinner. The ribs were fall off the bone tender and the BBQ sauce perfect, not too sour, not too sweet. The sides were perfect, and everyone was groaning by the time they finished.

"We'll have dessert later," said Kate, looking around the table. "I can tell no one will be able to appreciate my hard work right now!"

After the laughter subsided, they all agreed. Kate and Lucy volunteered for kitchen duty while the men and Marly went down to the basement.

Lenny looked around and commented, "This looks like a regular den. I think it's good enough to fool most people, but, we aren't dealing with most people. I still think the traps are a good move."

"We agree, Lenny," said Seth. "Can we help you in any way?"

"Probably, let's get in here and see what we have. Marly, is there anything you want to keep, because once the charges are set, you won't be able to take anything," said Lenny, looking at her.

She was silent for a few minutes, and then spoke, "No, I've taken everything out of there that I think is important. You guys can look more if you want to, but I'm not interested in finding anything else."

Lenny could tell this was upsetting to her and suggested that she return upstairs. "There isn't anything else you can do, Marly."

"Thanks, I think I will," said Marly and she left them, joining Kate and Lucy upstairs.

"This has really upset Marly," said Seth as he and Rafe stood with Lenny.

"It's obvious, but her whole life has been turned upside down. I think the quicker we can get this back together, the better it will be for her," said Lenny, picking up the duffel bag and squeezing through the hole in the wall. Seth and Rafe followed.

"Did they just check this desk, table, file cabinets and computer?" asked Lenny.

"I think so," said Seth. "They didn't see anything else to check."

"I wonder," said Lenny aloud. He walked over to the back wall and started tapping on it. It seemed okay until he got to one place that sounded dull when tapped. "Seth, can you punch a hole in this wall?"

Seth grabbed a hammer and started tapping and when the drywall broke through, there was a wooden box in a small niche. He pulled the box out, looking at the other two men.

"Look in it," said Lenny.

"Shouldn't it be Marly that looks inside?" asked Seth.

"Just make sure it isn't something that will hurt her," said Lenny.

Rafe nodded at Seth, and he slowly opened the box. Inside was a brooch, very intricate and covered in precious stones, the clarity of them denying they were fake. A note was underneath it. Lenny reached in and picked up the brooch, turning it over in his hand. Inscribed was the message, *'I'll love you forever, Giselle. Always yours, Randolph'*

"Randolph? Who's Randolph?" asked Rafe.

"Who knows? But, Marly needs to open the note. Maybe there is an explanation," said Seth and both men agreed.

Seth went to the bottom of the stairs and called out, "Marly, can you please come down here?"

They waited a few minutes and then Marly appeared, a question in her eyes. She saw the three of them standing there and Seth handed her the box. She opened it and saw the beautiful piece of jewelry and picked it up, turning it over in her hand. She then saw the inscription and looked puzzled. There was a note below it and Marly sat the box down and picked up the note, almost afraid to open it, for fear that it would be something else in her past that she didn't want to know.

Slowly sitting down, she unfolded the sheet of paper, smelling the faint scent of an old perfume, and slowly read the message within.

CHAPTER 29

'My dearest Randolph,

Things are getting very dangerous as the Duke is suspicious of our relationship. I know that you would erase my existence, but I don't want you to. If you made me disappear, I may never be able to find you again. Do you understand that I love you more than my life? Hold onto my brooch and one day I will return for it. Then we can be together, my love.'

Giselle Armenti

Marly asked the question they all did, "Who is Randolph?"

"Maybe there is something in those things you found," said Lenny.

Seth looked at Marly and asked, "Do you think your grandfather went by another name? Or maybe Oliver Anderson wasn't his given name?"

"Anything is possible, I'm finding out, Seth," said Marly. "I feel so betrayed by my past. Maybe I can find something on Giselle Armenti."

"That would be a good place to start," said Lenny. "I don't think there are any other hidden areas, but we'll check. Why don't you let Kate and Lucy help you research this person?"

Marly slowly walked back upstairs, wondering what she would learn next.

Lucy and Kate saw Marly appear with a box in her hand.

"What's that, Marly?" asked Lucy.

Marly handed it to her and Lucy opened it. "Wow, that is gorgeous! It's quite real, you know."

"Yes, I know," she said as she handed the letter to Kate. She and Lucy read it together.

"Oh my gosh, do you think she and your grandfather were in love with one another?" asked Lucy.

Kate picked up the brooch and saw the inscription and said, "Who is Randolph?"

"I don't know but we need to find out. Kate, would you try to find anything out about this Giselle woman and Lucy, you and I will look for anything with the name Randolph on it."

Kate went to the computer and Lucy and Marly went upstairs to look through the papers in the bin.

Kate searched for Giselle Armenti and didn't find anything. She didn't know what else to look for but then thought maybe Randolph was an alias for Oliver Anderson. She researched his name and oddly, the cabin in Gatlinburg didn't come up with his name only. Kate got a little excited and hopeful, going to look at deeds. She put in the address of the cabin which she still had in her phone from their girl trip, and she found a sealed file. She put in her attorney credentials and was given an access code. She entered it and the deed displayed on the screen. The cabin belonged to Randolph Vinson and Oliver Anderson.

"Marly! Lucy! Come here," she called out.

They both hurried down the stairs, seeing Kate at the computer.

"What is it, Kate?" asked Marly.

"I couldn't find anything on Giselle Armenti, but I decided to look for the properties under your grandfather's name. The cabin wasn't one of them, so I accessed the deed, and it is in the name of Randolph Vinson and your grandfather as secondary. Did you know that?" asked Kate.

"No...I absolutely did not know that," said Marly. "I never looked at the deed, and just assumed it was his."

"The deed file was sealed but I opened it with my attorney credentials and that's when I found his name. Since it was sealed, you were probably not meant to know about his other name," said Kate.

"Wow, who would have known your grandfather had a secret life?" asked Lucy rhetorically.

"Obviously no one, except the Andersons, and I doubt they knew the extent of it. I guess that Franklin Kennedy knows who they are and that's why he is so anxious to find this information. But why?" asked Marly aloud.

Kate sat there and thought, why as well. She typed in Randolph Vinson, and several entries populated the screen. She read through them quickly and found one that may be her grandfather. "Marly, do you want to see this?" she asked, turning the screen.

Randolph Vinson, a millionaire financier, was seen around Denver with Lady Giselle visiting from Europe, despite her being married to Duke Ramondo Breviat. It was becoming the scandal of the seventies as they attend all of the social events of the season.

"Maybe my grandfather was Randolph Vinson. I just can't think about this anymore tonight. I'm going to bed, if you don't mind," said Marly.

"Of course not, go on. We'll be up later. The guys might need something. See you in the morning," said Kate.

"We love you, Marly," said Lucy, hugging her friend before she disappeared upstairs.

After Marly left the room, Kate looked at Lucy and said, "I'm worried about her, Lucy. This has all been so emotionally draining for her and now all of this secretive information is coming to light. Plus, who knows what could happen with the Kennedy fellow."

"I know, I don't want to leave Wednesday, but I feel like I need to," said Lucy, torn.

"I don't have to go," said Kate. "I can stay with her and get her through whatever this is and Lucy...what if something is hidden at the cabin? You can bet Franklin Kennedy is researching too and if he finds that property, he may go there to search."

"You're right, Kate. Let's go down to the basement and talk to the guys. We need to figure something out before morning," said Lucy as they crept down the basement stairs.

Marly lay in the darkness of her grandfather's room trying to make sense of everything. Never in a million years would she have thought that her life was filled with deep, dark secrets and that she was probably not meant to ever find out about them. For the first time in a long time, she was unsure as to what to do. Everyone was leaving the day after tomorrow and then she would be alone and that scared her. Maybe she should call Marc and let him know what is happening. She was sure that he would come and help her, even though they were no longer seeing each other. She dismissed that thought almost as soon as she thought of it. No need in getting him involved, especially since Lenny was here too. That was like mixing oil and water. She thought about what Lenny was doing for her. He didn't have to, or take this job of watching her house, or even helping in the basement. She could tell that he was changed since Raven's death. She knew she could never repay him for what he was doing for her now. She whispered in the darkness, "Poppa, what have you done? What is hidden from me and where should I look? Help me, Poppa, please."

Exhausted from the emotional turmoil she was going through, Marly fell into a deep, dreamless sleep.

"Do you feel up to staying, Katie?" asked Seth, after hearing all of the information they had uncovered.

"I am doing good, Seth, and I don't have another follow up appointment for six months. I just don't feel as if I can leave Marly alone," said Kate, looking around at the others.

Rafe spoke up, "Lucy, do you want to stay as well? I can cover things back home."

"I want to, but I also have some things I need to take care of at the winery. I was thinking I could fly home as planned and then meet Kate and Marly in Gatlinburg to search the cabin. I think that needs to be done too, before Franklin Kennedy finds out about it," said Lucy.

"I agree," said Kate, "and I will speak to Marly in the morning to figure out when we can do that. I know she keeps it rented a lot when she is not using it."

Lenny was working silently as the others discussed their options.

"Done," said Lenny, picking up the remaining supplies and taking off his gloves, putting everything back in the duffel bag.

Lucy looked at him and said, "What do you think, Lenny? You are in this with us."

Surprised that Lucy asked the question, Lenny said, "I think Marly does need someone with her. She has found out a lot about her life and is probably on an emotional roller coaster. I'll be around, but I have to keep up appearances surveilling her house. It sounds like you have thought of everything that needs to be done. I'll do what I can."

"So, Seth, are you okay with me staying?" asked Kate, looking at only him.

"Of course, Katie, I love you and I love Marly. Whatever we can do to get her through this, I'm all for it. You just better give daily updates!" said Seth with a grin.

"It's settled then," said Lucy. "Lenny, you said everything is done. Can we start putting this room together tomorrow?"

"Yeah, it's ready. The desk, file cabinets and the computer are all wired. If someone tries to open or insert anything, it is set to explode. Not a lethal explosion but it will hurt. I also wired the space in the wall, just in case someone does tap around, looking for hidden places," said Lenny.

"Perfect," said Lucy. "We'll all help tomorrow and make a quick day of it. Then, we can go out for a nice dinner before we have to leave town."

"Sounds like a good plan, Lucy," said Rafe, putting his arm around her and hugging her close. He knew that she wanted to stay but she also is one of the hardest working people he knew, and she didn't want to shirk her duties at the winery. He admired that about her, and it made him love her even more.

"I'm headed to my motel," said Lenny. "I have to report to my employer. Hope you guys had a good golf game."

Everyone laughed at that and went upstairs, saying goodnight to Lenny and sitting in the living room just to decompress. A lot of decisions had been made and now to execute them.

CHAPTER 30

Lenny got back to his hotel and took a shower, after storing the duffel bag in a compartment in his SUV. He sat down and called Franklin Kennedy.

"Hello Lenny," he said.

"Hello Mr. Kennedy, sorry for the late call. I followed the group to lunch, and on the way back, the Anderson woman got out at an office building. They left but she didn't go with them. I stayed on her location, to determine who she was seeing. Apparently, she had a meeting with a financial advisor. The guy took her home."

"Did you find out his name? I just wonder what type of financial advising he does," said Franklin, curious.

"The name on the door was J.T. Fielding but I didn't hang around inside. Didn't want to arouse suspicion," said Lenny, giving the content that was Marly approved.

"Excellent work, Lenny," said Franklin.

Lenny continued, "I followed them back to the house and she went in. Her friends were at the house, and they stayed in, and I left when the lights went out. I'll go back before dawn."

Franklin was very impressed with Lenny and said, "I admire your conscientiousness, Lenny. You can get some rest as I doubt they will be up at dawn!" He chuckled aloud.

"I understand, but I believe in doing my best," said Lenny, laying it on thick.

"I am very pleased with you, Lenny. Keep up the good work. I also may need you to do another job for me. I'll give you the details later, but it is located in Tennessee as well," said Franklin, thinking he could send Lenny to the cabin in Gatlinburg.

Not wanting to appear overly eager, Lenny merely said, "Let's see how this goes, shall we?"

"Yes of course, we'll talk about it after this coming weekend," said Franklin, ending the call.

From his last comment, Lenny figured that Kennedy wanted to hire him to search Marly's cabin. That would be perfect because he wouldn't worry about someone hurting her. Everything seemed to be falling in place, he thought, as he retired for the night.

Lucinda, Thomas, and Tom sat at the dining table, eating potato soup with soft garlic knots that Lucinda had made earlier.

"This is delicious, Hon," said Thomas. "I had a heavy lunch today, so this is perfect."

"It is good, Mom, and easy to eat," said Tom, his mouth sore from his injuries as well as the dentist.

"What did Laramore say?" asked Thomas, as he continued eating.

Tom let his mom take the conversation and she filled her husband in. "He said the tooth replacement may be ready in a day or two, but he prepped Tom's mouth for it today."

"Yeah, you better watch out, Dad. Mom assisted Dr. Laramore, and he said she was a great assistant," said Tom, teasing his mom.

She blushed and said, "He was just being nice, Tom. I could never do that type of work."

"Well, I'm glad he got you in. Lord knows we have spent a lot of money in his office, and he should remember that," said Thomas.

"They worked us right in, Thomas," said Lucinda, thinking it always came down to money where her husband was concerned.

They quietly finished their dinner and Lucinda announced she had chocolate pudding for dessert when anyone wanted some.

"Thanks Mom, I should be able to eat that too," Tom smiled at his mother. He might get aggravated at her sometimes, but she did take good care of him.

Ethan and Brittany went to dinner and came back to the apartment. They decided they would watch another movie and this time, Ethan chose Ford vs. Ferrari. About the middle of the movie, Brittany made popcorn, and they shared it in the darkened living room. Brittany was watching the movie but thinking about Ethan. He was acting as if they were a couple again, talking about grocery shopping when they got back from this trip and it made her happy. She had hesitated to reach out to him after the way she left, but now, she was glad that she had. She knew that he would help her, and being here with him had ignited some of the feelings she previously shared with him. When their fingers touched as they both reached for popcorn, she took his hand in hers and entwined their fingers. She held his hand briefly and then let go, getting some more popcorn.

"Oh, so that is how you distract me to get popcorn? No fair!" Ethan laughed, enjoying her playfulness.

"A girl's gotta do what a girl's gotta do," she said, laughing with him.

They finished the movie, and Brittany was surprised that she really enjoyed it.

"That movie was really good," she said. "I wasn't sure when you suggested it."

"It had great reviews. I didn't get a chance to see it at the theater," said Ethan. "I enjoyed it too."

They went into the kitchen to clean up and Ethan turned her to him. Looking into her eyes, he didn't say anything at first.

"Brit, I can't lie and say you didn't hurt me when you left. But, having you here now, I feel happy again. I hope that we can start over and build our relationship, if you want that too," Ethan said.

Putting her arms around his neck, she leaned in and kissed him softly on the lips, her breathing shallow, "Ethan, I'm so sorry I hurt you. I made a mistake. I am happy here with you and I'm ready to start over. I promise, I'll make it up to you."

Smiling, Ethan kissed her deeply and said, "You already have, Brit, you already have."

After a few minutes, she pulled away from him.

"Okay, we better stop while we can," she said.

"I agree. I want it to be perfect when we move forward and maybe this weekend will be the right time," he said, kissing her again and letting her go.

She sighed but knew he was right. They would wait...for now.

Marly woke up to thudding sounds and for a moment was disoriented. Realizing that the guys must be at work in the basement, she hurried up and got dressed. She needed to make some breakfast for everyone. Going downstairs, she smelled something baking. Rounding the corner, she saw Lucy and Kate in the kitchen, with breakfast already underway.

"What is going on here? I'm supposed to be the host, not the guest," said Marly, laughing.

"Well sleepyhead, you have to get up earlier if you are going to feed us," said Lucy, pointing to the clock. "It's 8:30 a.m. little lady!"

"Oh my gosh, I haven't slept that late in forever!" said Marly, surprised.

Kate spoke up, "Marly, you were exhausted, physically, mentally and emotionally. Your body took over."

"I guess you're right," agreed Marly. "So, what can I do?"

"I'm making sausage gravy and there are biscuits in the oven. You can fix some mimosas and Kate, watch the grits," Lucy ordered everyone. It felt good to be together.

"We also need to talk, Marly," said Kate.

Not liking the sound of that, Marly asked, "What about?"

Lucy and Kate told her about their plans and that the men agreed. Marly was overwhelmed at the support her friends were giving her.

"Wow, Kate, are you sure? I mean, I would love to have you here, both of you, but I know that you have a life too," said Marly.

"I just have a few things to do and then I thought we would fly to the cabin and search it," said Lucy.

"I would imagine that Franklin Kennedy is also researching your grandfather and chances are, he has found out about the cabin," said Kate.

"You are probably right," said Marly. "It's rented for the next couple of weeks, but he would probably know that, especially if they look at the Airbnb site. But, I can reach out to renters and put them in another cabin to give us time to get there first."

"Would you be able to do that, Marly?" asked Kate, thinking it might not be that easy.

"I'll make some calls. I have friends in that area that rent their cabins too. I recall these people wanted something closer to town so I'll try to accommodate them," said Marly, already thinking of who she could call.

"But breakfast first!" said Lucy. "Kate, go get the guys and we'll eat."

After everyone was reassembled in the kitchen, they ate the delicious breakfast, talked and laughed and then discussed some of the things that needed to happen.

"We are going to finish by lunchtime," said Seth. "After that, we can spend the afternoon doing something fun."

"Did Lenny get everything done last night?" asked Marly. "I sort of flaked out on you guys."

"Yep, it's all done, and we have the dry wall up. We were starting to tape and mud when breakfast was announced, and we were ready for that!" said Rafe. "It was delicious, ladies."

"We'll help with the wallpaper when you get to that part," said Lucy.

"I found a plaid tablecloth upstairs too, Lucy, that we can use on that sideboard," said Marly.

"Sounds like everything is falling into place,"

said Kate, hoping that were true.

CHAPTER 31

Thomas had an early meeting and left before breakfast. Lucinda was making oatmeal when Tom limped into the kitchen.

"Morning, Mom," he said, groaning a bit as he sat.

"Oh Tom, what can I do to help you?" Lucinda asked.

"You're doing it Mom, and thanks," he said, glad to be home for the moment. He wasn't sure he wanted to go back to New York City.

Lucinda broached the subject of his sister, "I got a text from Cindy this morning. She wanted to check on you."

"That was nice of her," he said, surprised.

"She is off tomorrow and wants to come see you," Lucinda said quickly.

"Oh Mom, I don't know if that's a good idea. She and I haven't really spoken in a while, and we had that fight a couple of years ago about my girlfriend. I don't need any stress," he said.

"I know, Tom, I told her that and she agreed. But, she said she wanted to see you and was sorry she hadn't communicated with you," said his mother, trying to fix things between her only two children. She never considered Marly one of her children.

Lucinda put a bowl of oatmeal with milk and sugar in front of him. "Do you want some toast?"

"I'll try some, Mom," he said, deciding that the discussion about Cindy was done. He would see what she had to say and truthfully, he didn't feel much like talking.

Ethan's phone pinged and he looked at it. A text from Mr. Kennedy. NOT FEELING WELL. STAY HOME TODAY. Well, that opened up his day. Maybe he would take Brit shopping for a cocktail dress for a fancy dinner on the town while there were in Memphis. But, he would also review his notes about Marly Anderson and see if there was anything else he could do to persuade her to acquiesce to Mr. Kennedy's request. She seemed like a nice person but that didn't matter to Mr. Kennedy. When he wanted something, he didn't let anything, or anyone stand in his way.

He hadn't heard Brit stirring and he decided to let her sleep. It was late when the movie was over and then they had that little interlude in the kitchen. He felt happier than he had in a very long time. He knew he was probably considered weak, letting her back into his life so quickly, but he loved her. That hadn't changed. He was willing to forgive and forget if it meant having her back in his life. He hummed to himself as he brewed a cup of coffee, looking forward to the trip.

Franklin Kennedy was feeling very frail today. He rarely took a day for himself, but he didn't want to deal with anything. He instructed Victor that he wanted no visitors, no exceptions and he turned off his phone. After he ate a meager amount of his breakfast and sent it back, he lay back in his leather recliner in the library. His thoughts went to Giselle. Where was she? He was certain that Oliver Anderson had helped her to disappear. Not when he was trying to seduce her those many years ago but later. He had seen the articles in the Denver Chronicle back then, however, no matter what people thought, Giselle would never betray him. But, he had to admit, she was different when they returned to Europe. She was listless and did not participate in any of the activities she previously enjoyed. That's when we found out she was pregnant! I was over the moon about it, but Giselle was very sick and not excited. I had attributed her lack of enthusiasm to her physical ailments at the time. When she began to feel better, I could see more of the old Giselle, a spark in her eyes, a sweet smile on her lips. And then she was gone, disappeared. Of course, I was frantic and searched everywhere. I could find no trace of her. After traveling back to America, I visited with Oliver. He was just as distressed as I was with her disappearance. That's when we first began the Crimson Veil, to search for Giselle. But, we became very skilled at it and started helping others erase their pasts. It was quite lucrative, but we never found any trace of Giselle. Was his concern all an act? Did he know where she was all those years and what about my child? I have to find out if he was involved and if there is any evidence to help me find what happened to her. The nights he dreamed of her, of finding her dead, haunted him and he was so tired.

Marly called Bob and Judy Thornton, friends in Gatlinburg that had a cabin they rented on Airbnb.

"Hello?" answered Judy.

"Judy, this is Marly Anderson. How are you?" she said.

"Marly, it's so good to hear from you. We are doing well," said Judy.

Marly took a deep breath and crossed her fingers, "Judy, I was wondering if your cabin in Gatlinburg is rented for the next couple of weeks."

"It was, but we got a cancellation of the reservation today. I was going to make it available again," said Judy. "Why?"

"I have some renters coming Sunday and I forgot I had given my friends permission to use it. I was looking for a place to put my Airbnb renters. They wanted something closer to town which your cabin fits the bill. Would you be willing to let me switch my clients to your cabin, for your full fee of course? It would be a great favor to me," said Marly, hoping that the convenience of not having to repost it would appeal to them.

"Hold on a minute, Marly," said Judy. Marly could hear her muffled conversation with Bob. She returned to the call and said, "That would be great for us, Marly."

"Thank you Judy and Bob too," laughed Marly. "I'll contact my renters and give them your address. I think it will work out better for them and our cabins are about the same size, although I think yours is bigger."

"Thanks Marly, should we make any changes on Airbnb?" asked Judy.

"I don't think so. Both cabins will be occupied, so I don't think that will be a problem," said Marly. "I'll check and if so, I'll let you know."

"Great," said Judy. "Are you still selling books?"

"No, I closed the bookstore. With all of the digital options out there, I wasn't breaking even," admitted Marly.

"Oh, I'm sorry to hear that. We enjoyed it last year when we took our granddaughters there. They loved the story time," said Judy.

"I appreciate that, Judy. Oh, I've got another call coming in. Thanks again and send me your total fees and I'll send you the money," said Marly.

"Will do, Marly. Take care," said Judy, disconnecting the call.

"Whew, that was easier than I thought," said Marly to Lucy and Kate.

"Sounds like it," said Kate.

"How long do you need to be in Texas before you travel again, Lucy?" asked Marly, wanting to get to the cabin as soon as possible.

"I think I need about four days...we travel Wednesday, I can take care of my items by Sunday so I think I could meet y'all in Gatlinburg on Monday evening," said Lucy, thinking about all that she wanted to do when she got back to Blanco.

"I'd say that will work out great," said Marly. "I actually have a few things I want to do too. For one thing, I want to go see the fake Andersons."

Lucy and Kate looked at each other and then at Marly, "Are you sure you want to do that?" asked Kate.

"Yes, I do. I want them to know that they can go back to using their real names and that I will take them to court if I have to," said Marly. "They have been paid quite well to pretend to be related to me and I want to end our association."

"Good for you, Marly," said Lucy. "I don't blame you. Kate, you can go with her for moral support and step in if needed. Who knows how they will react when you approach them, Marly."

"True, but at this point, I don't really care. I decided last night that I was going to get my life in order. I wasn't going to share this with you two yet, but we never keep secrets. I spoke to Jerry yesterday about looking into selling my house here," said Marly.

"What? Are you thinking of moving?" asked Kate and Lucy clapped her hands.

"I was thinking that after all that has happened and no telling what I'm going to discover, I don't feel the same about this place as I did before. I don't know where I'll move but I don't think I would be opposed to living in Texas. I have some very good friends that live there, and I know I would be happy," said Marly.

Kate and Lucy both jumped up and hugged Marly.

"This is exciting, Marly," said Lucy.

"It really is," said Kate. "Could this mean we've gone full circle?"

"I don't know yet, girls," said Marly, smiling broadly, "but when I do make a decision, you two will be the first to know."

Seth's voice wafted up the stairs, "Hey, come down here!"

The three friends walked down the stairs into the basement. There was a wall, with striped wallpaper and a television mounted on it. The way everything was arranged, it looked like it had been that way for years. The tablecloth that Marly had found was on the sideboard and the guys had arranged the small fridge and snacks on it.

"This looks great, y'all," said Lucy. "Well done!"

"I totally agree," said Kate, taking in everything. "I love that picture on this wall."

"I never saw that picture before," said Marly, walking over to it, taking down the picture of a beautiful woman. Turning it over, she saw the handwriting and the message that read, *I think of you often and miss you more. I pray you found happiness. Giselle.*

Marly looked at her friends. "Another piece of the puzzle."

CHAPTER 32

Since the guys had completed the basement, they all decided to have a nice lunch and check out some of the local sights. They were going to Southern Hands restaurant to try out the local southern cuisine. They got ready and all got in Marly's SUV. As they pulled around the corner, Marly saw Lenny's car down the street.

"Pull in behind him, Seth, and I'll see if he wants to join us."

Seth pulled over and Marly got out of the vehicle.

Lenny's work was done and now all he had to do was finish out his obligation to Franklin Kennedy. As he sat down the street, he wasn't really paying attention to the house but thinking about the woman inside. He had been surprised to hear that she and Marc Rivers were no longer seeing each other. That should have made him happy, but somehow it didn't. Although someone like Marly would be great to have in your life, he didn't think that he had a chance. Their relationship hadn't started out on a good note, with him kidnapping her and serving her up to a crazy killer...but thankfully, in the end, Marly had been the bigger person. If not for her, he would be in prison, and his beloved cabin a mere memory. He owed her his life, and this small gesture was the least he could do for her. He figured that the job Kennedy wanted him for was to search her mountain cabin. He would have to let her know that Kennedy knew about it. Maybe she could beat him to it. He saw movement behind him and realized it was Marly's SUV. She appeared at his window, grinning.

"Sorry to sneak up on you, but what kind of detective are you?" she laughed.

He grinned back and said, "I'm not a detective...I'm a professional stalker."

"Not very professional either!" she said. "We're going to lunch, you want to join us?"

He thought about it but said, "Nah, I better just follow you guys. My employer seems to be a bit paranoid, and he might be having me followed!"

They both laughed but Lenny thought it might be the case. Better to be safe than found out.

"Okay, but if you change your mind, you'll know where we are!" she said happily as she sprinted back to the car, and it pulled out.

Starting up his SUV, he followed them to the Hickory Ridge Mall area, where the restaurant must be located. They all got out of the vehicle and went inside the Southern Hands restaurant, and he sat there, watching them. Picking up his phone, he checked in.

"Hello Lenny," said Franklin, his voice sounding weak, even to himself.

"Mr. Kennedy, are you okay?" asked Lenny, noticing his usual strong response was missing.

"Just a bit under the weather. What's happening?" he asked.

"It's been quiet, but they all just left together for lunch, I assume, since I followed them to a restaurant in Memphis," he reported.

"Probably their last hurrah before they leave town," mused Franklin. "Keep up the good work," he said as he ended the call. He really was very tired.

Lenny sat there and thought about joining Marly and her friends but in the end, he decided against it. This was their last day together and although he had helped them, he was not a part of their group. Sadly, that was very apparent to him.

Ethan finished up his coffee and heard Brit's door open. She came out and headed directly to the kitchen.

"Hmm, I thought I smelled coffee," she said.

Holding up his empty cup, Ethan said, "Yes, and it's delicious."

Brewing a cup, she looked at him and smiled.

"Are you going to the Kennedy Estate this morning?" she asked, picking up her cup and sipping the hot liquid.

"Not today," he said. "Mr. Kennedy is feeling a bit under the weather and told me not to come in. I have already finished my tasks for today and thought maybe we could go shopping for a fancy dress for a fancy dinner on our trip."

"You need a fancy dress?" she teased him.

He laughed out loud and said, "Yes, what color do you think?"

She pretended to think about it and finally said, "Maybe something in pink? But not short, because, you know, your knobby knees."

"Very funny, Brit," he said, feigning hurt feelings and then they both were laughing. It was going to be a fun day together.

Lunch was a fun affair, with much laughing and joking, and retelling stories, mostly about the girls' adventures.

"This one doesn't seem to be shaping up any better than the last few," said Lucy.

"I admit that when we are together, we are getting more and more involved in hazardous situations," said Marly. "But, thankfully, we always seem to land on our feet!"

Kate raised her glass of sweet tea and said, "To friends who have feline characteristics, nine lives and landing on our feet!"

Everyone laughed at that, all of them raising their glasses and not seeing the patrons at nearby tables smiling at them. It was obvious they were having a great time together.

They decided to play miniature golf and Seth drove them to the Putt-Putt Fun Center and they spent the afternoon, talking, bragging on their shots, and finally crowning Rafe the winner.

"Thank you, one and all," he said, bowing to the group.

"You were just lucky, Rafe," said Seth. "I almost made that last hole in one."

"In your dreams, brother-in-law," said Rafe, laughing.

The girls watched this masculine display until Lucy said, "We let you win."

That started up another banal conversation as they made their way to the car. It had been a wonderful afternoon together and the evening was a relaxing one. No one was hungry after the large meal earlier, so they snacked and tried out the basement media room. They watched a couple of movies and before they knew it, it was 10:00 p.m.

"I hate to be a spoilsport, but we have to get to the airport in the morning," said Seth.

"I know," said Marly, "I'm sure going to hate to see you go."

Lucy spoke up, "We hate to go, but Kate is staying, and I will see you guys in Gatlinburg on Monday evening. I'll get my flight scheduled and send you the information while we are waiting at the airport."

"True, and hopefully we will have all of this behind us soon. Rafe and Seth, thank you so much for all you have done. I don't know what I would have done without you," said Marly, sincerely,

"You are welcome, Marly," said Seth. "You're family to us."

"Glad to do it, Marly," said Rafe, "and besides, we got a few days of vacation."

"Some vacation," said Marly. "The next one will be better, I'm sure."

They all went upstairs and said goodnight, each to their own rooms.

Wednesday morning Marly hurried downstairs to find Lucy in the kitchen, toasting bagels.

"I thought I would beat you down here this morning," said Marly.

"I knew you would try," said Lucy, smiling at her friend. "We decided we would just eat light before we traveled. We'll have something in San Antonio before we drive to the vineyard."

"I'm going to miss all of you," said Marly. "It has really seemed like I had a family around me."

"You do, Marly. A blood relationship doesn't always make you family. We chose to love each other and be there for one another...that's family," said Lucy.

"You are absolutely right, Lucy," said Marly, giving her a quick hug. The sounds in the stairway indicated the others were coming down to join them.

After a light breakfast and some juice, the guys loaded up the rental, taking Lucy's bags too.

"Guess this is it," said Seth, wrapping his arms around Kate. He was glad she was staying but was going to miss her. He still worried about her recovery, but he was glad to witness that she was doing so well.

Kate held him for a few moments and then kissed him soundly. "There, that should hold you until I see you in a week or so."

"Don't you worry, Kate," said Lucy. "I'll keep him so busy he won't have time to miss you!"

"Don't I know it," said Seth, groaning aloud.

Rafe walked over to Marly and hugged her tight. "Call us if anything, and I mean, anything happens."

"I promise, I will. We will be careful," said Marly.

"I'll make sure of that," assured Kate to the others.

Lucy, Seth, and Rafe got into the car and drove off, waving goodbye. Kate and Marly went back into the house.

"Seems quiet now, doesn't it?" said Marly.

"Yes, but it probably won't last long," said Kate. Marly agreed.

CHAPTER 33

Franklin Kennedy was feeling much better today. He decided that he needed to get out more and eat better. Victor always brought nourishing meals, but Franklin wasn't always good at eating them. He had a mission ahead and he couldn't afford not to be in good form. He was expecting an update from Lenny Crocker this morning, confirming that Ms. Anderson's house guests had departed. Ethan will be leaving tomorrow and hopefully, he can persuade Ms. Anderson to allow a search. He wasn't very optimistic about it, but his patience was wearing thin. At that moment, Victor walked in silently with his breakfast tray.

"Good morning, sir, I hope you are feeling better today," said Victor as he sat down the tray.

"Yes, I am, Victor. I have new resolve as well. You work hard to take care of me, and I have to do my part. I intend to eat my meals and get my strength back. I have a lot left to do in this life," said Franklin.

"I'm pleased to hear it sir," said Victor. "Do you have any appointments today?"

"Ethan will be here sometime this morning but nothing else is scheduled. I think I may have Samson take me out this afternoon, get some fresh air," said Franklin.

"Excellent, sir," said Victor. "I will alert him to expect your summons."

"Thank you, Victor," said Franklin, dismissing him.

Removing the cloche, he saw his breakfast, and taking a deep breath, began eating.

Ethan was dressed and ready to go to the Kennedy Estate. Brittany was sitting at the bar, watching him gather his things.

"Will you be okay, here alone?" asked Ethan, worried about leaving her.

"Of course, Ethan. I can't go to work with you every day. Besides, I want to look for a job myself," said Brittany.

"You don't have to go to work right away, Brit," he said, thinking about the bruises that were fading but still evident.

"I know, I know, but I want to see what is out there. I want to contribute," she said, smiling at Ethan. "And buy my own clothes."

"I don't mind treating you, you know that," said Ethan.

"I love the dress we got yesterday. It is beautiful," said Brittany, remembering how good the sparkling pink sheath fit her slim body. Ethan was almost breathless when she modeled it for him.

"I love it too and can't wait to take you out in it," said Ethan. "But right now, I better get to Mr. Kennedy. He doesn't like anyone to be tardy."

"Tell him I said hello," said Brittany, giving him a quick kiss goodbye.

"Feel free to use the computer for your job search," said Ethan, rushing out the door.

Lucinda was cleaning up the dishes from breakfast after Thomas left for work. Tom was in the living room, watching a game show. As she was finishing up, a knock came at the back door. Walking over to it, Lucinda saw her daughter Cindy standing there.

Opening the door and smiling brightly, she said, "Good morning, Cindy! It's so good to see you."

Cindy came in and hugged her mother.

"Hi Mom, how are you?" asked Cindy, feeling a bit awkward.

"Good, good, come in and sit. Can I get you something to eat or drink?" Lucinda asked, feeling a bit nervous. This was her daughter, but they hadn't seen each other for a while and Cindy had always seemed aloof.

"Where's Tom?" Cindy asked, taking the offered orange juice.

"In the living room," said Lucinda. "He's pretty banged up, Cindy."

"What exactly happened, Mom?" she asked,

sipping the juice.

Lucinda relayed what Tom had told them. "They assume it was a random act of violence and don't expect to be able to find the person who did it."

"That sucks," said Cindy, feeling bad for Tom.

"Do you want to go in and see him?" asked Lucinda, hoping that they would call a truce.

"Sure," she said, finishing her drink and putting her glass in the sink.

They walked into the living room together and Tom looked up. Cindy was shocked at his physical appearance.

"Oh my god, Tom, you look terrible!" said Cindy.

Tom tried his pat joke, "You should see the other guy!" He tried to laugh but it hurt.

"Stop it, Tom," said Cindy. "This isn't a laughing matter. I'm so sorry this happened to you. Mom told me what happened."

"Yeah, she said she did. Mom, would you get me a glass of water?" he asked.

"Of course," and she left them alone in the living room.

Cindy sat down next to Tom and looked him over. "You really took a beating, brother."

"Yeah, I thought I wasn't going to make it, if you want to know the truth. I finally pretended I was unconscious so that the bastard would leave me alone. He did after he took my wallet," said Tom.

"Do you need anything, Tom? I can help you out financially for a bit. I've saved up some money and I still have some of the Anderson money," she said, referring to the last payment she was able to get from Marly.

"I'm okay, right now, and Mom and Dad are taking care of things here. I went to the dentist on Monday and I'm waiting for a replacement," he said, pulling back his lip to show her the empty space where his tooth once was.

"Geez, Tom, I'm sorry. And I'm sorry that I haven't been a good sister to you. I just had to get away from all of the lies we were living. I'm Dr. Weston in Nashville. I wanted to use my real name, just like you were doing in New York," said Cindy.

"I understand, Sis," he said. "It really wasn't fair to have us change our name. Why couldn't she have changed hers?"

At that moment, Lucinda walked in with Tom's water. Handing it to him, she said, "What are you talking about?"

Cindy said, "Just about the job I have in Nashville and that when he's better, he should come for a visit."

"That would be wonderful, Cindy. That makes me very happy," she said, heading back to the kitchen.

"That might be nice, Cindy, thanks," Tom said, responding to her statement.

"Are you planning to go back to New York?

And what about your girlfriend, Brittany wasn't it?" she asked.

"We broke up," he said, without any further comment.

"That's tough, brother," said Cindy. "Well, the offer was genuine and when you feel up to traveling, come to Nashville and stay with me. I bought a little house there and I really like my neighbors."

"Look at you, being an upstanding citizen and have a legitimate job," said Tom, smiling as best he could at his sister.

Cindy looked at him and smiled back, "It feels good, being honest."

"I know," he said.

Lenny called Marly and she quickly answered.

"Hey Lenny, everything okay?" she asked.

"I needed to talk to you. Could I come over?" he asked.

"Of course you can. Kate and I are just hanging out," said Marly.

Lenny was surprised and asked, "So Kate stayed behind?"

"Yes, for a few more days. Come on over," she said, ending the call.

Kate looked at Marly quizzically, "What did he want?"

"I don't really know. Said he needed to talk to me," said Marly and just then heard a knock at the door. "Must be him."

Marly opened the door and Lenny stepped inside. She led him to the living room where Kate was sitting.

"Hello Lenny, good to see you," said Kate, smiling.

"You too, Kate," he said, sitting down.

"What's on your mind, Lenny?" asked Marly, sitting down as well.

Lenny got right into the subject on his mind, "Kennedy has another job for me. He hasn't given me any details yet, but he said it was in Tennessee as well. I'm thinking that it is your cabin he is referring to, Marly."

Marly looked at Kate and then back at Lenny, "I wondered if he would find out about it and try to search it as well. So, do you know when he is going to have this job for you?"

"From what I can tell you, it seemed as if it would be a couple of weeks. I'm not sure why," said Lenny.

"Probably because it is rented until the end of the month and then will be vacant for a week. That's probably when he'll have you go," said Marly, not divulging that she and Kate were already planning to go there.

"Sounds about right," said Lenny. "If I do get the job, I'll just tell him I couldn't find anything although I don't know what he's looking for either."

"Neither do I, Lenny, but I wouldn't worry about it. There's not anything in the cabin. I've been there for years and have looked in every nook and cranny there is. It is just a vacation spot," said Marly.

"Then he will be disappointed," said Lenny, grinning, not aware of Marly's plans.

CHAPTER 34

After Lenny left, Marly and Kate discussed the cabin.

"He is really looking for something, if he wants to search the cabin too," said Marly.

"Yes, I wonder what it could be. Do you think it has anything to do with Giselle Armenti?" asked Kate.

"I've been wondering about her," said Marly. "Maybe he is looking for evidence of her and my grandfather. I just know that I want to look in the cabin before he sends anyone there, even if it's Lenny."

"I agree with you," said Kate. "What's on the agenda for this afternoon?"

"I think I want to go to the fake Andersons," said Marly.

"Are you ready for that, Marly?" asked Kate, concerned.

"Yes, I feel the need to confront them and let them know I am aware of their decades of deception," said Marly.

"Okay then," said Kate. "I'll be a witness to the conversation and if needed, I'll be your attorney."

"Perfect," said Marly. "Let's get ready and do it!"

When they were ready, Kate and Marly got into the car and Marly drove them to the Anderson's home. It was quite a large home in an upscale neighborhood.

"I guess they could afford this with your grandfather's money," said Kate.

"Yes, they did very well for themselves," said Marly. She drove up to the front of the house and she and Kate went up to the door, ringing the doorbell.

Lucinda walked through the living room, saying, "You two sit still, I'll get it. Probably a salesman."

When she opened the door and saw Marly Anderson standing there, she didn't know what to say. After a few moments of silence, Lucinda found her voice.

"What are you doing here?" she asked, angrily.

"I would like to speak to you, Lucinda," said Marly, the first time she addressed her by her first name.

Cindy called out, "Everything okay, Mom?"

Lucinda opened the door and allowed Marly and Kate to enter. She led them into the living room.

"What are you doing here?" asked Tom, seeing who it was.

"I needed to speak to your parents," said Marly, looking directly at Tom and Cindy.

"Thomas isn't here right now," said Lucinda,

"and I doubt that we want to hear anything you have to say."

Marly felt an anger she didn't know she had but she kept it in check.

"Lucinda, I have discovered that you and your husband entered into a contractual agreement with my grandfather," she began, speaking tersely.

Lucinda was momentarily at a loss for words but then spoke, "I don't know what you are talking about."

Taking out her phone, she turned it toward Lucinda who saw the image of the contract with both hers and Thomas' signatures.

"Cindy, call your father and ask him to come home," she said.

Cindy made the call, and Thomas Anderson immediately left his office, headed to the house. He didn't know exactly what was going on, but Cindy said it was urgent.

Thomas walked into his house and came into the living room where he was confronted by his family and Marly Anderson. There was another woman, but he didn't know her.

"What's going on here?" he asked.

Marly spoke up, "I came here today, Thomas, to let you know that I have uncovered the contract that you and your wife signed to pretend to be my family for quite a bit of money."

"That has nothing to do with you," said Thomas. "Besides, we treated you as if you were our own daughter."

Laughing mirthlessly, Marly said, "Then I pity your real children. I was just a paycheck to you. I was treated better at the orphanage I was in than at your hands. But I'm not here to discuss how you treated me. My purpose today is to inform you to return to using your real name, Weston."

Cindy and Tom looked at each other, smiling. It was what they wanted all along. But their parents didn't act like they wanted the same thing.

"It's not that easy," said Thomas. "We have property in the Anderson name. That can't be fixed overnight."

"Not my problem. Kate Butler here, my attorney, will bring this to a court if necessary," said Marly, watching Thomas and Lucinda.

"I'm known at my company as Anderson. I can't just change my name," said Thomas.

"But you did," said Marly. "And it wasn't a problem for you then, because it came with a large amount of money. I'm not disputing that you were entitled to that money because it was so stated in the contract. However, the money that you coerced from me under the guise of my family, can be sued for by me."

"You gave us that money!" shouted Lucinda. "It's ours!"

"Is it?" asked Marly.

Lucinda looked pleadingly at her husband, begging him to tell her.

It was obvious that Marly had somehow discovered the secret they had been keeping for years. Now, they had to figure out how to fix things without losing anything.

"What do you suggest?" asked Thomas, trying to buy some time.

"I suggest you go to court and change your name back to Weston and sever all ties with the Anderson name," said Marly, holding her ground.

"I don't know how quickly all of this can be done. I have a job and employees..." began Thomas.

Kate interrupted, "You need to obtain the necessary forms from your local court clerk's office, complete them and pay the filing fee. Then you will be given a hearing where you will obtain the court order needed to change your name on all legal documents. You can request them to expedite it for extenuating circumstances. I believe you encountered those when you tried to contest Oliver Anderson's will, did you not?"

While they were standing there in shocked silence, Marly said, "I expect this to take place within the month. If not, I will sue you for the money you extorted from me while pretending to be my family. Good day."

Marly and Kate walked out, closing the door on a silent group.

Marly and Kate were silent as they walked to the car. When they got in, Marly exhaled and started laughing.

"Are you okay, Marly?" asked Kate, not sure about this reaction.

"Oh yes, I'm fine. The look on their faces was priceless!" said Marly. "I can't tell you how liberating it felt. If they had treated me like family, I would have done anything for them, but they didn't. Am I a terrible person, Kate?"

Smiling at her friend, Kate said, "Absolutely not. I think they are getting off lightly, considering everything."

They drove back to the house, discussing plans for the trip. Marly had received the email information from Judy and notified her renters of the change of address and location. They were delighted and Marly had sent the funds for the rental to the Thorntons. Everything was working out. Now to get to the cabin and see if anything is hidden there.

When Marly and Kate left the Anderson/ Weston home, the family was quiet for a few minutes. Then everyone began talking at once.

"What are we going to do, Thomas?" whined Lucinda.

"Tom and I are already using our real name, so I don't think we have anything to worry about," said Cindy, looking at Tom.

"Do you have all of your legal documents in Weston?" asked Thomas.

"I do," said Cindy, "what about you, Tom?"

"No, I was using it as my stage name," said

Tom.

"Did you go to court?" asked Lucinda, curious.

"No, I got a friend to make a fake birth certificate with the name Weston and took that to the DMV," said Cindy. "I said I needed to take the driver's test. They tested me and I got my license in Weston. After I did that, it was easy to get everything in my name."

"I'll consult a lawyer," said Thomas. "If what that Butler woman said was true, it shouldn't be too hard to get the ball rolling on this but, I'm afraid the original contract will come into play."

Lucinda was pacing and wringing her hands, tears not far away.

"Mom," said Cindy, "calm down. Dad's got this and you didn't do anything wrong. Well, maybe the way Marly was treated but she's an adult now. I don't think that can be considered."

"She's right, Lucinda," said Thomas. "I'll consult with Dan Forsyth this afternoon and get some advice. I don't know what I'll do about work, but I'll worry about that later."

Thomas went outside and got in his car, headed to Dan's office, praying that he could get this taken care of with as little publicity as possible.

Lucinda's phone rang and she didn't move to answer it.

"Mom, your phone," said Tom.

She answered it and said, "Oh yes, Dr. Laramore. No, I'm fine. Tomorrow? Yes, we will be there at 9:00 a.m."

She looked at Tom after ending the call and said, "Your tooth replacement is in, and he will take care of it in the morning." Before he could answer her, she walked out of the living room and upstairs without another word.

"I've never seen Mom so upset," said Tom and Cindy agreed with him.

CHAPTER 35

Thomas walked into Dan Forsyth's office and spoke with the receptionist.

"Is Dan in?" he asked.

"Yes he is. Let me see if he is available," she said cordially.

After a few moments, she said, "Yes, Mr. Anderson, he can see you. Go on back."

"Thanks," he said, making his way to Dan's office.

"Hello Thomas, what brings you downtown?" asked Dan.

Looking at his friend intently, Thomas said, "I have a serious problem, Dan."

Realizing that Thomas was sincere, he said, "Sit down, let's discuss it."

Thomas told him everything about the contract, the child they were to raise as their own, how they were paid large amounts of money to change their name to match Oliver Anderson, and how, now, the woman who was his adopted granddaughter/daughter was demanding they change their names, or she will sue them.

"What would she sue you for? You were paid to change your name," said Dan, thinking this whole thing was bizarre.

"We did get additional money from her after Anderson died. She said she only complied because at the time, she thought we were her family. Can she do that, when she didn't know we weren't her family?" Thomas asked.

"It's a murky situation, Thomas, and I've never encountered anything like this before. I suppose it could be construed as extortion. Has she consulted a lawyer?" he asked.

"She had one with her when she confronted us," he said, clearly agitated.

"Calm down, we'll figure it out. I think you should complete the paperwork for a name change. I can get Evelyn to print it out for you from the website," said Dan. "You will probably have to produce the contract you had with her grandfather. Do you have a copy of it?"

"Yes, in the lockbox at the bank. I was hoping this wouldn't have to come out. What about my employees and my company?" asked Thomas.

"We'll worry about that after you get the name change taken care of," said Dan. "Just take it one step at a time."

Picking up his phone, he called his receptionist and asked her to print out the needed forms. While she was doing that, Dan looked at Thomas.

"Were you paid a lot of money, Thomas?"

asked Dan.

Thomas nodded but remained silent.

"There may be tax implications, if you didn't pay it at the time you received it, unless it is stated somewhere in the contract that it was a gift," said Dan.

"I don't remember, but I doubt if it was. Oliver Anderson was a shrewd man, and he had secrets of his own," said Thomas. "I just want to get this fixed."

"I'll talk to some judge friends of mine, see what we can do Thomas," said Dan. "Try not to worry about it just yet."

"Thank you, Dan, I really appreciate it," said Thomas. As he left Dan's office, he picked up the forms from Evelyn, thanked her and went outside the building, getting in his car and driving back to the house. He hoped that it would be as simple as it sounded.

It had been another fitful night for Franklin Kennedy. He had gone on an outing the previous day, but it did not improve his sleep. He received another 2:00 a.m. call.

"Have you found anything yet?" asked the voice.

"Not yet. I do have another place to check out and everything should be handled in two weeks. We'll find out something soon, I promise," said Franklin.

"This is taking too long! I can't hold them off much longer," was the reply.

"I don't know what you want me to do about it, François!" said Franklin angrily.

Silence filled the air.

"Just a bit longer. Surely, after all of this time, a couple of weeks more should be allowed," said Franklin, losing his own patience.

"Oui, we will wait," François agreed and disconnected the call.

Franklin must be tired, to break the cardinal rule of no names to be mentioned. Hopefully, he will be forgiven. After the call, sleep eluded him, and he was very fatigued this morning.

Ethan stepped off of the elevator and walked into the library.

"Good morning, Mr. Kennedy, are you doing well today?" he asked.

"I'm a bit tired, Ethan, but nothing a nap won't cure," he chuckled. "Is everything ready for your trip?"

"Yes sir, and Brittany is very excited. Thank you for allowing me to take her," Ethan said gratefully.

"Of course, she is a lovely young lady, and I hope, she is healing," said Franklin.

"Yes, I believe she is, inside and out," said Ethan, seeing the bruises fading each day and the easy smiles she now uses.

"Good. When you get settled in, contact Ms. Anderson as quickly as you can. I need to know what my next move will be," said Franklin.

"Absolutely, Mr. Kennedy," said Ethan, dreading the confrontation with Marly but knowing it was his job. "I'll report as soon as I speak to her."

"Excellent. I have nothing else for today, so you are dismissed. Enjoy the trip and I will see you back on Sunday, unless my plans change," said Franklin, hoping they would.

"Yes sir, Mr. Kennedy. Thank you," said Ethan and he left the estate, looking forward to his weekend with Brit.

Lenny decided he needed to report to Mr. Kennedy.

"Hello Lenny, I was wondering if I was going to hear from you," said Franklin.

"I'm sorry, Mr. Kennedy, I lost my phone in the hotel room and finally found it, but it was quite late," lied Lenny.

"You can call me at any time of the day, Lenny. Anything happening?" he asked.

"Three of the house guests left yesterday but one of her friends stayed behind. They haven't been out of the house since yesterday morning," report Lenny.

"Hmmm, someone stayed. I wonder if it is just a coincidence," said Franklin, more to himself than to Lenny.

"I'm not sure, sir. Do you want me to get closer and see what I can find out?" asked Lenny.

"No, no, I have someone on the way there so if

you see a young man and woman, they work for me," said Franklin.

"Okay, sir. Thanks for the heads up," said Lenny. "Anything else?"

"No, just keep up the good work," said Franklin, as he ended the call.

When the call ended, Lenny's phone rang, startling him. He answered it.

"Hello," said Lenny.

"Hey, Lenny, Jake Friar here," the caller identified himself.

"Hey Jake, how are you man?" asked Lenny.

"Can't complain. You still on the straight and narrow?" he asked.

"Yeah, sort of. I'm doing some surveillance work for a guy, not sure he is on the up and up, but I'm not doing anything illegal," laughed Lenny, thinking about the charges he set at Marly's house.

"Good, so what was the call about?" asked Jake.

"I have a friend who found some documents in her grandfather's house. There is a code book and then photos with codes on them. She wants to turn them over to someone but doesn't know who to trust," explained Lenny.

"Has she taken them to the police?" asked Jake, puzzled.

"No, her grandfather was apparently involved with some secret organization, Crimson something," said Lenny, trying to sound vague.

"Crimson Veil? Are you kidding me?" said Jake, incredulously.

"Why? Is that something important?" asked Lenny.

"It's something no one talks about around here, except in whispers. I really can't say much about it, but if what you say is true, it might be the key to finding a lot of missing people, or at least, finding out what happened to them," explained Jake.

"So, can she turn this stuff over to you? She wants to do the right thing," said Lenny.

"Is she involved in it?" asked Jake, excited and wary at the same time.

"No, she found it after her grandfather died but only after someone wanted to search her house. And they offered to buy it for millions," said Lenny.

"Wow, if I could produce evidence from the Veil, it would be a feather in my cap. Maybe I could get a promotion. And those are hard to get here at the FBI," said Jake. "Where does she live?"

"In Tennessee. Where are you located, Jake?" asked Lenny, hoping to get Marly a good contact.

"I'm in North Carolina," said Jake. "Can you give me her information?"

"You know, Jake, I'm going to let her contact you. I don't want to be in the middle of this, if you know what I mean," said Lenny. "I'll give her your number, okay?"

"That would be great. And let her know, Lenny,

that she can trust me. I'm sure she is a bit afraid. I'll help her all I can," said Jake.

"I'll let her know. It might be a few days before you hear from her because she has a house guest," said Lenny, not knowing what Marly's plans were.

"Sounds great, man," said Jake. "Thanks for reaching out to me. I'll look forward to her call."

"Thanks Jake," said Lenny, "it was good to hear from you."

CHAPTER 36

Marly and Kate were having breakfast and discussing their trip.

"Do you feel like a road trip, Kate?" asked Marly, as she was thinking about driving to the cabin.

"Sure," said Kate, "if we left tomorrow, we could have time to sightsee along the way, if there's anything we want to check out."

"Good, because I don't know if we are going to find anything and I want to be prepared, just in case," explained Marly.

"I totally understand, Marly," said Kate. "I was actually thinking the same thing. Besides, it would be fun!"

"I think so too, Kate," said Marly. "So, you want to leave tomorrow then?"

"Yes, when will the cabin be empty?" asked Kate.

"The renters are going to be moving to the new location tomorrow, so we could even make it to the cabin, if we felt like it," said Marly. "We can just play it by ear."

"Sounds good," said Kate, "I'll let Seth know

our plans and we can get things ready tonight."

"We'll just rest up today, if that's all right with you," suggested Marly.

"Perfect," said Kate.

Now they had a plan.

Thomas had left Dan's office feeling a bit better. He went home, spoke with Lucinda and the children and they had dinner together and then Cindy left. It was good to see her and Tom Jr. together and getting along. Last night they completed the paperwork Evelyn had printed for him, Lucinda and the kids signed them. Dan had suggested everyone petition for the name change since their birth certificates were in the Anderson name. He dropped them off at Dan's office on his way to work. He hoped that everything would be as simple as it sounded. He would be glad to go back to being Thomas Weston.

After speaking with Franklin Kennedy, Lenny called Marly.

"Hello Lenny," she answered.

He loved hearing her voice. "Hello Marly," he said. "I just talked to Mr. Kennedy and gave him my report. I did tell him that someone stayed behind with you."

"That's fine, Lenny. I'll be taking Kate home, but we decided to visit a little longer since she isn't working right now. How much longer are you watching me?" she said with a giggle.

Smiling, he said, "I guess until he tells me to go to the next job. He did say he had someone coming today, probably to see you, a man and a woman. He didn't mention any names."

"Probably that Ethan guy that works for him. Maybe he's bringing backup, thinking I'll cave if a woman is involved. They just don't know me very well," said Marly.

"No, they don't, Marly. You are quite a formidable woman," said Lenny, chuckling a bit.

"I don't know about formidable, but I am getting better at standing up for myself," admitted Marly. "I also appreciate you keeping me in the loop, Lenny. You didn't have to, but you cared enough to do it."

"I do care about you, Marly. No matter how our paths first crossed, I owe a great deal to you and if I can help you, I am going to do it," said Lenny. "Which brings me to another subject."

"Now what?" asked Marly, wondering what was coming next.

"I talked to my contact at the FBI, Jake Friar. I gave him a little bit of information, and he was very interested. In fact, the Crimson Veil is well known in his circles but is very hush hush. When you are ready to hand off whatever you've found, you can call him. I'll text you his number. And I trust him, Marly, with my life," Lenny said.

"Thank you Lenny, that means a lot. I'll call him when you send his number. I would rather get this stuff out of the house, if you know what

I mean," said Marly. "I don't know when Franklin Kennedy is going to come looking for it, but I know he will, sooner or later."

"You are probably right, Marly," said Lenny. "If I hear anything else, I'll let you know."

"Thanks Lenny," said Marly, and she ended the call.

Kate had been listening to her friend's end of the conversation and looked at Marly quizzically, "What's up?"

Marly told Kate about the couple coming and about the FBI agent that Lenny contacted.

"Good, maybe he can come before we leave and we won't need to take it with us, because I was thinking we shouldn't leave it behind," said Kate.

"I agree with you, Kate. You know, maybe we should bait the hook," said Marly.

Kate looked at her and said, "Bait the hook? What are you talking about?"

"Maybe I let it be known through Lenny that we are going to be gone, and the house will be vacant for a few days. Don't you think that Franklin Kennedy couldn't resist coming then?" explained Marly.

"I don't know, Marly, it seems a bit dangerous. What happens if he comes and realizes that there is a false wall in the basement and tears into it? He will search and the charges Lenny placed will go off. Then he will find nothing and realize we already found it," said Kate.

"But, what if I put a nanny cam down there,

in a stuffed toy or something? Then we would have proof he broke into my house and searched it. Even if those charges go off, I can deny I knew anything about them or a hidden room," explained Marly.

Kate thought about it for a few minutes. She remembered that Lenny was wearing gloves while working down there, so there wouldn't be any fingerprints to implicate him. It might work and she said so to Marly. "I want to run it by Seth and Rafe too, if you don't mind."

"Of course not, calmer heads prevail always," said Marly, "and I am very close to this situation."

"We'll call them tonight, when we are sure we can speak to them together," said Kate. "For now, I guess we need to go shopping for a baby cam!"

After his meeting with Mr. Kennedy yesterday, Ethan was free until Sunday. He slept in and decided to get packed. It didn't take him long to shower, dress and get everything together in a suitcase which matched the one he had given to Brittany. He walked out of his bedroom to find her already dressed and drinking a cup of coffee.

"Are you so excited you couldn't sleep?" asked Ethan, grinning at her.

"Yes! I'm very excited about this trip," said Brittany. "I've never been to Tennessee."

"I believe we will have some time to sightsee," promised Ethan, making a mental note to see what was in the area. Of course, everyone knew that was where Elvis had lived.

"I'm already packed too, so I can help you if you aren't," volunteered Brittany, her excitement evident.

Laughing at her enthusiasm, Ethan said, "I'm ready too. It's a little early to go to the airport but we can have breakfast somewhere. How does that sound?"

"Perfect! I'll get my bag," she said, coming out of her room with her bag and a backpack.

Smiling, Ethan got his things as well and they went outside to his car. This was going to be a great weekend.

Marly and Kate left and drove down the street, making it easy for Lenny to spot them. Smiling, he started his car and followed them at a distance. He figured they were going shopping and wasn't too worried. Soon, his assumption was proven as they pulled into the shopping mall. Marly waved at him as she and Kate went into the entrance. He would just wait here until they left.

"Why did we come in this way, Marly?" asked Kate. "There was an entrance to the electronics store a few doors down."

Marly looked at Kate and said, "I just didn't want to alert Lenny as to what we were doing. I'm sure he thinks we are shoe shopping or something. I trust him but I don't want him to interfere with my plans. Don't you think he would if he knew?"

"You are getting very cagey, Marly. I think your next line of work should be a detective!" laughed Kate, as they walked down the mall to their destination.

Kate had done some research, and they decided on a couple of options. Marly bought a photo frame with a hidden camera, that recorded video as well as audio that she could control with an app on her phone. It would also start recording when movement was detected.

"Should I get one for upstairs too?" asked Marly.

"It couldn't hurt and if anyone does come in, they will probably search upstairs too," said Kate.

Turning around, Marly went back to the salesman and asked for another exact model, and she made her purchases.

"I feel like Mata Hari," said Marly, laughing.

Kate laughed with her and said, "Let's just hope that you don't end up like her!"

"True! Now, let's go shoe shopping!" said Marly and they made several purchases before leaving the mall.

Seeing them come outside and noting the shoe bags, he smiled. Women, they always want to buy more shoes.

CHAPTER 37

After arriving back at the house, Marly found a picture of her grandfather holding her on his knee and another of him standing with her at her college graduation.

"I think these two will do, Kate, what do you think?" she asked.

"Perfect. This one of you on his knee is so cute! I think you should put the one when you graduated on his desk, because he was so proud of you and probably would have wanted to see it every day. The other one can go downstairs," suggested Kate.

"Yes, and we'll position it so we can see if someone is at his desk or the bookshelves," said Marly.

"You are good, Mata," laughed Kate. "I'll have to tell Lucy you have a new name!"

"Haha, very funny," Marly laughed with her friend.

She and Kate placed the frames and then Marly downloaded the app, testing out the cameras, having Kate walk by them and ensuring they were working properly.

"They work great, and the video is so clear," said Marly. "Now, even if someone invades my home, I will know what they are doing."

"Exactly," said Kate. "So, what next?"

Marly saw a text message come across her phone and it was from Lenny, with Jake Friar's phone number.

"I guess I will call the FBI friend of Lenny's," said Marly, showing Kate she had received the number.

"Are you planning to give him everything we found?" asked Kate.

"I'm not going to give him the brooch, letter or the picture, but everything else, yes," said Marly. "I don't think those things are relevant."

"I agree with you. I know I think like a lawyer, but I am going to create a transfer of custody form that he can sign when he picks up the documents. I will also make a list of everything in the bin, so that you will have a copy too," said Kate.

"Should I take pictures?" asked Marly.

"That would be a good idea," said Kate. "So, I guess we know what we're doing next!"

They went upstairs to Marly's grandfather's room and while she spoke with Jake Friar, Kate made the list of contents. She then took photographs of each item and emailed them to Marly and herself.

Ending the call, Marly looked at Kate.

"Well, it's done. He's flying here tonight," said

Marly.

Kate said, "Good, did you feel comfortable with him?"

"Yes, actually I did. He was very professional and said this would be a break for an ongoing case that had been going on for years. So, I guess I am doing the right thing," said Marly.

"You are doing the right thing," said Kate. "Now, let me get this list typed and a form created so we will be ready for Mr. Friar when he shows up."

Going downstairs, Marly fixed them a sandwich while Kate made the list and the forms. Everything seemed to be going smoothly...for now.

Ethan and Brittany arrived at the airport at the recommended time and waited for their flight to be called. The time went by quickly as they chatted and watched people. They boarded the plane, sitting in first class.

"Oooh, I've never flown first class, Ethan," said Brittany.

"I thought it would be a fun experience," he told her, although he had flown that way many times. Mr. Kennedy typically insisted on it.

"This is really going to be a memorable weekend, Ethan, thank you," she said in a low whisper.

"You're welcome," he whispered back, kissing her lightly on the lips.

The flight attendant made her announcements, and they sat back for the next two and a half hours, enjoying the perks of being in the first-class cabin.

Lucinda and Tom arrived at Dr. Laramore's office promptly at 9:00 a.m. The waiting area was crowded with patients, but the receptionist ushered them back to an examination room immediately.

When Dr. Laramore entered the room, Lucinda thanked him for not making them wait outside.

"Of course, I know how nosy people can be," he said with a wry grin. "I didn't want to put Tom through that, he's been through enough."

"Thanks, Doc," said Tom, glad to be getting this done today.

For the next thirty minutes, Dr. Laramore worked in his mouth, fitting the false tooth, taking it out, then cementing it and putting some kind of blue light on it.

"This is curing everything to keep it from loosening up," said Dr. Laramore.

Lucinda sat by Tom the entire time, watching the process.

"It's amazing what can be done these days," she said. "That tooth looks so natural."

"That's the intention, Lucinda," he told her. Turning his attention to Tom, he said, "No hard foods or meats for two days and then you can go back to a regular diet."

"We still have some potato soup, Tom, so we'll have that today," said Lucinda.

"Now that sounds like exactly what the doctor ordered," said Dr. Laramore. "Tom, how is everything else healing? You weren't limping as much today."

"Every day I feel a little better. Of course, Mom is taking good care of me," replied Tom.

"I have no doubt about that," said Dr. Laramore, smiling at Lucinda, causing her to blush.

"Do we need to come back?" asked Lucinda, trying to get back to business.

"Not unless Tom has issues with it, he should be good to go," said Dr. Laramore. "I better get back to the other patients. Good to see you Tom, Lucinda."

After he left the exam room, Tom and Lucinda walked through the waiting room and out to the car.

"I think Dr. Laramore was flirting with you Mom," teased Tom.

"Oh, I don't think so, Tom, he was just being nice," said Lucinda.

"I don't know, he seems quite taken with you," said Tom, smiling at his mother and feeling the new tooth with his tongue.

"Stop it, Tom!" Lucinda said, driving out of the parking lot. "He's just a nice man."

"And single," said Tom.

"Well, I'm not!" she said, pretending to be indignant as she drove them home.

Ethan and Brittany landed in Memphis, retrieved their bags and picked up their rental car. Ethan had rented a Murano SUV. It was roomy and a mid-sized car, which he thought would be good for sightseeing. They arrived at the River Inn of Harbor Town, and the valet took their bags and parked the car, handing him a claim card. Walking in, Brittany didn't know where to look first, it was so beautiful. Waterfalls, vases of fresh flowers everywhere and a bellman, taking their things to the room. Ethan tipped him and they walked in.

"Oh my gosh, Ethan, this is fabulous!" exclaimed Brittany. "This lounge is bigger than your apartment!"

"Yes, it is actually," laughed Ethan. "This is our home for three nights so enjoy it, Brit."

"I will," she said, going to the windows which were actually sliding glass doors to a balcony. "Oh my goodness, look at this!"

He walked over and saw that their room overlooked the Mississippi River.

"Wow, that's impressive," he said.

"I just love it," gushed Brittany. "Thank you so much Ethan, for bringing me with you!"

He grabbed her and hugged her, giving her a kiss full on the lips.

"You are welcome, and I think we are going to have a wonderful time," said Ethan, *right after I get that phone call over with*, he thought.

"Why don't you unpack your things in the bedroom, and I'll make that business call," he said.

She happily went into the suite, and he could hear her, 'oh my gosh' and 'wow' as she discovered all of the amenities. Resignedly, he sat down at the desk and made the call to Marly Anderson.

Marly's phone rang and she answered it, putting it on speaker so that Kate could hear.

"Hello," she said.

"Hello Marly," said Ethan. "I don't know if you remember me or not, but..."

"I remember you, Ethan," she said.

"I'm sorry to bother you but I was in town and wondered if we could speak," said Ethan.

"Do you have anything new to say to me?" asked Marly, winking at Kate.

"Mr. Kennedy is withdrawing his offer to buy your home, realizing that you do not need any financial gain," said Ethan.

"I'm glad that he finally realized that. You cannot buy someone's memories," she said.

"Yes, and he is willing to pay you a finder's fee, an amount you can decide on, and allow him to search for what he is seeking. Truthfully, I have no idea what it is," said Ethan.

"I believe you when you say you don't know what it is. I have concluded that Mr. Kennedy is the only one who knows what he is searching for, and no one can do the searching but him," said Marly.

"So, will you allow it?" Ethan asked, hopefully.

"I'm not sure, as you know, I feel it is a great invasion of my privacy. I would insist on being here," said Marly.

"Of course, I would expect nothing else," said Ethan.

"I'm leaving Sunday, taking a friend of mine back home to Texas and I'll let you know when I get back. We can arrange it then," said Marly. "I just want to get it over with."

"Thank you, Marly, you don't know how much I appreciate it," said Ethan, delighted.

CHAPTER 38

"I thought we were leaving tomorrow," said Kate.

"We are, but he doesn't need to know that. I want to give Mr. Kennedy time to fret about it and I am sure that he will not wait until I get back but break in while I am gone. I want us to be already at the cabin before he thinks we are leaving," explained Marly.

"Very sneaky, Marly," said Kate, as her phone rang. Seeing it was Seth, she answered it, putting it on speaker.

"Hello Seth," she said.

"Hi Katie, is Marly with you?" he asked.

"Yes, we are both here listening," said Kate. "Is Rafe and Lucy there too?"

"Yes, we're all here, so what's going on?" asked Seth.

Kate outlined their plans of leaving tomorrow and making it a road trip.

"I'm so jealous!" cried Lucy.

"It's okay, Lucy," said Marly, "we'll take another road trip together."

"Marly didn't want to try to fly back with

whatever we may find," said Kate.

Seth spoke up, "That makes a lot of sense."

Kate also told them about the hidden cameras and baiting Mr. Kennedy's assistant, who was back in town.

Rafe laughed at that and said, "Serves him right. He's caused a lot of stress for all of us."

"Agreed," said Lucy, wishing she was already at the cabin. "I'll be able to fly to you Sunday morning.

"Great," said Marly. "We won't search for anything until you get there."

"You better not!" said Lucy.

"Oh and by the way, an FBI agent friend of Lenny's is coming over tonight to get the stuff we already found," said Marly.

"Did you catalog it?" asked Rafe, who was used to doing wine inventory.

"Yes, I made a list today," said Kate, "and a form for the guy to sign, taking custody of the items."

Seth remarked, "I got myself a smart cookie!"

Everyone laughed and then Marly got serious, "I'm not turning over the brooch and letter or the picture, but I am taking it with me. I think all of that is related to a personal situation."

"I agree with you, Marly," said Seth. "We think your plan is a good one. Be careful on the road and check in, okay?"

"We will, Seth," said Kate. "I love you."

"I love you too, Katie," he said.

Lucy piped up, "Get a room, you two!"

They all laughed, and Seth disconnected the call.

"We have their blessings," said Kate, as she put down her phone.

"Yes, I'm glad they are okay with it. I feel a lot better about it and I will really feel good when Mr. Friar comes tonight and picks up that bin of stuff," said Marly.

"I know. I think you are doing the right thing, Marly. I don't know what kind of implications it will have for your grandfather, but it doesn't really matter now. He has eternal immunity," said Kate.

"That's true and I can't worry about that now," said Marly. "The wheels are already in motion."

Ethan was excited and put in a call to Mr. Kennedy immediately.

"Hello Ethan," said Franklin. "How was your trip?"

"It was good, Mr. Kennedy. Brittany and I are checked in at the hotel."

"Good and have you spoken with Ms. Anderson?" he asked, not expecting much.

"Actually, sir, I have, and it is encouraging news, I think," he said.

"Really?" Franklin asked, his hopes rising.

"I explained everything to her, and she is going to consider it, although she feels it is an invasion of her privacy," said Ethan.

"When will she decide?" asked Franklin, seeing a light at the end of the tunnel.

"Apparently she has a friend staying with her," began Ethan.

"Yes, yes, I know that," said Franklin, getting agitated.

"Oh, well, she is taking her home, back to Texas. They are leaving on Sunday, she said, and she will consider it when she gets back. That's good news, isn't it sir?" asked Ethan.

The wheels were turning in Franklin's mind, but he said aloud, "Yes, I think you have made progress with her. Thank you, Ethan. Enjoy the rest of your trip and I'll see you soon."

"Yes sir, Mr. Kennedy, thank you," said Ethan and he disconnected the call. Now he and Brit could enjoy the weekend without any more interruptions.

Franklin was ecstatic. She would leave the home on Sunday, and he would have a plan devised before then. He would not wait until she came back. He would arrange to travel to Tennessee and be finished with his search before she even returned. Knowing Oliver, he would have taught her to be cautious, and she probably has an alarm system. He would have to take someone with him that could disarm it. Maybe Lenny could do that sort of thing. He would check with him. Maybe he could find what he needed and also see if there was anything related to Giselle. He had to know if Randolph had anything to do with her disappearance.

Jake Friar reserved the FBI jet and was soon flying to Tennessee. He hoped that the trip did produce what Lenny had described. He didn't tell anyone except his superiors, and they were anxious to find out as well. The fact that they had authorized him to fly tonight let him know they wanted to see if the materials were legitimate. He wasn't planning to stay overnight, just meet with Ms. Anderson and then leave. Arriving at the hangar in Memphis, there was a rental car waiting for him. He put Ms. Anderson's address into the GPS and drove to Germantown. He arrived at her house about 7:30 p.m.

Jake got out of his car and strode up to the front door, ringing the doorbell.

Marly answered the door.

"Hello," she said to the man standing at her door.

"Hello, Ms. Anderson, I'm Jake Friar with the FBI," he identified himself.

"Could I see your identification?" she asked quietly.

Surprised by the request, he complied immediately, showing her his FBI credentials.

Marly opened the door and ushered him in.

"I'm sorry, but you can't understand what I've been through, with people trying to come into my home to search it," said Marly.

"Who has done that?" he asked.

"Come in, Mr. Friar, and I'll tell you," said Marly, and she walked into the living room, where Kate was seated.

"Mr. Friar, this is my friend, Kate Butler. She is also my attorney," said Marly.

"Please, call me Jake," he said. "Nice to meet you, Ms. Butler."

Wondering why she needed an attorney, Jake kept his questions for later, if necessary.

A plastic bin sat in the middle of the floor.

"Is this the information you wanted to surrender to me?" asked Jake.

"Yes, it is. I want you to know that a Mr. Franklin Kennedy of Denver has offered me ten million dollars for this building," she said.

He looked at her like she was crazy. "What?"

"Yes, that is exactly what I thought. This building is not worth one million, much less ten," said Marly. "When I refused, he insisted that he needed to look for something but would not tell me what it was or if I could look for him. Needless to say, I have been putting him off. But I, along with some of my friends, have searched the house and we found these things. They are connected in some way with an organization known as the Crimson Veil. Apparently my grandfather was associated with it for a time, but something happened, and he left, living under an assumed name. He has since died and apparently his whereabouts were discovered."

Jake couldn't believe the story Ms. Anderson was telling but she was very clear in her explanation.

"May I look at the documents?" he asked.

"Yes, please do," said Marly and she and Kate watched as he went through the photographs and the journals. Jake couldn't believe what he was seeing. It appeared to be a lot of the people that the FBI was interested in finding.

"Was all of this together?" he asked.

Kate spoke up, "No, the photographs were in some of the books in the bookshelves and the journals were in the basement."

"May I look in the basement?" Jake asked.

Marly figured he would request it and thought, *this will be a test of our work down there* and agreed.

They walked down the stairs and Marly turned on the lights.

"I found the journals in that old sideboard," she lied, the only one she would tell. "I never would have searched the house at all, had Mr. Kennedy not called and sent someone here."

Jake had heard the name Franklin Kennedy before and knew he was a person of interest in the Crimson Veil case, but he remained silent, not wanting to say more than he should.

"I've seen all I need to see here," said Jake, and he and Marly went upstairs.

Kate stood and handed Jake a form and a list. He looked at her, a question in his eyes.

This was something he did not expect.

CHAPTER 39

Marly spoke, "I don't know what all of this stuff is, Jake. But I do know at least one person who I think is desperate to find it. And from what Lenny said, you thought it was something of importance to the FBI. I want to ensure that I am not held responsible for anything that may come out of the investigation. I included a copy of a letter I found from my grandfather, but I kept the original. I don't know anything about this organization, and I don't want to be involved with it in any way. Can you understand that?"

"Of course, and I don't mind signing this form to prove that I took possession of the documents and that you willingly contacted me to arrange disposal of them to the FBI," said Jake.

Kate spoke up, "What if someone still comes after her? What recourse does she have?"

"Contact me immediately if you feel you are in danger," said Jake. "This investigation will probably go deeper than even I imagine."

"Attached is a listing of everything in the bin, but you are welcome to verify it before you leave," said Kate, wanting to be transparent.

"Yes, if you don't mind. I just wouldn't want to get back to North Carolina and something be missing that was listed," he said.

"Take your time, Jake," said Marly. "Can I get you something to drink?"

"Water would be great," he said as he opened the bin and started checking off the list.

It took Jake about an hour to verify everything was accounted for in the bin according to the list. He took a long drink of the water and sat down the glass.

He stood up, picking up the bin and said, "We at the Bureau appreciate you turning this information over to us. If we have any questions, I do have your number. I will be the one to call you so do not speak to any other agent about it. If someone else does call you from the Bureau, contact me immediately."

"I understand," said Marly, "and thank you for coming."

"Stay vigilant," he advised, and she opened the door, watching him walk to his car.

After he left, Marly let out a long breath, not realizing she had been holding it.

"I'm glad that is over," she said.

"Me too," said Kate. "Now, tomorrow, we'll be on our way to possibly more discoveries."

"I hope so, Kate," said Marly. She punched Lenny's number in her phone, and he answered it quickly.

"Hey Marly, what's up?" he asked, having just

gotten ready to relax.

"I wanted to let you know that Jake Friar was here tonight and he picked up the things we found. Thank you for putting me in touch with him," said Marly.

"You're welcome. He's a good guy and he will treat you right," said Lenny.

"I think you're right. Oh, and by the way, Kate and I are leaving tomorrow for Texas. I'm taking her home," said Marly.

"I wonder if I'm supposed to follow you to Texas," laughed Lenny.

"Lenny, I did hear from that Ethan guy, and I told him I was leaving Sunday, but that I would consider Mr. Kennedy's request when I got back. Would you still watch the house until then because I don't want him trying anything," said Marly.

"Okay, Marly, I will," said Lenny. "I don't trust that Kennedy guy or anybody that works for him. But I will be there for you, if you need me."

"That means a lot to me, Lenny and you don't know how much I appreciate what you've already done for me," said Marly.

"I'll keep an eye out and keep in touch, won't you?" said Lenny, feeling that this was a final goodbye.

"I will," she said, not knowing if that was the truth.

Lenny called Franklin Kennedy to give his

daily report. He was pretty tired of this job and figured he wouldn't take another one. He missed his solitude at his cabin. Kennedy answered quickly.

"Hello Lenny," he said, with some pep in his voice.

"You sound chipper today, Mr. Kennedy," said Lenny, recognizing it in his voice.

"I am feeling very good today, Lenny. What's happening in Tennessee?"

"Not much, a shopping trip, lunch, typical things women do when they are together," said Lenny, in a bored voice.

"I can tell this is getting laborious to you. I did get some news today," he said.

"Hope it was good news," said Lenny, trying not to sound eager to hear it.

"It was very good. My associate Ethan Longmire spoke with Ms. Anderson. It appears that she will be taking her house guest home and is leaving on Sunday. My plan is to travel there on Sunday and, with your help, search her house," said Franklin excitedly.

"My help?' Lenny questioned. "I'm on probation, Mr. Kennedy, and I am not going to break and enter into anyone's home."

"I will do that with my associate," said Franklin, not even batting an eye. "I need help with the alarm system that she probably has in place. Are you skilled at disarming something like that?"

"No, I don't have that skill set," he lied. He wasn't going get involved or set up by anyone.

"No matter then, I'll figure it out," said Franklin, curious as to why Derrick didn't mention Lenny Crocker was on probation. Oh well, he couldn't worry about that now.

"Do you want me to follow her on Sunday?" Lenny asked, knowing that he probably wouldn't.

"That's not necessary, Lenny. She is going to Texas, and I don't need to know what she is doing while there. After Saturday, our contract will be over. I did have another job for you, but in light of your situation, I will get someone else. It would be, I'm afraid, against your probation," said Franklin.

Lenny was relieved but said, "I'm sorry to hear that, Mr. Kennedy. It's been nice working for you."

"You too, Lenny. I'll reach out again if I have any more surveillance jobs," said Franklin, already thinking about Sunday.

"Sure, and I'll see if I can accommodate you," said Lenny, disconnecting the call before Kennedy.

Lenny thought, *so Marly planted the seed with Kennedy's associate that she would be leaving on Sunday when in reality she was leaving tomorrow. Pretty cagey Marly. Was she trying to get back and catch Kennedy red handed? Is she actually taking Kate home? Or, are they going to search the mountain cabin in Gatlinburg? He figured the latter and thought, good for her. She needs to be the one to do that anyway. He hoped she found what she was looking for, but he was glad she was going to beat Franklin Kennedy to the punch.* And he was glad to be heading back to Colorado on Sunday.

Ethan and Brittany were enjoying the amenities of the hotel. They had changed into their bathing suits and gone to the hot tub in the outdoor grotto, looking down on the Mississippi River. Brittany was glad Ethan had suggested she bring a swimsuit. As they lounged in the water, Ethan watched her face.

"Are you having a good time, Brit?" he asked, smiling at her.

"Oh yes, Ethan, it is so beautiful here and this hot tub is so relaxing. Can you believe the view from up here?" she answered him.

"It is beautiful but not nearly as beautiful as you are, Brit. Thank you for calling me that night. I didn't think I would get a second chance with you," said Ethan, looking into her eyes.

"I didn't know if you would take my call or even try to help me, after what I had done to you," said Brittany. "But I'm so thankful that I did and I feel like the luckiest girl in the world."

"Just so you know, all of our times together won't be this fancy, but let's take advantage of it while we are here," said Ethan. "I thought tonight we would relax and have room service for dinner. We'll go out tomorrow night and paint the town, how does that sound?"

Smiling at Ethan, she said softly, "It sounds absolutely perfect."

Brittany reached over and pulled Ethan to her and kissed him deeply, slipping her tongue inside his mouth. He tightened his grip on her, matching her kiss, feeling himself aroused. He pulled back, grinning at her.

"I want to be able to walk back to the room unnoticed, so we better cool it, for now," said Ethan and Brittany giggled.

After a little longer in the hot tub, they got out and wrapped themselves in the thick towels provided by the hotel and went back to the room.

As they entered the room, Ethan's phone was ringing. Looking at it, he saw that it was Mr. Kennedy. Holding up one finger to Brittany, as if to say hold on, he answered it.

"Hello Mr. Kennedy," said Ethan.

"Hello Ethan, I needed to speak with you about this weekend," he began.

"Hold on just a minute, Mr. Kennedy," Ethan said, not knowing the direction their conversation was going to take. "Brit, go ahead and get dried off and into some comfy clothes."

"Ah, sorry, did I interrupt anything?" asked Franklin, not caring if he did.

"No sir, we just got in from the hot tub. What are we doing?" he asked.

"I need you to find someone to disarm the house alarm at Ms. Anderson's home on Sunday. Lenny Crocker can't do it or won't do it, I'm not sure which it is," said Franklin.

"I can find someone, of course. Do you need me to stay in town then?" he asked.

"Yes, that would be ideal. Send Brittany back to Denver though. No need to involve anyone else," said Franklin.

"Understood. I'll reach out to my sources for what we need, and I'll see you on Sunday," said Ethan, ending the call and figuring out how to tell Brittany to go home without him.

CHAPTER 40

Franklin called Victor to the library after his call with Ethan.

"Yes sir?" asked Victor when he entered the room.

"I will be traveling on Sunday, Victor. I need to get a charter flight to Memphis. Can you arrange that for me please?" asked Franklin.

"Of course, Mr. Kennedy, will anyone else be accompanying you?"

"Yes, I believe I will have Samson go with me. Ethan is already there, but he will be traveling back with me," said Franklin.

"Very good, sir," said Victor. "I will pack your bag for you. Will you need any formal attire or casualwear?"

"Just casual this trip, Victor," said Franklin. "I will cancel any appointments for next week as well so no one will be expected."

"I will take care of it sir," said Victor. "Will that be all?"

"Yes Victor, thank you. Let me know when the charter is arranged and please let Samson know I will need his presence on this trip," said Franklin, going back to the notebook in front of him.

"Yes sir," said Victor, as he quietly left the room to take care of Mr. Kennedy's requests.

Franklin Kennedy smiled to himself, feeling that everything was finally falling in place.

Ethan called Davis Berg, his friend and fellow hacker.

"Hello Ethan," said Davis. "How's it going?"

"Actually, Davis, Brit and I are in Memphis for the weekend," said Ethan.

"Brit? Your Brit?" he said, curious.

"Yes, it's a long story and one that I'll share with you when I'm back in town, but I need you to do a hack job for me," said Ethan.

"What is it?" he asked.

"I need a house alarm deactivated. I can send you the address, but I don't know what type of system it is," said Ethan.

"That shouldn't be a problem, as they are all very similar. I can find out which one online. When do you need it done?" asked Davis.

"Sunday morning, but I'm not sure of the time. I'll find out and let you know via text," said Ethan.

"Okay, sounds good. It won't take but a few seconds," said Davis confidently.

"Great," said Ethan, wanting to get everything taken care of quickly so that he and Brit could enjoy their time together.

Calling Mr. Kennedy, Ethan told him that

he had Davis lined up to deactivate the alarm system and asked what time to do it.

"I'm not sure what time she will be leaving, but with such a long trip, I would imagine early in the day. I feel confident we can do it at 10:00 a.m. Sunday," said Franklin. If it was too early, she just wouldn't be able to set it when she left and she probably wouldn't let that deter her plans. Yes, everything was going perfectly.

Marly and Kate packed everything and loaded it into the car so they could be ready to leave early tomorrow morning. Marly put the brooch, letter and picture in the spare tire compartment in the back of her Tahoe.

"I looked it up and it's only about seven hours, Marly," said Kate.

"I know, but we are going to take our time and do some sightseeing too," said Marly. "I thought we might stay overnight somewhere on the road and make it to the cabin on Saturday."

"So fun!" exclaimed Kate. "I wish Lucy could be with us too, but she will have to do it the next time."

"I know, but I do understand that she has obligations at the winery," said Marly. "We will definitely do another girl trip, maybe even one with no drama!"

They both laughed at that, recalling the disasters they had experienced together. When they had everything except their toiletries packed, Kate looked at Marly.

"Are you okay with everything?" she asked, knowing she was referring to Jake Friar and giving him what they had found.

"Yes, I am. I'm not going to worry about what will happen afterwards because I did the right thing," said Marly.

"I think you did too," said Kate. "We better get some sleep because we have a busy day tomorrow and a fun one too!"

Kate went to her room and called Seth, giving him the details of their trip and Marly went into her grandfather's room. As she got into bed, she thought about the life she had with her Poppa. Even though this part of it was not what she expected, she had a wonderful life because of him. He prepared her for her future, and he provided to her the financial means she needed to do whatever her heart desired.

"Thank you Poppa," she said aloud in the darkness. "I love you."

Jake Friar sat on the jet, headed back to North Carolina. He couldn't believe the information he had at his feet. He could tell it was credible information and there was so much of it. He knew that his superiors were going to be pleased, and he hoped that they would reward him for it. Of course, he had Lenny to thank for it, but the FBI had already cut him a sweet deal after the kidnapping and his association with that Silvers woman. That had been a mess. The plane landed around 12:30 a.m. and Jake picked up the bin and walked down the steps. An SUV was waiting for him, and he got in the backseat, putting the bin at his feet.

"Is that everything?" asked Agent Mathison, Jake's superior.

"Yes sir," he answered.

"Do you think it's legit?" he asked.

"It's definitely legitimate, Steve, and you aren't going to believe the people that are listed. Many of them we have been searching for as missing persons or defected persons. It's a goldmine of information and I think you are going to be happy with what I have," said Jake.

"Great job, Jake. I can't wait to review it with you," he said as their driver took them to the Bureau offices, even though it was nearly 1:30 a.m. when they arrived.

Friday morning, Kate and Marly took the last of their bags to the car as well as a basket of snacks that Marly had prepared for the trip.

"I don't know if I can wait until we get on the road to try these muffins," said Kate, the smell was so delicious.

"They do smell good. It's an orange and cranberry muffin with a light glaze," said Marly. "It is a new recipe I'm trying out."

"I can already tell they are going to be a winner," said Kate, getting in her seat and buckling in.

Marly backed out of the garage, closed the door and set the house alarm on her phone. Taking a deep breath, she pulled into the street, and they were on the road. Lenny saw them leave but didn't acknowledge them and he didn't think they saw him on the side street. *Good luck, Marly* he thought and drove to a restaurant for breakfast.

Ethan was watching Brittany sleep. She looked beautiful, even without makeup. In a few minutes, she started stirring.

"Good morning," said Ethan.

Stretching her arms over her head, she smiled, "Good morning. How long have you been awake?"

"Long enough to watch you a while," said Ethan.

"I'm sorry I fell asleep last night while you were working," said Brittany. "I guess I was more tired than I thought after we ate. I'll make it up to you, I promise."

"Yes you will," said Ethan, laughing. "We are going to sightsee today and then tonight, we will go to dinner, and you will wear that beautiful dress."

"Gladly," said Brittany. "So, what's first?"

"Room service will be delivering breakfast soon so get dressed in comfortable clothes and shoes. We're going to take in the sights and sounds of Memphis!"

Dan Forsyth received a call from Judge Williams regarding the petition for a name change for the entire Anderson family.

"Dan, this is very unusual. What the hell is going on?" he asked.

Dan relayed to him what Thomas had told him. "I agree, it is bizarre."

"Bizarre is an understatement! I knew Oliver Anderson and I would never in a million years thought he would orchestrate anything like this," said Judge Williams.

"I know but the Anderson heir is insistent that they discontinue using the Anderson name and all that it entails. They are happy to do so and want to use their legal names," explained Dan.

"I know there is a lot of money in the Anderson estate because the pseudo-Andersons contested the Oliver Anderson will, but it was iron clad," Williams stated. "It is my leaning to grant this petition without a hearing, so we will complete the documents for all of the family members. I don't want to complicate my court," he said.

"I totally understand, Judge Williams," said Dan, secretly glad that there wouldn't be a hearing. That would be the best news that the Andersons could have possibly received. He thanked the Judge and prepared to call Thomas and give him the good news.

CHAPTER 41

Thomas was seated at his desk, looking at the properties they had listed. His real estate company was thriving, and he had some excellent employees that were motivated to sell. Last year had been their best revenue cycle yet. But the state of the company wasn't on his mind but the impending court hearings and the questions that would be asked about their family. He knew at the time it wasn't the right thing to do, but Anderson offered so much money, knowing they needed some financial help. This was going to complicate their lives and may even impact his livelihood. The worry was constantly on his mind. He was startled when his cell phone rang.

"Hello," he said.

"Thomas, Dan Forsyth here. How are you this morning?" he asked conversationally.

"Fine, fine, Dan, how about you?" he asked, wondering what the call was about.

"I heard from Judge Williams this morning," said Dan.

Thomas cringed. Judge Williams presided

over the contesting of Oliver Anderson's will.

"Really? Is he the judge who will be presiding over the hearing?" he asked.

"No, actually, he was baffled by the facts of the case. He knew Mr. Anderson and he was aghast at the arrangement he had made with you and your family. He actually doesn't want to complicate his court, meaning there would be too many factions regarding this case. He wants to grant the petition without a hearing," explained Dan.

"Really? Are you kidding me?" asked Thomas, feeling some relief of pressure.

"Yes really," said Dan. "He is going to grant all four petitions, and the name changes will be granted. I'm not sure when it will be finalized but I know that he wants to have it done as quickly as possible."

Thomas was speechless. "I don't know what to say," he said to Dan.

"This is great news, Thomas. All of your fears were unfounded. As soon as we get the paperwork in the office, I'll have all of you come in and sign the documents. Then, you can start making those changes on your legal documents," outlined Dan.

"Thank you, Dan," said Thomas simply.

"You're welcome, Thomas. I'll be in touch," he said, disconnecting the call.

Thomas sat there dumbfounded. He never dreamed this would be the outcome. He was extremely relieved and happy. Now he needed to let Lucinda know, because she had been a wreck since all of this occurred.

Picking up his office phone, he called her.

"Hello," said Lucinda.

"Lucinda, I just heard from Dan Forsyth," he began.

"Oh my god, what is it? I don't know if I can take any more bad news this month," said Lucinda.

"Calm down, Lucinda, it's good news," he said.

"Really? You aren't just saying that, are you?" she asked.

"No, I'm not. Apparently, Judge Williams was assigned our case," he began.

"Judge Williams? Oh no, he was the judge when we contested Oliver's will," said Lucinda.

"Yes, he is, but the case is so bizarre, that he is going to grant the petitions without a hearing. Dan is going to call us to come in and sign the papers when the court sends them to his office," said Thomas.

"Oh my, that is wonderful news, Thomas," said Lucinda. "What about your company and your employees?"

"I'm not worrying about that now. I'll figure something out, but in the meantime, stop worrying. Everything is going to be okay. Do you think Cindy will come back to the house this afternoon? I want to take the family out for a celebratory dinner," suggested Thomas.

"I'll call her right now," said Lucinda. "Oh

Thomas, this is the best news we could have gotten."

"You're right. So stop worrying and let's go out as a family," said Thomas, ending the call.

Lucinda called Cindy immediately.

"Hello Mom," said Cindy, recognizing the number.

"Cindy, are you busy today?" asked Lucinda.

"We are only open a half day on Fridays, Mom. I'm not on call either," she said. "Why?"

"We had some good news today about our petitions for a name change and it has been granted, without a hearing," exclaimed Lucinda.

"Wow, Mom, that is good news," said Cindy.

"Can you come back home this afternoon? Your dad wants to take us all out for a celebration of sorts. He wants you to be here too," said Lucinda.

"I was just going to do some housework, so yes, I can come back. I'll leave soon and will be there about 6:00 p.m. Will that work?" asked Cindy.

"That will be perfect," said Lucinda. "See you then. Drive safely."

"Okay Mom, bye," said Cindy, disconnecting the call.

Lucinda went upstairs to tell Tom Jr. the good news and that they were all going out to dinner. Lucinda felt happy.

Marly had driven the route to Gatlinburg

many times but this time she was nervous because of what she might find at the cabin. But, she was trying not to worry and wanted to have a good trip with Kate. They chatted along the highway, talking about everything except for the one thing that Marly was avoiding. Kate realized it and let her talk about anything she wanted because she knew that Marly was anxious about what she was going to find, if anything, at the cabin.

"Okay, I can't wait any longer. I want a muffin!" said Kate, laughing.

Marly laughed too and said, "I think there is a park up here somewhere. We can stop and walk around, after we eat a muffin."

"Great," said Kate, "we probably need to stretch our legs anyway."

Marly turned off of I-40 onto the exit for Cookeville and the Burgess Falls State Park. She parked and they got out, muffins in hand, and found a picnic table. Marly had also packed some small bottles of juice to complete the perfect breakfast on the road.

"Marly, this muffin is delicious. I know you went to culinary school so have you thought about a bakery adventure seriously?" asked Kate.

"I have thought about it, and I haven't completely ruled it out. It would have to be the perfect scenario and now that I am thinking of leaving Germantown, I have a whole new set of decisions to make," she said.

"True, but you could certainly keep baking on the back burner," said Kate, taking the last bite of her muffin. "I'm glad you made extras because I see another one in my future tonight!"

"Thank you, Kate," said Marly. "I'll keep it on the list. Now, with that said, are you ready for a little bit of hiking? The River Trail is a mile and a half, round trip to see the falls. Are you up for it?"

"Yes, I think I am. I can always stop and rest if needed but my strength has been returning," said Kate.

"Okay, but if we need to turn around, just let me know," said Marly.

"Alright my friend, lead on," said Kate, following Marly to the trail.

For the next forty minutes they trekked along the path, taking in the beautiful waterfalls along the Falling Water River. It was breathtaking and Kate kept taking pictures and video with her phone.

"I wish Seth could see this!" she said, sending him some of the videos.

"Maybe you can come back together one day," said Marly, taking pictures herself.

It was a fun outing and by the time they made it back to the car, Marly could tell that Kate was fatigued.

"We may have pushed it too much," said Marly, feeling concerned.

"I'm fine, Marly, just a bit winded. But I loved it and wouldn't trade that experience for anything.

Thank you for showing me," said Kate.

They got back on the road, seeing beautiful scenery and mountains in the distance. It was a great road trip but the closer they got to Gatlinburg, the more pensive they became.

Ethan and Brittany had a full day of sightseeing, going to Graceland and seeing Elvis' estate, the garden, as well as the airplanes. They did a little bit of shopping and ate at a place located near Graceland. They walked down Beale Street and noted the many clubs that lined the street, boasting of jazz, fun, and BBQ.

"We need more than one day to see all of this, Ethan," said Brittany.

"I know, I had no idea there was so much to see," agreed Ethan. "But, I also have dinner reservations for us, and I absolutely want to see you in that dress. I think we need to head back to the hotel."

"So, where are we going?" she asked.

"We're going to try the Porch & Parlor Prime Steakhouse," said Ethan. "It has great reviews and is a bit swanky."

"I can't wait," said Brittany. "Thank you for this weekend, Ethan. I haven't done anything like this in such a very long time."

He looked at her and smiled, "That is a crying shame, Brit. A woman like you deserves to be treated like this, every day of the week. However, I can't afford it every day, but I definitely can afford it periodically. And we will."

Taking her hand, they walked back to the car and headed to the hotel, to relax and get ready for dinner. It was an evening they were both looking forward to sharing together.

CHAPTER 42

Thomas got home around 5:00 p.m., anxious to take the family to dinner. He walked in the kitchen and Lucinda wasn't to be found. He went into the living room, and she was seated in a wingback chair, reading a book.

"Hello Lucinda," he said, "are you ready for dinner?"

She had on a white sheath dress with tiny cherries on it and a red jacket. "Yes, I am. Is this okay? You never said where we were going," she answered him.

"The news was so good, that we are going to Porch & Parlor Steakhouse downtown," said Thomas, smiling.

"Thomas, that is very expensive," said Lucinda, who was always conscious of costs.

"Tonight is a celebration, Hon, and we deserve it. Especially after all that Oliver Anderson has put us through these many years," said Thomas emphatically.

"I agree with you there for sure," said Lucinda. "Tom said he would come downstairs when he was ready. Maybe you can check on him when you go up to change."

"Yep, I'll do that now," said Thomas, as he took the stairs two at a time. He was looking forward to this dinner, one that he thought of as their liberation from the Andersons.

Stopping by Tom's door, he asked, "Hey Tom, you need any help in there?"

"No Dad, I'm just about ready. I'll head downstairs in a few minutes," he said, slipping his feet into his shoes.

As Thomas got ready, Tom Jr. walked down the stairs to where his mother was waiting.

"Tom, you look so handsome," said Lucinda, smiling at him. The bruises on his face were fading and he was moving better.

"Thanks Mom, you look pretty," he said, smiling.

"Thank you," she said. "Cindy should be here in about twenty minutes. She just called to let me know."

"That's good. Dad seems to be in a good mood," said Tom. "I guess he is happy with the news from the attorney."

"Yes, and it's the best news we could have received. It won't be long now that we can go back to being the Westons," said Lucinda, starting to feel some excitement about it.

Thomas came down the stairs, smartly dressed in a red shirt and black slacks. "I thought I would try to match you, Lucinda," he said, smiling at her.

She was flattered that he thought about that and told him how handsome he looked. "I'm very fortunate to have two men taking me to dinner."

Looking at his watch, Thomas asked, "When's Cindy going to get here?"

"She should be here in about fifteen minutes, Thomas," Lucinda said, just as Cindy's car pulled up. "Oh, I guess she got here a little sooner than expected."

Cindy came in the front door and was wearing a yellow sundress with white daisies on it and carried a white jacket. "Hey, I got here pretty quickly, Mom, and no, I wasn't speeding. I just got a lot of the green lights."

Refusing to comment, Lucinda said, "You look lovely. Thomas, we're all ready."

They got into Lucinda's Cadillac and Thomas drove them to the restaurant located in downtown Memphis. They were all looking forward to a wonderful evening.

Marly and Kate continued toward Gatlinburg when Marly asked Kate if she wanted to stop at a motel for the night.

"How much longer to the cabin?" asked Kate.

"About an hour, because we are almost to Pigeon Forge," said Marly, mentally calculating.

"Why don't we stay at the cabin, if we can get there before dark," said Kate. "We can spruce up if we need to."

"No need for that," said Marly. "I contacted my cleaning service and asked to have it done today so all we need to do is show up."

"That's even better," said Kate. "We'll be able to just come in and totally relax."

"That's right," said Marly. "And, I sent them a short grocery list and that should already be done as well."

"You've thought of everything, Marly," said Kate, impressed.

"It's the least I can do for you, Kate, since we drove instead of flying," said Marly.

"Don't be sorry about that, Marly, I have totally enjoyed the road trip. You miss so much when you fly!" said Kate.

The next hour went by quickly, and Marly pulled up the long driveway to the cabin. There were no lights on, and it seemed quite deserted.

"Looks like the renters did get moved to the new location," said Marly, as she opened the back of her Tahoe and she and Kate unloaded their bags. She keyed in the door code, and it unlocked, and they entered, turning on some lights as well. Everything was in order and cleaned.

They claimed their rooms and took the time to unpack. When Kate came out of her room, Marly was in the kitchen, taking out ingredients to make quesadillas for dinner.

"Does that sound okay?" asked Marly.

"Sounds perfect," said Kate. "What can I do to help?"

"You could pour us a glass of wine," said Marly, indicating the two glasses on the counter and

Kate laughed.

"Gladly!" she said, pouring them a crisp Riesling from the wine fridge. Taking a sip, Kate closed her eyes and said "Ahhh, delicious. The best way to end a long day."

Picking up her glass, Marly took a drink and agreed, "You are so right."

"After dinner we will call Lucy and get her flight time," said Marly, putting the ingredients together and laying the tortillas onto the hot grill pan.

"Mmmm, I didn't realize I was hungry until I started smelling those peppers and onions grilling," Kate said, sitting on a bar stool and watching Marly work.

When dinner was done, they sat at the island, eating the hot and spicy quesadillas and drinking the cold wine, reliving some of the memories of the day.

Thomas drove up to the front of the restaurant and the valet was there to take their car and another person ushered them into the restaurant.

"This is so fancy, Dad," said Cindy, walking in with him. "You certainly are going all out tonight."

"I think the occasion calls for it, Punkin," he said, calling her his pet name for her.

They were escorted to their table, and the hostess gave them menus and a wine list, saying their server would return in a few moments.

"Thomas, this place is so nice. Thank you for bringing us here," said Lucinda, looking around the restaurant's interior, noting all of the décor.

"I've been here once," he said, "but everything here is top notch. I want you all to order whatever you like because this is a celebration. Soon we will be the Westons, and we won't have any of the Anderson past attached to us."

The server appeared at their table, taking drink orders and asking if they wanted to order an appetizer.

Thomas answered for the group, saying," We will have the Duck Confit Ravioli and the Fried Oysters Rockefeller. Anything else?"

Everyone was satisfied with his selections and the server left to put in their requests.

They were in a good mood, drinking their drinks and when the appetizers were served, they tried both of them. It was a great start to what promised to be a memorable evening.

The server returned to take their orders for dinner. Lucinda ordered the Scottish Salmon, Cindy chose the Surf and Turf, Tom was having the Wagyu Tasting and Thomas chose the Tomahawk Ribeye. As they were enjoying the appetizers and waiting for the main course, Cindy looked over at the door and noticed a woman in a stunning pink sheath dress, that sparkled like diamonds.

"Wow, Mom, look at that gorgeous dress," said

Cindy.

"Very nice, I guess if I had a figure like that, I'd wear it too," said Lucinda, impressed as well.

When the woman and her date turned around to head to their table, Cindy recognized her.

"Oh my god, Tom, it's your ex-girlfriend with some dude," said Cindy.

Tom turned around and saw Brittany on the arm of a guy that seemed vaguely familiar to him.

"What the hell?" asked Tom, finally realizing that she was with Ethan Longmire. "She's with the guy she left for me."

As they got closer to the table, Thomas said, "I guess they'll let anyone in here."

When they were close enough to hear his remarks, Tom said, "Well Brittany, did you find another sucker to fund your habits? Looks like Longmire has the funds!"

Brittany blushed and Ethan stepped forward, "Who are you?"

"Don't remember me, Ethan? I'm Tom Weston, Brittany's lover from New York," he said smugly.

Ethan pulled his fist back to hit Tom, who had the decency to flinch, but Brittany grabbed his arm and said, "He's not worth it, Ethan. He'll crawl back under his rock soon enough."

"Go on to the table, Brit, I'll be right there," said Ethan. As she left, he leaned down to Tom and whispered, "Careful, Tom, or you might get attacked in another alley somewhere."

Leaving their table, Thomas saw that Tom was shaken up by what the man had said.

"What is it, Tom? Do we need to call the police? Did he threaten you?" asked Thomas, looking at his son.

"No Dad, just a jealous prick trying to pick a fight. Let's forget about it," said Tom.

CHAPTER 43

When Ethan arrived at the table, Brittany was waiting for him. He sat down as if nothing had happened.

"Are you okay, Ethan? Did Tom say anything else to you?" asked Brittany.

"Nothing that was important," said Ethan. "Let's forget about him and have a lovely dinner. Have you had a chance to look over the menu?"

"Not yet, but I'm going to do that now," said Brittany.

The server asked about drinks and Ethan ordered a bottle of champagne.

"What's the occasion, Ethan?" asked Brittany.

"Being here with you," said Ethan, smiling, and the fact that he got to scare the shit out of Tom Weston.

In a few minutes, the server was back with the champagne, and he uncorked it, and poured their glasses before setting it in the ice bucket beside the table.

"Are we ready to order?" he asked.

"For our appetizers, we'll have the King Prawn Cocktail and the Lobster Thermidor

Mushrooms," said Ethan. "Is that okay with you, Brit?"

"Perfect," she said, having been overwhelmed by the sheer volume of choices.

"To the most beautiful woman in the room and in my world," said Ethan, raising his glass in a toast.

Brittany raised her glass and smiled. Tom could see her from his seat in the restaurant. He saw them toasting and he got angry. *Probably celebrating my injuries*, he thought. He couldn't really say anything, but he wanted to so badly.

Ethan was ready with their order when the server returned. "She will have the Petite Filet with the Creamed Corn Brulée and the Brussels Sprouts & Bacon, and I will have the Signature Filet with the Maple Roasted Sweet Potato and Glazed Carrots."

"Excellent choices, sir," said Pierre, their server, and he disappeared to put in their order.

"These prawns are so big," said Brittany, "and delicious."

"I agree but the mushrooms are excellent. Here, try one," he said, popping one in her mouth.

Watching them from afar, Tom couldn't enjoy his dinner. His mother noticed his frown.

"What's wrong, Tom, is your steak not good?" she asked.

"No Mom, it's excellent. I'm just peeved watching Brittany and Ethan," he said.

"Don't worry about them, Son, you're better off without a gold digger like her," said his father. "It's obvious she follows the money."

"Yeah, you're right, Dad," he agreed although he regretted losing her.

"Britt, do you want some dessert?" asked Ethan.

"Where would you like me to put it?" she said, laughing. "I'm so full now I think I need to walk back to the hotel!"

When their server returned to offer dessert, Ethan asked for the Toffee Bread Pudding to go and handed Pierre his black card.

He quickly left the table and returned with the dessert in a box and the check. Ethan paid it and left a hefty gratuity for the server who thanked him profusely.

"It was an excellent meal and the service was extraordinary," said Ethan. "Thank you."

Ethan got up and helped Britt to her feet and said, "If I didn't already tell you, that dress is stunning and you do it justice."

Smiling and blushing at the same time, she boldly said, "Just wait until I take it off for you."

"I can't wait," he said, walking with her, pausing when she wanted to go to the ladies room.

While he waited, Thomas walked up behind him to go to the men's room. He stopped and commented, "Hope you enjoy my son's leftovers. You better be careful, she's a gold digger."

Ethan pulled out his phone and scrolled to the pictures of Brittany's bruised body and said, "No, she isn't his leftovers. She was his punching bag and he better be glad that she isn't pressing charges."

Brittany came out of the ladies' room and was shocked to see Tom's dad speaking with Ethan, but Ethan walked directly to her and escorted her out, not looking back to see the horrified look on Thomas' face.

They walked outside as the valet pulled up with their Murano. Ethan handed him a fifty-dollar bill, and the valet helped Brittany into the car. They drove off into the night, headed toward their hotel.

As the Andersons/Westons got ready to leave, Thomas paid the bill, and they walked outside. The valet brought their car, the women got in the back and the men in the front, and they drove off. On the way home, Lucinda spoke up.

"Cindy, are you going to spend the night?" she asked.

"I think so, Mom. It will be a long drive tonight and I did have a couple of drinks. I'll drive home in the morning sometime," Cindy said.

"Good, I made up your bed with fresh sheets this morning," said Lucinda. As they chatted in the backseat. Thomas spoke low to Tom.

"That guy Ethan showed me something," he said.

"Yeah, what?" asked Tom, not really wanting to talk about Brittany and Ethan.

"He showed me pictures of her, beaten and bruised and said you did it," said Thomas.

"That's a lie, Dad," said Tom, fidgeting in his seat.

Thomas could tell his answer was a lie. "Why did you do it, son?"

"She's a bitch, Dad. And why does he have pictures of her?" he asked, trying to deflect.

"Maybe for evidence. He said you were lucky she wasn't pressing charges," Thomas said.

"What are you two talking about in whispers?" asked Lucinda.

"Probably man talk, Mom," said Cindy and they laughed together.

Thomas was concerned about his son. What if they did decide to move forward with a legal battle. He needed to do something about it but wasn't sure. He better call Dan.

Marly and Kate were exhausted from the long travel day and all of the sightseeing. After they ate, they called Lucy to get her flight information.

"Hey Lucy," said Marly and Kate chimed in as well.

"Hello, you two, how was your day?" asked Lucy.

"Long," said Kate, "although I'm sure Marly is really tired after driving all day!"

"It was a piece of cake," said Marly, smiling.

Kate asked Lucy, "What time will you be flying tomorrow?"

"Actually, I got finished with my projects and I got an early morning flight. Rafe and I are in San Antonio tonight. He's going to take me to the airport in the morning, and my flight is scheduled to land at 10:05 a.m." said Lucy.

"Oh a little getaway for you two," said Marly. "That is nice."

"Yes, we decided it would be easier, and he'll be home before I take off," said Lucy.

"Okay then," said Marly, "we will be there early to pick you up!"

"Sounds great," said Lucy, "I can't wait to see you both. Have you done any searching yet?"

"No silly," said Marly, "we are waiting until you get here!"

"Oh good," said Lucy. "I hoped that was what you would do. Kate, be sure you call Seth. He's been anxious about the road trip."

"I plan to as soon as we head to bed, which will not be long after this call," said Kate.

"I'm excited," said Lucy. "See you in the morning!"

"Goodnight," said Marly and Kate and they disconnected the call.

"It will be good to see her," said Kate.

Marly agreed, "Yes, it will be. I'm so lucky to have you two in my life. I'm glad that I don't have to do all of this on my own."

"We wouldn't have it any other way," said Kate, hugging Marly.

"Do you want to watch television or anything," asked Marly, yawning.

Laughing, Kate said, "I think I feel the same way you do. Let's head to bed because we need to get up early in the morning. Besides, I need to check in with Seth, according to Lucy!"

"Honestly, that sounds good. I think I'm going to sleep soundly tonight," said Marly, heading to her room as Kate did the same.

Kate got ready for bed and laid down. It was so quiet here in the cabin and peaceful. That is what she missed about the Blanco house. She picked up her phone and clicked her favorites and touched Seth's name. It immediately rang.

"Hello Katie," his voice came over the phone.

"Hello to you too, Seth," said Kate, smiling even though he couldn't see her.

"Long day?" he asked.

"Yes it was, but a good day. We saw some really beautiful waterfalls that you would love. Maybe we can take a trip together to see them," said Kate.

"That would be fun," said Seth. "How are you feeling?"

"Truthfully, I am good but exhausted. Even though Marly drove the entire way," said Kate.

"I'm glad to hear it," said Seth. "I was a little worried about a long road trip for you."

"I know you were, Seth, but I'm doing so good.

I think that when I get home, I'll have to decide about returning to work or not. We'll discuss that when I get back," said Kate.

"Whatever you decide, Kate, will be fine. I love you, Katie," said Seth.

"I love you too, Seth," said Kate, ending the call and quickly falling asleep.

CHAPTER 44

Ethan and Brittany arrived at the hotel and went to their suite. The night would have been perfect if Tom Weston had not been there. But, Ethan thought he took care of him by letting his father know what a creep he is.

"Ethan, tonight was magical," said Brittany.

Ethan smiled at her, knowing that he still loved her, "I'm glad you enjoyed it. I thought the food was fantastic as well as the service."

"It certainly was posh, and I loved it," said Brittany. "I'm sorry we had to see Tom there. What a weird coincidence."

"Right? Oh well, we don't have to worry about him," said Ethan.

"I'm not," she said, smiling seductively. "Want to meet me in the bedroom?"

"I most certainly do," he said, hearing his phone ping that he had a message.

"You take care of that, and I'll be waiting for you, awake this time!" she said, giggling.

As she disappeared into the bedroom, Ethan looked at his phone and saw that it was from Mr. Kennedy. He quickly called him.

"Hello Ethan, how is it going?" asked Franklin.

"Very good, sir," said Ethan. "We had a lovely day sightseeing and then dinner out tonight."

"I'm glad you're having a good time," said Franklin. "Did you speak to her about your staying behind on Sunday?"

"I did and she is okay with it. I told her you were traveling here, and I needed to work with you on a project. Everything is fine," said Ethan.

"Good, I wanted to make sure," said Franklin.

"We did have a surprise tonight though," said Ethan. "Tom Weston, the guy from New York, was at the same restaurant having dinner with his family."

"Oh really?" said Franklin, surprised as well. "How did he look?"

"His arm was in a cast, and I could tell he had some bruising but otherwise, he was fine. Well enough to be a jerk," said Ethan.

"Oh? What happened?" asked Franklin.

Ethan told him what occurred, and Franklin laughed when he heard what Ethan had said to him.

"I believe he will think twice before bothering her or you again," said Franklin.

Ethan also relayed his interaction with Mr. Weston, Tom's father. "I think that put some fear into him."

"It should. I think you handled everything perfectly, Ethan. Enjoy tomorrow with Brittany and I will see you at the address on Sunday morning," said Franklin.

"I'll be there as soon as I drop Brit off at the airport," said Ethan.

"Excellent," responded Franklin, ending the call.

Ethan walked into the bedroom to find Brittany propped up against several pillows, wearing nothing but a smile. He stood there for a few moments, taking in her beauty. The bruises she had before were almost gone and her alabaster skin glowed in the soft light of the lamp. He didn't say a word but undressed while she watched. He walked toward the bed and slid in beside her, pulling her close to his chest. Her hair smelled faintly of roses, and he started lightly kissing her, working his way from the top of her head to her pouty lips. Slipping her arms around him, she deepened their kiss, pressing her body against his, feeling his arousal.

"Mmmm, I like this," she whispered.

"So do I," he said, letting his hands wander down her body, cupping her breasts and then moving to the warmth between her legs.

She moaned slightly when he touched her, spreading her legs apart to give him more access. Slipping his fingers inside of her, he pushed them in deeply and then set up a thrusting motion, whispering, "Yes, Brit, you feel so good."

It didn't take long for her to have an orgasm, and he pulled his hand out of her wetness and kissed her neck, moving to her breasts. She pushed his shoulder down and climbed on top of him, looking down into his eyes.

"I've missed this, and I've missed you, Ethan. I'm sorry, I was such a fool," said Brittany.

"Let's have no regrets," he said, guiding her onto his hard cock.

She slowly eased down and then up, each time pushing him deeper inside of her until they were locked together. She started grinding her hips as he sucked her breasts, both of them moaning and grunting. They climaxed together and Brittany laid against his chest, his skin glistening with a light sheen.

"Brit, that was wonderful," said Ethan, rubbing her back and then her buttocks.

Brittany lifted her head and looked at him, "Yes it was."

They stayed together for a little while and then Brittany slipped off and laid beside him. Her hands began rubbing his chest, then his flat stomach, moving lower and he was already getting hard again. She straddled him, this time with her mouth encircling his hard shaft as he moaned. He pulled her hips to him, slipping his tongue in and out of her hot wetness while she sucked his cock. She slipped her hands under his butt, pulling him closer and deeper into her mouth. She moved in a steady rhythm until he almost exploded. He quickly pushed her down on the bed and entered her, thrusting in and out while she panted. They came together again, and they laid still, spent.

After a few quiet moments, Ethan smiled at her. "We didn't have our dessert."

"I did," she said, grinning at him and he kissed her, knowing that sleep wasn't going to be coming any time soon.

Marly and Kate were up early to head to the Gatlinburg airport. Marly was glad that Lucy was coming earlier than expected because she was anxious to get started at the cabin. They had a quick breakfast of another muffin and some juice before heading into town. They left at 9:00 a.m. since it was Saturday and Gatlinburg was always busy on the weekends. They arrived at the airport at 9:45 a.m. and went inside to the baggage claim where they had arranged to meet Lucy. Checking the flight board, Kate saw that her flight was going to be on time.

"Just a few more minutes, Marly, and we'll all be together again," said Kate.

"I know, I'm excited," admitted Marly, her eyes scanning the groups of people entering the area.

A few minutes after 10:00, Lucy came around the corner, carrying a backpack.

"Lucy!" Marly and Kate screamed in unison as they hurried over to their friend, hugging her tightly. By-standers were watching and smiling at this obvious reunion.

"You'd think we hadn't seen each other in

years," laughed Lucy. "I have one bag, because I didn't know how much time we were going to need."

They walked over to the carousel and watched the baggage drop onto it as they chatted about the last few days. Lucy identified her bag and soon the three of them were walking to the car to head back to the cabin.

"Are you hungry, Lucy?" asked Marly.

"No, Rafe and I had breakfast before he left me at the airport to head back to Blanco," said Lucy. "I'm good right now."

"I saved you one of Marly's muffins at the cabin, but it was hard to do. They are so delicious!" said Kate.

"Isn't everything she makes delicious?" asked Lucy as they drove back to the cabin.

"At least it's daylight and we shouldn't hit anyone on the side of the road," said Lucy, laughing as she referred to their infamous girl trip.

"Thanks for the reminder, Lucy," laughed Marly and Kate joined in.

They arrived at the cabin and got Lucy settled before they sat down in the living room.

"Okay, what is going to be our plan of action?" asked Kate, knowing that Marly was ready to start the search.

"I'm not sure that there would be anything hidden in the bedrooms, other than the one that my grandfather used. We can start in that room and then I thought the mudroom next. We may even want to search the old shed out back, even though Marc cleaned it out when he was pretending to be Mac," said Marly, remembering more about the girl trip.

"That was such a bizarre time, Marly. Come to think of it, maybe all of this stuff happens because you are around!" said Lucy, laughing.

"Very funny," said Marly. "Remember, you have been around in all of those situations too, so maybe it is you who is the jinx!"

"We've all been there," said Kate, "so, let's get this mystery figured out!"

The three of them got up and headed into the room that was the one Marly's grandfather used when he stayed at the cabin.

"Are you ready for this, Marly?" asked Kate, looking at her friend.

"Yes, I'm so ready to get all of this over with and think about what I am going to do for the rest of my life," said Marly.

"If you need help deciding," said Lucy, "I have some ideas."

"Why am I not surprised, Lucy?" smiled Marly at her friend. "I'm looking forward to hearing about these ideas."

They got to work searching the room and hoping to find something that would give Marly the closure that she needed.

CHAPTER 45

Jake Friar and Steve Mathison stayed at the Bureau all morning, going through the bin of photographs, matching codes on the back of them with the codes in the journals, making notes and attaching names to the people when they were able. It was a long process but they both were so excited, they couldn't think about stopping until they had reviewed everything.

"This is tremendous, Jake," said Steve. "I never thought we'd find anything on some of these people."

"I know, Steve," said Jake, looking at the copy of the letter Marly's grandfather had written to her. "Read this, Steve," he said, handing the letter to him.

Steve scanned the letter and said, "Wow, poor kid. To have all of this laid on you by your grandfather, someone you trusted. I recognize the name Franklin Kennedy. He is in Colorado, if I'm not mistaken. He has been on the radar off and on over the years, but he is extremely wealthy and apparently has friends in high places."

"He is and he was the man who contacted Ms. Anderson and prompted her search because of his demands. I guess we are lucky that she reached out to someone who put her in touch with me," said Jake, not wanting to give up Lenny as his source.

"Lucky we are," agreed Steve. "This will save years of research and follow up on people. Look, I'm beat, and I know you are. Let's call it a day and reconvene on Monday. I'll lock this information in the safe in my office."

"Sounds good," said Jake, stifling a yawn. "I'll see you on Monday, Steve." With that, Jake walked outside to his car and drove off, wondering where all of this was going to lead.

Lenny called Kennedy to report in and surprisingly, the call went to voicemail. He left a message. SUBJECTS STAYED IN BUT LEFT THIS MORNING FOR SHOPPING TRIP TO BIG BOX STORE. I FOLLOWED INSIDE AND TRIP PURCHASES BEING MADE. BACK AT HOUSE NOW. ADVISE IF ADDITIONAL SURVEILLANCE IS NEEDED.

Lenny wasn't even going to the house anymore, since the girls left yesterday. He just had to keep up appearances for Kennedy. It wasn't long before his phone rang.

"Lenny, Franklin Kennedy here," he said. "Sounds like they are getting ready to leave tomorrow. I see no need for you to hang around and watch them. We know what they are going to do. Thank you for your services, and maybe we will work together again someday."

I highly doubt it, thought Lenny, but aloud he said, "Maybe, you never know. Nice doing business with you, Mr. Kennedy. Bye."

Lenny ended the call first, leaving Franklin holding a dead phone. *Oh well*, he thought, *I got what I wanted by hiring Lenny Crocker. Now, I will take over this operation personally.*

Lenny packed up his things at the motel and loaded his SUV. The sooner he got out of here, the better. He didn't want to be anywhere around when the fireworks started, literally. Hopefully, he wouldn't be implicated in any of it. He had been very careful when setting the charges, didn't leave any signatures or fingerprints. He was ready to be back in the solace of his cabin on the mountain, at the top of Snake Hill Road.

Cindy had breakfast with her family before heading back to Nashville.

"Do you have to leave today?" asked Lucinda, having enjoyed her visit.

"Yes Mom," she said. "I am on call tomorrow and I need to do some errands before then."

"I understand but it has been so nice having you here. Come back again when you can," her mom said.

"I will and Tom, take care of yourself. Don't let anyone else jump you!" she said, laughing.

Tom didn't find it funny but played along, "I'll try not to piss off any more muggers." Although, after what Ethan had whispered to him, he was sure that it wasn't a mugger.

"Seriously, I'm glad you're okay, and on the mend," she said, hugging Tom goodbye.

"Thanks Sis," he said.

Thomas hugged her as well, "Goodbye Punkin, drive safely and I'll let you know when Dan calls us to sign the papers. Hopefully, you will be able to get away."

"If I know in advance, I can get someone to cover for me, Dad," said Cindy. Gathering her things, Cindy walked out the back door to her car and backed out, leaving her family behind.

Lucinda started cleaning up the kitchen while Thomas and his son went into the living room.

Thomas looked at Tom and said, "I'm going to call Dan today and ask him if there is anything we need to do, in case that woman presses charges."

"Dad, leave it alone, I'm pretty sure she won't," said Tom.

"How can you be so sure?" asked Thomas. "The pictures I saw were horrific. How could you do that to someone?"

"Look what someone did to me?" Tom asked, getting angry.

"A woman didn't beat you up, Tom," said his father.

"A woman caused it," said Tom, not realizing

what he had said.

"What do you mean by that?" asked Thomas, looking at his son.

Tom had to do some quick thinking and said, "I mean, if Brittany hadn't left me, I probably wouldn't have been out that late by myself."

"I see," said Thomas, but he didn't. He could tell Tom was hiding something and getting mad. That was the last thing he wanted because he just wanted to protect his son from any ramifications of his actions.

"Look Dad, I messed up and Brittany left me. That's it. If she was going to press charges, don't you think she would have right after it happened? But she didn't. She ran back to her old lover in Colorado," Tom said.

"In Colorado? So why are they here?" asked his father.

"I don't know, Dad. Ethan works for some high-powered guy there and I'm sure he travels. It was just a coincidence," said Tom.

"I hope you're right, Tom," said Thomas. "I'm going to play a round of golf. You want to join me?"

"No Dad, I think I'll rest for a while," said Tom, getting up to go to his room.

Lucinda walked in and saw them together, "I'm so glad that my boys are together. What are we talking about?"

"Tom is going upstairs to rest, and I was thinking about playing a round of golf today. Are you okay with that, Lucinda?" he asked his wife.

Surprised by his consideration of her, she said, "Of course, Thomas. Enjoy yourself. Tom probably needs to rest, and I have a book here that I'm reading." She picked up her copy of *Coastal Justice* and said, "I'll take it upstairs to my reading nook."

Thomas kissed his wife goodbye and left, heading to the club. While he was driving, he put in a call to Dan Forsyth.

"What's happening, Thomas?" asked Dan.

"Headed to the club for a round," he answered. "What about you?"

"Honey do's," he said, laughing.

"Dan, I want to ask you a question. A guy approached me last night and showed me some pictures of my son's ex-girlfriend and she was beaten up pretty bad. The guy said Tom did it and I wondered if there was anything we needed to do in case she pressed charges," said Thomas.

"Wow Thomas, you are really getting hit from all sides," said Dan. "Why did the guy approach you?"

"He was with my son's ex at the restaurant where we had dinner last night. I think my son is guilty, but he says he doesn't think she will press charges. I just want to be prepared, just in case," said Thomas.

"When did it happen?" Dan asked, giving Thomas his full attention.

"I think it was two or three months ago," said

Thomas. "That was when I learned they had broken up."

"I think the only thing you can do is wait and see," said Dan. "I know that isn't the answer you were looking for, Thomas."

"I don't know what I wanted, except to be prepared. I guess I'll just have to wait and see if the other shoe drops," said Thomas. "Thanks for talking to me, Dan."

"Just sit tight, Thomas. Don't borrow trouble, because if that much time has passed, she probably won't press charges," said Dan. "But, if she does, call me, okay?"

"Thanks, Dan, get your honey do's done," said Thomas.

"I'd rather be on the course with you," said Dan, "have fun."

Thomas disconnected the call and drove on to the club for some relaxation, he hoped.

Marly, Lucy, and Kate were searching in her grandfather's old room at the cabin. Everything seemed normal, no books to search, no false walls that could be detected. They looked behind pictures on the wall and through an old desk, but it yielded nothing.

"I don't think he had any hidey holes in here," said Lucy.

That stopped Marly in her tracks. "What did you say, Lucy?"

Looking at Marly, she said, "No hidey holes in

here."

"Hidey holes. Poppa called the little door under his bed, his 'hidey hole'. I had completely forgotten about that. I found it one day when I was playing hide and seek with him and I was pretty little. I crawled under his bed and saw a trap door."

Excitedly, they moved the large four poster bed and saw a rug under it, nailed to the floor. Marly found a hammer and pulled out the nails, moving the rug aside. There a small trap door was in the wooden floor. The hidey hole.

CHAPTER 46

The three girls looked at each other and Marly knelt down. She pulled on the clasp on the hinge, but it was stuck. Lucy found a screwdriver and handed it to Marly, and she pried it under the hinge, Suddenly, it gave way, and Marly pulled the small door open. There, in the bottom of the secret compartment was a small box, about the size of a shoebox. Taking it out of it's hiding place, Marly placed it on the bed and looked at her friends.

"Are you okay, Marly?" asked Kate.

"I don't know, I guess I'll let you know in a minute," said Marly. She opened the box and there was a stack of letters, tied with a ribbon. She pulled them out and saw the same handwriting that had been on the back of the picture. Giselle Armenti.

"I think these are from Giselle," said Marly.

"No return address either, since the envelopes are gone," noted Kate.

"He probably didn't want her to be found," said Lucy. "Can you imagine having to live that way?"

"I can't," said Marly.

"We can leave you alone, Marly, so that you can read these," said Kate.

"Really? Aren't we in this together?" she said. "Let's take them into the living room and go through them."

They went into the living room and started reading the letters.

Kate said, "In this one, she tells your grandfather that she is settled, in an undisclosed place. She said her time was near. I wonder what she meant by that. Was she sick or something?"

"Uh, yes, something. She writes '*the baby was born yesterday. He is healthy and we will stay here until I think we should travel again. I wish you could see him Randolph.*' Lucy looked at Marly, "I think your grandfather had a son!"

"Oh my god," exclaimed Marly. "Do you know what this means? I have a brother!"

Kate looked shocked and said, "You have some real family, Marly, not a fake one. Do you think your grandfather knew where she was but didn't want to endanger her secrecy?"

"I don't know," said Marly, picking up another letter. Opening it, she read, *Timothy is growing up so quickly. He started taking steps today. You would be so proud of him, Randolph.* She was letting Poppa know about them without giving away their location. I wonder if he ever knew where she was living?"

"There aren't any envelopes so we can't trace the postmarks," said Kate. "Unless…."

"Unless what?" asked Marly, looking at Kate.

"What if he separated the letters from the envelopes as another layer of protection but I'm sure he would have wanted to keep track of where they were. Maybe he put the envelopes in a different place. Were there any other hiding places around here?" asked Kate.

Marly thought and then said, "There used to be another small cabin on the property, but I haven't been there in years. I'm not even sure if it is still standing. Do you think he may have put something there?"

"It can't hurt to look," said Lucy, "and he might have made another hidey hole there."

"Oh this is exciting," said Kate. "Where is this cabin located, Marly.

"It used to be on the other side of the lake. We will need to wear good shoes because I have no idea how rough it will be," said Marly.

They got ready for the hike and headed out the back door in the mud room, heading down the path that Marly remembered taking with Marc. She pushed that memory aside and when they got to the big rock, she pointed to the right.

"Now, we need to go in that direction," she said.

The three of them hiked around the lake, not speaking, but watching the trail, which was rocky with roots growing up in it. When they made it around the bend in the lake, there it was; a small cabin that looked to be in pretty good shape.

"Is this it, Marly?" asked Lucy, assuming that it was.

"Yes, this is it. Poppa always said I shouldn't come here because it was dangerous," she said.

"Maybe he was protecting something there," Kate said, as they approached the front door.

Marly opened the door and walked into a small living area that was furnished. It was dusty and evident that no one had been here in a very long time. A small kitchen was there as well as two doors leading into what must be bedrooms. Marly opened one and saw a small toddler bed with a stuffed teddy bear on it. Tears filled her eyes, and she turned away. She opened the other door, and a small bed was there with a little wardrobe. Opening the wardrobe, she saw a couple of dresses and an empty hatbox.

Kate and Lucy lagged back, letting Marly take it all in.

"Should we pull back the bed and see if there is a secret compartment?" asked Marly.

"Sure," said Lucy and the three of them moved the bed with little effort.

A rug was nailed to the floor and Marly pulled on it. The material was dry rotted and tore easily, Underneath it was a compartment, identical to the one at the other cabin. The hinge was rusted shut and Marly went to the kitchen and found an old knife. She knelt down and pried at the hinge until it gave way.

Looking at her friends, Marly said, "It's now or never," as she opened the door of the hiding place. There was a stack of envelopes as well as a jewelry box. Marly took them out, handing them to Kate and Lucy as she got up.

"It seems that Giselle was here for a short while, wouldn't you agree?" asked Marly.

"Yes, I think so," agreed Lucy and Kate.

"Let's take these things to the main cabin. I feel there are too many ghosts here...a permeating sadness," said Marly.

They made their way back to the main cabin and went inside. It seemed bright in comparison to the dim cabin they had just left. Sitting down in the living room, they put the envelopes in date order by the postmarks.

"She lived in so many places," commented Lucy, looking at them. "New York, Florida, Montana, Nevada....poor Timothy, no place to call home. But no return addresses."

"I know, I wonder if they ever settled down. If they ever felt safe enough to stay in one place," said Marly, saddened by the thought.

"What's in the jewelry box, Marly?" asked Kate.

Lifting the lid, sparkling against the velvet was a fortune in jewelry.

Ethan and Brittany woke up and ordered room service for breakfast.

"What do you want to do today, Brit?" asked Ethan.

"More sightseeing?" she suggested.

"We'll try to see the things we missed yesterday and then get back here for an early dinner. I have to get you to the airport early and unfortunately, I will be staying behind," said Ethan.

"I know, but Mr. Kennedy needs you. Hopefully you will be home in a day or two. I am going to keep looking for a job too, so I can do that while you are gone," she said, smiling at Ethan.

Wishing she wouldn't get a job, Ethan just let her talk. Maybe he could talk her out of it when he got back home.

"Okay," he agreed and there was a knock at the door. It was room service, and a young man came in and set up the meal, taking the tip that Ethan slipped in his hand.

Brittany and Ethan enjoyed a leisurely breakfast and Brittany said, "I'm going to take a shower. You want to join me?"

"Absolutely," said Ethan as they walked into the bathroom and it was a very long time before they were finished.

Lenny was driving toward Colorado, thinking about Marly and wondering if she found anything at the cabin. He knew he shouldn't, but he called her.

"Hello," said Marly.

"Hey, Marly," he said, "Lenny here. I just

wanted to let you know that I am headed back home. Mr. Kennedy doesn't need me to watch you anymore since you are leaving tomorrow."

Marly laughed. "Well good, now you can get back to your favorite spot."

"That's the plan," he confirmed. "Let me know if you need me to help you in any way. Oh, did you find anything?"

"Nothing that I think Mr. Kennedy is looking for," said Marly.

"Keep looking," he said, "you never know where people will hide things."

"That's true, Lenny. Thanks for calling," said Marly, ending the call.

Taking a deep breath, Lenny knew that he probably would never hear from Marly again. If things had been different, if he had been different, maybe they could have gotten to be closer than friends. But life plays tricks on us sometimes and he felt that he ended up with a pretty good hand. He was living as a free man, thanks in part to Marly, in a place that he loved, and to be honest, his life was pretty good. He didn't want for anything, and he could live comfortably for the rest of his life. All in all, he had no complaints. His thoughts then went to Raven. She could have had such a different life, but she chose the wrong path. Unfortunately, he had helped her on that path and sadly, she had ended her life. Lenny didn't like where his thoughts were going. He switched on Sirius XM and put it on an oldies station. The music lifted his spirits as he traveled down the highway, looking forward to his front porch at the cabin. Yes, life was good.

CHAPTER 47

As Marly took the pieces of jewelry out of the box, they glittered with diamonds, rubies, sapphires, emeralds and amethysts. There was also a beautiful diadem set with sapphires and diamonds.

"Wow," said Lucy, "this would bankroll your travels for sure."

Kate agreed with Lucy, "Maybe this was how she funded her travels."

"If that were so, why are they still here?" asked Marly rhetorically.

"Good question," said Kate. "And the envelopes were put with the jewelry, so your grandfather had to have done it. Maybe she gave them to him for safekeeping."

Marly was thinking and said aloud, "Or maybe this was to be Timothy's inheritance, if anything happened to them."

"Where was the last envelope postmarked?" asked Kate.

"Tennessee," said Lucy, her eyes widened. "Oh my god, do you think she is still in Tennessee?"

"Could it be that simple?" wondered Marly

aloud.

"Maybe she didn't want to be too far from your grandfather so that Timothy would be able to see his father, if what we assume is true," said Kate.

"Poppa apparently knew how to communicate with people without traces and maybe he visited them, wherever they were located," said Marly, which made her feel happy if that were the case.

"It's getting late," said Kate. "Why don't we put this aside, distract ourselves with a movie and order a pizza?"

Lucy and Marly agreed on that plan and while Marly called a local pizzeria to place the order, Lucy and Kate were deciding on the movie.

"Let's eat first, get showered and ready for bed, then the movie," said Marly, after she finished the call.

"Sounds like a perfect idea," said Lucy, "because I'm hungry."

"When are you not hungry, Lucy?" asked Kate, laughing at her friend.

"I don't think I'm hungry when I'm asleep but now that I think about it, I wouldn't know. I'm usually hungry when I wake up, so, I must always be hungry!" Lucy exclaimed, laughing with her friends. It felt good to be together again.

The pizza was delivered, and the girls ate their fill, putting the leftovers in the fridge. They took showers and got in their pajamas, ready to watch Sweet Home Alabama, one of their favorites.

They sat on the sofa and Marly was getting

ready to start the film when suddenly, she stopped. "Kate, didn't you find an article that said Lady Giselle was married to Ramondo Breviat, a duke or something from Europe? Maybe Giselle signed that note and photograph with her family name, Armenti!"

"Duh, why didn't I think of that?" Kate said.

"I think I have been so emotional about the entire situation that I shut my mind off, because I didn't want to think about it," said Marly. "But, since we couldn't find her using Armenti, do you think she might have used Vinson?"

Kate ran to her room and grabbed her laptop. She brought it back into the living room and she started searching for Giselle Vinson in Tennessee. After a few minutes, she had to admit defeat as she couldn't find a Giselle or a G. Vinson.

"Dang, I just knew you were going to find something," said Lucy, just as disappointed as Marly.

"What if we looked for Timothy Armenti or Timothy Anderson? I know that Franklin Kennedy is Ramondo Breviat, according to the letter from my grandfather. So he would have known about the Armenti and Vinson name but not the Anderson one at that time."

Kate was already typing in the search bar, and she stopped, looking at Marly.

"What?" asked Marly.

"I can't believe this, but there is a Timothy

Anderson listed in Sevierville, Tennessee," said Kate as Lucy and Marly sat in silence.

Marly broke the silence, "That is nearby. It's only about thirty minutes from here."

"We can go there tomorrow, Marly!" exclaimed Lucy. "At least see if he is related in any way to Giselle."

Kate had also been thinking, "Marly, the article said she was married to Duke Breviat. What if those jewels are the crown jewels of whatever country in Europe they were from? That would be a big reason for them to be recovered."

"This just keeps getting more and more complicated," said Marly. "All of the what ifs are making me crazy, just thinking about it."

"So? What are we going to do?" asked Lucy.

Marly looked at her friends and said, "I think we are going to Sevierville tomorrow."

Ethan and Brittany had a full day of sightseeing, and they found a great place on Beale Street to eat and listen to some Delta blues.

"This place is so cool, Ethan," said Brittany as she tapped her foot to the music.

"Yes it is," he said and at that moment, their server brought the rack of ribs and sides they had ordered.

"Oh my gosh, Ethan, do you think we can eat half of this?" she asked, looking at the large portions.

"Probably not, but remember, I am staying

over so I can make another meal out of it. Besides, I don't want to walk around without you by my side," he said, smiling at her.

"That's sweet, Ethan. I'm just grateful that we didn't order an appetizer because then I couldn't walk around!" she said, laughing.

As the music played, they started eating and they both agreed it was the best BBQ ribs they had ever eaten.

"This meat just falls off of the bone," said Ethan, setting the bone in the tray beside the ribs.

"These baked beans are so flavorful. I wonder if they give out the recipe?" Brittany asked.

"I would guess probably not, but you can ask. You are pretty persuasive," said Ethan, looking at her and knowing she could persuade him of anything.

"I'm just going to enjoy it, but not too much because I have my eye on that Southern Pecan Pie Ala Mode!" she said, grinning at him.

"We'll see about that," said Ethan, grinning back. He was enjoying this trip a lot more than he thought he was going to, and he knew it was because Brit was with him. He would hate to see her go, but he didn't want her to be around when he met Mr. Kennedy at Marly Anderson's home.

Jake Friar finally got some sleep, and it was 2:00 p.m. when he woke up. He brewed a pot of coffee and poured himself a cup, going out onto the balcony of his apartment. There was a breeze blowing across the lake which cooled the air a little bit. He was thinking about all of the information they had reviewed last night and the far-reaching implications for Franklin Kennedy. It would have been just as bad for Oliver Anderson but not now, not since he had died. It might have involved his daughter, Marly Anderson, but the transfer of custody form her lawyer drew up released her from any culpability. Lenny had trusted her, and he doesn't trust anybody. Thinking about Lenny, he called him.

"Hello," he said.

"Hey Lenny, it's Jake. You on the road?" asked Jake.

"Yeah, my job is done in Tennessee, and I'm headed to Colorado. What's up?" asked Lenny.

"I was up all night with Agent Mathison, going through that box of information I picked up from your friend, Marly," said Jake.

"Hope it was worth your time," said Lenny, trying to be vague.

"Oh, it was definitely worth it. It is going to help us find several high-profile people that have been on our radar for a long time. Also, your friend made me sign a form that released her from all responsibility of anything that might come from the investigation. She's a pretty smart cookie," said Jake.

"She is but she isn't involved. She just

happened to find it and I put her in the right direction to get rid of it. She lost her grandfather and now she is finding out all kinds of shit about him. I think that is punishment enough for her, don't you think?" said Lenny, hoping that Jake wasn't going to pursue it.

"Yeah, I can't imagine what she's going through. I just thought I'd touch base with you," said Jake.

"Listen, I am going to give you a tip, but you didn't hear it from me. I think that Franklin Kennedy is going to break into Marly's house while she's out of town," he said.

"What makes you think that?" asked Jake, very interested.

"Because he wanted me to help him disarm her house. I told him I didn't know how to do that kind of thing," said Lenny.

Jake laughed. "I think you know how to do all the things, Lenny. So, when is this break-in supposed to happen?"

"Sometime tomorrow morning. He thinks Marly is leaving in the morning on her trip, but she left yesterday. He wants to search for something, which is probably the stuff you guys already have," said Lenny.

"Interesting. I will have the Memphis office send some plainclothes agents there tomorrow morning. I'll let you know if you were right," said Jake. "Safe travels, man."

"Thanks, Jake," said Lenny, disconnecting the

call and smiling broadly.

CHAPTER 48

Franklin Kennedy was in the back seat while Samson drove him to the charter plane hangar. It was early and he had to admit he had been unable to sleep because of the excitement. He hoped that today he would find that elusive clue as to where Giselle is hiding. Not that he wanted her back in his life, but she had something that she was not entitled to...the crown jewels of the Duke of Magenta. When he recovered them, he planned to return to Europe and restore them and reclaim his reputation. He also wanted to ensure that Oliver had not kept any Crimson Veil information. If he did find it, he would destroy it as well. Soon Samson announced their arrival at the airport and the hangar.

"Excellent, Samson," said Franklin, preparing to exit the car.

"I will check to ensure all is ready, sir," said Samson, walking inside the hanger.

After a few minutes, Samson returned to the car and opened the door for Mr. Kennedy.

"It's ready, sir," he said, accompanying Franklin to the plane and walking behind him as he boarded.

Franklin chose one of the seats and soon Derrick Porter got on the plane, sitting across the aisle from Franklin.

"Good to see you, Derrick. Are you ready for this?" he asked.

"Yep, I told my wife I had a business trip," said Derrick.

"That's not a lie, you do," said Franklin. "Were you able to employ Mr. Ricter for this assignment?"

"Yes, he will meet us there at 10:00 a.m. Anyone else going to be there?" Derrick asked.

"My employee, Ethan Longmire will be there as well as Samson," said Franklin, pointing him out in the back of the plane.

"Should be enough," said Derrick.

"Yes, more than enough. But it must be a thorough search. We are dealing with an old acquaintance of mine who was an expert at concealing information. I want every room searched," said Franklin.

"You got it, sir," said Derrick, pulling out his phone when Franklin reclined his seat and closed his eyes.

Ethan was up early, ordering their last room service breakfast, wanting to have it ready when she woke up. Soon there was a soft knock on the door and Ethan admitted the hotel staffer pushing a cart. They set up the meal and Ethan slipped a tip in his hand. He quickly left while Ethan moved the silver vase with a rose in it to the middle of the small table. He hated for her to fly back alone but he didn't think this thing with Mr. Kennedy would take very long. He sent a text to Davis to remind him to disarm the house at 10:00 a.m. and then he waited. He didn't have to wait long.

Brittany came out of the primary suite wearing the soft robe provided by the hotel, looking more beautiful than he remembered.

"Good morning, Brit," said Ethan, smiling at her.

"Oh my, how beautiful," she said, picking up the vase and smelling the rose.

"I wanted our last breakfast here to be special," he said, pulling out a chair for her. When she sat down, he sat beside her.

They ate the meal and talked about all of the memories they had made on this trip.

"I've had such a wonderful time, Ethan," said Brittany, biting into a big strawberry.

"I have too, Brit. I'm so glad that you came with me," he said. "As soon as we are done here, we need to get you ready and to the airport, although that is the last thing that I want to do right now."

"I know, Ethan, but it's only going to be a day or so. We will have plenty of time to be together and make more memories, right?" Brittany asked.

"Of course," he said as they finished up breakfast. They got up and he helped her gather her things and get them packed. He called for the bellman to come pick up the bags and call for the car from the valet. As they waited for the notification, Ethan took Brittany into his arms, holding her close. "I never want to let you go," he said.

His phone pinged and he moved to check the message.

Brittany laughed and he asked, "What's so funny?"

"You did let me go, to answer your phone," she said. "Timing is everything."

He laughed too and said, "That was the bellman. Valet is getting the car. Are you ready?"

"No but okay, let's go," she said, looking back one last time into the room and then they went downstairs to head to the airport.

Marly woke up early. She didn't sleep very much, going over everything in her mind. Were they on the right track or would they be making the biggest faux pas in history? It was such an unbelievable story, but stranger things had happened. She got up and dressed in jeans and a floral shirt, wearing tennis shoes. She pulled her hair back into a ponytail with a matching floral scrunchie. Looking at herself in the mirror, she thought, *here I am, I think I'm your sister, what do you think?* Thinking she better rephrase that in person, she laughed at herself. Worse case scenario, she can say she was mistaken, and they can leave with some dignity.

She quietly went into the kitchen so she wouldn't wake Kate and Lucy but to her surprise, they were already dressed and in the kitchen. Lucy was making pancakes and Kate was cooking bacon in the microwave.

"Good morning," said Marly. "What are you two doing up so early?

"Do you think any of us slept very well Marly?" asked Lucy, laughing. "I thought I would surprise you both with breakfast, but Kate was already in here, rummaging around in the fridge!"

"I think we all were thinking about today," said Kate. "I have to admit I was."

"I've thought about everything, all night. Do you think I'm doing the right thing? I mean, this could change his life forever and hers, if she is still alive," said Marly.

"I think of it like this," said Kate. "Would you want to know, Marly?"

"Yes, I would, no matter what it was," said Marly truthfully. "Okay, what can I do?"

In unison, Kate and Lucy said, "Mimosas!"

"I can do that," Marly said, pulling down glasses and getting the orange juice.

Ethan pulled up to the airport and helped Brittany out of the car. He went to the back and got her suitcase from the trunk, pulling up the handle to make it easier for her to get into the terminal.

"Here you go, milady," he said, formally, followed by a hug and a kiss.

She giggled and said, "Why thank you, sir, you are so very kind," she said, kissing him again.

"I better go because I can't hold up the departure lanes," said Ethan.

"I know, Ethan, call me tonight, okay?" she said, waving to him as she disappeared through the glass doors.

Getting back into the car, he drove to the rental service and turned the car in. Next, he called for an Uber to take him back to the hotel. He figured it would be easier to do it now than when Mr. Kennedy was ready to leave. He sat down in the rental office and scrolled on his phone until he received the Uber notification. Walking outside, he verified the car and the tag number, and the driver introduced himself as Kevin, which matched his reservation. He gave the driver the name of the hotel and he settled back in the seat, wishing this day to go by quickly so that he could be with Brittany.

The girls finished breakfast and cleaned up the kitchen, laughing and talking about anything except going to Sevierville. When they completed the cleanup, they sat down in the living room, to discuss how they would approach Giselle or Timothy.

"I think you just tell the truth," said Lucy. "If they know about your grandfather, you will be able to tell, and they may be glad to have someone else know the secret that they have had to live with all of this time."

"I agree with Lucy," said Kate. "Sometimes it's better to rip off a band aid quickly and not prolong it by pulling it off slowly."

"Good analogy, Kate," said Marly. An alarm went off on Marly's phone. "What in the world?"

Looking down, she saw that it was the motion cameras in her house. Kate and Lucy sat on either side of her so that they could see what was happening too. Marly saw several men in her living room. She heard an older man, probably Mr. Kennedy, directing them.

"Search the desk over there as well as the bookcases," he said.

"Look, that's Ethan Longmire, the guy that came to my house," said Marly, pointing him out on the screen.

"Oh my gosh, should you call the police?" asked Lucy.

"No, we want them to try in the basement, remember? It's wired," said Marly.

"Oh yeah, I forgot," said Lucy.

"Look, it's the guy that was stalking us," said Kate. "He's headed upstairs."

"This makes me feel so violated," said Marly. "I'm glad I didn't put a camera up there because I don't want to see them touching my things."

They continued to watch, and no one found anything. You could tell Mr. Kennedy, if that was him, was getting frustrated. Marly heard someone shout out there was a door to a basement.

"Let's head down there," said Mr. Kennedy, and they all disappeared from the screen.

CHAPTER 49

Jake Friar contacted the Memphis police for backup and sent a task force from the Memphis FBI field office to Marly's home. Jake had informed his boss, Steve Mathison, of the intel he had received from a credible informant about an invasion on Ms. Anderson's home while she was out of town.

"I understand that they may be searching for some of the Crimson Veil information or other items that possibly Ms. Anderson did not find," said Jake.

"We can't let that happen, Jake. Contact Memphis, detach a task force and get backup from the MPD," ordered Steve.

Now the police and the FBI were surrounding the home in Germantown. The police were to stay outside and make sure that no one escaped the building while the FBI infiltrated it.

The group of men made it to the basement, and it looked like any ordinary media room.

"This doesn't look like anything important," said Derrick, glancing around.

"Don't let looks deceive you. Be diligent and

look for hidden compartments," said Franklin, moving around slowly, his piercing eyes searching every corner of the room.

"I've searched this old sideboard, and I don't find anything," said Ethan. "I'll check this old desk too."

Dan Ricter had made it down to the basement, having come up empty upstairs.

"Nothing upstairs but bedrooms and empty drawers," he reported.

Samson stood silently, ready to assist Mr. Kennedy when needed. He had noted the retail space and was looking at this room, noting it was not the same size. He walked over to Franklin and whispered into his ear.

Smiling, he spoke, "Derrick, check that wall where the television is located. Samson has pointed out that this space is smaller than the retail space, which should be exact."

Derrick walked over to the wall and tapped on it. He did this several times, saying, "I think it's a false wall."

Excited, Franklin said, "Find something and break through it."

"I'm not sure that is such a good idea," said Derrick, having some common sense. "We can't fix the wall after we destroy it."

Ethan was listening to him and thought he was right. "I agree, Mr. Kennedy, that might not be the right move."

Looking at his men, Franklin said, "This is

the key to what I am searching for, and we will breach the wall. I will worry about the ramifications later. I'll pay to have it repaired. After all, Ms. Anderson has no idea that it is here. She should thank us for making her home safer."

Derrick nodded to Dan, who looked in the garage and found some tools. He brought back a hammer, a screwdriver, and a saw.

"I found these we can use," he said, and he hit the wall, breaking through the drywall, revealing a hidden room.

Gleefully, Franklin shouted, "I knew it! Oliver was the type of person who would hide something in plain sight. He was a genius."

The men kept working until a couple of openings that were big enough to squeeze through were done. Franklin pushed in, seeing a computer, file cabinet and desk. He was elated, thinking he was finally going to have the information that he needed.

"You want me to do that for you, sir?" asked Ethan, moving toward the file cabinet.

"No, no, I'll look first," he said as he pulled open the top drawer.

Suddenly, there was a bright light and an explosion, which knocked Franklin over and paper pieces shot up into the air. Ethan was bleeding on his cheek as part of the file cabinet had become a projectile and hit him. Samson ran to Mr. Kennedy to check on him and Derrick called out to everyone.

"Don't touch anything else! It may all be booby trapped," he said.

"What are we going to do? I didn't sign up to get killed," said Dan, shaking from the nearby blast.

"Let me think," said Derrick, while Samson was lifting up Franklin and putting him on the sofa.

The FBI heard the blast from their positions outside, and motioning to the MPD to watch, they pushed through the front door. Two agents went upstairs while two searched the ground floor. Hearing commotion downstairs, they found the entrance to the basement, and with firearms drawn, they creeped down the stairs.

"Freeze!" shouted the leader of the group.

The four men turned around and saw the FBI. Derrick started to move when he thought better of it.

"FBI, no one make a move. Is he okay?" he asked, indicating Franklin Kennedy on the sofa.

Ethan spoke up, "He opened a file cabinet, and it exploded. He was knocked down and he is not well."

The agent radioed outside to the police officers to call the bomb squad as there may be additional explosives that haven't been detonated.

Franklin was coming around, and seeing everyone standing still, asked, "What is going on? Let's keep looking."

All of the men looked in the direction of the FBI agents that had stormed the basement.

"Oh, hello officers, we were just conducting a search for a missing object of mine," he said calmly, belying the beating of his heart. He was so close.

The agent spoke, "I'm Darius Stone, FBI agent in charge. Do you have permission to search Ms. Anderson's home?"

Always quick to think, Franklin said, "I believe she was allowing it, but she had to go out of town. Since I had already traveled here from Colorado, I didn't think it would do any harm. I tried to contact her, but no answer."

"And who are you, sir?" asked Agent Stone.

"I'm Franklin Kennedy," he said, as if that were all the information needed.

"Mr. Kennedy, I have been instructed to detain all persons here until further notice. The Memphis PD is waiting outside to take you downtown. Your vehicles will be impounded," said Agent Stone.

Nodding to the other agents, they moved in to take the men upstairs and outside. Seeing Ethan's face, he also ordered EMS to the address.

"Wait, you don't understand," said Franklin, getting agitated, "I have something here that belongs to me."

"What would that be, Mr. Kennedy?" asked Agent Stone.

"I believe my former colleague, Mr. Anderson,

held some jewels for me and they are hidden here. I must find them as well as some confidential documents," explained Franklin.

"If we find them, we'll let you know. For now, no one is going to search here until the bomb squad has swept it for other explosives. Now, let's go." Agent Stone walked behind the men as they followed his team up the stairs.

Lucy, Marly, and Kate watched the entire scene unfold on Marly's phone.

"Oh my god," said Lucy. "Did you see that explosion? Lenny did good, didn't he?"

"Yes, he did. Can you believe that Kennedy guy, still trying to search after the FBI arrived? And, how did they know to come to my house?" wondered Marly.

Kate thought she had figured it out. "I think Lenny probably put a bug in Jake Friar's ear. They definitely don't want anyone else to have the Crimson Veil information and now that they have the files, they want to control what happens with it."

"You are probably right," agreed Marly. "Wow, I can't believe all of the hard work we did down there has been ruined. I will definitely have someone come in and repair it but make a door to the hidden room as storage."

"That is a great idea," said Lucy.

They saw the group come into view upstairs and be escorted outside.

"I guess the show is over," said Lucy.

"I'm so relieved that it is over, for the most part," said Marly. "Now a bomb squad is going to disarm the rest of the explosives."

"Yes, and I think that your best bet would be to tell them, when asked, that you knew nothing about it," said Kate. "I say that as your lawyer and your friend."

"I know, and I don't want to give Lenny away either, so I will assume that Poppa set those explosives when he sealed up the room," said Marly. "I have no problem with believing that as a matter of fact."

"Now that it is over, for now, you know what the next step is, don't you?" asked Kate, looking directly at Marly.

"Yes, it's time to find Timothy Anderson and possibly Giselle too. I've got her picture and the brooch my Poppa gave to her as well as the other jewels we found in the little cabin. There's no time like the present," said Marly.

They all headed to the door and Marly locked it, getting in the car with her best friends and driving to Sevierville, where she was probably going to change the life of an unsuspecting man. But, maybe she was also bringing closure for a chapter in his life and maybe Giselle's too. She could only hope she was doing the right thing.

CHAPTER 50

The bomb squad went into the basement and found explosives in the desk as well as the computer. After they disarmed everything, they gathered up the pieces of the detonated explosive for forensics and bagged all of the other devices. Agent Stone came downstairs to check on their progress.

"How's everything going?" asked Darius.

"Everything is clear. We found two more devices. They were old school, probably been here a while," said Randy Sims, explosives expert.

"Yeah, from what I understand, this was a hidden room from years ago. The guy who probably set it up is deceased now. His daughter is working with the FBI on some stuff she found herself. I'll put that in my report," said Agent Stone.

"What about the damage done here?" asked Randy.

"I'll let the agent in charge of this operation know and let him handle it. We were just dispatched to take care of the intruders. Guess they got surprised themselves," said Darius.

"Probably more than they bargained for," laughed Randy. "We've got the evidence here and will take it downtown. Forensics will dust for prints but if the guy was smart, we probably won't find any."

"You're probably right," said Darius as they all walked upstairs and left the building. Agent Stone locked the door behind him and called Jake Friar, letting him know what had occurred.

"Thanks Agent Stone, just send your report when you have it completed," said Jake.

"Will do, and thanks for an exciting Sunday!" he said, laughing.

"Anytime," said Jake, laughing with him.

Jake hung up the phone and called Steve Mathison, letting him know the details of the raid.

"Sounds like we got there in the nick of time," said Steve.

"I think so, Steve. The perpetrators are being taken downtown by the Memphis PD and will hold them until we give clear instructions. Probably be tomorrow though, because today is Sunday," said Jake.

"Give them something to think about," said Steve. "See you tomorrow."

"Okay," said Jake, ending the call.

It was chaos at the police station with everyone trying to speak at once. Each man was trying to get permission to make a phone call, except Derrick Porter. He was sitting there silently, trying to think of a way to salvage his career.

Vic Evans, Police Commander, was trying to make sense of what happened. Everyone had given a statement except one guy, Derrick Porter. He wasn't talking to anyone yet. Dan Ricter was a private eye. He stated he had been hired to watch the Anderson home and report to Derrick Porter. Ethan Longmire stated he was in Memphis with his girlfriend when his employer called him to come to Ms. Anderson's address. Samson, Franklin Kennedy's chauffeur stated he drove Mr. Kennedy to the address he was given and Franklin Kennedy said he had permission to search for his missing jewels. Apparently no one thought the place would be rigged to blow up. The FBI gave clear instructions not to contact Ms. Anderson as she was out of town, and they would contact her about what happened at her home. So, it was his job to figure out the mess in his precinct. He decided to start with Porter, calling the desk sergeant to escort him back.

In a few minutes, Derrick Porter walked in and sat down. Commander Evans looked at him without speaking and then said, "What's your story, Porter?"

Derrick was ready and began his speech, "I'm an FBI Agent, undercover. I have been feeding information to the main office about Mr. Kennedy's movements and directions. I did hire

Dan Ricter to watch the Anderson home, but I had to stay undercover. You surely understand that, right?"

"You have your badge?" asked Vic and Derrick Porter produced it. He was definitely an agent but was he an honest one? "Of course, in our line of work we have to be careful, especially when working undercover," said Vic, trying to figure out how much of his story was truthful. Even though he had the report in front of him, Vic asked Porter to recount everything that happened when they reached the house. While he was spinning his story, Commander Evans pretended he was taking notes when he was actually sending a communication to the field office to check out Porter's story.

Porter was ending his recap of the events and Commander Evans asked him, "Do you need to check in with your superior?"

"I will do that tomorrow because I don't want to break my character, you know?" he asked.

"Sure, but we are going to have to hold you here with everyone else, so that you look legitimate. You understand?" asked Vic.

"Oh sure, sure, I get it. I can sleep in a tank for one night," he joked, trying to insert some humor in this disastrous situation.

Commander Evans rose and escorted Derrick back outside and had the desk sergeant take him to a holding cell.

Ethan was giving his statement and saying he

needed to call his girlfriend and let her know he wouldn't be back in Colorado tonight. After his statement, he was allowed to call at the officer's desk, with him listening.

Brittany answered the phone, "Hello Ethan, I just got home about an hour ago. How are things going there?"

"Brit, there was a mix-up with the assignment and all of us have been detained. We won't be traveling home tonight. I wanted to let you know," Ethan explained.

"What? Are you okay?" she asked.

"I'm fine, don't worry. I'll probably be heading home tomorrow. Get some rest and I'll see you soon," said Ethan.

Looking at the officer, he said, "Thank you," and was escorted to a holding cell.

Samson was not cooperating with the police, and they finally put him in a cell too as well as Dan Ricter. That left Franklin Kennedy.

Franklin was escorted into Commander Evans office. Vic knew of Franklin Kennedy and that he was a very wealthy and powerful man. However, he wanted to see what he had to say.

"Mr. Kennedy, we certainly have a situation here," Vic began.

"Yes we do. If you would allow me to contact my attorney," began Franklin but Vic stopped him.

"Mr. Kennedy, you have been detained for unlawful entry into the home of Ms. Marly

Anderson and searching it. You destroyed her property and fortunately for you, the explosion you set off didn't kill anyone. I understand you think something is hidden there but you did not have permission to look for it," said Vic. "Does that about cover it?"

"I really need to speak to my attorney," said Franklin. "Surely, you aren't going to deny me my rights?"

"Of course not, but you will need to explain everything to me in detail," said Vic, looking directly at Franklin.

Not one to back down, Franklin stated, "I believe I will speak to my attorney first, if you don't mind."

Realizing he wasn't going to get anywhere with Mr. Kennedy, he smiled, "Certainly. We'll put you in a holding cell until we have gotten everyone's statements. Then you will be given your one phone call, Mr. Kennedy."

Vic called the desk sergeant and instructed him to take Mr. Kennedy to a holding cell. His computer pinged and he saw an interoffice memo regarding Derrick Porter.

Derrick Porter is an FBI Agent in Denver, Colorado, He has been under investigation regarding his relationship with Mr. Franklin Kennedy. Bank records indicate large sums of money changing hands for possible assignments that are illegal. Detain him until he is picked up by our office tomorrow. Jake Friar, FBI Senior Agent.

Commander Evans read the memo and shook his head. *Agent Porter, I believe your time as an FBI agent is coming to an end.*

Finally all of the men were in holding for the night and Commander Evans informed the desk sergeant to let Mr. Kennedy make a phone call in two hours. Maybe that would make him a bit more cooperative.

The girls pulled up to the address in Sevierville, Tennessee and got out of the car. Marly picked up the bag with the things she had brought with her, and they walked up to the front door of a pretty white cottage on a country road. A stream ran along the side of it, creating a comforting sound. Rocking chairs were on the porch and pots of bougainvillea brightened the area with their bright pink and red blooms.

Lucy and Kate stood behind her as Marly knocked on the door. In a few minutes, a young man opened the door, looking so much like her Poppa, Marly nearly fainted.

Noticing her reaction, he asked, "Are you okay, miss?"

Nodding, she asked the question that she already knew the answer to, "Are you Timothy Anderson?"

Puzzled, he said, "Yes, how can I help you."

Marly took a deep breath and then said, "My name is Marly Anderson, of Germantown, Tennessee. My father, who I thought was my grandfather, was Oliver Anderson, also known as Randolph Vinson. I think we are, in some way, family."

CHAPTER 51

Timothy Anderson looked directly at her and smiled. Marly figured he thought she was playing an elaborate joke on him.

"Just a moment please," he said, and he closed the door.

Marly didn't know what to say and looked at Kate and Lucy. "Should we go?"

"No, let's wait a few minutes," said Kate, wondering herself what was going on.

"I vote to go. He just passed up the gift of a lifetime in Marly," said Lucy, indignantly.

"Thanks, Lucy," said Marly, smiling. "We'll wait."

After about five minutes had passed, the door opened again. Standing there was an elderly woman, with her hair upswept in a French twist, wearing a beautiful floral dress with a crocheted collar. She was beautiful and her blue eyes matched the ones in the picture Marly had seen.

"Apologies for my son, but he wanted me to confirm your identity," she said. "Please, come in."

They walked into a living room with beautiful

antique furniture and lovely décor.

"You have a beautiful home," said Marly, not really knowing what to call her.

"Please, sit down. Timothy, would you please make a pot of tea," she requested.

Without a word, he left the room, presumably to go to the kitchen to make the tea.

Marly couldn't wait any longer. "Are you Giselle Armenti?"

Smiling, the woman answered, "Yes, I am. I am curious as to how you found us. I have always hoped that we made it impossible to trace me here."

"It wasn't easy, and I mean you no harm. I'm Marly Anderson, Oliver Anderson's daughter," she said.

"Yes, I know, Oliver, or Randolph as I knew him, spoke of you many times. He loved you so much and was so proud of your accomplishments," she said.

"I want to know so much but I don't know where to start," said Marly, looking at Giselle, sitting across from them.

"We will start at the beginning, but first, introduce your friends," said Giselle.

"I'm so sorry, this is Lucy Cavanaugh and Kate Butler, my very best friends," said Marly.

"I'm happy to make your acquaintance. It is good to have best friends," she said.

Marly wanted to fill the gap in conversation and said, "I'm sorry that we interrupted your day, but I was afraid that if I called, you may not want to see us. I didn't really know if you were here, but I had hoped."

"Ah, here's Timothy with the tea. Sit down son and let's pour," said Giselle, as if this was any ordinary day.

It was not an ordinary day for Marly. She was like a clock wound too tight, her nerves on edge.

There were tea biscuits as well as dainty floral teacups, sugar and milk in containers matching the teapot. Timothy poured the tea, letting each person prepare it the way they wanted it and then they all sipped the tea. It was quite delicious.

Timothy spoke up, "Marly, when I saw you at the door, I recognized you from pictures that my father, your adopted father, sent to us over the years. But, I had to protect my mother's anonymity until she was ready to reveal herself."

"I have to admit that I knew nothing about you, Timothy, or Giselle, until recent events made it evident," said Marly. "I wish I had known about you."

"I think Poppa wanted to protect my mother so much that he did not tell you about us," said Timothy, looking over at his mother sipping her tea.

Marly realized that he called Oliver by the same name she did, Poppa.

"I think we discovered the reason why and it involves Franklin Kennedy, or as you probably know him, Ramondo Breviat," said Marly, noting that Giselle's hand shook a little.

"Yes, he is the reason for the secrecy and the hiding. Poppa let us stay in the small cabin when I was little, but we moved to many homes, just to keep Maman and I safe," Timothy continued. After many years, he decided we were safe enough to settle down and he chose this place for us."

"I'm so glad he did that for you. It must have been very difficult to live that way for so long," said Marly.

"But, you also had to endure the wicked stepfamily, did you not?" he asked. "Poppa regretted that decision, but he felt it was best at the time."

Marly realized that Poppa had shared everything with them, which made her feel many emotions. She was glad, happy, a bit hurt, but mostly seen.

"I didn't know about their role in my life until recently," said Marly, and she told them both about the events from the beginning until the recent arrest of Franklin Kennedy and his men who were searching her home.

"Oh miséricorde," said Giselle. "I'm so sorry this happened to you."

"I'm sorry that Poppa died before we could all be together," said Marly, sadly.

"I regret that too," said Timothy, "but now we can be as a family."

Touched by their openness to accept her as one of them, Marly's dark brown eyes became teary, and the tears escaped down her cheeks. Kate quickly handed her a tissue.

"Ah, Marly, do not cry or you will cause me to do the same," said Giselle, her blue eyes glistening.

Gaining her composure, Marly reached into the bag and pulled out the picture that Kate had found in the basement. She handed it to Timothy.

"This started the search for Giselle, but we had no idea who you were or where you were. We also found this brooch," she said, pulling it out of the bag.

"My brooch," Giselle said wistfully. "I didn't want to give it back to Randolph, but Ramondo was very suspicious. I had hoped one day to get it back, but I did not."

"Poppa kept it for you in a hidden place. We found it, trying to figure out why Mr. Kennedy wanted to search my house," said Marly.

Giselle sat her teacup on the marble top coffee table, taking the brooch from Marly. "I am sure he is looking for the crown jewels of the Duke of Magenta. But, he failed to tell people that he became a duke when he married me, the Duchess of Magenta. The crown jewels are not his to have. They belonged to me, but I do not have them any longer," she said. "I gave them to Oliver to sell, to help with supporting me and Timothy."

Reaching in the bag again, Marly pulled out the jewelry box they had found in the small cabin and handed it to Giselle. "We found these in a secret compartment in the cabin. I guess Poppa put them there after you left."

Opening the box, Giselle gasped, "Oh mon dieu, it is the crown jewels! Timothy, look! But why didn't he use them?"

"I imagine he wanted to support you both himself. Poppa was very resourceful and smart, and he amassed a great fortune. I inherited all of it when he died, but I want to share it with you," said Marly, not realizing that she was going to say that but felt good about it.

Timothy spoke up, "No Marly, that was for you from our father. He left a trust for me which was quite enormous, so I do not have to worry about anything. He left me well off."

Marly didn't know what to say. Today had been a revelation that she never expected. To actually have a real family that was ready to welcome her was almost more than she could take in.

"I am overwhelmed," said Marly.

"I am sure that you are," said Giselle, "there is so much to talk about together. How long will you be here?"

Kate spoke up, "Lucy and I need to fly back to Texas, so we will probably leave Tuesday."

Marly said, "I can stay as long as I want because I closed my bookstore and right now, I'm making some big decisions regarding my life."

Timothy spoke, "We would like to get to know all of you better so would you agree to return tomorrow and have dinner with us? I would like you to meet my fiancée, Alaina Cosetta, who is flying in tonight from New York. She is a dress designer."

"Oooh I would love to meet her," said Lucy. "I love unique designs!"

"Then it is settled," said Giselle. "I cannot tell you how happy you have made us today, Marly. We have spoken of you often through the years and now our hopes and dreams are becoming a reality."

Marly rose from her seat and went to Giselle, embracing her. While she had her arms wrapped around Giselle, Timothy stood. When Marly stood up, he held his arms open to her and he hugged her tightly, his blue eyes like his mother's, glistening with unshed tears.

"Until tomorrow then," said Timothy as Lucy and Kate stood up as well.

"Yes," said Marly. "What time?"

"Come early so we can visit," said Giselle.

Smiling Timothy said, "Come at 2:00 p.m. and Maman will be up from her afternoon rest."

The girls left, waving goodbye to Timothy as he stood on the front porch of the white cottage.

Driving away, Marly said, "Can you believe this day? I never in a million years expected anything like this to happen!"

"But aren't you happy, Marly?" asked Lucy.

"Oh yes, I am so happy," she said.

Kate spoke up, "And we are happy for you too, Marly. I'm looking forward to tomorrow."

Marly said, "Me too. Now I need to find out what is happening with Franklin Kennedy and my home invasion," driving back to the cabin to do just that!

CHAPTER 52

Franklin Kennedy was sitting in the holding cell, desperately wanting to talk to his attorney. This was a disaster! There had to be a snake in the woodpile, but who was the snake? Snake! Snake Hill Road! That has to be it, Lenny Crocker. He must be the one that tipped off the authorities. He hadn't had time to think about Lenny Crocker and his story that he didn't know how to disarm a house. A man with his talents surely had that skill in his toolbox. Franklin regretted stopping the deep dive into Crocker now, but it was too late. He would deal with him later. Right now, he had to speak to Simon Rockford, his attorney, to get himself out of this situation.

Franklin was about to call for someone when the desk sergeant came to the cell, escorting him to the desk to make his call.

"Could you give me some privacy, please?" he requested haughtily.

"No sir, you call from here like everyone else. You don't want to discuss it, wait until your lawyer gets here," said Bill, the desk sergeant.

"Fine," said Franklin, dialing the number.

After a couple of rings, Simon Rockford answered.

"Hello?" he said, unsure as to why he was getting a call from the Memphis Police Department.

"Simon, it's Franklin Kennedy," he identified himself quickly. "I'm in a bit of a spot and need your assistance."

"Mr. Kennedy, are you in Memphis?" he asked.

"Yes, and I've been detained by the local police," he said. "I need you here ASAP."

"I have to be in court in the morning," Simon said. "Can you tell me what happened?"

"I'm sitting at the desk of the sergeant in charge, and he is present as I make this call. I would rather not," said Franklin.

"Have you been charged with anything?" asked Simon, still a bit confused.

"Just a moment," he said, handing the phone to the desk sergeant, Bill.

"Hello, Bill Edwards, desk sergeant. Can I help you?" he asked.

"Has my client been charged with anything?" asked Simon.

"Let me pull that up," said Bill, who then said, "Breaking and entering, unlawful search, destruction of property and detonating an explosive device."

"That wasn't me! I was almost killed because I didn't know it was there!" shouted Franklin, grabbing at the phone.

Bill calmly handed the receiver back to Franklin.

"Did you get that, Simon?" he asked his attorney.

"Yes and it sounds pretty bad, Mr. Kennedy. I'll send my second chair to court and get on a plane early tomorrow. I'll get there as soon as I can."

"Thank you, Simon. I'll see you tomorrow," said Franklin, placing the receiver on the phone. "You can take me back now."

Bill Edwards escorted Franklin Kennedy back to his holding cell and left him to contemplate his fate.

When the girls arrived back at the cabin, Marly called Jake Friar.

"Hello," he said.

"Hello Mr. Friar, this is Marly Anderson," she acknowledged.

"Yes, Ms. Anderson, how are you?" he asked.

"I was calling to find out what happened at my house today," she said.

"Did someone notify you?" he asked.

"No, I had cameras set up and saw the whole thing. When were you going to let me know that my home had been invaded and that an explosion happened? Was anyone hurt?" she asked.

Surprised that she had cameras, he quickly became transparent. "I received a tip from Lenny Crocker that he suspected a search would happen since you had left town. I had a task force raid the house as they were in the process of searching it. There was an explosion in the basement from a charge that had been set where they were searching. Mr. Kennedy was blown back but suffered no injuries, although I suspect he will claim he did. Ethan Longmire did receive medical attention for a laceration on his face but that was all. Mr. Kennedy was also checked out but had no issues. I apologize for not informing you today, but I was going to contact you after I talked with all of the officers that were present."

"Thank you for your honesty, Jake. I'm glad no one was injured but why was there an explosion?" asked Marly, feigning innocence.

"I don't have all of the reports in yet, but it must have been set years ago. We are running forensics on the pieces to see if there are any prints," he said.

Marly hoped Lenny was careful not to leave any. Aloud she said, "I have the footage of the intrusion if you want that for your evidence as well. I guess I became paranoid after Mr. Kennedy approached me and felt the need for cameras."

"I can certainly understand that, especially a woman living alone. The footage would be very helpful in this case. Can it be sent to an email account?" he asked.

"Yes, if you will send me the address, I will send it to you right away," she said. "I'm not sure when I will be returning but please keep me informed. I will keep you updated on my return home," said Marly.

"Great, Ms. Anderson," said Jake, "I'll send that address and do let me know when you return. The police may need additional information from you for this case."

"Of course, Jake, and thank you," she said, ending the call.

"Whew!" said Marly, taking a deep breath. "I hope I sounded plausible."

"You did," said Lucy. "I almost couldn't tell you were lying!" They all laughed.

"I hope Lenny didn't leave any fingerprints," said Marly, a bit worried.

Kate said, "I don't think he did because I saw he was using gloves."

"That makes me feel better. Jake wants me to send the footage to him, and I'll do that when I get the address," said Marly. "I will be so glad when this part of my life is over!"

"But remember, Marly, that you never would have known about Giselle and Timothy had Mr. Kennedy not approached you about searching your house," said Kate, looking at the positive side of it.

"You're right Kate, but what a way to find out you have a brother!" said Marly, and they all joined in the laughter, lightening the mood.

They got in pajamas, cooked burgers, and talked until midnight about Giselle and Timothy.

Monday morning was a busy place at the Memphis Police Department. Simon Rockford had managed to get on a red-eye flight from Denver and was waiting for Commander Evans to arrive. The desk sergeant Bill Edwards was back on duty and notified the Commander that Franklin Kennedy's attorney was waiting for him.

Commander Evans walked into the precinct and went directly to his office. He buzzed the desk sergeant and said, "Bill, you can bring Mr. Kennedy's attorney."

Sergeant Edwards motioned to Simon Rockford to follow him and took him to the Commander's office.

"Mr. Rockford from Denver, Colorado, Commander Evans," Bill announced and closed the door as he left.

"Hello Mr. Rockford, I'm Commander Vic Evans. You certainly got here quickly," he said.

"I try to be available when my clients need me, Commander," said Simon.

"Especially one with the money and power such as Mr. Kennedy, wouldn't you say?" said Vic.

"No, I work hard for all of my clients," he said, pretending he was offended.

"Good for them," said Vic. "Now, what can I do for you?"

"Firstly, I wanted to discuss with you the charges against my client and to inform you that there must be some mistake. This is not something that Mr. Kennedy would be involved in," said Simon.

"We have very clear evidence that he was involved and actually, that he spearheaded the entire operation," said Vic. "As a matter of fact, I received video evidence this morning from the FBI that shows the entire home invasion, and Mr. Kennedy was calling the shots."

Unprepared for this information, Simon wasn't sure what he was going to do next. "Why was the FBI involved?"

Vic was loving this exchange. "Actually, it was an FBI operation, and we were just the back-up. However, we agreed to hold the men involved until we were given further instructions."

"I think I need to speak to my client now," said Simon, trying to figure out what was going on. "I will need to see the video as well."

"I'll let the FBI make that call, Mr. Rockford," Vic said, calling Sergeant Edwards to escort Mr. Kennedy's attorney to the interview room and then retrieve Mr. Kennedy.

As he was being escorted to the interview room, Vic said aloud, "Poor schmuck, he doesn't know what he's getting into."

Simon sat down in the interview room and waited for Franklin Kennedy to be escorted in. After a few moments, Mr. Kennedy was brought in, and they were left alone.

"Thank god you made it here," said Franklin.

"Mr. Kennedy, I don't know what's going on here, but you better be honest about everything because the FBI just sent a video of the supposed home invasion to Commander Evans and he seems pretty sure you were leading the charge," Simon said, as a shocked look came across Franklin's face.

CHAPTER 53

Marly woke up early after a restless night. So much had happened and she was still trying to make sense of it all. She knew that Lucy and Kate were still sleeping so she just stayed in bed. She was also worried about Lenny and decided to give him a call.

"Hello," said a sleepy voice.

"I'm so sorry, Lenny. I didn't mean to wake you!" she said.

"Marly? Is everything okay?" he asked, wide awake now.

"Yes, I'm fine. I was just worried after I spoke to Jake Friar last night. He said that the explosive pieces were being checked for fingerprints," explained Marly.

Lenny chuckled saying, "I was careful Marly. They won't find my fingerprints on anything. I even wiped the surfaces when I was done. So, there was an explosion? I guess they got caught."

"Yes, they are all at the Memphis PD. I don't know what's going to happen next, but I set up hidden cameras and got it all on video," admitted Marly.

"I'd love to see that," Lenny laughed.

"I can send it to you," she said, laughing softly.

"No, better I don't have anything that connects me to you. I'm pretty sure old man Kennedy will figure out that I was the one that tipped off the FBI," Lenny admitted.

"You did?" asked Marly, surprised herself.

"Yeah, Kennedy asked me if I could disarm your house, but I told him I didn't know how to do that," said Lenny.

Marly laughed. "You can set explosives, but you can't disarm an alarm system? Lenny, that is funny."

"I guess it is and that's why I figure he will be on to me," said Lenny. "I'm not worried though. I can see anybody coming to my place and I have alarms too."

"Good," said Marly, relieved. "I just didn't want you to suffer for helping me. I don't know how this will all turn out, but thank you for being my friend, Lenny."

Lenny smiled and felt happy. "You're welcome and that goes both ways."

"I better go, Lenny. Take care of yourself," she said, ending the call.

"You too, Marly," he said, shutting off his phone and turning over to go back to sleep.

Simon stared at Franklin Kennedy, waiting for his version of what happened at the Anderson home. If the FBI had a video, Franklin knew that he better tell his side very carefully, so he went about explaining that his old business partner had died and had something of his. He wanted to find it and had asked the granddaughter for permission to search for it, but she hadn't given it. He knew she was going to be out of town, and he thought he could search, find his property, and then be gone without any problems and none the wiser. But he didn't find what he was looking for and the cabinet he opened had explosives wired to it and it blew up.

"Explosives? Good god, Mr. Kennedy, were you injured? Did you receive medical attention?" asked Simon, who was recording this interview.

"Yes, the FBI called EMS and my employee, Ethan Longmire was treated for a cut, and they checked me out at the time as well," admitted Franklin.

"Why were there explosives?" asked Simon, unsure about Mr. Kennedy's story.

"I think my old business partner wired it up, in case I ever came looking," said Franklin.

"Why would he have done that?" asked Simon.

"To keep me from finding it," said Franklin. "I tried to be nice to his granddaughter who inherited everything when he died and asked but she was so stubborn. It's my property!"

"What are you looking for?" asked Simon, his look telling Franklin to tell the truth.

Franklin told his version of the truth, "At one time, I was the Duke of Magenta in Europe, and my wife stole the crown jewels and fled the country. She was having an affair with Oliver Anderson, and I know she went to him for help. The government of my country is demanding the return of the crown jewels."

"Where is your wife? Do you even know where she is?" Simon asked Franklin.

"No, I have been unable to locate her after these many years. I don't even know if she is still alive," Franklin Kennedy admitted.

"I don't see how this is something you can do anything about. The man is dead, the woman is missing, the jewels, if they exist, were probably sold on the black market and will never be found. You committed this crime just to retrieve these crown jewels which may not even exist anymore? It sounds more like an obsession to me," said Simon, upset about flying to Tennessee for this mess.

"There is a powerful man in Europe who is demanding them," said Franklin, for the first time exhibiting some frustration.

"Look, Mr. Kennedy, I'm going to do all that I can to get you out of this situation, but I'm telling you now that this story is preposterous and has a lot of holes in it. I am not going to risk my reputation by bringing up some old story that no one knows or cares about," said Simon.

"I care about it!" shouted Franklin.

"That's just it, Mr. Kennedy, you care about it. You are the only one who does and if you continue to push this story, you will have to find yourself new counsel," said Simon Rockford decisively. Mr. Kennedy may be rich and powerful, but he was eccentric as well and everyone knows it.

Sitting in silence for a few minutes, Franklin was seething but he knew he probably sounded crazy. Still, he knew he wasn't. But, he needed Simon to help him get out of jail, so he agreed to drop that part of the story.

"Good," said Simon. "I will push for your release as well as your associates, if I can, but you will have to do exactly what I say. Do you understand?"

"Yes, I understand. Will it be today?" asked Franklin, anxious to get home.

"I don't know. I will see if we can get your arraignment scheduled today. Let me make some calls and I'll get back to you," said Simon, crossing his fingers that all would go smoothly.

Simon got up and opened the door and the officer on guard took Franklin back to his cell until his attorney got back with him. Things were not going the way he had planned. Damn you Randolph Vinson!

CHAPTER 54

Marly had cinnamon rolls baking when Lucy and Kate came into the kitchen.

"Mmmm, that wonderful smell!" said Lucy. "I'm ready for one!"

Kate agreed. "It smells great, Marly. What time did you get up?"

"Early," she admitted. "I had trouble sleeping and I was worried about Lenny too. I called him this morning, and he assured me he left no fingerprints. So, I got up and made cinnamon roll dough."

"I'm sorry you didn't sleep well but if the reward is homemade cinnamon rolls, I'm good with it," said Lucy, grinning.

"I figured you would be, Lucy," said Marly smiling, "and I think they're done." Marly pulled the pan out of the oven and the big, beautiful rolls filled the cabin with aroma. Marly iced them quickly with the frosting she had made and said, "Voila! Breakfast!"

They all took one and a mimosa that Kate had made while Marly was icing the rolls and made their way to the couch. This was a breakfast you could eat anywhere!

"Oh wow, Marly, this is divine!" said Lucy, licking the icing off her lips.

"I must agree with Lucy, the best cinnamon roll ever!" said Kate, pulling it apart.

"Thanks my friends. I have a confession to make," said Marly.

"Oh my goodness, do we need more mimosas?" asked Lucy, laughing.

"No, I was thinking about finding a property in Fredericksburg, Texas and opening a small bakery. I think I would enjoy that but..." started Marly.

"Awesome Marly!" shouted Lucy and Kate said, "Great!"

"Uh oh, what's the but?" asked Lucy

"Since we found Giselle and Timothy, I want to have a solid relationship with them. They are my family, and I think it is what Poppa would have wanted. I am definitely going to sell the building in Germantown, and I think I will move here to the cabin. That way, I'll be closer to them, and we can bond and learn things about each other. What do you guys think?" asked Marly, anxious to have their opinion.

Lucy put down her cinnamon roll, "Marly, I think it sounds perfect. As much as I would want you to live in Texas with us, I can understand the importance of your family. I wouldn't give mine up for anything."

"Honestly, I think it is a great plan, Marly," said Kate. "You already have the cabin, it's the perfect location to them, giving you both space, and you can always open a bakery in this area, if you wanted to."

"But you have to be available to cater events at the winery! We have a reputation to uphold!" said Lucy.

Marly laughed and said, "Of course, Lucy. I will cater all of the winery's events."

"Okay, then you have my permission," said Lucy, getting back to her cinnamon roll.

Kate and Marly shook their heads at Lucy as they all finished their breakfast and were deciding what they were going to wear to Giselle's today. They hadn't brought any fancy clothes, except for Kate who had all of hers in her suitcase.

"I have a solution," said Kate, finishing up her cinnamon roll.

"And, what would that be?" asked Lucy.

"I know," said Marly, "let's go shopping this morning!"

"Exactly," said Kate, and they hurried to get dressed to do just that.

Commander Evans was sitting at his desk when the desk sergeant called, stating FBI Agent Sean Carlson was here to see him.

"Okay, bring him in," said Vic, figuring this was the agent for Derrick Porter.

As Agent Carlson was escorted in, Commander Evans rose to greet him, extending his hand.

"Good morning," said Vic cordially.

"Good morning, Commander," said Agent Carlson formally.

Not wanting to assume his reason for being here, Vic asked, "How may I assist you today?"

"I am here to take custody of Derrick Porter. He is being transferred to the North Carolina office for further investigation," stated Agent Carlson.

"I thought so," said Vic, picking up his phone and requesting Derrick Porter be brought to his office. "He'll be surprised to see you, I'm sure."

"I'm counting on it," said Agent Carlson, grinning a little.

At least he has a sense of humor, thought Vic.

A few minutes later, one of the officers on duty brought Derrick Porter to Commander Evans' office. At first he didn't see the other person in the room, smiling at Vic.

"Nice digs you got here, Commander. I slept like a baby," he boasted.

Without comment, Vic pointed to Sean Carlson in the corner of the room.

"There's someone here to see you, Porter," said Vic.

Turning his head, his stomach flipped over when he saw Sean Carlson, the equivalent of IAB for the FBI.

"Hello Sean, long time no see," he said. "What brings you to Memphis?"

"You do, Derrick. I'm escorting you to the North Carolina office for further investigation," said Sean, with no facial expression.

"What's the charge?" he asked, knowing there was one.

"I'm not privy to that information. I just have my assignment. Let's go," said Sean, as he rose to take custody of Porter. "Hands behind your back."

"Come on, we don't have to do that, do we?" Derrick asked, knowing it was futile. Sean Carlson was a by the book agent.

Vic interjected, "You ought to know the rules, Porter. And you should have known not to break them."

Putting his hands behind his back, Derrick Porter resigned himself to this treatment, hoping that he would be able to worm his way out of this situation. If Mr. Kennedy is available, maybe he can help.

After handcuffing Porter, Agent Carlson shook hands with Vic, "Thank you, Commander Evans. I will send you a follow up report for your case file."

"Thanks, Agent Carlson, I appreciate it. Safe travels," he said, as Agent Carlson and Derrick Porter made their way to the SUV outside.

Simon went to the courthouse after his interview with Franklin Kennedy. This was going to be a circus and unfortunately, he was the ringmaster. He appeared before the court clerk and was informed that the arraignment for four of the arrested was scheduled for 3:00 p.m. that afternoon.

"What about the fifth man?" asked Simon.

Looking at the notes, the clerk stated, "The FBI has taken custody of that person and will handle his case in their jurisdiction."

Walking out of the courtroom, Simon was worried. The FBI was involved in this case, and he knew it wasn't for some old crown jewels that Franklin Kennedy was raving about. He had read everyone's statements and felt that he could get them released with fines, but there was something else going on that no one was talking about. Either they didn't know all of the facts or they were all involved in something deeper.

Malorie Hackett, the district attorney in Memphis was reviewing the docket for arraignments. She paused when she saw the name Franklin Kennedy. She looked further and saw that it was the Franklin Kennedy of Denver, Colorado. Reading the arrest documentation, she was puzzled why a high-profile individual such as Mr. Kennedy would be involved in a home invasion. She also noted that the FBI was involved in the matter. She saw the name Jake Friar and decided to contact him.

"Hello," said Jake, sitting in Steve's office. He had held up his phone so that Steve could see who was calling. He put it on speaker.

"Hello, Mr. Friar?" she asked.

"Agent Jake Friar with the FBI," he responded.

"I apologize, Agent Friar. My name is Malorie Hackett, District Attorney and I am going to appear in court this afternoon for the arraignment of several men involved in a home invasion and one of them is a very prominent figure in Denver, Mr. Franklin Kennedy. Is there anything I need to know before I attend this hearing?"

Before Jake could respond, Steve spoke up, "Ms. Hackett, Steve Mathison here. I'm the lead investigator on a very sensitive case in which we believe Mr. Kennedy is involved. The home invasion is a part of the case, but we do not want you to hold him. We are gathering evidence for an arrest at a later time."

"Okay, so I have reviewed the arrest warrants, and I am good with setting fines and releasing them. Are you in agreement with that?" she asked.

"Yes, we are not yet prepared to take anyone into custody except our agent that was investigated for bribery. He is already en route to North Carolina," said Steve.

"Thank you, Agent Mathison and Agent Friar, for your information. I will proceed and dismiss with fines. Good luck with your investigation," Malorie said, ending the call.

That will make her job a whole lot easier this afternoon.

It was 11:00 a.m. and the girls had reached the shopping district in Gatlinburg. There were a couple of boutiques that looked promising.

They walked in and started browsing, trying on different outfits and modeling them for each other.

Lucy walked out in a straight red skirt, white blouse with a lace bodice and a short bolero style red jacket. It was the perfect ensemble for her jet-black hair in her signature braid.

"Okay girls, what do you think?" asked Lucy.

"I love it," said Kate. "Only you could pull that off."

"I agree," said Marly. "You always look great in bold colors."

The salesperson heard them and came over, commenting, "Oh my goodness. I love that on you. When I ordered it, I didn't think it would appeal to everyone, but I always like to have some unique pieces."

"I'll absolutely take it," said Lucy. "Won't it look great with my red Luchese boots?"

"Yes!" said Kate and Marly in unison.

Next Kate came out in palazzo style pants in black with a cream tunic blouse, lace trim at the bottom and three-quarter length sleeves with the same lace trim, and pearl buttons down the back for decoration.

"Always elegant Kate," said Marly. "That is perfect. Seth would love it."

Lucy looked at her future sister-in-law and said, "I agree with you, Marly. It would be a perfect honeymoon outfit."

Blushing a little, Kate said, "It feels so good too, very comfortable. This is my choice. Now Marly, we have got to find you something just as awesome!"

They looked a bit longer and Marly found a mid-dress with ruffled sleeves in a sage green with small dark orange flowers on the bodice and plaid on the sleeves and skirt. She walked out with her hands in the pockets of the dress.

"Marly, you look adorable!" said Lucy. "You are just so dang cute!"

Laughing, Marly said, "You are prejudiced my friend."

"I am in total agreement with her, so I guess I'm prejudiced too," said Kate.

"I am not prejudiced, but you look beautiful in that dress, and the colors suit you," said the saleswoman, impressed with the taste of these three women in her shop.

They made their purchases and drove back to the cabin, to have a quick bite of lunch and get ready for their afternoon with the Andersons.

Marly made a quick chicken salad, and they had sandwiches with some lemonade. As they were discussing their shopping trip, Marly's phone pinged.

Getting up from the bar, she walked over to her phone on the coffee table. Picking it up, she read the text message.

'WE ARE NO LONGER THE ANDERSONS. WE ARE THE WESTONS. WE ARE DONE WITH YOU AND YOUR FAMILY.'

"What is it, Marly?" asked Lucy, noticing the expression on her face.

"I guess our visit to the Andersons was effective, Kate," she said, taking her phone over and showing them the text message.

"They certainly got busy getting that done. I think they were worried about you suing them for the money you gave to them under the assumption that they were your family," said Kate.

"Thank you Kate, for helping me with that and now, another lie in my life is done and I can move on," said Marly, smiling at her friends.

CHAPTER 55

Malorie requested to speak with the judge prior to the arraignment hearing and she explained the case as clearly as possible.

"The FBI is working a case on which this home invasion is connected but they do not want us to hold these individuals," she explained to Judge Homan.

"Very unusual, to say the least, Malorie," said Judge Homan.

"I thought so too, but Eric, it makes our jobs easier this afternoon," said Malorie, smiling at the judge who was also her fiancé."

"Yep, sounds good to me. Let's do this!"

Malorie left the judge's chamber and sat at her table in the courtroom. In a few minutes, a police officer escorted in four men, an elderly man she assumed was Franklin Kennedy, a middle-aged man who was probably the private eye, a tall muscular man which must be Mr. Franklin's driver, Samson, and the younger man with a face laceration she deduced was Ethan Longmire. At the other table was their attorney, a Simon Rockford. Smiling to herself, she *thought he probably got teased a lot about his last name. Her dad used to love the Rockford Files when it was on television.*

"All rise," announced the bailiff as Judge Homan walked into the courtroom. "The Honorable Judge Eric Holman presiding."

Then it began. Simon was prepared to fight for the release of his clients as they were all first-time offenders and ultimately, nothing was taken. Also, one of his clients had been injured in what appeared to be illegal explosives that were set in the home.

The District Attorney stated she had no objections to the release of the offenders, with the condition they all paid a $1,000 fine.

Judge Homan looked at the men and said, "I'd say an explosion would be enough to deter you from going into someone's home uninvited. Judgement granted with fines. Pay the bailiff in the office and you are released without restriction."

And that was it. No arguing, no crazy talk about crown jewels, nothing else. Thankfully, they only had to pay a fine and then they were free to go.

As they walked out of the courthouse, Dan Ricter thanked Simon and left, leaving Franklin Kennedy, Samson and Ethan Longmire with Simon on the courthouse steps.

"Thank you, Simon, for your rapid response when I called you. I am ready to leave this town for sure. Do you want to fly back with us? I have a charter plane," said Franklin.

"That would be great, Mr. Kennedy," said Simon. "I appreciate it."

"Mr. Kennedy, do you mind if I take another flight? I wanted to get something for Brittany," he said.

"Of course not," said Franklin. "I am pretty sure you are thinking of something very special for her."

"I had a lot of time to think about it, sir, and I'm not getting any younger. I love her and I want to marry her," said Ethan, surprised that he had come to that conclusion while he was in jail.

"We'll plan a reception at the estate after you propose. I'll let Victor know," smiled Franklin, as he, Samson, and Simon made their way to the airport and his private plane's hangar.

As they got on the plane to head back to Denver, Simon asked Franklin, "Is that the young man you made your heir?"

"Yes, he has been like a son to me over the past ten years. I have no one else to leave my wealth to and he is very loyal. I think I'll have he and Brittany move in with me after they are married" said Franklin, smiling to himself.

They prepared to leave, and Simon opened his laptop to do some work on the flight back. Samson sat behind Mr. Kennedy and Franklin closed his eyes, but he wasn't sleeping. He was thinking about François. He would have to tell him this mission was a failure, but he would keep looking. Simon didn't think they existed or that they were sold on the black market. He knew that wasn't true because he had Derrick look for them there. Unfortunately, he wouldn't have Derrick to depend on any longer as he was arrested by the FBI. He must have been sloppy keeping his movements secretive. Tsk, tsk.

It was 1:00 p.m. and the girls were dressed and ready to go visit with Giselle and Timothy. Marly drove to Sevierville, and they pulled up to the white cottage with five minutes to spare. As they walked to the front door, it opened, and Timothy stood there smiling at the trio.

"Welcome back, ladies," said Timothy. "Please come in," he said as he held the door open wide.

They walked in and Giselle was sitting in the wingback chair, and another woman was also there.

"Let me introduce you to my fiancé, Alaina Cosetta," said Timothy, beaming.

"It's so nice to meet you, Alaina," said Marly and Kate and Lucy agreed.

"It is lovely to make your acquaintances," said Alaina, hugging each of the women. "I must say, I didn't know I would be meeting such fashion-conscious women!"

They all laughed, and Marly said, "We didn't bring anything with us we thought suitable, so we got to do a little shopping, which is always fun."

"Absolutely," agreed Giselle, smiling at the women. "You all look C'est magnifique."

"Thank you, Giselle," said Marly. "We wanted to look our best today."

Giselle smiled and spoke," We are honored you are here, Marly, and your friends. I have asked Alaina to show Kate and Lucy her studio here while we speak. Is that alright?"

Marly looked at Kate and Lucy, not sure how to respond. She wasn't expecting this but realized that Giselle may have some private things she wanted to discuss.

Kate said, "Of course, we would love to see your studio, Alaina. As a matter of fact, Lucy and I are both planning weddings and maybe you could give us some dress ideas."

Alaina smiled brightly, "Yes, of course. I would be so happy to do that. Maybe you would want me to design them for you. Come, let's go this way," she said as she led them into the back of the cottage.

"I hope that you did not think me rude, Marly," said Giselle. "I thought we may need to discuss things you would not want to in front of them."

"It's not rude, Giselle. Although I share everything with them, I understand your request. First, I would like to know what I may call you. I think Giselle is too familiar," said Marly.

Timothy spoke up, "I would be pleased if

you called her Maman, Marly. She would have been, had things worked out the way Poppa had planned."

Clapping her hands in glee, Giselle said, "That is parfait, Timothy."

Smiling, Marly said, "Thank you Maman and Timothy."

For the next hour, Giselle told Marly about the years she and Randolph had been able to be together. Timothy added the times he remembered, and each story was filled with love and warmth. Marly was a bit jealous that she had not had that close of a relationship with Poppa as a child and young adult because of the deceit with the Andersons.

"I know this is hard for you to hear, Marly, but I wanted you to know that Randolph loved you so much. He was trying to protect you in case he got implicated in the Crimson Veil," said Giselle.

"What do you know about it, Maman? I have found bits and pieces of information, but what exactly did he do?" asked Marly.

"Ah, Marly, he was very upset about it. He thought that Ramondo was involving him in an effort to help refugees find asylum in this country. But when he was actually admitted to the circle, he found out quickly that they were not what they represented. Some of the first people that Randolph helped seemed legitimate and that was what Ramondo wanted. He is a ruthless man and threatened your life if he didn't do as he was told. Please do not think any less of your Poppa," said Giselle, her eyes glistening.

"I don't, Maman," said Marly. "I wish we could have been together as a family and that he would have told me."

"He spoke of it many times," said Timothy, "but he was afraid, even until the end. The Veil still operates but I'm not sure to what capacity."

"I turned everything we found over to the FBI and now it is their problem. Poppa will not be incriminated as he is no longer here," said Marly sadly.

"I'm sorry that you didn't have the best relationship with him when you were young but your later years, he bragged about how close you were. I think it was his happiest times when you were there in his home. When you graduated from college, it was one of his proudest moments," said Timothy.

"I'm sorry that you lost your Poppa too, Timothy," said Marly and looking at Giselle, she said, "and that you lost your true love, Maman."

About that time, Lucy and Kate came into the room with Alaina, all of them smiling.

"What have you been up to?" asked Marly.

"Well, we are going to have Alaina design our wedding dresses! She is amazing, Marly," said Lucy as Timothy smiled at his fiancée.

"You were not supposed to be drumming up business, Alaina," he admonished her teasingly.

"I didn't. My designs sell themselves," said

Alaina, laughing.

Kate agreed, "They certainly do, and I can't wait to come back for a fitting! But first, we have to set a date."

"We do too," said Lucy, "but I plan to do that as soon as we get back to Texas!"

Everyone laughed at that, and the conversation turned to fashion, wedding dresses and New York Fashion week. It was a wonderful afternoon, and they had a delicious dinner of chicken Cordon Bleu that was cooked and served by Timothy and Alaina. Lucy and Kate told everyone goodbye as they were leaving in the morning for Texas and Giselle said, "Thank you for helping Marly find us and uniting our family as it should have been."

CHAPTER 56

Ethan didn't know why they had gotten off so easy in court today, but he wasn't going to question it. It seemed to him that with the FBI involved, there was more to the story than Mr. Kennedy was sharing with him. He was also worried because Derrick Porter had been arrested by the FBI. Ethan had called his friend Davis and filled him in on what happened.

"Shit!" said Davis, after hearing Ethan's account.

"I know, and I wanted to give you a heads up because who knows what they can trace, even the disarming of the door," said Ethan.

"I don't think so, but I'll go back and make sure it looks like a glitch. Wow, that's scary. Sorry you got hurt, man," said Davis.

"It wasn't too bad, just a few stitches. The doctor said it would leave a slight scar, but he did the best he could, since it was on my face," said Ethan.

"Thank god for that," said Davis. "Is there anything I can do for you?"

"No, I stayed behind because I want to get an

engagement ring for Brit," Ethan confessed.

"Really? That's great man, as long as it makes you happy," Davis said to his friend.

"She does make me happy, Davis, and as long as we're talking about it, I would be honored if you would be my best man," said Ethan.

"You know I will, Ethan. You're my best friend," said Davis, touched by Ethan's gesture.

"Okay, I better go and find the most gorgeous ring I can on short notice and get to the airport. I'm scheduled to fly out at 7:00 p.m." said Ethan.

"Okay Ethan, safe travels and we'll talk soon," said Davis, ending their call and making sure his hack was clean.

Ethan went downtown to a jewelry store he noticed when Brit was with him. He walked in and was greeted by a woman behind the counter.

"May I help you sir?" she asked, smiling.

"I hope so," he said. "I'm looking for a unique engagement ring."

"What price range were you looking for, sir?" she asked, not wanting to show him something he couldn't afford.

"I have no price limit," he said, causing the woman to press a button and summon the manager.

A gentleman came to the counter and said, "Please come with me and we'll look at some one-of-a-kind creations."

Ethan followed him to the back and through a door to a small showroom.

"My name is Bernard, and I am a jeweler. If you do not see something you like, we can always create something for you," he said.

For the next hour, they looked at multiple rings and Ethan settled on a flower shaped setting with diamonds and rubies, with a matching band featuring tiny diamond flowers with ruby centers, sparkling brilliantly. They were the right size fortunately. Ethan handed his black card to the jeweler who completed his purchase, putting everything into a small gold bag.

"Thank you, Mr. Longmire," said Bernard, "for being a highly valued customer."

Ethan thanked him for his help and called for an Uber to take him to the airport. He would be so glad to get home and hold Brit in his arms. This experience made him realize how much he wanted her in his life.

Simon and Samson were sleeping on the plane, and Franklin was looking out the windows, as darkness was growing outside. The pilot came over the loudspeaker stating there would be some slight turbulence as some thunderstorms were reported in the path of their flight. Franklin was used to turbulence and didn't think much about it. Simon roused awake and asked Franklin if everything was okay.

"Yes, just a little bumpy ahead... thunderstorms," said Franklin, unconcerned.

"I hate to fly anywhere," said Simon.

"I don't very much," said Franklin. "I'm getting too old to maneuver in airports. I don't mind a private plane though because they are less restrictive."

At that moment, the plane jerked, and lightning flashed, causing the plane to plummet down. It quickly evened out and even Franklin had been alarmed.

"I didn't expect that," he said, chuckling a little.

Simon was not amused. "That was scary. How much longer until we get to Denver?"

Franklin checked his watch and said, "About half an hour. Relax, we're almost there."

Simon tried to relax but he wanted to be on solid ground. The storm continued outside and then it was quiet. Almost too quiet. Samson was now awake and observing but remained silent. He had felt doom during this entire trip.

"Mr. Kennedy, have you heard from the pilot that everything is okay?" he asked.

As Franklin started to assure Simon everything was fine, he heard the pilot saying "Mayday, Mayday. C5148 engine failure, Mayday, Mayday."

Simon started screaming, Samson was praying and Franklin sat there, stone silent. So this is how it will end. He wasn't upset. He was tired of the frailty of his body, and he had failed in finding Giselle. Was the child mine, Giselle, he thought as the plane hit the ground, bursting into flames and the last thing Franklin heard was Simon's screams.

The girls got back to the cabin, talking about the day. It had been full of fun including the shopping, the visit with Giselle and Timothy, Alaina's fashions and her studio, dinner which was delicious and now it was coming to an end. Kate and Lucy were getting their bags ready for in the morning when Marly would take them to the airport and they would fly home. She knew that it was time, but she was going to miss them terribly. The only silver lining was that she was going to get to know her brother Timothy and her Maman. Her phone pinged and Marly picked it up, seeing a text message from Jerry Fields.

'OFFER FOR HOUSE. $800K INVESTOR. WANTS FOR RETAIL. ADVISE.'

Marly was stunned. She just put out feelers through Jerry. She thought about waiting but thought, why? This was a sign that she should move forward with her plans. She sent a text back to Jerry to accept it as it is, thinking about the damage in the basement and when they wanted to close. He was quick to respond, 'END OF MONTH.'

She replied, 'DO IT' and suddenly relief flooded through her.

Marly turned on the television while waiting for Kate and Lucy to join her in the living room. They were going to watch one more movie together. A breaking news story came on the screen, and the reporter was in a deserted area with the remains of a small plane still in flames behind him.

"A charter flight from Memphis to Denver experienced turbulence due to a thunderstorm and lightning struck the plane, taking out the engines. The pilot sent out a Mayday message and the plane crashed in this field near the Colorado state line. There were no survivors. The victims have been identified as Walt Johnson of Denver who piloted the plane, Simon Rockford of Denver, Franklin Kennedy of Denver and his employee, Samson Travers."

The reporter continued but Marly didn't hear anything else. She sat down in a state of shock. She couldn't believe what she was hearing.

Lucy bounded in the living room, saying she was ready, when she noticed Marly.

"What's wrong, Marly?" asked Lucy, as Kate walked into the room.

Marly looked at them both and pointed to the news story still going.

"Franklin Kennedy was on that plane. He was killed," said Marly.

"What?" exclaimed Lucy.

Kate walked over and turned up the volume as the reporter was repeating his story along with the names of the victims of the crash.

"I can't believe it," said Marly.

"I can't either, Marly," said Kate. "I guess this will change the course of the FBI investigation but at least they may be able to find the people that the Crimson Veil worked with."

"I hope so," said Marly. "I need to call Timothy and Giselle."

As she called them to tell them about the plane crash, Lucy and Kate listened to the reporter again.

Brittany sat there in shock. Ethan was with Mr. Kennedy. Why didn't they mention him on the news? Did he survive? Did he walk away? Tears were streaming down her face when she heard a knock at the door. She went to the door.

"Who is it?" she asked, still crying.

"Brit, it's me, open up," said Ethan. "What's wrong?"

She flung the door open and grabbed him tightly. "Oh Ethan, thank god you're alright."

"Whoa, baby, I'm fine. What's wrong?" he asked.

"I thought you were with Mr. Kennedy..." she began but he interrupted her.

"I was, but I flew back on a commercial flight because I had to run an errand," he said.

"Oh Ethan, I'm so glad, but Mr. Kennedy...Mr. Kennedy..." she tried to speak.

"What Brit? What about him?" asked Ethan, confused.

"His plane crashed, Ethan. He's dead!" she said,

grabbing Ethan again, holding onto him as if her life depended on it.

Ethan couldn't believe it. Mr. Kennedy dead? Brittany had saved his life. If he hadn't wanted to buy her a ring, he would have been on that flight as well. He held onto her as she sobbed, and they stayed that way for a while. Eventually she let him go.

"I'm sorry, Ethan. I know you were very close to him," said Brittany. "He was a nice man."

"Sometimes he was, but Brit, I wasn't on that flight for a reason," said Ethan, as he pulled out the ring box and got on one knee, "Will you marry me?" he asked as he flipped the box open and the diamonds and rubies glittered against the black velvet.

CHAPTER 57

Brittany looked at the gorgeous rings in the box and then at Ethan. Was this really happening? Had they come full circle. Her heart was full.

"Yes," she said, smiling through her tears. "Yes, I will marry you!"

He took the ring out of the box and slipped it on her finger.

"Does it fit?" he asked, hoping he had guessed the right size.

"It's perfect, Ethan and it's beautiful," Brittany said. "I've never seen anything like it."

"And you won't," he said, smiling at her, happier than he had been in a long time. "It is a one-of-a-kind creation."

"Oh Ethan," she said, kissing him hard and pulling him close.

"I love you Brittany and I want you to be in my life forever," Ethan said, full of emotion.

"And I love you, Ethan and am so thankful you are here with me, safe," said Brittany.

Ethan's phone rang and he saw that it was Victor. He answered it.

"Hello Victor," said Ethan.

"Have you heard?" he asked solemnly.

"Yes, I just did, Victor. I took a different flight. This is unbelievable," said Ethan.

"Samson is gone too," said Victor, saddened by his friend's death.

"I'm sorry, Victor. It's unimaginable," he said.

"I'm glad that you were not on the plane, Ethan," said Victor.

"Me too, but I feel guilty thinking that," said Ethan but Victor reassured him that everything happens for a reason.

"Do we need to contact anyone else tonight, Victor?" asked Ethan, wanting to be sympathetic and do everything he could but also wanting to comfort Brit.

"I don't think so, Ethan. Come to the house tomorrow and we will go over things," said Victor, as he ended the call.

Not knowing what things Victor was referring to, he put his arm around Brittany, and they walked into his bedroom, to make the comforting a bit more intimate.

Marly was taking Lucy and Kate to the airport, and they were talking the entire way about everything that had transpired.

"Can you believe that Franklin Kennedy is dead?" asked Kate.

"No, it's almost hard to believe," said Marly. "Giselle was upset, and Timothy was taking care of her. I'll have to check on them today."

Lucy spoke up, "Well, I have to tell you Marly, that this trip was about par for girl trips with you."

"Hey now," said Marly, laughing, I didn't have control over a lot of it. For that matter, I didn't on any of the trips. You and Kate had your share of contributing to the chaos!"

They all laughed, and Kate said, "I agree with you, Marly. Maybe we shouldn't travel together anymore!"

"That is not the answer, Kate," said Lucy. "Where's your sense of adventure?"

"Hopefully the only adventure we have together next will be a nice wedding and reception. Think we can manage that?" asked Kate.

There was unanimous agreement!

Lenny was watching the news and saw that Franklin Kennedy had perished in a plane crash along with several other people. He was glad that he had severed his association with Franklin Kennedy, or he might have been on that flight. This should make things easier for Marly now, at least he hoped so. He figured she knew about the crash, so he didn't bother to call her. Their paths would stay separate. His phone rang and he looked down, seeing it was Jake.

"Hey Jake," said Lenny, "what's up?"

"Hey Lenny, did you see the news?" he asked.

"Yeah, what a turn of events. What does that do to your case?" asked Lenny.

"Not much of a case, in terms of holding anyone responsible. Apparently all of the actors are dead," he said. "I'm sure Marly Anderson will be glad that it's over, at least for her."

"I'm sure but she will be sad the way it ended. She is that kind of a person," said Lenny.

"Sounds like you like her," said Jake.

"I do. She is a good friend, and I owe her a lot," said Lenny truthfully. "But she's just a friend."

"Too bad, man," Jake said. "She's real pretty."

"Yes she is," said Lenny.

Not getting a rise out of Lenny, Jake said, "We'll go after these missing people and some of them we can bring to justice or help them clear their names. We have a lot to thank Marly for in that respect. I just wanted to see if you heard the news."

"Thanks Jake," said Lenny. "If you want to go hunting this winter, let me know. I got a lot of room here at the cabin."

"Great, I'll probably take you up on it. Talk to you later, man," said Jake, ending the call.

Thomas Weston closed the door to the real estate office and locked it for the last time. He and Lucinda had sold their house in Germantown and were going to move back to Michigan, where their families lived. Of course, Cindy was going to stay in Nashville as she had a great job there and Tom Jr. was going back to New York to try to make it in the theater. Thomas and Lucinda weren't happy about it, but he was a grown man, and they wanted him to be successful. He had healed from his mugging injuries and was doing well. Thomas had convinced him to take some anger management classes which he did before he left for New York. Hopefully that will help him in future relationships. He was opening up a real estate office in Michigan, Weston Properties. He had high hopes that he would be as successful there as he had been in Tennessee. Fingers crossed.

Marly had finally settled in the cabin near Gatlinburg. The sale of the building in Germantown had gone smoothly and she sold most of the furniture she had. She did keep her wingback chair and her Poppa's recliner and moved them to the cabin along with her personal things and kitchen stuff. It had seemed strange at first, actually living here. She did love the beauty of the area and the silence at night. It was peaceful and calming.

She talked to Maman every day and Timothy helped her at the cabin, getting things situated and was great at fixing things for her. It was great to have someone to call family. Alaina came to the cabin sometimes, when she wasn't in New York, to spend the night and she and Marly loved cooking new recipes together. Marly considered opening a bakery in the area but thought she would wait a while. She wanted to fully immerse herself in her new family and her new home. She had made some friends in the area as well as meeting in person, Judy and Bob Thornton who helped her out when she needed to move her Airbnb renters.

Marly had a new family and a new life in an old and familiar place. It was comforting and she felt closer to her Poppa now that she was here. She had resolved the feelings from her childhood and loved her Poppa even more, knowing what he had sacrificed for her. At times she found herself saying aloud, "Thank you Poppa, for my life and my family. I love you forever."

EPILOGUE

There was a flurry of activity at the Vine to Vino Winery in Blanco, Texas. Two weddings in one weekend! It was madness! Lucy and Rafe were getting married on Friday night in the newly completed Chapel of Bliss on the winery property. Kate and Seth were getting married on Saturday afternoon in the Chapel of Bliss as well.

Marly, Maman, Timothy and Alaina had flown to San Antonio the Monday before the weekend to get everything ready. Marly and Alaina had been working on the wedding cakes and the food for the receptions. Alaina had completed the wedding dresses and shipped them to the girls and was here to make any alterations as needed. There were photographers for the weddings and some from New York to capture the wedding dresses for Alaina Armenti Designs.

Friday arrived and Lucy was so nervous. You would think someone with her sassiness wouldn't let a little old wedding shake her up, but it did. Rafe's family from Fort Worth had arrived a couple of days before and they were helping anywhere they could. The winery had added six more guest cabins, and they were all full. Rafe was a basket case, not knowing what to do with himself. His brothers were keeping him occupied but it was fun to watch. It was getting close to 7:00 p.m. and the music started playing.

Marly and Alaina had taken on the task of decorating the chapel as well and it was stunning. The stained-glass windows glowed with candles and wildflowers in each window, and the pews were decorated with white ribbon, silk Texas bluebonnets and red roses. It was simple but elegant and the chapel was full of family and a few close friends. Seth had done an amazing job building the chapel with the rich, exposed beams forming an arched ceiling with etched lanterns hanging from them, making the room glow in soft light.

Standing at the front of the chapel was the officiant, Rafe, and his two brothers, waiting for the bride. Lucy was in the anteroom of the chapel, Alaina straightening her veil. Her gown was stunning, sleeveless with a V-neckline, fitted closely on the bodice. Tiny seed pearls and iridescent sequins sparkled on the full skirt of the white dress. A small train draped from the waist had embroidered bluebonnets in white, showcasing the Texas state flower. On her feet, Lucy was wearing ankle high white boots, with rhinestones sparkling.

"Do I look okay?" she asked her attendants,

Kate, Marly, and Alaina.

"You look perfect," said Marly, putting the white sparkling cowboy hat atop her head, with her long dark braid, entwined with pearls.

"Let's go," she said, smiling and looking radiant.

The ladies lined up to lead Lucy and Seth into the chapel and when Lucy entered, the entire group gasped, she was so beautiful. Everything about her was unique and breathtaking, all at the same time. Rafe teared up when he saw her, his heart full of love for this spitfire of a woman. He knew that his life was going to be the best one ever.

After the short ceremony, everyone went to the winery's tasting room which was decorated in the same flowers and candles that had been in the chapel. The huge crystal chandelier could not hold a candle to the bride. The reception was a fun and happy event, with a lot of wine and laughter. When Lucy and Rafe started to cut the cake, Seth shouted out, "We're going to do this again tomorrow, everybody!" Laughter filled the room as Vine to Vino employees made sure everyone had everything they needed.

Kate was nervous. She had wanted Seth for so many years and the fact that it was happening was almost surreal. Here she was, standing in the same place Lucy had been yesterday, with Alaina making sure her veil was perfectly set.

Kate's gown was a scoop neckline and short sleeves in white satin. A lace overlay draped over her shoulders, with tiny gemstones and pearls, sparkling every time she moved. The sheath of satin fell softly to her feet where she wore small low-heeled mules, sparkling with the same pearls and gemstones. The train was attached at the waist and fell approximately three feet behind her, embroidered with pearls and gemstones. Her veil was attached to a crown of pearls and gemstones with the veil flowing to the floor. She looked angelic. She wore small pearl and diamond earrings, and her short blonde curls framed her face.

"Same song, second verse...are we ready?" asked Kate.

"You look radiant, Kate, just like we knew you would," said Lucy to her friend and now her sister.

"Absolutely Kate," said Marly, her heart full of love for these women, her best friends.

They walked into the chapel, now decorated with pink and white roses, candles in lanterns in the windows and the pews decorated with the pink and white roses. It was exactly Kate. Seth was watching her closely as she walked slowly toward him, smiling with the knowledge of the life they were going to have together.

After the ceremony, it was back to the tasting room which had been decorated again with Kate's choices and the party started. It was another fun evening, with dinner being served today. It was the perfect second wedding of the weekend.

Lucy and Rafe were going to fly to Hawaii tonight and Seth and Kate were going to the honeymoon cabin on the property. But at this moment, Marly, Lucy, and Kate were huddled together at the back of the room, talking and laughing together.

"I know this isn't the end of our friendship, but it will be different," said Marly.

"No, we won't let it be different, Marly," said Lucy.

"We'll still take trips together and probably get in all kinds of trouble," said Kate.

Raising her wine glass, Marly said, "To the best friends a girl could ever have and I'm so thankful that you two have been with me through thick and thin!"

Lucy raised her glass and said, "To the friends that made me a better person and loved me in spite of myself!"

Kate, raising her glass as well said, "And to the friends that became my family when I had none and rearranged their lives when I needed them!"

"Here, here," they said in unison, as they drank from the wine of friendship.

Best friends, forever.

The End

ABOUT THE AUTHOR

Lois E. Lane

I am from Mobile, Alabama and worked for 35 years in the medical industry. After retirement, I wrote my first book, Gulf of Deception. I enjoyed it so much, that I wrote a sequel. I was then hooked and realized that I loved writing. The Best Friends Series is based on the relationship I have with my two besties, but thankfully, we do not have the same type of adventures! I plan to continue writing and hope you will continue to enjoy the stories I tell.

BOOKS IN THIS SERIES

Girl Trip

Three best friends since their college days seem to find murder, suspense, or mystery everywhere they go...not to mention some handsome men. Follow Marly, Kate, and Lucy on each of their adventures and through it all, their friendship prevails.

Girl Trip

Marly, Kate, and Lucy plan to have a relaxing week in Marly's family cabin in Gatlinburg, Tennessee. But relaxing was not in the picture...they bring a man, who they believe they hit on a dark, mountain road, back to their cabin. Marc at first pretends to be a maintenance man but later reveals his true identity and that his father has been shot and is in the hospital. The next shocking fact is that he is the prime suspect! Find out the real truth as the girls unite to help Marc and solve the mystery of his father's assailant.

From Vine To Vino

Lucy and her brother Seth are finally seeing their dreams come to fruition as they build their winery in the Hill Country of Texas. Financial difficulties halt their progress while a California wine mogul builds a winery and is their competition before they can even open. An investment from a close friend helps them get their project back on track but not before Thomas Preston's children come to wreak havoc for the Cavanaughs. Take a journey into the wine country of Texas and see if the Cavanaughs' dreams come true.

Fear In The Alamo City

Kate is relocating from Amarillo to San Antonio with her employer and is excited about a new city with new opportunities. She will also be living close to Lucy and her brother Seth, her best friend and the man she loves. The excitement is replaced with anxiety and fear when a woman's body is discovered near the iconic Riverwalk and the entire city is on edge. See how Kate navigates her new life, job, and the added fear of the happenings in the Alamo city.

Secrets Of The Crimson Veil

Marly is approached by an eccentric billionaire with an offer to purchase her home for millions of dollars. She doesn't want to part with her cherished home and refuses. However, he will not take no for an answer, wanting to search her home for some unidentified object. Wondering why he is so insistent, Marly becomes suspicious that her home may have a hidden secret. Marly and her friends, Kate and Lucy, try to uncover the secrets the house conceals, not knowing that it will change the course of Marly's life forever.

BOOKS BY THIS AUTHOR

Gulf Of Deception

Coastal Justice

Girl Trip

From Vine To Vino

Fear In The Alamo City

Secrets Of The Crimson Veil

Made in the USA
Monee, IL
05 September 2025

23828637R00277